PRAISE FOR JAY BRANDON

AND HIS PREVIOUS NOVELS

RULES OF EVIDENCE

"A wild novel that has its own surprises. . . . The court-room dialogue and drama are some of the finest I have seen in recent years."

—Francis Moul, *Lincoln Journal-Star*

"Brandon involves the reader in rich descriptions of the courtroom, verisimilitude of dialogue, a compelling plot, and the workaday lives of bigger-than-life characters. . . . A singular tour de force."

—Charles P. Thobae, *Houston Chronicle*

"The tension-filled relationship between Boudro and Stennet . . . propels *Rules of Evidence* to its highest level. Because they see crime and punishment from far different perspectives, their story raises fundamental questions about racism and the law."

—Richard Martins, *Chicago Tribune*

"A compelling, explosive conclusion. . . . Jay Brandon is a talent to be reckoned with."

—Toby Bromberg, *Rave Reviews*

FADE THE HEAT

"Scathingly pointed ... a suspense story of great tension."

"Better than Turow.... I'll go a step further and add a comparison to the classic *To Kill a Mockingbird,* because Brandon's focus encompasses more than merely the courtroom.... I kept having to remind myself I was reading fiction."

"First-class writing and high drama all the way."

"In the tradition of Scott Turow's *Presumed Innocent,* a category that is full of pretenders to the throne, *Fade the Heat* is a real prince."

"Its knowing view of the American justice system chills to the bone."

Books by Jay Brandon

Deadbolt
Tripwire
Predator's Waltz
Fade the Heat
Rules of Evidence
Loose Among the Lambs

Published by POCKET BOOKS

LOOSE AMONG THE LAMBS

JAY BRANDON

POCKET BOOKS

New York   London   Toronto   Sydney   Tokyo   Singapore

This book is a work of fiction. Names, characters, places, and incidents are products of the author's imagination or are used fictitiously. Any resemblance to actual events or locales or persons, living or dead, is entirely coincidental.

POCKET BOOKS, a division of Simon & Schuster Inc.
1230 Avenue of the Americas, New York, NY 10020

Copyright © 1993 by Jay Brandon

ISBN: 0-671-76033-5

First Pocket Books paperback printing November 1994

10 9 8 7 6 5 4 3 2 1

POCKET and colophon are registered trademarks of Simon & Schuster Inc.

Cover art by Ben Perini

Printed in the U.S.A.

for Dan Thornberry and Mark Stevens,
who are the best
on their respective sides of the street

Acknowledgments

I would like to thank all those who shared their expertise with me for this and the other books in my Bexar County legal series: Beth Taylor, formerly (I'm sorry to say) of the Bexar County District Attorney's office; Lyndee Bordini, assistant district attorney; Cruz Morua, San Antonio Police Department Identification section; Dr. Robert Bux, deputy Medical Examiner of Bexar County; Dr. Nancy Kellogg, Medical Director of Child and Adolescent Sexual Abuse Intervention Services; and counselor Dorothy Le Pere.

I also thank Bill Grose, Virginia Barber, and Mary Evans for their thoughtful, thought-provoking appraisals of the manuscript; and Dudley Frasier for his professional and kindly treatment of the book and its author.

PART ONE

The price one pays for pursuing any profession,
or calling, is an intimate knowledge
of its ugly side.

James Baldwin

1

When word came that Eliot Quinn was in the building, he was still on the first floor. Some enterprising clerk had called upstairs with the news, and Patty stuck her head in my office door to pass it on.

Eliot Quinn. *The boss is coming,* was my first thought. I found myself on my feet, as if I'd been caught sitting in his chair. "I guess I should go escort him up," I said. "Or would that be presumptuous? Maybe he's not even coming to see me."

"Of course he is," Patty said.

"Well—I'll give him a few minutes. For God's sake, tell Joan to buzz him right in if he does come up." If Eliot made it as high as the fifth floor he *would* be coming to see me, because the fifth floor is nothing *but* the district attorney's offices.

"I'll tell her," Patty said on her way back out, "but I'm not sure Joan even knows what Eliot Quinn looks like. She's only been here five years."

I gave him a while. Eliot would have lots of people to see on the way up. He'd picked his day shrewdly, a Thursday, when the week's trials would be winding down but the judges had not yet skipped town en masse. I walked to the end of my office, surveying it. This had never been Eliot's office. We had been in the new building almost a year. My office was a little smaller than the one in the old courthouse, but this one looked bigger because of the windows. The old office had been a burrow, hollowed out of the heart of the building. This one was an aerie, perched on the top corner of the Justice Center. I often found myself at the view, which wasn't much but at least reminded me there was an outside world. It was the middle of August, the buildings looked as if they were painted on a rippling scrim; the whole landscape was liquified by heat. We'd already thought the heat unbearable back in June. By now it seemed to have been with us half our lifetimes.

After a while I worked my way down through the building to find Eliot. The fourth and fifth floors were all DA's office, warrens of offices. From the third floor down the building was all courts. All criminal courts. The new Justice Center wasn't big enough to hold all of Bexar County's courts, so the county commissioners had decreed a segregation. The civil courts had remained in the old courthouse, stretching out and breathing a sigh, undoubtedly, when the riffraff were booted across the street into the Justice Center.

I picked up my own small crowd of gladhanders at the third floor. Two or three defense lawyers lingering in the hallway said, "Mark!" and shook my hand warmly, as if we were old friends well-met in a surprising place. Pete Fortune, who had tried to block my promotion years ago and later had stolen a client or two from me, glanced up, cried "Blackie!" happily, and waved me over. I was happy to return his wave and keep moving. The really bogus insiders use that old nickname on me. Friends know I detest it.

I was not above my own gladhanding. "Hello, Judge," I said to a sixtyish man who looked uncomfortable in his suit and in the hall. He was not a judge, hadn't been for two years, but would carry the title for life. I'd never liked him, had contributed to the campaign of the woman who'd unbenched him, but it nonetheless saddened me to see him in the building carrying a briefcase and a load of worry, having to hustle for a living again. The uncharitable would have said there was an element of the personal in the sympathy I felt. I shook his hand warmly, asked after his family, and wished I had some business to send him.

One of the youngest of my assistants was so startled to see me when I peeked into his courtroom on the second floor that he called me "sir." I could tell from his face he regretted it immediately. We were all supposed to be colleagues here. But he tried through the remainder of our brief conversation to call me by my first name and couldn't make his tongue do it.

"Hi, Bill. I was looking for Eliot Quinn; have you seen him?"

"Who, mmm—uh. Who?"

"Eliot Quinn. You don't know him?"

"Quinn, Ma—? Well, it sounds familiar. Is he a lawyer?"

Paula Elizondo, the court coordinator, who had seen a thousand young lawyers like Bill during her years in the courthouse, and found each new one more ignorant than his predecessors, leaned around Bill to give me a little smile and a destination. "Judge Hernandez's office. He's been stuck there for the last twenty minutes."

"Thanks, Paula." On my way out I heard twenty-six-year-old Bill ask her who Eliot Quinn was. Paula's only response was, "You *were* born yesterday, weren't you?" I decided to reward Bill's sudden historical curiosity.

"Eliot Quinn was district attorney here about five times as long as I've been," I said.

"Oh, *that* Eliot Quinn," Bill said, and anyone could see he wanted again to slap himself in the face for sounding such a fraud. Paula laughed out loud. It was good to see one of the people who actually ran the joint laughing at a lawyer.

After making my way through another small crowd of well-wishers I did find Eliot in Judge Hernandez's outer office. I could see that Eliot had worked his way back out that far from the inner sanctum but hadn't quite been able to make that last bolt out the door. When I said his name Eliot leaned in to me as if greeting me intimately. What he murmured was, "Get me away from this old fool."

"Hello, Judge. Hope you don't mind if I steal Mr. Quinn away for a few minutes. I only have a minute before I have to be across the street in Commissioners Court."

"Certainly, certainly," Judge Hernandez said, as hearty as I. He was still wearing his robe, though I would have guessed his day's work was done. "The two of you must have much to discuss. The old gives way to the new, eh,

Eliot? Eh, Blackie? Stop back and see me on your way out, Eliot."

"Of course, Judge, of course. So good to see you again." The door barely closed behind us—I had his arm, as if literally dragging him away—when Eliot said, "That man destroys your respect for institutions. I should have fired him while he was still in Misdemeanor.

"Hello, Mark," he said more warmly. "You're the one I came to see. I should have just taken the elevator straight to the third floor. But you know these elevators."

"It's the fifth floor in this building, Eliot. And these elevators are pretty fast."

"A man could get lost in this building," Eliot said quietly. "I don't want to sound like one of those old dodderers lost in the past, but this is an awful building, Mark. This ministry of justice. We could be anywhere in the world in here. There's a building like this in every city in America. The old courthouse is unique, and so is every courtroom in it. You could be taken into one blindfolded and know exactly which court you were in. This, this is a cold, joyless place. All the courtrooms exactly alike, and all the furnishings gray and bolted into place." He shook his head. "The courthouse has style. Stupid style, but style. It looks like a man out on the town on Christmas Eve, wearing a red vest and a green hat, stepping with great dignity because he knows he looks ridiculous."

"But everything works here," I said. "Everything isn't falling apart." My defense of the new building was half-hearted. I missed the stupid old courthouse myself. The shiny new Justice Center is too uncomplicated, too clean. The old courthouse is a living entity, so infected with humanity that it breathes.

"But this is your building," Eliot said as if finishing my thought, but he was only interrupting his own speech. "I shouldn't criticize. I'm sure you've invested it with your own fond memories."

I gave him the brief tour, Eliot nodding and peering as if interested. He didn't stop to admire anything until the fifth floor, where he gazed up at the foot-tall letters of my name: MARK BLACKWELL. DISTRICT ATTORNEY. I ushered him under them and briefly through the maze of hallways, concluding

6

in my office. "And this could have been yours," I said, "if you hadn't decided to bail out so early."

"Ha ha," Eliot said. His laugh was that precise; I could hear the syllables. He dropped his hat on a chair. I saw he still had a full head of white hair. "Try for two lifetimes in office instead of only one? No, no, I retired right on schedule. Of course, I never intended for that *civilian* to usurp my position." As if he couldn't bring himself to say my predecessor's name. "I wish you'd run four years earlier than you did, Mark. But at least you took the office back. I'm glad it's in good hands again."

It was so strange to see Eliot Quinn in my office. I saw him regularly, every few months, but never before here in the office. His presence seemed to drag us into the past; the room darkened and expanded in imagination, became the old office, and I felt myself turning into a midlevel assistant to the man before me. That time was not so long-gone. Eliot wasn't old. Sixty-two, sixty-three. But he embodied a past era. He had been district attorney of Bexar County for almost twenty years. He'd been the only boss I'd had during my eight years as an assistant DA, from the late sixties to the midseventies. I was forty-eight now—older, I suddenly realized, than Eliot had been when he'd hired me. But he'd been so steeped in authority he'd seemed Olympian to me.

He had hardly changed in the seven years since he'd declined to run for reelection again. It appeared to me he'd coalesced. He was smaller than I'd remembered, and thinner. His gray pinstriped suit was lint-free, his white shirt casually glistened, and his tie was held out by a collar pin. Eliot's jaw, which in final arguments he would clench into a vise of determination, as if he had a grip on the defendant and would never let go, was still firm. He hadn't taken to glasses. When he glanced at me his blue eyes still pierced, from across the room.

We still heard about him from time to time, though he avoided the criminal courts, his old venue. Occasionally he was still hired as trial counsel in a federal or civil case. Representing personal-injury plaintiffs allowed Eliot to prosecute again, in a sense. Recently he had mounted a rather spectacular prosecution—it could be called nothing else—of the managers of an office building who had sought to discourage an old homeless woman who frequented the building's lobby. What should have been a routine slip-and-fall case, with considerable jury sympathy for a business that only wanted its customers to go unmolested, had turned in Eliot's hands into an account of vicious persecution of a helpless victim that bordered on Nazism. The jury's punitive damage award would keep the old woman off the streets for several lifetimes.

"How's Mamie?" I asked.

"Fine as ever. But still not used to having me underfoot during the day. She kicks me out when I spend too many days in a row at home. And how are you doing, Mark? Will you be keeping the job?"

"That's not up to me, is it?" It was election year. I'd won the barely contested primary back in the spring. The party had done its job, seen that I, its best candidate, had no serious challengers. The general election coming up in November promised to be more harrowing.

"Yes, it probably is," Eliot said seriously. He continued studying me, quite frankly. "Half the battle of keeping the job is really wanting it. Do you want it, Mark? Are you enjoying it?"

"Enjoy? Enjoy." I tasted the word again, but couldn't make it work in my mouth. I knew what he meant. When I'd been an assistant DA there'd been a touch of nasty joy in getting a really ugly case, one in which the testimony would make the jurors wince in disgust and start thinking in punishment terms of decades rather than years. A great case, a prosecutor would call it. But now I was *the* District Attorney, I saw all the great cases, and there was no joy in them, just a weariness at the idea that new batches of ugly facts would appear on my desk every morning, day in and out forever, no matter how well I did my job. "It's not a job you can enjoy, is it?"

"You can't?" Eliot asked. His gaze at me had changed from friendly interest to concern. He looked like my doctor, studying me for symptoms of a disease he'd just diagnosed.

I gave him an ironic smile to show I was okay, but said, "Tell me how to enjoy this one." I sat down behind one of the files I'd been studying that morning. "This is one of the tough ones. We've got a man here, a male prostitute. He's tested positive for the AIDS virus. But he hasn't changed what we like to call his lifestyle. He won't quit. It's his living and his life. After his last arrest he told the cops he *wants* to take as many with him as he can. So he's out there killing people, and all I can charge him with, the one time out of a hundred when he's caught, is prostitution. A class B misdemeanor. He does ten days in jail, then he's screwing somebody new the next day. He's going to turn out to be the biggest mass murderer in San Antonio history, and I can't stop him. Tell me, Eliot, did you have problems like this? Somehow the job seemed simpler when you did it."

I had hoped to perturb him just a little, but I hadn't. I could see that his only concern was for what he considered my overreaction.

"Maybe it was simpler," he said. "Or maybe I'm just a simpler man than you are, Mark. But I know one thing. You're taking this job too seriously. You're not the guardian of San Antonio. It's not your job to protect everyone."

"If I'm not then who is?"

"No one is," Eliot said. "No one can be. People have to look out for themselves. As for you, being district attorney is the easiest job in the world. Other people have to make all the tough decisions. Judges, juries. Some poor hapless defendant has to decide whether to take the plea bargain offer or try his luck. Defense lawyers have to decide whether to have their defendant sit silent and be thought a criminal, or take the stand and remove all doubt. But you—you just go full steam ahead. All you have to do is hold a press conference once in a while after some particularly heinous fiend is arrested and say"—he leaned forward, forearm resting on one knee, head thrust aggressively forward—"'We're going to throw the book at this guy. We're going to make him wish he'd never been born.'" Eliot leaned back and laughed. "Then take a nice vacation. Go to a conference somewhere. You're not getting the fun out of this you should, Mark. My God, we used to enjoy power. Your generation just seems to see it as a burden. Take it easier, Mark, or you won't last."

"I know. I fret too much," I said.

"Maybe that's the only difference between us," Eliot said. "We do the job the same way, but I basked in it and you brood over it." He was looking at me happily. "Mark, I'm proud of you. I'll bet you don't hear that very often. But I am. I keep up with things in my own small way. I hear things you wouldn't hear yourself. I know what kind of district attorney you've been for four years. You are the best. Even defense lawyers don't have anything bad to say about you. You had a rocky first year." He waved away that understatement as if it were smoke in the air between us. "Most people didn't expect you to get out from under it. But you did. You do the job just the way it should be done, without partiality. I don't hear anything about you except that you're strictly fair. That you treat everybody exactly the same."

"I try," I said.

"No. You *do*. If the public understood how well you do your job this election would be a walk. But I'm not sure they do. Lawyers do, but the public—well, most people go through life without being exposed to the criminal justice system, and of those who are, few emerge happy.

"I try to tell people," Eliot continued. "It's silly of me to take this pride in you, as if I made you what you are, when in reality I had nothing to do with it."

"You taught me everything I—" I began, but he waved me silent.

"I guess I take pride in it because I feel you've finished the work I began," he said, looking out the window reminiscently. "You know the way this office used to be run?" He laughed. "You would have thought it a horror, Mark. I remember when I was interviewed for a job here, in the fifties, fresh out of law school and damp all over. If I'd been a puppy my eyes wouldn't have been open yet. They weren't, in fact. I sat right there— Well, no, this was in the old office, in the first assistant's office. The first assistant himself interviewed me for the job. Dan Blake, did you ever know him?" I shook my head. "Fat old blusterer," Eliot continued. "He talked to me for a while, and asked me the same silly questions people always ask at interviews, then all of a sudden he excused himself and left the office. It confused me a bit. He'd left so suddenly he'd forgotten to close his desk drawer. It just sat there beside me, gaping open. I thought he was testing my trustworthiness, seeing if I'd snoop while he was gone, so I sat there rigid as an altar boy, staring straight ahead, until the interviewer came back. When he sat down he glanced in the drawer and got a sour look, like there was something rancid in there he'd forgotten about. And all of a sudden the interview was over."

Eliot nodded at my chuckle. "You're laughing, you're not as naïve as I was. I didn't realize it even after I got the letter saying they couldn't use me. I had no idea what had happened.

"But I had an uncle, he wasn't a lawyer but he knew how things worked. He asked me why I hadn't been hired and I told him I didn't know, I thought the interview went okay. When I mentioned the desk drawer business to him he scowled just like the first assistant had done and he said, 'Idiot. You were supposed to put money in it.'

" 'No,' I said. I thought he must be wrong. But my uncle made one phone call and came back and told me the proper amount. And I called the first assistant to ask for a second interview. He seemed disinclined, but when I said, 'I think you'll be surprised how much I've learned in such a short time,' he agreed. And we went through a briefer version of the same charade again, and again Mr. Blake was called away so suddenly that he left his desk drawer open. This time I deposited my bills in it. When he came back he looked in, he smiled, he closed the drawer, he shook my hand, and he said, 'Welcome to the district attorney's office.' "

My smile had died long before the end of the story. I'd heard of the practice before, and it had seemed like a funny anecdote, but as Eliot quietly sketched it I pictured it happening, such an interview being conducted here in this office.

Eliot was sober, too. "I never got to fire that man," he said. "He died long before I got the chance."

"But, Eliot," I said, "there was a vestige of that system even when you were DA. Even when I interviewed for the office, you needed some kind of connection to get in. I'd worked for Harold Adams when I was in law school, and if Mr. Adams hadn't put in a good word for me—"

"Yes, but you didn't have to pay," Eliot said, so sanctimoniously he could hear it himself, and we both laughed. "And if you hadn't worked out you would have been bounced."

He gave me a belated surprised look. "You say 'connection' as if it were a dirty word. Connections are just a way of sorting people. I get a hundred applicants a year fresh out of law school, what do I know about them? That they won the mock trial competition? You know what that's worth once you shove them into a real courtroom. But being a prosecutor is a people job. If you don't work well with police officers, you don't work well in this job. If you can't establish a rapport with the judge, you're no good to me in that court."

Unconsciously, Eliot had started talking as if he were still district attorney. I listened as if being instructed.

"Anyone with those kinds of people skills can make contacts," he continued. "You don't have to be born to them. I wasn't. You weren't, yet you met Mr. Adams, and did good enough work for him that he'd recommend you. You see? You made a contact, so there was someone I knew who I could ask about you. Can he cut it, can he do the job? That's all a connection is worth. It won't get you in if you're no good, if you're just somebody's nephew."

He gave me a grin. "And now that you've become a politician, you need all the connections you can get."

"Yes indeed," I said, and we sat in companionable silence, thinking about the distasteful aspects of the job of district attorney, until Eliot suddenly stirred himself.

"Drat me for an old fool, Mark," he said. "Don't let me talk your day away. I came for a reason." He leaned toward me. "I came to help you with your problem."

"What problem is that?"

"That one." He pointed at the newspaper lying discarded on the floor beside my desk. I picked it up, ignoring the blaring front-page headline, and handed the paper toward Eliot to leaf through and tell me what he was talking about. But he didn't take it out of my hands.

"That problem right there," he repeated, pointing at the headline, the one that screamed, WHERE WAS LOUISE? It was the newspaper's way of keeping alive a story that had kept the city buzzing the previous week. A four-year-old girl had wandered or been taken from her parents' apartment complex and been gone overnight. By late the second day volunteer search teams were combing the neighborhood, the nearby woods, culverts, the dark, crawly spaces under front porches. Hope of finding a living girl after two days in the August sun died quickly. People began searching with their noses as much as with their eyes.

And after sundown that day Louise came toddling home. She was happy, unexposed to the heat, but she couldn't say where she'd been, only that a "nice man" had taken her to a nice house. A new search commenced immediately as the old one reached its only partly joyous conclusion.

"That's not my problem," I said, "that's a police problem." Indeed, the chief of police was feeling the heat. Reporters, digging into the story, found Louise's was not an isolated case. A boy had been missing overnight the month before, another boy earlier in the summer. The newspapers and TV news hatched the phrase *serial child molester* and found ways to insert it into every day's otherwise barren news summaries. I thought it was overblown, myself. There were always such cases, and the police weren't even sure these could be blamed on the same man; children's descriptions are notoriously sketchy. But the chief of police, finding it increasingly difficult to fade the heat of that hungry media attention, had accepted the public theory, and had just assigned more detectives to the cases.

"I'd be just delighted to prosecute anybody they can arrest, but they don't seem to be having much luck at that. Until they do—"

Eliot said, "If you think this is just a police problem, you don't understand the public relations aspect of your job. The public doesn't make distinctions between law enforcement agencies. The only thing the news-watching citizens know is that a wolf is loose among our lambs. Rest assured, they will blame all the shepherds. And you're up for reelection. You're the one they can exercise their fear and outrage on."

Eliot Quinn was a much shrewder politician than I. His two decades in office had proven that. I could see he was right.

"Well, thank you," I said quietly, already trying to think of solutions. I should meet with the chief of police—

"I didn't come just to offer advice you don't need," Eliot interrupted my thoughts. "As I said, I'm here to help you."

He had my attention. He didn't immediately use it. Eliot seemed not quite to agree with the course on which he was about to launch. When he spoke it was slowly, the way a man steps on half-submerged rocks to cross a creek.

"I have a friend," he said. "An old friend. He has a client. The client wants to turn himself in."

"The client is the man who abducted the children?"

"Yes. It's only a case of indecency, Mark, not aggravated rape. Only some touching. He's a sick, ashamed man—"

"Well, it's also kidnapping," I interrupted. "Maybe aggravated. If—"

"Now we're plea bargaining," Eliot said, "and that's not why I came. I don't represent the man. Thank goodness," he added fastidiously.

"No," I agreed. "But what does he want? I can't agree to anything before he's even arrested. He has to turn himself in—"

"That's it," Eliot said. "That's exactly what he wants to do. He's overborne by guilt. But he's also afraid. The frenzy this city seems to be in, he's afraid for his life. He has a deathly fear of police. Unreasonably, but we can understand. How many people in this city would say the best solution would be just to shoot him on sight?"

"Yes. But then?"

Eliot cocked his head at me, as if I were something to regard. "He'll turn himself in to *you*, Mark. You personally. You see, you do have a reputation in some quarters. He trusts you to do the right thing."

"He does?"

Eliot acknowledged my look. "Well, *I* do. And my friend does, his attorney. This seems best for all concerned. For you too, Mark," Eliot added. "It will not be at all bad publicity for you, at a time when you can use it. You'll have the arrest yourself, you'll be the one who ended the crime spree."

That had already occurred to me. I searched briefly for any trap into which my self-interest could be leading me, and saw none. Eliot must already have made the same search himself. "But we have no deal," I emphasized. "No agreement, except that he'll turn himself in."

"That's the only agreement," Eliot confirmed. "You and Austin can work out the details later. Austin Paley, that's his attorney. You know Austin, of course. You and he can strike some sort of agreement later on as to sentencing."

"All right." Eliot and I shook hands, as if he *were* representing clients, as if he had acted for them. And of course he had, but just as an intermediary, an old friend in the middle. He bestowed his fond smile on me again.

"I hope this will do it for you, Mark, give your campaign the momentum it needs. I want to see you reelected. With you in office, Mark, I can feel my tradition is continuing."

He stood up to lean closer to me. "And I tell you frankly, you can use the help. I mentioned your reputation for treating everyone equally. The voters may not be as aware of that as they should, but it's well known in the circles that matter. And you know, not everyone likes it. A reputation for doing no favors is actually harmful to you in some cases. Because some people expect favors. This town runs on favors. Why do you think Leo Mendoza is running against you? Leo's not the smartest lawyer in town, but he's pretty shrewd politically. He's got money behind him, and more than money. Men who'd like to have a district attorney who's beholden to them. You remember that, Mark. Don't treat him lightly."

"I didn't think I had been. But thanks."

Eliot shrugged. "Advice is cheap. I've ignored more of it than you'll ever hear."

He retrieved his hat. " 'Twere best done quickly," he said, more loudly, returning to our earlier topic. "As soon as Austin gets his client in hand we'll be in touch. Done?"

"Done."

Eliot nodded once, briskly, and strode out, as confidently as if he were leaving his own office, as if this new building weren't an unfamiliar maze to him. I remained at my desk, regarding again the bold, tall type of the newspaper headline. Next week it would be my name in print that striking. And as Eliot had said, that couldn't hurt, could it?

I wish I had the gift of invisibility, to turn on and off at will. I enjoy being recognized, I enjoy the notoriety of being district attorney, but to do the job properly I need to be able to slip unobtrusively into courtrooms, and that's a gift usually denied me. I'd like to drift into the room completely unobserved, to watch my assistants when they're chatting with the judge, or plea bargaining with a defense lawyer. I don't mind them looking a touch bored at docket call, as long as they remain professional; boredom is a part of any job. But as soon as I walk into a courtroom, backs straighten. Mouths set in grim determination. Everything turns life and death.

To diminish this air of importance, I've made it a practice to be constantly at large in the building. At least once a day I drift down and cruise the courts. People don't get that startled look when they see me any more.

That Thursday afternoon after Eliot left I made my usual run downstairs. In August the weeks seem to run short, the building clears out faster than usual. By Thursday afternoon it was already deadened, as if I were intruding on a weekend. I had to glance into three courtrooms before I found anything going on. In Judge Ramon Hernandez's court a jury trial was in progress. I took my seat among the scattering of spectators and identified the trial participants. The defense lawyer was a twenty-year veteran of the courts who had probably stopped learning anything new his first year out of law school. The first chair prosecutor was Becky Schirhart, who had been a prosecutor only slightly longer than I'd been district attorney. She was about thirty, the newest first chair felony prosecutor in the office. I'd followed her career with more than usual interest since a couple of years earlier, when Becky, still fairly new to the felony courts, had jumped at the chance to prosecute a police detective for murder.

Becky had the kind of appearance that made her the topic of occasional speculation; I'd overheard some of it. She looks both innocent and intense in the office and the courtroom, leading some men to wonder what she's like after work, whether she devotes that intensity to anything else.

I didn't recognize her second chair, which disturbed me. Even from the back, I should know everyone who works for me. This was a woman, Mexican-American, small and a little slumped. When she turned her head toward Becky I could see not only that she was very young but that she was no one I had ever seen before. What was she doing sitting at the State's counsel table?

The jury was watching a young Mexican-American man testify. He was wearing a white shirt for the occasion, but no coat or tie; he looked as if he wouldn't own either. His knees were cocked outward, leaving his feet lying on their outsides, a boyish pose that looked unstudied.

The chair beside the defense lawyer was empty. The witness was the defendant. His lawyer was questioning him, in the time-honored words of a lawyer not quite in possession of the facts himself: "And then what happened?"

"I decided I better go," the young man said. "I didn't want no trouble. So I went outside and around to the back where I was parked, but I heard somebody running after me, so I turned around quick, but it wasn't the guy, it was her."

"By her you mean Miss Flores?"

"Yeah, her." The defendant nodded toward the woman at the prosecution table. His eyes didn't quite snag on her.

So it was a witness Becky had sitting beside her. Now I was genuinely perplexed.

"What did she do?" asked the defense lawyer.

"She came up and she grabbed my arm and she said she wanted to go with me. I told her no, you better go back, but she wouldn't. I think she'd been drinking some. I don't mean she was swaying or anything, but maybe she was loosened up more than usual. I don't know, I'd just met her."

"What did you do?"

"I kept walking toward my car. And she kept following me and when I got in she got in. So I thought, okay, and I drove us down the street to a house I knew."

"Was it your house?"

"It wasn't nobody's house. It was empty."

"Did Miss Flores say anything while you drove?"

"No, she just scooted over beside me and put her hand on my leg."

"And did that have some effect on you?"

"Well, yeah."

The defense lawyer didn't ask him to specify the effect. The defendant reached for his shirt pocket, but the cigarette pack that obviously belonged there had been removed for the solemn occasion. He went back to twisting his hands together in his lap while his lawyer led him through a tale of sudden youthful passion followed by feminine remorse and shame. As the defendant talked, my attention was drawn to the victim—that was obviously who she was, as this was obviously a sexual assault trial—the young woman sitting up front at the State's table. Early in the defendant's recital she turned animatedly toward Becky, clutched her arm, and whispered something. Becky calmed her. The victim sat quietly for the rest of the testimony. I couldn't see her face, but something in her expression kept drawing the attention of the jurors, and repelling the defendant's gaze. He would glance toward her but couldn't look at her. I wasn't alone in noticing his inability.

When he was passed to Becky for cross-examination, Becky stood and took two steps to the side, so she was standing directly behind the victim. The defendant found something interesting on the other side of the room.

"So when you left the restaurant," Becky began, but interrupted herself. "Mr. Arreola, could you look at me, please?"

"Objection," the defense lawyer said hastily. "The witness doesn't have to take direction from the prosecutor."

Oh good, Joe, I thought. *Go ahead and tell everyone your guy can't bring himself to look in the direction of his victim.* Judge Hernandez said mildly, "That's true, he doesn't."

"So this young woman forced her attentions on you, Mr. Arreola? You couldn't shake her off?"

"No, I couldn't get away."

"How much would you say she weighs, Mr. Arreola?"

"I don't know." Nor could he estimate very well, because he glanced at the victim but his glance wouldn't take hold.

"She didn't overpower you physically, did she?"

It was a silly question, but no one laughed. Becky's tone wouldn't permit it. The jurors looked very solemn as they stared at the expression I couldn't see on the victim's face.

"In fact it wasn't immediately after you left the cafe that Ms. Flores came out, was it? And it wasn't only the parking lot that was outside, the restrooms were too, weren't they? You had to skulk around the ladies' room for some twenty or thirty minutes waiting for Ms. Flores to come out, didn't you, Mr. Arreola?" Becky's questions grew more and more harsh, but her hands were on the victim's shoulders, asking *her* to bear up.

Even after both sides rested and the judge gave the jury

a recess, Becky Schirhart didn't seem to see me. She spoke quietly to the victim for a minute or two, until the woman left, giving the defendant a wide berth, to join a small family group in the audience. It was as Becky followed Ms. Flores with her eyes that Becky saw me. I stood, and she came to talk. But I spoke first.

"I've seen it done coldly," I said, "as if the facts were so plain only idiots could fail to see them. And I've seen it done passionately, as if the victim were the prosecutor's sister; that usually sounds forced. But this is the first time I've ever seen it done angrily and compassionately at the same time."

Becky shrugged. She looked worried. "It was a risk, of course. Having her in the room while he testified meant I couldn't call her in rebuttal. But she'd already told her whole story, I didn't think I'd need to call her back. The defense objected, but the judge let me try it."

"Something this novel—" I began. Becky was already nodding.

"I know, I should check with someone first. But I didn't plan it. It was a spur-of-the-moment thing. You should have seen that little bastard while *she* was testifying. He squirmed, he rolled his eyes, he groaned out loud. He turns to his lawyer and says, loud enough for everyone to hear, 'I can't believe she's saying all this shit.' "

Becky turned to look at the defendant. "For once I wanted to give one of them a taste of his own medicine. They always get to sit there and put on a show while the poor victim's struggling to tell her story. I wanted to see him try it. And I wanted the jury to see if he could look her in the face while he tried to spout that load of crap and he *couldn't!* They saw it. That lying little creep."

I've seen prosecutors animated by cases, but I've rarely seen one so personally involved. It is, after all, just a job. After this case was over there'd be a thousand more in line behind it. I didn't remind Becky of that.

"It was very effective," I said. "But let's not try this experiment again until we see what happens to this one on appeal."

"No," she agreed. "But if this guy gets reversed I'll try him again."

"Assuming he's convicted this time," I said gently.

"He will be. Can you picture that jury coming back in here and facing her and saying not guilty?"

I left her to her waiting. I felt restored by having watched someone so unjaded in her work. I wondered how I could spread Becky's enthusiasm through the rest of the staff, rather than allow the more common reverse effect.

Becky's performance and Eliot's visit had given me a greater sense of well-being than I'd enjoyed in some time. Events were flowing my way. I was the head of a professional, well-trained staff, and by the following week I'd be a public hero as well.

The hallway outside the courtroom was empty. There was no one lying in wait for me, which had been a problem for a while. Three years ago, shortly after my election as district attorney, my son David was arrested for rape. He'd protested his innocence and I had supported him, of course, supported him so publicly that ever since some people saw me as peculiarly vulnerable to emotional appeals. Mothers, sisters, uncles of defendants caught me in the hallways of the Justice Center to tell me that what had happened to my boy had happened to theirs, too. But I never intervened. I was not a judge; I did not usurp the jury's function. It had been three years, and the emotional pleas had slowed.

I checked the other courtrooms, but they were empty. It was time to go home. The only alternative was to watch Becky's final argument and wait for her verdict. I have seen a thousand final arguments. I've given hundreds. On the other hand, I know my empty townhouse very well, too.

I headed back to the courtroom.

2

Once I had a partner. I'd had a family, as well. Now I had the office of district attorney. I didn't think I'd given up the rest of my life for the office, but I could see how a neutral observer might disagree.

Fresh out of law school, I'd been an assistant DA for eight years. I loved the work, but no one with any ambition remains a prosecutor forever. Tired of being a bureaucrat of justice, and of my layers of bosses, I left the office after eight years. When I did, I wanted to learn about the only aspect of criminal law I didn't know: representing clients. I didn't want just instruction, though, I wanted a partner. Someone I could talk to about my cases; someone I could rely on to back me up.

Linda Alaniz was the partner I found. I'd opposed her in several cases, enough to be singed by her skills. But Linda was not just a capable defense lawyer. She was as true a believer as there ever was. I wanted to learn from her the secret of her faith, how she committed herself so passionately to the defense of the guilty.

Linda believed in our clients. If she didn't believe their stories, she still believed in them. She saw them as victims themselves, lost children whose causes no one else had ever taken up.

I learned from her, but she did not convert me. I couldn't treat our clients the way Linda did, like family members who'd gotten a bad break. We were good partners, maybe *because* I was the skeptic and she had the passion. If we'd been more similar, Linda and I would have gone our separate ways after I'd spent a year or two learning from her. Instead, our differences kept us together for ten years.

Ten years can pass like a long weekend, but always perform a decade's worth of change. We look around and find we are not the people we thought, we are not living the lives we'd assumed. Early in my partnership with Linda I was a happily married man, with a teenaged son and an infant daughter. A few years later I discovered that leaving the office at night and going home to my wife Lois seemed backwards. I went on feeling this dislocation for more than a year, until a moment came when Linda and I felt the same way at the same time, and we became partners completely, privately as well as professionally.

When we did, it was as if Lois knew, as if she'd expected it before I had. My wife and I didn't separate. We remained friendly partners in raising our daughter Dinah; pleasant roommates. Linda didn't want a husband and I didn't want to leave my home while my daughter was still in it, so we all drifted along for a few years.

It was the district attorney's office that finally separated us all. When I was offered the chance to run for DA I found I wanted it, I wanted it badly. Linda must have been dismayed to see me seeking so arduously the world I'd left behind to become her partner, but she understood. She helped me campaign. When I won she even came into the DA's office with me, as my first assistant.

As for Lois and me, I think we could have continued to live as we had, maybe into old age, but the terrible events of my first year in office—David's arrest and its aftermath—broke us apart. We had been divorced for two years now.

Being chief prosecutor pried me loose from Linda a little more slowly, but just as certainly. Linda was no prosecutor. She didn't last as first assistant for a year before returning to private practice. Even then we thought we could maintain our private relationship while remaining occasional public adversaries, but we were naïve. The absolute difference in our work emphasized our private differences as well. What we did was what we were. For months we did nothing but argue, until the arguments became so wearisome we began seeing less of each other to avoid them. And when we'd put a certain distance between us we found there was not much reason to bridge that distance.

But I hadn't found anyone to take Linda's place, and I don't think she'd replaced me, either. She had her clients. I had my duties and my reelection campaign. And after all, there's nothing more satisfying than work, is there?

The arrest went off without a hitch. That's what it is when a suspect is taken into custody, an arrest, even though in this case police weren't involved. *I* was the arresting officer, a first for me, one I didn't enjoy. I had tried to make sure this silly business wouldn't damage my relationship with the police department. As soon as the plans were set I'd informed the chief of police, Herman Glower, who, it was said, had "cleaned up" the department during his six years as its chief. As far as I could see he'd just made the PD colorless, like himself. Chief Glower had unsmilingly instructed me in the basics of arrest.

"There's nothing to it," he'd said. "Just remember to take a firm grip on his arm. That settles them down. You'd be surprised how many want to bolt at the last minute, even when they're turning themselves in voluntarily."

And that had been the end of my prearrest dealings with the police department. I assumed they'd closed their files on the cases once I'd informed them of the imminent arrest.

The spectacle was to take place in the well-lighted hall outside the fifth-floor entrance to the district attorney's offices. I would make the arrest out there in the hall. It had to be a public event. My campaign could use the publicity of my putting a stop to a series of horrifying crimes, and the suspect presumably wanted a very public view of his going quietly into custody, not like a monster brought to bay.

The whole hallway was secured, with our investigators, two uniformed cops, three sheriff's deputies, and the sheriff himself to take over the transport to the jail, and a sprinkling of assistant DAs who wanted to watch. With the media arriving and angling for camera positions, the small hall must have been jammed already. I was in my office, regally awaiting the appointed minute. I wished I had Eliot there to joke with. But Eliot had refused my invitation to be part of the arrest, modestly claiming he'd had nothing to do with it.

My intercom buzzed. "Ready," Patty said, and I was already at the office door, to ask her in person in the outer office if the satellite coverage was in place.

"Everybody but Oprah," she said.

I went down the long interior hall toward our front door, picking up acolytes along the way, including the chiefs of the felony and sex crimes units. They stayed discreetly in my train, waiting to do the dirty work once I'd intercepted the glory.

As soon as I emerged into the public hallway the lights hit me, making it impossible to distinguish faces. I was sure I knew everyone there, the reporters, the prosecutors, my colorful friend the sheriff, but the lights isolated me. I could picture my assistants smirking at the edges of the crowd. That would have been my reaction to this silly waste of time.

But it hadn't been, I recalled. When I was an assistant DA there'd been occasions like this two or three times a year, press performances in the hallway starring Eliot Quinn. And Eliot, a man of sharp, solemnity-deflating humor, took them very seriously, so seriously that his assistants learned not to smile at them either. "This is as much a part of the job as pointing your finger at the defendant in court in front of a jury," I'd heard him say once. "You can't just do a good job, you have to let them know you're doing a good job. Otherwise some other bumblewit will be doing this job four years from now."

I'd nodded soberly then, and the memory of it kept my face straight as I stepped into my own public performance.

"Where are they?" I asked softly into the blazing void, and a voice answered, "That sound is their elevator arriving."

A few moments later my eyes had adjusted well enough that I could see the blond man in the suit with no tie pressing through the crowd toward me. Austin Paley was right behind him, so I knew this was the suspect. The arrestee. He looked scared to death, as if the crowd were calling for his blood.

What they were calling were questions. The lights abandoned me, to center on the child molester and his attorney. Austin Paley stopped, touching his client's arm, to allow him to answer a question or two if he chose. The man to be arrested kept his head down and spoke shortly if at all. I had a moment to study him. This was my first view of Chris Davis, the man who'd chosen me to arrest him. He was about forty, I'd been told, but looked far more youthful. I fancied I could understand his fascination with children. He looked like a boy himself. His open collar made the suit look a little too big for him. He kept his eyes shyly downcast.

It was a horrible occasion for him, the worst of his life. I wondered what had made him do it. He must have believed the police were very close to arresting him anyway. But why not just quit and disappear, move to another city, rather than subject himself to this—arrest and prison and pain? Maybe it was guilt that had forced him here; a childhood churchgoing upbringing he couldn't shake, or a recent conversion, or a deep-seated revulsion at what he was.

But if conscience had been Davis's goad, it seemed to have deserted him. Now he just looked scared. I saw him hear the elevator doors closing, saw him look across the hall to the head of the stairs. "Take a firm grip on his arm," Chief Glower had said, and I realized he'd been right.

Austin Paley had taken over the press coverage. "Yes, I made this arrangement," he was saying. "Mr. Davis came to me to say he wanted to turn himself in and put all this behind him, but he was afraid. One or two experiences with San Antonio police officers in his youthful past had left him fearful of the reception he'd receive at the hands of outraged police. When I told him that I knew from personal experience that District Attorney Mark Blackwell was eminently trustworthy, and has an impeccable reputation for fairness, Mr. Davis came up with this scheme. Everyone concurred, so here we are."

Austin glanced at me. He didn't wink—he couldn't have, it would have shown up on the news footage—but that was the impression he gave me. Austin was a man who could rise to any occasion but in the midst of solemnity or passion slip one a look that said, "Only you and I know how full of shit I am." I smiled back at him, though Austin hadn't smiled. I quickly erased mine.

Austin was only five years younger than I, but like his client he bore his years very lightly. He could, in fact, have been Chris Davis's slightly older brother, a more successful, infinitely smoother guardian used to pulling his sibling out of scrapes.

They came toward me and I laid hands on the suspect. "Mr. Davis, you're under arrest," I said, managing to avoid adding, *in the name of the law.* I held him long enough for a good photo opportunity, justifying the time in the spotlight by explaining to him in careful detail just what would happen next. Davis nodded along as if I were his friend. I kept my face stern.

Finally I passed him off to the contingent of sheriff's deputies who took him into actual custody, hustling him into the offices out of sight. Chris Davis looked like a wave-borne glint of sunlight in that tide of dark men.

I stayed to answer a few more questions, confident that one of them would give me the opening to make my tough speech. When it did I said, "No, we have no deal between Mr. Davis and my office. Our only arrangement was that he could turn himself in to me rather than to police. Now the case will take its normal course. Whether I prosecute it personally or not, there will be no favors. As in all cases. I'm flattered by the faith Mr. Davis and his attorney place in my fairness, but I'm sure they realize that my job is to prosecute people like this suspect. These are particularly heinous crimes that have thrown this city into an understandable panic. It's my responsibility to prevent their happening again. I won't be taking it easy on Mr. Davis."

That was as good as it was going to get. I ignored the rest of the questions and retreated into my offices, Austin Paley at my elbow. He patted my back in greeting, I touched his arm, and we proceeded down the interior hall to my private office, loosening up further with every step, until we were laughing.

"Gosh, Mark, but you told me we had a deal, right? Two years' probation and no fine, wasn't that it?" he extemporized.

"I'm sorry, Austin," I responded in kind. "That was just a lie to get you in here. You don't mind, do you?"

We didn't do any real plea bargaining in my office; in

fact, we hardly mentioned the case at all. We made cocktail-party chat about how long it had been since we'd seen each other, what we were busy with, how our friend Eliot seemed to be doing in retirement. After a few minutes Austin stirred himself and, with a small frown, as if it were indelicate to refer to his reason for being there, said, "Well, I'd better go find my client. Where are your men keeping him?"

"In the torture chamber, beating a confession out of him."

"It will cleanse his soul, no doubt," Austin said, and shook my hand again, taking me into his confidence as he said, "We'll talk soon."

After all the waiting, the event seemed to have passed quickly, leaving me alone again, though the clock told me it was almost lunchtime and I'd done nothing else all morning. It had been campaign work, not prosecution. In atonement I worked late into the afternoon, finding myself still in the office when it was time for the six o'clock news. I turned on the TV in my office and watched my act again. My God, I looked formidable in my few seconds on the screen. There was no hint of the foolishness I'd felt. *This will do me some good*, I thought. All over the city, burglars in appliance stores must be dropping their tools and repenting their trades at the sight of my stern countenance. Tearful private citizens would be murmuring, "Thank God we have this man watching over us."

It wasn't until I saw myself on screen, hours after the event, holding Chris Davis's arm, that I remembered the vileness of the man I was touching, remembered the ordeals of little Billy and Louise and Kevin. It was impossible for me to picture the frightened Davis as the villain of our collective imaginings. He looked like a victim himself.

3

The building hums on Mondays. I can feel it, even in my remote perch. I remember Monday mornings perfectly well, from both sides of the docket, prosecutors getting files together, arguing with defense lawyers, the defense lawyers gliding from court to court, trying not to look in a hurry, all of them wondering if they'll be in trial that afternoon.

My morning is more predictable. My time is scheduled. I meet with the county commissioners to ask for money. I meet with my staff to ferret out recurring problems. Community leaders come to ask me to do more, or less. I seem never to hear from happy people.

Austin Paley was a welcome diversion that afternoon. Part of his appeal was that he wasn't scheduled. He was one of the rare people who could expect to drop in on the district attorney, not because of some special access, but just because of his impenetrable insouciance. I postponed a scheduled meeting to see him.

He looked fastidiously out of place. Austin was rarely seen in the criminal courts any more, though at one time he had been one of the familiar crowd. Sometime in the last eight or ten years he had moved beyond us, though, into the corporate realm where lawyers were as unfamiliar with the courthouse as was an average law-abiding citizen. But Austin hadn't lost touch. He made the social rounds, contributed to judges' campaigns, occasionally even personally steered an important client through the hazards of a DWI charge.

"How did you get into this one, Austin?" I asked after our cheerful, clubbish greetings were done.

He rolled his eyes. "Friend of a friend," he said lazily. "Chris thought— Well, you can imagine. He felt like a hounded man. Hearing footsteps. He just wants to get shut of the whole thing."

"I imagine," I said mildly, not taking up the implied invitation to make an offer.

"One reason I allowed his arrest to be so public," Austin continued, as if he had arranged it all, like a reception for a visiting dignitary, "was so that people could see how harmless he is. You saw him, Mark, so befuddled. He's really a child himself." His mouth turned wry. "That's his problem, I suppose. Children are peers to him."

I opened my desk drawer, to let him know immediately where we stood. "I've gotten letters, Austin." I dropped a representative sampling on the desk. "Saying they're breathing easier now that the child rapist's behind bars. Asking me please to put him away well into the next millennium."

That was the shorthand rendition, but someone with Austin's political savvy wouldn't need more. His gaze fell on the letters momentarily with a flicker of distaste. "Well, you will get reactions like that, won't you? But they can't dictate what you do. First of all, of course, you couldn't get a lot of years."

"For aggravated sexual assault of children? I couldn't?"

Austin's eyes had been roaming idly around my office. For a moment they returned to me, searchingly. He smiled again, as if I'd made a joke.

"I think you'll find it's only indecency. You can't prove penetration. But you know that. You've talked to the children, of course."

"Yes. Well, I've read their statements."

"And of course the defendant gave a statement too."

I had read that one, too. Davis's confession was a little more precise, and much more articulate, than the average defendant's, but still damning.

"Yes. One that would revolt a jury."

"Oh, juries," Austin said dismissively, and we both laughed.

"What he needs is treatment," Austin continued. "Ten years of probation would be a much more effective deterrent in this case than any term of imprisonment. It would make the streets safer." Acknowledging my letters.

I shook my head. "I can't do it, Austin. Not probation."

He understood. And he was thoughtful enough not to make me spell out the political realities we were talking about. Austin waved his hand as if we'd passed beyond his attention span. We were only talking about a defendant, after all.

"All right, if it has to be years, how many?"

Years means prison. It's the word we use. A term of probation may last years, too, but they're different sorts of years.

"Thirty," I said.

"I'm telling you, Mark, you can't get thirty. If you went for aggravated you couldn't get it. There's no physical evidence, the girl's too young even to make a witness, and if the boys do remember accurately they'll just prove indecency."

Indecency with a child, basically fondling, carries a maximum sentence of twenty years, as opposed to the maximum of life for aggravated sexual assault of a child.

I shrugged. "We'll see what a grand jury says," I said, and immediately felt like a bully.

Austin sounded mildly exasperated. "You're not going to make me try this, are you? Do you know how long it's been since I tried a case? Come on, Mark, I brought this to you. I promised him you'd be fair. *Be* fair.

"Look," he went on, in the confidential tone that came naturally to him, "this is easy. You can come out of it golden. Someone leaks a copy of the statement to the media. People read that it was just some mild fondling, rather pathetic at that. The children remain anonymous, of course, but they're safe, and too young to remember much. And you, you'd like to put this man away forever, but the damned legislature has tied your hands, they put a maximum of twenty years on this crime. And in view of the relative mildness of the offense—that's not the word, we'll think of a better word—and the fact the defendant is so torn by remorse he turned himself in, you think a sentence of say, eight years, is more than adequate to protect ..."

Austin was leaning forward, talking animatedly. I thought I was seeing him now as he must be at his best, in private meetings throughout the city, in the highest rooms of many an office tower. His client was forgotten, I was sure. Strategy itself was the enticement. We were collaborators.

That made me wonder anew how Austin had come into the case. Friends of friends, he'd said. Was Chris Davis politically connected? I'd never heard of him, but that didn't mean much. There were power brokers in San Antonio I hardly knew. I certainly couldn't keep track of their extended families, and friends and lovers, and friends of lovers.

Davis could even have been a relative of Austin's. I remembered their resemblance. It would have been rude to inquire too closely.

"Let's say twenty," I interrupted his flow. "You know he won't do much time, in that range." Due to early paroles because of prison overcrowding and intervention by a nobly humanitarian federal judge, prison sentences in Texas have become largely symbolic. A twenty-year sentence could mean as little as two years actually served.

"Whatever," Austin said. "We're in the ballpark." He exhaled, suddenly bored with the subject. "How's the campaign going?" he asked, switching to something more in his line.

We talked politics for another ten minutes. Austin was too discreet to offer me a campaign contribution on the spot, instead talking about people I should meet, the kind of people who don't normally get involved in something as low-level as a DA's race.

"We can get this settled quickly, can't we?" Austin said in leaving. "I'd like to drop back out of the limelight. I've tried to deflect it all back on you."

"I appreciate that," I said, remembering his nice speech at the time of the arrest. Austin waved away my thanks. It had been a favor too small for him even to keep track of. We shook hands at the door and Austin hurried off down the hall, with many calls on his time, I imagined, but he'd drop in on old friends on his way out of the building. *Like Eliot,* I thought. *Like Eliot's private shadow.* Austin Paley was almost unknown to the general public, but in his quiet way he wielded more influence than most public figures. I realized I felt flattered by his small courtesies.

Later that week, at a political fund-raiser, I thought I felt Austin's ghostly fingers slip into my pocket, leaving not cash but something much more valuable.

"I got a call from the firefighters' union," my campaign manager told me in a quiet corner, momentarily aside from the smiling, swirling crowd. "They want you to speak to their next meeting. You manage not to set fire to anything, I think we'll get their endorsement."

"Good, Tim. Why firemen should care who the DA is I don't know, but anybody's welcome on this bandwagon."

Tim Scheuless, my campaign manager, and I weren't friends. We'd hardly even known each other a year earlier. He'd come recommended from more-veteran campaigners. Tim owned a local ad agency, one he'd staffed so ably that he had too much time on his hands, and had gotten interested in politics. Tim understood politics better than I, but he wasn't a lawyer, and he didn't have a very good grasp of the nature of my job, as he often demonstrated in conversation.

"That's the trouble with the district attorney's race, there aren't any issues," he said, shaking his head. Tim should have been a candidate himself. He had broad shoulders and a large head that photographed well, and his teeth when he flashed them were truly impressive. "Tough on crime," he went on. "That's it. But who's gonna run for the office and say he'll be weak on crime? Where's an issue?"

"There's character," said a voice at my elbow. I knew the voice, but I was amazed to turn and see Linda Alaniz at a political function. She hated politics almost as much as she'd hated being a prosecutor.

Linda was wearing a dress held up by straps that showed off her shoulders, and the brownness of her skin. Her eyes glittered. She looked tired, but as if she'd abruptly thrown off weariness at the prospect of a good fight.

"You know some dirt on Leo?" Tim asked her. That was what "character" meant to him.

"I mean fitness for the job," Linda said acidly. "Fairness.

Setting a standard to which the entire office must adhere. That's what Mark has done during his term."

"Oh," Tim said. "Yeah, sure. I mean of course, obviously. But tough on crime—that's what sells." He turned back to me. "That's where you've got the real advantage, and I don't see you using it enough. Mendoza can talk about being tough on crime, but you can do it. You need to try something, soon. Some big case, with gruesome details. A laydown, of course; God forbid you lose it. Something long, too, so you could be in the paper every day looking tough, and there's no chance of losing. Surely you've got some case like that around the office? I read about 'em all the time."

Sure, they all look easy when they happen, when the TV reporter says police have arrested a suspect. People want to see that suspect on trial the next day. They ignore or never hear about the details that make trial an adventure—the contradictory statements from victims, the alibis false or true, the witnesses who are less than pristine themselves.

"I could do that, couldn't I?" I said to Linda.

"I could help," she said. She was looking at me, ignoring Tim. "I'll pick one of my most disgusting clients, and instead of trying to get him a good plea bargain I'll let you try him."

"Good. And if the case isn't going too well during trial— for me, I mean—"

"I'll advise him to testify, so you can tear him to pieces," Linda finished.

All this sounded like a good idea to Tim, but he knew when he was being kidded. "All right, all right," he said. He raised a finger. "But look, why do you have a campaign manager? So do what he says once in a while, okay? You listen to me, and we'll win this thing going away."

"I'll work on it, Tim, I promise."

He saluted me with an eyebrow, patted Linda's shoulder, and slipped away to work the crowd. "It's good to see you," I said to Linda. "It's *amazing* to see you here."

Linda gave me an ironic smile. "You deserve to be re-elected, Mark. I support you."

Well, political support. But I was delighted to have Linda beside me again, for whatever reason. I wished it could be permanent.

I looked around at the crowd. Linda was eyeing them too,

as if she might have to talk to some of them. "Aren't you glad you don't have to do this kind of crap to keep your job?" I said.

"I make no judgments," Linda said, causing me to laugh so boisterously that several people turned to smile at me.

Austin was right about the child-molesting cases. He had done his homework more thoroughly than I had. I started catching up a few days later, beginning with rereading the children's statements. The statements might have relieved a parent, but they were poor material from a prosecution point of view. The crucial part of one boy's statement read, "I was just about asleep when I felt him touching my leg. His face looked funny. He put his hand inside my shorts. I laid very still. Then I went to sleep."

As Austin had said, it proved indecency with a child, not sexual assault. Only fondling, no penetration or contact between intimate body parts.

"What about the girl? There's no statement from her."

The advocate shook her head. "It's a good thing this is going to plead. You don't want to depend on little Louise."

The advocate works for me, supposedly. We have three of them in the sex crimes section. They're counselors who help prepare children for trial, take statements from them, sit with them and play with anatomically complete dolls for the video camera. Sometimes they accompany the child to court. They're supposed to be neutral, just assigned to protect the child, but as defense lawyers always point out, the advocates work for the prosecution.

This advocate, Karen Rivera, was a pale, bony woman who smoked, even in my ashtray-free office. She didn't seem the kind children would respond to, but they did. I've seen her. Her face changes when a child comes into the room. Even her body grows more maternal somehow. With children she is wonderfully protective and reassuring. She uses up all her patience on them.

"Why?" I asked.

"Because she'd kill you," the advocate snapped. "Ask her the same question three times and get three different answers. I know, I've done it."

"What about medical? What could I prove there?"

She shook her head. "Like he knew it would come to trial. Nothing. No redness, no damage. She doesn't remember much, and I don't want to push her. Maybe she's better off not remembering."

"How is she?" I asked.

The advocate shot her half-smoked cigarette into my metal trash can from five feet away. "She's fine," she said, but her tone said something different. "If everybody'll stop asking her about it she might forget it. She might fall to pieces ten years from now on her first date, or twenty years from now when she's married and has kids herself, but right now she's okay. She doesn't know what happened. Everything's new to her, she doesn't know this was something awful. If I can save her from her damned parents she'll be fine."

"What do you mean?"

She gave me a hard look, like I was after her babies, too. She said, "They get victimized three times. First by the molester. Next by the parents. That's the most important one. The child can forget what happened, maybe, but they're much slower to forget what Mommy and Daddy did when they found out."

"Like what?"

"Like not believing. That's the worst. The kid gets up her nerve, she's scared, she suspects something's wrong, so she goes to the only people she can rely on. And if they tell her she's lying—and a lot of them do, I'll tell you; they don't want to believe it so they say the child's making it up—if Mom and Dad don't believe her, if they don't take her in their arms and promise her they'll never let it happen to her again, then she's all alone in the universe. And she knows it could happen again, because nobody's on her side."

"Who's the third one who mistreats her?" I asked.

"Us. The system. Once the parents are convinced, or half-convinced, so they call for help, then the cops come. When the cops come to a child's house because of something the child said, then she knows she's done something terrible. She thinks she's going to be arrested. Then she gets taken to a doctor who takes her clothes off and sticks a flashlight up her behind, and god damn, this is worse than what happened with the nice man in the field or the motel room.

35

Then the prosecutors get hold of her, and some sweet friendly bitch like me who's going to be her friend just as long as we need her and not a day longer. Sometimes I think we're the worst. You and me, the whole justice system."

She'd lit another cigarette, on automatic pilot, and inhaled half of it. "You need some time off, Karen?" I asked quietly, the tone used to avoid scaring someone off a ledge.

She laughed, causing a cloud of smoke to obscure her face. "I need Green Lantern's ring. I need to scour the whole world clean. When is everybody going to wise up and put me in charge of everything?"

I could already see how difficult the cases would be to prosecute. Austin knew that. Luckily, his guy wanted to plead guilty.

"I need to meet with all the parents," I said. "We don't want them to read in the papers that it's going to be plea bargained. They'll be expecting trials."

Karen rolled her eyes. "Be gentle with them," she said. "The kids're all right, at least for now. It's the parents that're falling apart."

But they came into my office very bravely, faces set. I met with each set of parents individually, telling them what we were proposing. I talked about avoiding the trauma of trial. Kevin's parents took up my theme almost before I'd announced it.

"Yes," Mr. Pollard said. His head bobbed. "We understand. Don't worry about us."

He was Kevin's father, a big man with a heavy dark mustache and work-hardened hands. Six-year-old Kevin sat silently beside him, his mother on the other side. She reached for Kevin's hand when she remembered. Other times she worked a tissue in her hands.

There was something about Mr. Pollard I didn't like. His quick acquiescence to a plea-bargain agreement was a relief, but it surprised me and put me off. I turned my attention to Kevin, a slight boy with pale eyes anomalous beneath his shock of black hair. Kevin must be tired of being looked at by adults the way I was looking at him; appraisingly, but with mouth retaining a smile at all costs. He looked down, away from me.

"Kevin?" He wouldn't look up. "Do you understand what I'm saying? The man would go to prison, far away from you, and you wouldn't have to tell anyone else what happened. Does that sound good to you?"

"He understands," his father said. "We've talked to him about it. He'd be glad to get it behind him. Don't worry about Kevin," he said heartily.

That was what bothered me. Mr. Pollard's concern with not causing us bother. I'd seen that reaction in victims before, but I was more accustomed to those who demanded justice, who demanded more than I could provide. The suspicion crossed my mind that Mr. Pollard planned to obtain justice in his own way. He could have taken Chris Davis apart in the time it took a bailiff to cross the room.

"Does that sound all right?" I repeated to Kevin, my insistence aimed less at him than at his father. By staring intently at the boy I imposed silence on everyone else until Kevin looked up at me. His eyes were watery.

But he kept his voice from wavering by speaking softly. "Yes," he said. His eyes held me. He wanted something more. I wanted to speak to him privately. For a moment he looked as if he were still a kidnapping victim, and it was the people on either side of him holding him captive.

"Yes," he said more clearly. "That's what I want to do. Not testify in court. As long as he'll stay away."

"He will," I said. Kevin looked down again. "Karen, why don't you take Kevin down the hall and get him something to drink. And maybe something to play with."

Karen seemed glad to get the boy away, and Kevin went with her without hesitation. Karen turned at my door, took in both parents with her flat gaze, and looked at me. I nodded, and she left with Kevin.

Mr. and Mrs. Pollard were looking at me. Neither moved over to take the vacant chair between them.

"We're lucky," I said, "that this was not a violent or—extended—case of molesting." There was no good way to put this. I didn't want to minimize the harm to their son, but legally he hadn't been as much of a victim as he might have been. "I know it's frightening, but it could have been much worse. Kevin should outgrow it without much trouble. If he doesn't seem to be recovering, you should get in touch with this office and we'll recommend a counselor. We know some good ones." I assumed.

"The bad part is, *because* it wasn't worse than it was, I can't obtain a very high sentence for this man. Even if we put Kevin through a trial and did the very best we could do, it would only be twenty years."

Steve Pollard was nodding along with me. Once again I felt irritated at having him on my team.

"I can get almost that much in a plea bargain," I went on flatly. "Probably fifteen or so. I'm sure that doesn't sound like enough, but—"

"Yes, it does," Pollard said. "We won't make trouble about it."

"It's your decision," I said, giving up. "Whatever you tell me to do I'll do. Mrs. Pollard?"

"Yes?" She looked startled, as if she'd forgotten what we were discussing. Then she stiffened. Nothing had happened, husband and wife hadn't exchanged a glance. Pollard was suddenly stiff, the muscles standing out in his neck as if he had his jaws clamped. And his wife sat up alertly as if he'd grabbed her arm.

"Have you understood everything I've said?"

"Yes," she said hastily. "Yes, this is best. For Kevin. We don't want him—to have to relive it."

We had our agreement, that's what I'd wanted from them, but I found myself both anxious to get them out of my office and reluctant to let them go. We hadn't connected. I hoped Karen was doing better with Kevin.

"Is he going to be okay?" I asked her a few minutes later, after the family Pollard had taken their joyful leave of us.

"Kevin?" she said, and shrugged. "How good was he going to be anyway?"

It had been interesting to see Karen in the room with all of us. She'd been in her kinder, gentler persona because the boy was with us, but she'd been sitting behind him, behind his parents, and her eyes had told me she was still there, inside her motherly disguise, the bitter woman for whom the world was arranged all wrong.

"I hope you didn't let that Norman Rockwell family-togetherness scene fool you," she said now that we were alone. "That was the most time they've been in the same room for a year. The parents are separated."

Ah. Click, click. Nothing was ajar any more. I found myself feeling slightly relieved. "I'm stunned," I said. "They seemed such a happy family."

"That boy's going to need help," Karen said. "They haven't even bothered to get divorced, so the father doesn't have to pay support or have regular visitation. He just drops by whenever he feels like it, and he hasn't felt like it much since Kevin spent the night with a strange man. You saw him—his biggest concern is that his kid's going to turn out to be a fag instead of a fullback. He's doing his duty now, but after this is done he'll drop Kevin like a hot rock. And Kevin knows it. He's smarter than both of them, he knows his dad wants nothing to do with him. You stay in office long enough, you'll see Kevin back in this place. Nine, ten years from now. You watch. I only hope what he's charged with is killing his old man. I'll testify for him."

I sighed. This had been the last of the interviews, the hardest and the easiest. I had all the parents' agreements. All of us, the defense included, just wanted the cases to go away quietly.

"Let's do it," I said abruptly. "Let's get these things indicted and get it over with.

"What?" I added harshly, after silence had forced me to look at the advocate again. "What do you want me to do? All I can do is prosecute somebody who's already done something. Everybody else has to get on with their own lives. I'm no more in charge of the world than you are, Karen."

When everybody wants something to happen it can get done quickly. I took the cases to a grand jury the same week, and had three indictments for indecency with a child an hour later. The cases landed in Judge Hernandez's court, and when Austin and I appeared together to ask for an early disposition setting, the judge was happy to oblige. We had a date set the week before Labor Day.

The only surprise was the call I received from Mrs. Pollard. She spoke very quickly, as if afraid she was wasting my time or as if somebody might step in and pull the phone out of her hands.

"I know you said we didn't have to be there for the guilty plea, and it won't be like a regular trial, but I wondered if it would be all right if we do come. Kevin and I. Not to talk or anything, just to watch. I think it would help for Kevin to see it happen, to see the man taken away in handcuffs. He still doesn't— Some nights I have to sleep with Kevin. He—"

It was none of my business. "Of course," I said. "It's a public event. You're free to be there. But do you really think—"

"He won't get near Kevin, will he? I've never been in a courtroom." She sounded apologetic, as if telling me she'd dropped out of school.

"No, ma'am. You and Kevin will be in the audience, with a railing between you and the front of the court, and the defendant will be brought in through a side door. They won't be close."

"Good. Then we'll be there."

I wanted to ask if Kevin's father would be there too, but didn't want my tone to alert her that I'd noticed anything wrong in her family. Let them think they could fool anyone.

The day of the plea, we gathered by ones and twos as if for a secret meeting. Judge Hernandez had graciously given us a day in the middle of the week when nothing else was set in his court. The Justice Center was almost empty on the hot summer afternoon. My footsteps echoed in the stairwell.

But there was a flock of media outside the third-floor courtroom. We hadn't kept the occasion secret; to the contrary, publicity was part of the plan. It was a campaign appearance for me, and I allowed myself to be sidetracked into one of those dashing courthouse interviews—"Yes, Jim, I can take a moment to reassure your viewers, while on my way to do justice and serve the people"—so beloved in the spot news biz in which we were all engaged.

Two print journalists and a couple of their TV counterparts were inside the courtroom, scattered through the pews. There were no spectators. It wasn't an entertaining occasion. There was no potential for drama as there would have been if it had been a trial, I thought.

Halfway up the left aisle I saw a black-haired head that barely reached over the seat back. Beside him, Mrs. Pollard turned to look at me. She had no expression. Karen was with them, protectively placed on the aisle. No man.

I nodded to them gravely as I passed, but didn't think I'd do them any favor by calling further attention to them. As I passed them, another figure, inside the rail, arrested my attention. I walked faster as he turned toward me.

"Eliot!" I pumped his hand. "I didn't know you'd be here."

"Just watching out for you," he said quietly.

I chatted with him, aware that we were standing before the bench of a criminal courtroom in which he had never tried a case and never would. I wondered how Eliot felt as a spectator at the scene to which he'd once been so central.

Becky Schirhart arrived. As the regular first chair prosecutor in the court she was there to do the actual work of taking the guilty plea. She looked quite at ease. It wasn't her case, it was just a guilty plea, she had nothing to worry about. But I remembered her new to the office, when I'd still been a defense lawyer, and later when she was made insecure by having me as a new boss, when an occasion like this would have sent her spinning with worries of everything that could go wrong. She was an old pro now, relaxed in the courtroom. Becky was summer-casual, wearing a long-waisted dress instead of a suit. Her brown hair, loose to her shoulders, showed traces of exposure to sun. Her eyes, I noticed for the first time, were hazel, some subtle shade that seemed to shift as she did, as the light moved across her face.

I introduced her to Eliot. Becky wasn't as callow as many of my young assistants; she had enough sense of history to know whom she was meeting and treat him accordingly, not as if Eliot were a civilian lost inside the bar. Becky was as tall as Eliot, making him look older, though he was tanned and steady and made us both laugh with a casual story about an occasion when the judge of this court had worked for him.

I was looking past Becky's shoulder down the aisle. Kevin Pollard's reaction told me something had happened. He was suddenly sunk even deeper in his seat. Karen was leaning over him.

Austin Paley was coming up the aisle, glancing to either side, pleased, I was sure, by the sparse population of the courtroom. This appearance was slumming for him; he wouldn't want it widely observed. He stopped as he came abreast of the two women and Kevin, glanced at them disapprovingly, then hurried toward us. But he wasn't looking at either Eliot or me. Finally I turned and saw that Chris Davis had entered through the quietly sliding door behind the bailiff's desk.

He was wearing his Bexar County Jail uniform, a white coverall. His hands were handcuffed in front of him. The cuffs seemed to drag down his arms, showing their white undersides, the thin muscles apparently incapable of lifting the heavy metal cuffs.

He hadn't even shaved for his appearance. He looked fifteen years older than the last time I'd seen him. His eyes were sunken in reddened sockets, his nose had grown so thin it looked incapable of drawing breath, and his hair looked lank and thinner. He shuffled toward me in his jail thongs, his bare feet pathetically bony.

I looked back at Kevin. This was why he was here. I didn't see how anyone could be frightened of this apparition before me, but Kevin visibly was. Both Karen and his mother had their arms around him, but Kevin looked all alone, lost in a foreign landscape. He'd raised his left arm so that only his eyes showed, and I suspected beneath the cover of the arm he was sucking his thumb.

"You should have warned me we'd have an audience," Austin said, rather snippily.

"The boy's mother thought it would be good for him to see it," I said formally.

"Let's hope it's good for all of us," Austin said. "Hello, Eliot."

"Austin. How odd to see you in this place."

"And you," Austin said, recovering his good humor. "Let me just make sure my client is as happy as possible."

He went to confer with the defendant in the jury box, Eliot resumed his seat, and Becky and I went over the paperwork for the plea. Judge Hernandez kept us all waiting. I looked from Chris Davis to Kevin. The defendant never looked at the boy. He did nothing threatening that I could see, but Kevin never grew calmer. He stared at the jury box where Davis sat with his lawyer. The sight of the defendant should have reassured him. Davis looked helpless and beaten himself. It was impossible to picture Kevin letting this crazed-looking man near him.

Finally Judge Hernandez, a man of middle age and more than middling girth, entered, and we few scattered souls rose to acknowledge his sovereignty. "The State of Texas versus Christopher Davis," the judge announced.

"The State is ready," I said. Becky rose and approached the bench to represent us.

"So is the defendant, Your Honor," Austin said, always only as formal as the occasion required. He brought the defendant forward to stand between Austin and Becky, in the direct glare of the judge's majesty.

"Do we have an agreement?" Judge Hernandez asked.

As Becky read the terms and Austin agreed she had it right, I moved to the side so I could see Davis's face. It also gave me a chance to look back at Kevin. The details of the guilty plea droned on, a ritual I'd performed or watched thousands of times, until it had lost not only meaning but reality. But Kevin Pollard's frightened face opened the proceedings to the outside world, made this quasi-public ceremony hopelessly inadequate. It would be over in ten minutes. Kevin needed more.

As did the defendant. I noticed Chris Davis shuffling to the side, almost edging Austin out of his path. Austin had to put a hand on his arm. Davis saw his fate coming. Until this moment he'd probably still hoped to get away free, even after agreeing to accept a fifteen-year prison sentence. I've seen defendants, I've listened to them. Many of them harbor foolish hope up to the last moment that when the time comes they'll be able to say something, or a sign will appear on their faces, turning aside the wrath of the State and persuading the judge to exercise compassion.

For a defendant, the guilty plea, though he'd accepted that it represented his only chance to receive a lighter sentence than he had coming, also meant giving up his one chance to tell his story. It meant that the judging authority heard only the guilty details, not the compelling reasons. The defendant lost his chance to evoke sympathy, to make people see that nothing had happened as he'd intended, that he had been as much a victim of events as anyone else. Sometimes I could see their faces twitch with the desire to explain themselves.

Chris Davis had that look. I thought the bailiff was going to have to restrain him. Maybe it was Davis's nervousness that was making Kevin so fearful. Davis did look like a man about to bolt. I walked through the low gate in the railing and back down the aisle to stand next to Kevin. I leaned over and put my hand on Kevin's shoulder, only for a moment, then just stood there looking as determinedly protective as I could. Damn his father.

It should have been over in minutes. It's hard to derail a guilty plea. Chris Davis found a way to do it, though.

"You understand," the judge was telling him, "that by entering a plea of guilty you are waiving your right to a trial by jury?"

Davis murmured something that must have been acceptable to the record. "Very well," Judge Hernandez said. "How do you plead?"

I didn't hear what he said. But the proceeding halted. Austin looked at his client. Becky looked back at me.

"What?" the judge said.

"No," Chris Davis said distinctly, obviously repeating himself. He shook his head. He said it again—"No"—not noisily but adamantly.

Judge Hernandez looked displeased, as if suspecting he was the victim of a prank. "Do you mean 'not guilty'?" he asked in deep magisterial tones.

"No," was all Davis would say. "No, no, I won't." He began shaking his head and wouldn't stop.

"A moment, please, Your Honor." Austin pulled the defendant aside and began speaking to him with obvious growing harshness. Davis wouldn't stop shaking his head. Austin's hand came up as if he wanted to slap his client. Chris Davis's head was down, he couldn't look at Austin. He might still have been repeating his litany of "no, no, no, no."

"Cold feet," Becky said, beside me. "Send him back to jail, bring him back in another month, he'll come around."

"Well, hell," said a low, fierce voice behind my other

44

shoulder. Becky and I turned in surprise to see Eliot Quinn standing there, as if he had joined our discussion, but his troubled gaze was directed across the room at the recalcitrant defendant.

When Eliot realized we'd heard him, he turned toward us. "I'm sorry, Mark," he said. "I got you into this. I'll get you out again. Perhaps this young lady is right." He gave Becky a more than perfunctory glance; she became self-conscious. "Let him stew for a while, he'll come around."

"It's no problem, Eliot. This gives me a chance to try him. Even better exposure for me." Neither Eliot nor Becky would have understood that I was joking, because they hadn't heard my campaign manager's suggestion that I do just that. They took me seriously. Eliot looked concerned, started to speak again, then changed his thought to goodbye. "I'll get it straightened out," he told me just before he left.

"Will I be like that?" Becky asked, watching him go. "Still wanting to prosecute people long after I'm gone?"

"I don't know. How strong is the urge now? Do you want to prosecute this one?"

She turned to look at the defendant. To me he hardly looked worth prosecuting. He looked as if he'd expire on his own in another day or two. But there was no sympathy in Becky's stare. She looked as if she were seeing the crime enacted. It is a rare quality in a prosecutor, or anyone else, to be able to resurrect from bare written details the immediate horror of crime. The cases pass before your eyes so fast you just have time to translate details into sentencing guidelines—abuse, gun, pain, fear: thirty years—not to bring them to life. This one had slowed suddenly so that Becky seemed to see it. Her gaze only softened when she looked up the aisle to the boy huddling next to his mother.

"Sure," Becky said. "I'll try it."

"Have you ever done a child sexual assault before?"

"I've sat second on two or three," Becky said.

"Then you know you have to win that boy's trust completely. Think you can do that?"

She said, absolutely unconvincingly, "Children love me."

I touched her arm, lightly, and walked up the aisle. "Okay?" I asked, and Karen said, "Yes," but her deep look at me belied it.

"What's happening?" Mrs. Pollard asked. I was looking at Kevin rather than her, so I was startled when she reached across and grabbed my hand.

"The defendant can't bring himself to say guilty," I said, as if it were no big problem.

"They won't let him go?" She tugged at me, saw she was being inappropriate, and released me.

"Oh no," I said forcefully, answering her question, but it was Kevin I was looking at and speaking to. He had sunk to the size of a child half his age, and he was trembling. *My God,* I thought, *what did Chris Davis do to him?*

"This is bad for him," I went on. "He'll go straight back to jail, and after he thinks about it for a while he'll probably beg to come back here and plead guilty. And if he doesn't I'll just prosecute him, and we'll do each case separately so the sentences will be stacked on top of each other and he'll be in prison a lot longer than he would have if he'd taken this offer. Kevin."

Maybe it was a mistake. I'm certainly no child psychologist. But I wanted to involve him, not conduct the whole discussion over the boy's head as if he were inanimate. I knelt to put my face on a level with his. "Do you think you could sit up there on that witness stand and tell what happened to you? Not today," I reassured him, "but someday, if we needed you to do that? We'd practice with you, you'd know what to say. Could you do that, Kevin?"

The challenge, as I'd hoped, made him sit up straighter instead of cowering further. "Yes," he said softly.

"Good." To his mother I said, "It might not come to that, but I want to know. Kevin would be our best witness."

When I stood up it had all fallen apart. Austin Paley threw up his hands and stalked away from his client. The judge had already left the bench. Austin said a word to Becky, then looked at me and stopped. He looked as if he didn't want to approach me. But then he steeled himself, as if forcing himself to do the right thing by someone against whom he'd committed some social faux pas, and came through the gate in the railing. He only glanced at the little group in the seats beside me. When he reached me he took my arm and drew me further up the aisle toward the courtroom doors.

"I'm sorry, Mark. I had no idea I was involving you in a fiasco like this."

You and Eliot have been too long out of the daily grind, I thought. A busted plea bargain is no big deal, it happens all the time. "I'll just set it for trial," I said.

Austin looked disconcerted, but he didn't protest. "Maybe that's what it will take. But we'll work something out. I'll give you a call."

He glanced behind me as if the whole setting gave him a pain, and hurried away. The room was clearing. The bailiff had swept up the remains of the defendant and whisked him back through the door into the clandestine passages that led to the jail wagon. Mrs. Pollard and Kevin were coming toward me. I tried to reassure her again, telling her I'd keep her informed, when two small hands gripped mine and tugged me down to Kevin's level. He was dressed up, in black slacks, a white short-sleeved shirt, and a green tie, making him look even more betrayed. He'd gotten dressed for a special occasion and been left waiting.

My face was only a few inches from his. For the first time I was close enough to see some strength in his little face. He had a good grip on my hand, too.

"Don't let him come to my house," he said.

"He won't get near you, Kevin. I promise."

He held my hands and my eyes a few moments longer, until my sincerity convinced him. He exchanged my hands for his mother's, and they walked slowly out.

A newspaper reporter named Jenny Lord was in front of me when I turned around. Without preliminaries she asked, "If these cases have to be tried now, will you prosecute them yourself?"

I motioned to Becky. "If my schedule permits," I said routinely.

"Come on, Mark, you can give me better than that."

I looked at Jenny, remembering the times we'd joked in halls and courts about the silly doings in the courthouse. "Hey, come on, it's not fair to pretend you know me. You wouldn't take advantage of our friendship, would you?"

"If we had one, no," she said, raising her pad, pencil, and eyebrows.

"All right," I said, accepting the challenge like a schoolboy. "Here. Since becoming district attorney I have personally obtained two death penalties, two more life sentences, and other convictions amounting to hundreds of years in prison. I'm not afraid to try a case. However"—I looked at Becky—"I have also assembled a professional, excellent staff. If this defendant is foolish enough to ask for a trial, he'll find a formidable prosecutorial team opposing him, and sending him to prison."

The reporter finished writing and looked up at me, bored. "That it?"

"All right, how about this?" I deepened my voice. "We're gonna throw the book at this guy. We'll make him wish he'd never been born."

"Oh, that's good," Jenny said, writing furiously.

Becky was looking at me, trying to keep her face expressionless. She wasn't very good at it. When I looked at her I remembered what she had said when I'd rebuked her ever so mildly for not clearing with a superior her plan to have the victim sit with her in the rape trial I'd watched her prosecute. "I know," Becky had said. She'd known she should, but she hadn't. Becky was the most deferential of my assistants, but in trial she was perfectly sure of herself.

I took her out with me. "I want to look at these cases a little more thoroughly," I said. "Would you like to join me?"

"Does that mean I'm the formidable staff member who gets to hammer this guy?"

"If you ask me nicely," I said.

4

The story about the ruptured plea bargain ran on that night's news. The TV anchor reminded viewers of the panic before the defendant was arrested and pointed out that the saga wasn't over yet. They also reran the video footage of Chris Davis's arrest in the hallway. We were all preserved in the melee—Austin shaking my hand, the defendant hangdog beside him, I the stern guardian of the community peace.

Unknown to me at the time, a ten-year-old boy I hadn't yet met was in his living room when the tape of the scene ran on the five o'clock news. The boy stopped what he was doing to watch, then watched for the story again at six. This time his parents were in the room, but they didn't notice his concentration. They thought nothing of it until the boy climbed out of his bed that night, sat unnoticed behind them until the footage appeared yet again, on the ten o'clock news, and said quietly, "He molested me, too."

His parents didn't believe him. They accused each other of overexposing the boy to the wrong kind of TV. But the next day the boy told his fifth-grade teacher, as well. The teacher, flustered but concerned, took the boy to the school nurse. After pondering her official options of giving the boy aspirin or sending him home, the nurse instead called a doctor she knew. The doctor made an appointment for the boy and called his parents.

And so Tommy's story began to make its way to me.

*　　*　　*

In the meantime, though, the cases I already had against Chris Davis were giving me fits. This was not going to be the laydown my campaign manager had asked me to find to prosecute. Becky and I began preparing the cases for trial, which involved much more careful study than merely talking to the parents. Since the defendant was no longer going to cooperate to convict himself, we had to see what we could prove against him, and that began to look slimmer and slimmer. Louise, the four-year-old girl, as Karen had warned me, proved useless. She identified Chris Davis from a spread of six photographs, yes. But the second time she identified another of the six. When we changed the lineup, with only Davis the same, she took another stab and missed.

"Adults are all the same to her," Karen said. "She doesn't even look at our faces. Put *your* picture in there and see what she does. You might look familiar to her by now."

I declined the experiment.

The third boy identified Chris Davis's photograph, but his story of what had happened between them had weakened to the point that the behavior he described may have been inappropriate, but it was no longer a crime. "He's successfully repressing it," Karen said. "Maybe that's best for him."

"It's not best for me," I growled.

I knew I could rely on Kevin Pollard. I'd heard him identify Davis in court. My only worry was that he'd be too scared to testify. Becky and I went to his home, hoping he'd be more comfortable there. It was seven o'clock at night, but Dad wasn't there, having abandoned the pretense of normal family life. I was glad not to see him.

As a way of easing into the idea of identifying the defendant in court, I showed Kevin my little spread of six photos. "In court," I told him, "you'll say that I showed you these pictures, and I'll ask if you picked one out. Now take your time, Kevin. Just show me the one of the man who picked you up in the car and took you home with him and touched you the way you didn't like."

The pictures were similar, young blond men, but not that similar. I expected the one of his molester to leap out at the boy. But he went through them slowly, pushing them apart with his finger. His mother leaned over his shoulder to look at them too. Somehow the mug shots, more than the court proceeding, seemed to make the experience her son had endured more real to her. Kevin lingered over the photo of Davis, but then kept going. Becky returned my look.

"He's not here," Kevin finally said.

"Could you look again, please?" I cajoled, trying to keep the exasperation out of my voice.

The little boy obliged. I watched Kevin. He no longer looked frightened. Was he successfully repressing the experience too? Were all my victims going to heal on me before I could put together a case?

"Not one of these," Kevin finally said in his thin voice. "Can I go play now?" he asked his mother.

"But you told me ..." I started over, trying to take the whine out of my voice. "Remember the day in court, when you told me he was the one who'd touched you?"

"Not him," Kevin repeated. His mother looked up at me, as innocently as her six-year-old son.

Out on the sidewalk, as we walked toward the car, I said to my assistant, "These have now become your cases, Becky."

"Oh, thanks."

"Being a first chair prosecutor, I'm sure you know the principle by now. When the case looks perfect, the first chair plans to try it. If a glitch pops up, it's no longer worthy of the first chair's attention; it's become a second chair case. If it gets bad enough it can become a third chair trial, and that's just one step above dismissal. And that's where these cases are headed."

"Well," she said as we settled into my car and I took off too fast, eager to leave this slightly shabby middle-class suburb behind, "I couldn't really picture myself trying a case with the district attorney." A beat. She was looking out the window. "But I was looking forward to it."

"I would have liked working with you too, Becky. You know, I wouldn't have let just anyone prosecute Mike Stennett." A rogue cop accused of murder. Becky had tried him in with the chief of the special crimes section. "Tyler thinks he handpicked you for that case, but I wouldn't have approved other choices he might have made. And I followed your trial work very closely."

"Really? I never saw you." Becky was still looking forward, not at me, but now she seemed deliberately to be forbidding herself from looking at me. Some strain showed in the profile of her neck and cheek.

"You were rather caught up in the trial," I said dryly. "I dropped in to the courtroom now and again. And of course I got daily reports from Tyler."

"I wondered."

We drove in silence for a few minutes. The atmosphere in the car was warmer but still a bit strained. Often I could forget my official position—there were a few people in the world who treated me the same as they always had—but from Becky I felt a steady awareness that I was her boss. I felt her watching me, waiting for her cue.

My thoughts returned to the case. I couldn't understand Kevin. He'd told me in court we had the right man. I would have known from his reaction anyway. Why was he denying it now?

Becky was also thinking of the boy. When the Justice Center loomed in sight, and the parking garage where we'd left her car, she cleared her throat and said, "Are these really my cases? And do you really think they're on their way to being dismissed?"

"At the moment. Have you thought of a brilliant way to resurrect them?"

She turned sideways in the seat to face me as I pulled to a stop. "No, it's probably something stupid. But if we're about to lose them anyway, maybe you wouldn't mind trying something a little unorthodox."

"Try me," I said.

In the incidental crevices of time between work and campaigning, I tried to have a personal life, too. Luckily, I didn't have much of one to squeeze in.

When I picked up Dinah on Friday afternoon Lois invited me inside. I went just a few steps into the house, into the dining room beside the entry hall. "Hello, precious," I said to Dinah, holding her against me. Lois smiled at me over our daughter's head. "Have a good week?" I asked Lois.

The question became more than perfunctory when the

phone rang, Dinah yelled, "I'll get it," and streaked out of the room.

"Not bad," Lois said. "You?"

I laughed. "Hard to say."

She nodded as if she were still following my career.

"Is everything okay around here?" I asked. "The house seems to be holding up. You look great." I stopped and looked at her, at her raised eyebrows. "I didn't mean that to sound as if you're part of the house."

She laughed again. "I seem to have more time now, Mark. Dinah helps me out. I can even leave her alone for an hour or two. I get chances to go to a workout again once in a while. It's nice."

Our togetherness had been extended longer than we'd expected by the length of Dinah's phone call. Lois led me farther into the dining room. "Sometimes David comes over to stay with Dinah, or take her somewhere while I do something else," she said. "Have you talked to David lately?"

"Of course."

She looked at me as if she knew I was lying. It had been almost two weeks since I'd spoken to our son, twice that long since I'd seen him.

"He doesn't seem very happy," Lois said.

"I guess not. I don't understand why he's still married." David's marriage had always been rather mystifying to me, and had grown more so in the last three years.

"Well, you know." Lois didn't want to criticize. But, "I wish you'd talk to him," she continued. "I don't know what's wrong. Maybe he'd tell you what he won't tell me."

I just looked at her. She acknowledged the family history with a shrug. "But maybe it's the kind of thing he wouldn't want to tell his mother."

"My God, Lois, I think I've put off telling him about sex too long."

She didn't smile. "Well, when the chance comes up, I just thought—"

"Sure. I'll try, don't worry." Talking of David reminded me, and I'm sure Lois as well, of our marriage, and how it had ended. We cleared our throats and our sentences trailed away to nothing, until Dinah rejoined us. "Let's go!" I said heartily.

"Don't forget," Lois said softly as I went out the door.

There were two slight problems with my cases against Chris Davis. Technical difficulties, we would call them: He wouldn't plead guilty, and I couldn't prove he was. I had a sudden brilliant insight. Davis now said he hadn't done it. So did the victims. Could it be—? I hoped a chat with the defendant might allay this silly fear.

Austin Paley had to be there. I couldn't talk to a defendant without his lawyer being present. So Austin Paley met me at the jail the following Monday morning. Sheriff Marrs was kind enough to let us use an office rather than one of the booths where inmates normally met with their lawyers. While we waited for Davis to be brought in, Austin and I exchanged greetings more formally than usual.

"What a mess," Austin said, shaking his head. "I'm sorry, Mark. What are we going to do now?"

I found Austin's calm assumption that we were working to solve the mystery together, on the same team, annoying, but I answered anyway. "I thought I'd see if your client's changed his mind about pleading."

"Maybe you can better the offer just a touch?" Austin suggested helpfully.

"Would that help?"

Austin shrugged. A short, jumpy-looking deputy brought Chris Davis into the room. I didn't think the handcuffs were necessary, but some deputies use them at every opportunity.

"I'll be right outside," the deputy said vigilantly.

Davis sat down, manacled hands in his lap. Austin and I remained standing across the room, as if we both were his interrogators.

"I want to ask you a few questions," I said. "It's up to you whether you want to answer, but it might help if you did."

Davis looked at Austin, who said offhandedly, "I'm sure Chris doesn't need me to tell him that he doesn't have to say anything. But if he feels he should—"

Austin extended a hand, offering his client to me, and I sat in front of the defendant. He glanced up, then back down.

"I just have one question," I said. "Why did you change your mind about pleading guilty?"

Davis wouldn't look at me. "Because I didn't do them," he muttered.

"But you confessed, Chris."

His gaze shifted still farther away, to the side. After a minute of silence I said, "Then I have to assume you *did* do them."

He looked at me sharply. Chris Davis's blue eyes were already watery. He looked scared, as I wanted him. But not scared enough to talk.

"And you knew the right details," I went on. "Facts that weren't in the newspapers. Things you couldn't have known to confess to if you weren't the one."

"No, but I—" he said quickly, then stopped again.

I could see he was tormented. I had a good idea that Davis was no innocent, as Eliot Quinn had told me, but I also had that growing suspicion. He had been on the verge of confirming it for me, I was sure, when he'd stopped himself.

I leaned my head in close to his, and spoke confidentially. "You didn't have to be here, Chris. You turned yourself in. You confessed."

"I felt guilty," he muttered.

"But you didn't do these, did you?"

He looked past me, at his lawyer. I couldn't see Austin. I kept my attention riveted on Chris Davis.

"No," he said.

I leaned back. Now I had a terrible problem: I believed him.

"Why on earth would you confess, then?"

I think if we'd been alone he would have told me. But it was a secret so awful he couldn't say it in front of Austin. I put the question a different way. "What could they threaten you with that would be worse than this?"

I didn't mean the police officers who had taken his confession, and he knew it. I meant whoever had sent him into the glare of publicity to absorb the heat of the public's fear and indignation.

"Who put you up to it?" I asked. But whatever the hold

on him was, it held still. Davis clamped his jaw and shook his head.

Behind my back, Austin chimed in as if we were working together. "You can tell him, Chris. Who sent you to me?"

The defendant just shook his head again. He was growing older every time I saw him. His white jail coverall seemed to be leeching color from his skin. He was so pale I could see his veins running blue under his skin. The only dark spots on his body were around his eyes. His frightened eyes were retreating into the caves of darkness under his brow.

We hammered at him for twenty or thirty minutes. Once in a while I'd throw up my hands and say something like, "Well, I've got him, and I need somebody. I'll just convict him anyway. I can do it with my witnesses and his confession." And Austin would say, faithfully trying to good-cop his client, "You hear that, Chris? You're the only one who can save yourself." But we were wasting our dramatic talents. Chris Davis kept shaking his head at first, even spoke a few times, evasively, but after a while he began to withdraw from us. His thin arms, with the hands lying limply in his lap, began to draw closer across his chest. His head lowered. By the end of the session he looked like an overgrown autistic child, his response to the outside world reduced to one shaking foot.

I looked at Austin, who looked back alertly, ready to follow my lead. But I was done. Not bothering to lower my voice, I said to Austin, "I'm going to dismiss one of the cases, where the child says positively Davis wasn't the one."

Austin nodded. "That was honest of him."

"But the other two I'm keeping pending. As soon as he wants out of jail he can have it, in exchange for a name. I assume he understands that."

"Let me talk to him for just a minute."

I went out into the hall. The deputy who'd promised to remain on guard had deserted his post. I looked back to see Austin leaning earnestly over his client, a hand on Davis's shoulder. Austin had managed to animate him sufficiently that the defendant was nodding again. It was only a minute or two before Austin straightened and walked out to where I was standing.

"Let's walk out together, Mark. Um—" He saw that we were locked in too. "I'll get a guard."

He walked farther down the hall. I returned to the doorway of the office, feeling a vague obligation to keep watch over the prisoner. He looked too pitiful to guard, though. At the sound of my footsteps he looked up. He must have been expecting Austin again, but he kept watching me so intently that I reopened the conversation.

"Who could have made you do this?" I said, shaking my head. It was a rhetorical question, I thought.

But Davis swallowed and looked past me and said, "Ask him. Ask my lawyer."

5

But I'd realized that already. Austin Paley hadn't been tricked into this scheme, he was part of it. Austin was connected. If a powerful manipulator wanted to arrange this substitution scheme, he'd go to Austin. And Austin had arranged it beautifully, even conning someone I'd trust blindly, Eliot, into fronting for him. But who was Austin's real client in this business? It must have been a complete insider, someone who knew where the bodies were buried. Maybe he'd blackmailed Austin, too, into helping arrange the scheme. I wouldn't have thought Austin would willingly do something so unethical. But I also knew I'd never find out the name of his shadowy client from Austin or, apparently, from Chris Davis. Davis probably didn't even know. So I had to try the back door.

If someone had devised this scheme to get a substitute, Davis, to take the heat for these crimes, it must have been because the real molester felt the heat himself. The police investigation must have been getting uncomfortably close.

I went to see the detectives who'd worked the cases. From the one who'd taken Chris Davis's confession I got only disappointment that he was back at work on the cases. "Shit, you close a case—three cases, this time—you take some satisfaction from putting some jerk away, you go on to the hundred other cases you got, then *boom!* it all falls through. What happens to these things over in that damned courthouse?"

His partner was cagier. Lou Padilla, his name was. He was older, probably old enough for retirement, and in anticipation he'd started letting himself get fat. But his face was still hard when he wanted it to be. He didn't stand up from his desk and shake my hand, just grunted as if he wasn't surprised to see me.

My entering his office had reduced the floor space almost to nil. I sat in the metal visitor's chair, my knees hitting the front of his desk.

"I guess you've heard these child-molesting cases are open again?" I said after the preliminaries. Padilla nodded toward three files open in front of him. I had a sudden conviction that the files had never left his desk. "You have any other good suspects?" I asked.

"Got several." The two words must have hurt his throat terribly, because he didn't try any more.

"Such as?"

He waved a hand. "Just suspects, you know? The usual. I don't wanta blacken anybody's reputation by droppin' their name before I'm sure."

I didn't say anything else for a minute or so, because there wasn't any point. Suddenly the whole conversation was between our eyes. He was looking at me languidly, but steadily. There was something he didn't like about my being there. I looked back at him hard, trying to pry it out. He managed to bear up under my stare.

"Any of your suspects what might be called highly placed?"

"Highly placed?" he repeated, as if I were speaking over his head.

"Rich, or politically connected, or the son of somebody who's got some influence somewhere, that sort of thing?"

"I don't concern myself with that kind of crap," Lou Padilla said.

The hell he didn't. "What is it?" I asked. "Somebody you're afraid to go after? Who are you protecting?"

"Just being careful, sir." He had a way of saying "sir" that made you think it was his dog's name.

"Somebody forced Chris Davis to fade the heat for them. That means somebody with money or power or both."

"Good theory," the detective said. He hadn't moved from

his slumped position in his desk chair. He didn't break into a sweat, either, under the weight of my suspicions.

"How about if I glance through your files myself?" I asked, reaching for them.

"Be my guest," he said, so I knew it would be useless. He wouldn't have written the name down.

I had expected that at least the investigating officers were doing their jobs. I hadn't thought the cover-up would extend this far. This seriously disrupted my theory that the child molester had thrown Chris Davis up as a screen because the police were getting close to the real offender. Maybe he'd done both, devised the substitution scheme *and* bought off the cops. He was a careful man, in some matters.

Suddenly I was furious. I'd been duped, but here was a man deliberately neglecting his job. I stood up. "So who're you going to come up with as a suspect this time?" I said on my way out.

"Look," his voice called me back, with an edge of anxiety, but when I turned back he looked imperturbably the same. "I'm a nobody," Lou Padilla said. "I put in my ten hours a day in this pit, I go home and eat supper, I sit in front of the TV with a beer. I don't own a tux. I don't run for office. I'm not looking for an in with anybody."

If he felt he had to justify himself, then it must have been bothering him. "Tell me what you know," I said, closing his office door.

"Just leave me out of it," he said, glaring, but not at me, at an empty corner.

"You're not," I said. "You're right in the thick of it."

He shook his head as if he'd just shake me off. When I didn't leave we stayed encased in silence for a long minute. I decided I wouldn't ever leave. Detective Padilla acted as if he'd read the thought in my mind. For a moment his voice sounded uneasy again, just a shade.

"Why don't you ask somebody who *would* know?" he said. "Some insider. Somebody who collects those things."

"Like?"

He looked at me. He studied me. Then his face grew hard again. This would be the last word I'd get from him.

"Ask Eliot Quinn," he said.

* * *

At first I thought, *Yes, it makes sense now. Eliot has known from the beginning.* Then I thought, *No, Eliot would never set me up that way. Especially not to protect a criminal.* Then I thought, *But maybe once I tell him it was all a hoax, he'll have a good idea who might have been behind it.* There was nobody who knew more about the dirt in San Antonio, for the last thirty years, than Eliot Quinn. And then I thought, *No, Padilla was just being sly, throwing me off the track.* Then I thought—

This array of thoughts kept me from going to see Eliot. In my state of mind, it wouldn't have been helpful, because I couldn't have trusted whatever he chose to tell me anyway. I kept putting it off, while trying to develop my own investigation.

"This is the crazy thing you wanted to try?" I asked.

"I don't think 'crazy' is the word I used," Becky Schirhart replied.

"You realize you could hopelessly taint the witness? If this came out at trial—"

"What good is he to us now anyway?" Becky answered.

She was right. The risk was minimal.

"Besides," she said, again reasonably, "Kevin was already in the courtroom. How much more could this taint him?"

So we found ourselves once again at Kevin Pollard's house two evenings later. It was nice to have something to do at night. After seeing Linda at the campaign rally, I'd almost reached the point of calling her again. Work postponed the decision for me.

We settled cozily in the living room. Becky sat beside Kevin on the couch, but I took a seat to the side, so I could see the boy as well as the TV screen. Mrs. Pollard stayed on her feet. We'd politely refused her offers of coffee and dessert, but she wanted to be ready in case we changed our minds.

Becky had called ahead to make sure they had a VCR. She had to eject a tape of turtles or dinosaurs in order to insert ours. Kevin stared at the screen like a born addict. As Becky straightened and resumed her seat she explained.

"I obtained this videotape from the TV station. It's very short, Kevin." She had to say his name again to tear his gaze from the screen. "Remember we showed you pictures

61

before, and you identified the man who touched you? But then later you said it wasn't him." Kevin nodded. He was very quiet, waiting for us to tell him what he'd done wrong, and what his punishment would be. Becky smiled at him reassuringly, but she spoke like an adult who had no children of her own, overelaborately, making too much of everything.

"But sometimes pictures don't really look like the people," she continued. She looked up at Mrs. Pollard and me and laughed. "I'd hate to think I look like my driver's license photo." Kevin's mother smiled back politely.

"So we thought we'd show you this instead. A videotape where people move and turn different ways and look more like themselves." As she started the tape she said, "Now don't get nervous, Kevin. Just tell us if you see the man who molested you. Who touched you. And if he's not here, tell us that too."

The screen came to life. It was the tape of my heroic arrest of the infamous serial child molester, in the crowded courthouse hallway. There was no sound. The speed seemed slightly off, so that the figures moved like some weird breed between humans and cartoon animations. This was not such a crazy idea of Becky's, at that. The videotape was as good a lineup as a defendant could ask for. Chris Davis edged into the scene, but he wasn't handcuffed, nothing shouted that he was the suspect. And there were many other men in the picture, some of roughly similar appearance to Davis. We weren't influencing Kevin with a hopelessly suggestive showing.

Kevin looked much calmer than he had in court, but he still grew stiff as the figures filled the screen. When Chris Davis entered the picture with his lawyer, Kevin's eyes grew big. A minute later the scene was over.

"Did you see him?" Becky asked. Kevin said nothing.

"Run it again," I said.

This time as the scene started Kevin stood up. His back was to his mother and Becky, I was the only one who could see his face. His mouth was pinched into a tiny circle. His eyes were watery again, but he didn't just look as if he were on the verge of tears. He showed a mixture of emotions. I couldn't believe, looking at him again, that he hadn't seen his molester in court. Tonight's was a much diminished version of his reaction then, and it was still disturbing.

"Him," he said, touching the screen.

I looked at Becky and rolled my eyes.

She couldn't see the screen, Kevin was blocking her view. She moved around him, but by that time the figures had moved so that Kevin's immobile finger rested on nothing. Becky ran it back and asked him to try again. "Him," Kevin said again. This time Becky froze the picture.

"Which one?" she asked, and Kevin made sure we all could see. Becky and I looked at each other, she ruefully, as if the label I'd applied to this experiment had proven correct.

But Kevin was convinced of his choice, however wayward. He was trembling again. I wanted to reach out and hold him, but I was afraid to touch him. To my relief, Becky put her arms around him, murmuring reassurance, but Kevin remained stiffly standing, staring at the screen.

"Something happened to that boy all right," Becky said later in the car. "But by now he's so confused I don't think he knows what."

"No," I said. "But somebody knows." I was beginning to think I should take Detective Padilla's advice. Ask Eliot Quinn.

The sun hit me as soon as I stepped out of the Justice Center. It was barely noon, but already one of those days. The sky was cloudless but not blue. It had been bleached of color, white as the sun that burned in its center. It made people scurry for cover the way heavy rain would. I had to walk across rubble to cross one street. Workers had excavated a ten-foot hole to get at something and had the tar bubbling ready to replace the pavement. Its fumes blended with the heat to make it seem we were under noxious attack. The downtown streets were always torn up, in a pattern seemingly designed for no reason but to frustrate motorists. Something was always broken. Five thousand years from now archaeologists will uncover this city and conclude that it was built by a race of titans who mysteriously died out and their city was taken over by a lesser race who couldn't maintain it and eventually smothered in their own garbage.

Even the short walk left me feeling a little light-headed. The office building was pleasantly cool and the elevator brisk, but I still arrived at the entrance to the dining club feeling clammily inappropriate for the dim, elegant surroundings. The maître d' looked as if he agreed with my thought. "This way," he said.

On the way we collected Eliot, who was in the bar talking and laughing with a man who appeared to me underdressed until Eliot introduced us and I realized the man could dress any way he damn pleased, because he owned the building.

"Drink?" Eliot asked when we were seated, but I declined, both because I was still a bit sun-dazzled and because I didn't want what I had to say to sound merely like the product of a loosened tongue. When Eliot finished the amber drink the maître d' had carried for him from the bar the waiter brought another, with no signal from Eliot.

Our chairs were very comfortable, and our table bore a white cloth. There was only a scattering of other lunchers, all of us far enough apart to be private. All through lunch I tried to bring up what I wanted to say, but the elegant surroundings seemed to impose a murmuring inconsequence on the conversation. Eliot kept up an amusing flow of stories about other rich, important men he spotted around the room, but he punctuated it with questions for me about running the office. Once in a while he'd smile at my answers as if to say there was nothing new beneath the broiling sun.

The next time the waiter replaced Eliot's glass I said, "Me too." It turned out to be a bourbon old-fashioned, not one of my favorites. The taste made me suck in my breath, and it emerged dragging the train of words I'd been rehearsing.

"Something's happened that points away from Chris Davis, Eliot. I'm beginning to suspect Austin Paley set me up, trying to protect someone. How he forced Davis to confess I don't know, and it doesn't matter. What I want to know is who he was trying to protect."

Eliot didn't answer. With one finger he swept the table, clearing the space between us. I barely even saw the waiter's hands. Eliot dropped his boulevardier's air but didn't look perturbed. He just gave me his full attention.

"The cases are crumbling," I began, before I remembered I wasn't sure whether what I said would find its way into the enemy camp. I stopped so suddenly Eliot must have sensed my reason, but he didn't say anything. The silence grew as we watched each other.

I realized, looking at him, that I would never be Eliot. I'd never match his record of longevity; my current term as district attorney might be my last. Even if I did remain in office I'd never develop Eliot's contacts. At his age I'd feel as out of place in this quiet, rich club as I did now. I lacked that combination of toughness and gregariousness that gave Eliot such ease anywhere he found himself. It seemed to me as I sat there that an old ambition of mine was falling away. The feeling made me change the subject.

"When I was one of your assistants," I began, "I never had delusions about my place in the hierarchy. I didn't picture myself as felony chief. I knew I was just one of the troops. But it did seem to me I had a peculiar string of luck in one way. Once in a while I'd have a problem with a case. Like knowing the case would be tough to prove, maybe impossible, but not wanting to let it go. The defense lawyer's pressing me for a dismissal or a low offer and I know he has it coming, in the normal course of things, but the *crime* was worth more. Yes—" I grinned. "Once in a great while I stepped outside the system and thought about the crime itself instead of how good or bad a case it was, and I'd get angry. But I knew it wouldn't do any good to try a case I couldn't make. It certainly wouldn't make my stock in the office rise any higher."

Eliot cleared his throat. "And often on one of those occasions," I hurried on, "not every time but often enough that it seemed more than coincidence, you would appear. You'd come into my court to talk to the judge or my first chair, or you'd be passing in the hall and step into my office to ask how it was going. You must have done that a lot, but the times I remember were the ones when I was having a problem. As if you'd come because you knew about it, like some sort of"—I didn't say what I was thinking, which was "fairy godmother"—"guardian. Not just like the boss. And you always said something that helped. You'd tell me to go ahead and try it and let the chips fall where they would, or that you'd assign another investigator who might dig something up. One time just the fact that you appeared in court and seemed to confer with me about the case made the defense lawyer think there was more weight behind the case than he'd been thinking, and he agreed to plead to what I'd offered."

Eliot and I both smiled, at having put one over so long ago. There was something I wanted to say, but even now I was too embarrassed. Instead I said, "You must have been all over that building all the time, dropping in on courts and offices, to leave all your assistants with that feeling. It's something I'd like to learn."

"Mark." Eliot shook his head slightly, still smiling. "I *did* take a special interest in your career," he said. He'd heard the thing I couldn't bring myself to say. "I watched you, I watched your cases. Eventually I made you a first chair prosecutor, and you know there were people who stayed in the office years longer than you who never made that. I'm sure you know why, now that *you're* the office guardian. You have assistants you watch more fondly than the others."

"But you didn't know me well enough—"

"I did," Eliot said. "Oh, I know, I didn't have drinks after work with you, or bring you to my club. But it doesn't take socializing. You know who you can count on, don't you? It doesn't take many times of watching in court or strolling through the halls after five o'clock. You can tell the real prosecutors, the ones who believe in what we do, from the ones who are just in the office to get trial experience or a paycheck. Can't you?"

Yes, I made those distinctions, usually unconsciously. It was no random chance I was working with Becky Schirhart on these important cases.

"I think you've proven I was right about you," Eliot said.

Then why did you help Austin Paley screw me? That was my question I didn't ask. Intuitive as Eliot was, I was sure he heard it, especially when I returned to the topic.

"I'm sure Austin lured you in just as he did me, Eliot. But now that you know it was all a fraud, you should have a good idea who he's trying to protect. You know his associations. You must have heard rumors." Eliot didn't look like a man searching his memory. He began to look like a cagey opponent. Damn. "There's something old about this case, Eliot. Austin himself, for one thing. How long has it been since he was in a criminal court? And the investigation seems to be leading back in time." That was a wild shot, based on Detective Padilla's age and attitude. "Something that goes back to your administration, maybe. Tell me."

Eliot said, "I'm glad you don't think I took any knowing part in duping you. If that's what it was. I'm still not convinced—"

"Because I couldn't imagine you doing that without being forced. And no one could have forced you. Who could threaten you, Eliot? You know where all the bodies are buried."

He smiled gently into his fading drink. "No, I dug them all up. I prosecuted all the crimes I knew about."

"Bullshit. I know better than that, Eliot. You can't have been district attorney of this town for twenty years, somebody as sharp as you, without learning things you couldn't prove in court. Hell, I know a few myself, and I haven't even been in office four years. Some underling is stealing from the customers and you know damned well he couldn't have done it without kicking back some to his boss, but he won't admit it, so the employee goes to jail or gets probation and you keep running into his boss at public functions and saying, 'Hi, how you doin',' but you know he's a fucking thief and he knows you know it. Somebody else knocks his wife around every time he gets drunk, but she drops the charges every time he sobers up. You can't make a case out of everything you know. But you know." I emphasized the pronoun. "Tell me who to suspect, Eliot."

He was no longer smiling. He sighed deeply. That made me hopeful. It sounded like a man who knew his disguises had been penetrated. But it also sounded like a man stalling for time. Eliot drained the last of his drink and made a gesture of negation that may have been aimed at the waiter rather than me. And his answer seemed off the subject.

"In the old days," he began, "even before my time, this was what was called a wide open town. Meaning it was completely closed up. If you knew the right people—and I mean maybe five men—you could get things done without anyone ever knowing. I don't mean get away with murder. The people one knew didn't commit murder. Murderers have very little influence on society. I mean you could get a historical building torn down without any fuss, if you needed the lot for a good reason. In crime it was DWIs, that sort of thing. That was something people could understand. Everyone ran the risk of being DWI once in a while. Nobody would mind if the case went away. Even reporters would keep it quiet. Once in a while something bigger, too. A rape case, maybe, if the girl wasn't from a good family and the boy was. She got compensated. Nobody got hurt.

"It filters down, you know? It wasn't just the big boys working things out. It's a way of life. No one wants to be unreasonable.

"But one thing leads to another. Once you start trading favors, even *receiv*ing favors becomes capital. 'You did me one before, I'd hate somebody to find out about that, how about another one now?' It wasn't that bald, but you know what I mean."

I knew. But I'd grown up in a different, less genteel system, thanks to this man across the table from me. "But you changed all that, Eliot."

He smiled. As usual, being with Eliot made me feel young and naïve. "Nothing ever changes, Mark."

"Austin Paley's a part of that old system, isn't he? He's too young, but somehow he's connected to everyone. I've always known Austin moved behind the scenes, but—"

"Austin's not very forward," Eliot agreed. "He likes his position in the deep background. Men like him usually have a longer life than people who get right out in front and have to stand for reelection."

"But he's not rich," I said. "Is he? It's not just about money, the kind of influence he wields. Politicians can always find other money cows. Tell me about him, Eliot."

There was no reason why he should, except the pleasure Eliot took in sharing a story. And perhaps the amber drinks were having some effect on him. "I can tell you exactly how to become Austin Paley," he said. "Austin did have some family money. Father was a lawyer, you know."

No, I hadn't known that. I couldn't think who Austin's father might have been.

"He didn't leave Austin a fortune," Eliot continued, "not enough to live on. I remember when Austin first started out he was scrambling like every other young lawyer fresh out of law school. You'd see him in county courts looking for appointments to DWIs, that sort of thing. Just trying to make a living.

"But Austin had plans, even back then. He got interested in politics early on. He used that money his father had set aside for him, and he made contributions. He did it smart, too. He didn't try to go over his head. The governor would never have heard of him. Even a state senator would have been out of Austin's league in those days. But you know, Mark, in local races, especially back then, the budgets were tiny. They didn't get big contributions. That's where Austin made his mark. A county court judge running for reelection would have been enormously grateful for a hundred dollars. Five hundred would get a city councilman's attention."

Or a district attorney's, I thought. But Eliot didn't have a confessional attitude. He was a man of the world offering some of his stored knowledge.

"Still, there must have been more than campaign contributions," I said. "How deep do Austin's connections go?"

Eliot sounded almost cheerful again, as he got to continue his explanation. "It only *started* with campaign contributions," he said. "You can't buy your way in to the inner circle, not with the little amount of money Austin had. But it can get you noticed. You can buy your way a little closer to the candidate. Austin didn't just contribute to campaigns, he worked on them. He did favors. He was at the right spot. For a couple of people he was indispensable. He came through for them right when they needed it.

"That's what you have to do, you see. Work your way far enough inside to find out the way things are done. Who did what to whom, and why. You don't do favors just to win favors in exchange, you do them to show you can be trusted. Do something a little bit unethical so insiders will know you're not judgmental, they can let you help with even worse things they have in mind. Or they'll tell you things other candidates did. People love to talk. You know that, don't you, Mark? They'll spill secrets they've held for twenty years if you happen to be there when they're in the right mood, and they think they know you enough to trust you. It doesn't take long to learn where the bodies were buried."

And next they'll trust you to bury one or two yourself. At some point, past favors admit the bearer to real corruption. On one level it was fascinating to hear a real insider tell me how things worked on the real inside. But it was Eliot. It scared me to hear Eliot reveal knowledge like this. A few minutes earlier he'd denied knowing about any crimes he hadn't prosecuted. Now he sounded as if there were a rampant underground of crime, or at least sleaze. And as if he were a full member. He couldn't have been talking about the dim past, either, before his time as district attorney, because we were discussing Austin Paley, who'd been a teenager when Eliot first became DA.

Eliot must have sensed what I was thinking, because he stopped talking. His lips were pursed, his eyes downcast.

"Give me an example," I said.

Eliot answered my unasked question instead. "He never did anything for me. I never had a need for anything like that." He looked up at me. Eliot's eyes were limpid and sincere. He could have sold me the courthouse. "You know yourself, Mark, I ran unopposed for my last two terms. I didn't need favors from anybody."

Not necessarily. That could have meant the favors were done far backstage, that any potential opposition had been dissuaded very early on. I believed I would have heard rumors of that kind of activity, though. After all, any lawyer thinking of running for DA would mouth off about it to other lawyers long before taking any official steps. All I remembered hearing during Eliot's years in office was that Eliot was too popular and too highly regarded for anyone to want to challenge him.

"I don't understand the kind of favors Austin could have done that would win him this kind of support," I said.

Eliot grew reminiscent again.

"A few years ago," he said, "we had a little political scandal here in town. A developer wanted to build an office complex, but there was a community center in the way. The county government issued the permits, but the city couldn't let the land go while the community center stood on it."

Little political scandal was typical of Eliot's downplaying. It had been the biggest scandal in recent memory. "I remember," I said.

Eliot looked at me indulgently, as if I were a child who

had just told him I knew all about World War II. "Somebody torched the community center," I said, to demonstrate my familiarity with the details.

"Yes. Somebody. And after that it turned out a couple of the officeholders who'd helped the project along had an interest in it."

"Financial interest," I said.

"Yes." Eliot smiled quietly again.

"Heads rolled," I prompted him.

"One or two," he acknowledged. "But when something like that breaks, what the public hears is the least of it. Somebody resigned, somebody else got defeated at the next election. But the ones who took the fall, Mark, might not have been the dirtiest. They were the ones who failed to protect themselves. Who didn't have enough markers to call in. When a story like that starts breaking, there's frantic damage control going on subsurface—bodies being thrown overboard to lighten the load; promises made. 'I'll take care of you down the road, trust me.' The people who were really in deep, you never heard about them."

"And Austin was one of them."

Eliot chose his words carefully. "Austin—helped out. He wasn't in on the deal from the beginning. But after the first torpedoes struck he happened to sail by in his yacht, and he took a few survivors on board. Am I being too metaphorical for you?"

"No." I thought about what I wanted to ask. What first occurred to me was, "Did Austin keep *your* name out of it? Is that one of the favors he did you?"

Eliot shook his head again. "I was never in it. I'm not rich and I was out of office by then. Nobody asked me into the deal."

I still had the illusion that Eliot wouldn't lie to me. I *knew* it was illusion, but I felt it nonetheless. I believed him.

"But Austin helped cover up for other people," Eliot continued. "Men who are still in office. That's the main source of Austin's power now. People owe him."

I thought we had neared the end of what Eliot would tell me by implication and example and speculation. It was time to confront him. "And what has Austin Paley done with this power of his?" I asked.

Eliot's answer was oblique. He wasn't looking at me. "I should never have let you inherit this problem. I should have settled it once and for all. I thought I had."

I stood up. "Eliot, I'm developing a terrible suspicion. You know what it is. Tell me I'm wrong."

"Sit down, Mark. Don't run off half-cocked. I'll take care of this."

He was looking at me sternly, and he spoke with his old authority.

But it wasn't his any more.

To get the answer I had to find someone with nothing to lose, someone who might even take pleasure in telling me. I knew where to start. Ben Dowling had been the courthouse reporter for one of the papers when I was a young prosecutor and for twenty years before that. He was a press-pass-in-the-hat kind of guy, not literally, but he harked back to that era. He continued to wear a suit every day even after his younger colleagues were prowling the courthouse halls in jeans and Nikes. Ben was retired now. He'd talked about finding a small-town weekly that needed a senior editor, but he couldn't bring himself to leave San Antonio. After my lunch with Eliot I found Ben that night at home, a freshly painted three-bedroom house on the near south side, with small rooms that were much neater than I'd expected. There were two walls of crowded bookshelves, but very few things on the walls otherwise. It didn't look like an old man's house. Ben saw me glancing around as he led me into the living room.

"You should've seen this place before my wife died," he said. I sank into the comfortable chair he gestured me into. "She not only couldn't throw anything away, she'd put it up on the walls. We didn't have an inch of wall space. And I mean just crap. Framed seashells and menus from places we'd eaten in once on trips. After she was gone I got rid of it all. Looked at everything one more time and remembered where we'd gotten it and cried like a baby, but I don't want to be looking at that junk every day for the rest of my life. Besides, I knew the kids would dump it all later on, so I saved them the trouble. Now once in a while I think— Ah, but the hell with it. Drink?"

"No, thanks."

Ben frowned at me. He was still on his feet. "You worry me, Mark, don't you know how to do this? You come to pry information out of some old codger, first you ply him with drink. I got more stories that way than with my good looks, and you don't have that advantage."

He laughed and I joined him. "All right. Whatever you're having," I said. He disappeared into the kitchen for less than a minute. He must have had it already prepared. He returned with two small but brimming liqueur glasses.

"Sherry," he said. "Now you know my terrible secret, but there's nobody left down there you could tell it to who'd give a damn. Salud."

He drained his glass, so did I, and he carried them away and returned quickly. He was enjoying himself and making me start to enjoy it too, though I'd come on a bitter errand.

Ben was tall and thin and his curly hair was still thick. He moved like a dancer. He must have been over seventy, but age hadn't slowed him.

We chatted about times old and new. He showed more interest in the latter. It was five minutes before I realized he had painlessly dug out of me not only facts about pending cases but a statement or two about my personal philosophy of running the office I wouldn't have revealed to the current crop of reporters. "This is all off the record," I finally said.

He laughed and spread his hands. "What record?"

We worked around to my reason for coming. Ben had heard about Chris Davis's uncompleted guilty plea.

"I'm looking for background," I said. I gave him a quick sketch of developments in the case, not everything, but enough details that hadn't been in news reports to make him think he was hearing the real skinny. Ben sat forward restlessly on the edge of the couch, eager to interrupt with questions. He wasn't used to being the interviewed. I fended off his questions until I could conclude. "So it seems obvious the real molester is somebody with influence. And I have a strong feeling this has happened before. I was hoping maybe you could tell me anything you might have heard about other dropped cases."

I've never heard a reporter talk about a story who didn't know more than had seen print, and they are most passionate about the stories that never got written. Ben settled back with a happy look in his eyes that didn't reflect the emotions of the story, only of his pleasure in sharing inside information.

"Eliot Quinn is right about the old days. We had a sort of gentlemen's agreement to let certain stories pass. And in return they gave us others. They made us feel we were all in the same club, and you didn't betray fellow club members. I remember there was one state senator, a real family-man type, who practically had a police escort on his way home from his girl friend's every Thursday night, to make sure he didn't bang into cars and pedestrians on the way home. Everybody knew. But it didn't seem like a story, it seemed like a family secret, and we were all family. If there'd ever been a rumor that he was stealing votes or state funds, all bets would have been off. We would have been all over him. But the other indiscretions, they seemed like his own business. We didn't want to embarrass his wife and children.

"And like I say, we were fed stories in return. The press was almost like another arm of government in those days." He gave an apologetic sort of shrug. "This was when I was just starting out. I chafed under it a little, I'll tell you, but I couldn't have bucked it. There were no mavericks then, because it went all the way to the top. And I mean the *top*. You think no reporters knew about Jack Kennedy back then? Or even Eisenhower and his jeep driver? But it would have been bad manners to report it. If I'd tried to print one of those stories my editor would have killed it and I would have found myself writing obituaries for the next six months.

"Nowadays reporters have got no manners, and I say that's a good thing."

Ben sounded nothing at all like a crabby old fart complaining about the kids today. He sounded still in the thick of things. But he had a long perspective.

"So what are you telling me," I asked, "that none of you would have reported on some rich guy who couldn't keep his hands off children?"

Ben thought about it, uninsulted. "I don't think the gentlemen's agreement would have covered that. But it doesn't matter. I'm talking forty years ago. I don't think you need to worry about somebody who was active back then. You want something of more recent vintage. And by then things were different. I don't need to tell you. You were in the DA's office twenty years ago. Would you have ignored a case like that, just because of who the defendant was?"

"No."

"No. Or even a DWI. And I wouldn't have either, by then. The gentlemen's club disbanded around the early seventies. And you know one of the people who killed it."

"Eliot," I said.

Ben nodded. "When Eliot Quinn became DA, all agreements terminated. One of the first things he did was prosecute a city councilman's son for assault. Personally. He pissed off a lot of people in the early days, Mark, but by the end of his first term he was so popular he didn't even draw an opponent. The old boys even took him under their wings. He's one of the reasons things are different now."

This didn't do me a damned bit of good, but I was glad to hear it. I didn't want to believe Eliot had taken orders from fat-assed criminals. I didn't want my memories twisted; to think I'd naïvely accepted his preachments that we treated everyone the same, unaware there was one stratum of offender laughing at us all.

Ben sat quietly on the couch, lost in thought. His face showed no trace of the pride that must have suffused mine. He wasn't here to praise Caesar. He was just reporting the facts.

I made a small joke, as prelude to departure. "So, Ben, forty years as a reporter in this town and you don't know any dirt that could help me?"

He ignored my tone and spoke from a deep well of thought, still staring off into the past. "I was just trying to think," he murmured. Then he revived, and looked at me. "There's nothing I can specify. But there were rumors.

"Your old boss, Eliot Quinn, was as tough a prosecutor as this town's ever had. Once a case was indicted he'd take it as far as it could be taken. But once in a while over the years there was just a whiff, nothing anyone could confirm, about a case that would get derailed, somewhere between the police investigation and the courthouse. It would never get as far as a courtroom. It just went away."

Ben reached for his sherry glass, found it empty, kept

holding it as if he'd get up in a moment. "I can't tell you it was true," he said. "I tried to dig into it a couple of times, but it was the kind of thing if you tried to track it to its source it dried up into nothing. Some people claimed Eliot knew about the lost cases. That was the kind of rumor that would follow any public figure, in these mean-spirited times of ours. No one believes in saintliness, you know?" He laughed. "Neither do I."

My unease returned, like the chill from the breeze he stirred as he walked past me back into the kitchen, because I don't believe in saintliness either.

"But you can't give me a name?" I called.

Ben reappeared, with two full glasses. "Wish I could. If I'd ever found it, it wouldn't be a secret."

"You said maybe Eliot knew about the cases. But some of them might have gotten lost before they reached the courthouse. Like where?"

Ben said, "I'll tell you how I think it would work. It would have to be someone with a lot of influence, at several levels. When he starts feeling the heat, a city councilman or a councilman's aide goes to see the chief of police. Now, the chief serves at the pleasure of the city council, so he needs every council vote he can get, all the time, because if he ever loses a majority he's out. So he listens."

"When the councilman tells him to halt an investigation?"

Ben shook his head. "It wouldn't be that ugly, Mark. The councilman would just say that he's heard his good friend is being investigated, and that he happens to know that this man is a very solid citizen, so he'd better not be being harassed by police without good cause. And the chief passes the word on to his detective that before he makes an arrest he'd better be damned sure of his facts." Ben shrugged. "A case like that, one involving a child witness, it could never be that good a case."

No, not that could stand up to that kind of scrutiny from above.

"It would be very discreet and gentlemanly," Ben said.

"But of course there'd have to be something ugly back of it, to provide the mystery man with his clout in the first place."

"True, true."

Ben Dowling snapped his fingers, then pointed one at me. "I'll tell you who you should talk to. McCloskey. Did you know Pat McCloskey?"

"Sure. Detective McCloskey. Is he still alive?" That was out before I realized it might offend my septuagenarian host, but Ben took no offense.

"Oh yes. Pat's younger than I am. But you know cops, they take early retirement, put in twenty years at something else, too. I don't know any old cops who aren't drawing two pensions. But then, I don't know too many old cops, come to think of it."

There was nothing good to say to that.

"But Pat," the old reporter continued. "He only retired seven or eight years ago. He might still have all his faculties. I talked to him once, I don't know how many years ago, when I was following up one of these rumors. He stonewalled me from 'Hello' on, but I thought— You know, I should have followed that up when he first retired. I thought, maybe once he's had his last promotion and nobody's over his head any more, he might tell me something. But I forgot." He shrugged, forgiving himself. "It would have been an old story by then anyway."

"Maybe not," I said. It might have been a story of renewable interest. Ben knew what I meant.

"You track McCloskey down, then. There was something, he didn't like it but he had to take it. He might have just been mad at his boss that day, who knows? You let me know, will you, Mark? I'd be very curious."

"I will," I lied. Well, it might not turn out to be a lie; it depended. I thanked Ben most politely, and made my last glass of sherry last another hour, to let the old man talk. He was quite entertaining, too. Told me a good deal of local history I'd never heard.

Pat McCloskey, former vice detective, twenty-year veteran of the San Antonio Police Department, retired, had a new job that wasn't law enforcement–related. He was the manager of a cafeteria. "They've got great benefits," he said.

He and I were having a cup of coffee, sitting in the middle of a sea of empty tables at three o'clock in the afternoon.

The place was closed between the lunch and dinner shifts, but Pat was on duty, supervising the cleanup.

Pat was barely over fifty, but he'd been retired for ten years. He looked like a man with ready access to food, but as if he still put in time in the gym, too. His arms stretched the short sleeves of his shirt almost to the breaking point, and his chest and stomach did the same to the shirt's buttons. Similarly, his head was thrusting through the top of his hair. His wide nose rested atop a bushy brown mustache.

"That guy," he laughed, shaking his head. He was referring to Ben Dowling. "Still tryin' to get to me. 'S been a long time since anybody asked me anything newsworthy."

"This isn't for the news." I didn't know McCloskey well, I didn't know if that would reassure him or if he missed being in the thick of things. So I got right to the point. "Was Ben right? Did you know something?"

McCloskey sipped his coffee, stirred it, tried to fish a speck out with his spoon. He was stalling, trying to decide whether to bullshit me. After a minute he realized he'd paused too long to say no, he'd never known anything. He twisted his mouth to acknowledge that he'd given himself away, but he still didn't speak. If he'd been bought off, I thought, it had been years ago. Had he given his money's worth of silence yet? But if it was something else that had kept him from talking, as Ben had implied, the pressure should be off now. No one was going to demote him now.

"It's happening again," I prompted him. "Maybe it's been happening all along. Now we have the extra added attraction, of course, that this guy may not just be fucking children, he may be fatally infecting them, too."

"I read about these new ones," McCloskey said quietly, "and I wondered. But there's so many perverts around now, there's no reason to think these are my guy."

"I have reason to think so," I reminded him.

He nodded. "I'm not even sure I knew anything," he said, beginning to tell his story.

"I was working on a case. This was ten, eleven years ago. Kid in an apartment complex. Eight-year-old boy. He started acting funny, doing things with his toy soldiers his mother thought was damned peculiar. Took the boy to a doctor and the doctor thought yes, he might have been abused. Mother reported to us. And she also kept an eye on a guy in her apartment complex who'd been friendly with the boy. Babysat for her sometimes, even. She'd been glad to have his help. She was single, she was trying to work and go to school too, she didn't have any money." McCloskey shrugged, not making a judgment. "She told me the guy's name, but it didn't mean anything. I couldn't even prove he existed. And apparently he'd sniffed the wind, 'cause he was gone. She never saw him again.

"She knew where he lived in the complex, of course, she'd taken her son to his apartment before." The former detective gave that thought a moment of silence before continuing. "But when I got a warrant the apartment was empty. Furnished but empty. The manager told me it'd been vacant for months.

"It didn't make any sense. I asked him who else would have a key and he said nobody. I checked out the manager, I checked his friends, nobody fit the description. Then I did something just silly, I thought. I tried to find out who owned the apartments. You ever try something like that? Go through a management company into a holding company into a parent organization. I must've been real bored."

I had my doubts about that. I wondered what had become of the eight-year-old boy in the last ten or eleven years. I wondered if McCloskey had children of his own.

"Pretty soon I was in thick among more blue suits than you could sort out in a year. I tried to find out who was enough into the actual hands-on business of managing the apartments to get a key to one. That narrowed it a little, but at that level nobody'd have a key to any individual apartments. If for some reason they wanted to see one they'd just have the manager let them in. I asked if anybody'd done that a few months earlier, about the time the boy's mother remembered this friendly neighbor appearing. People with important things on their minds don't remember little things like that, but I knew who to ask. A secretary remembered getting a key one time. She couldn't say when. It wasn't for her boss, it was for some consultant the company'd hired, who had some expert coming in for a couple of weeks who didn't want to stay in a hotel. That's what the boss had told her, anyway.

"I checked out the boss and the consultant—some hotshot lawyer the company'd hired to do something I didn't really follow: bribe somebody, probably—and the expert, who was from Dallas. This was really far afield by this time, you know. I felt sure I was wasting my time. But I managed to get pictures of all three of these guys, without them knowing. They didn't have mug shots, needless to say. These were pictures from business journals, the company's annual report, that kind of thing."

He was talking faster, assuming I'd know what followed. I could guess. "I mixed the pictures in with some fillers and showed them to the boy," he said. "And he picked the lawyer right out. So did his mother."

The hair on the back of my neck had stirred at the word *lawyer*. But there are a lot of lawyers, representing a lot of people. "What did you do?" I asked.

McCloskey looked at me and laughed. "I finished out my career in Internal Affairs."

"What?"

McCloskey had the same free and easy tone as he finished his tale, but I could hear behind his voice what this had once cost him. "I took what I had to my boss," he said. "I knew for what I wanted to do I needed more clout than I had. I wanted to do a live lineup, and for that I needed to make an arrest. I went to the captain and told him what I had, who my suspect was, and what I wanted to do. He listened and said he'd get back to me, and the next week I was reassigned. To Internal Affairs."

He looked at me to see if I understood the import of that, then he spelled it out. "Internal Affairs is where you finish out your career. At least I did. You don't make a lot of friends. Not too many people outside the division want to work with you after that. I just held on long enough to get my twenty and quit."

"And the case with the little boy?" I asked.

McCloskey watched me. "Left it behind, of course. Oh, somebody else took over my cases, but nothing ever came of that one. I checked."

We sat quietly for a minute. I was starting to grow stiff from the plastic chair I'd been sitting in for half an hour. The cafeteria served good food at good prices, but it wasn't designed to encourage leisurely dining. McCloskey looked around his kingdom of chairs and tables, wondering, I imagined, if he was safe now, if they could get to him here. His right fist was clenched, making me think his shirt sleeve really was going to pop.

"That just leaves one thing," I said. "The name."

He looked at me hard, trying to judge my interest. I realized it was the same look I'd gotten from Detective Padilla. A sort of standard-issue department stare.

"Would I know him?" I asked, trying to ease it out of him.

"I'm pretty sure you've run into him," McCloskey said.

Padilla was so delighted to see me that his emotions must have embarrassed him. As soon as I walked into his office he stood up and turned his back on me.

"I have more now," I said.

I'd expected some sarcastic reply, but he didn't say anything. He pulled his jacket out of a locker as if he were going somewhere; somewhere preferable to here, because I wouldn't be there.

"I owe you an apology for what I was thinking about you," I said. "And you owe me one, too."

He glanced at me over his shoulder just long enough to let me know he didn't find me amusing.

"You might as well sit down and listen," I said, "because if you leave I'm going with you. I don't think you can outrun me." I continued as if I didn't care what he did.

"I owe you an apology because I thought you were on the take. I thought you were covering up for this molester. But that wasn't it, was it, Padilla? You wouldn't tell me who your suspect was because you've seen what happens to cops who suspect this guy."

He hadn't turned around, but he'd stopped pretending to be leaving. All I could see was his motionless back.

"You thought I was here just to see if you were on to him. That's why *you* owe *me* an apology. You thought I wasn't really trying to find out the name, you thought I knew it. You thought I was part of the cover-up when your chief told you I'd said the cases were closed, and it turned out I was taking a guilty plea from a guy you knew wasn't the molester."

Detective Padilla turned around. His wide shoulders were sloping, his arms dangled at his sides. He looked wary. I hadn't disarmed him with my honesty. "I don't know that," he said quietly.

"Well, I do. That was all a setup and I fell for it. It would've been nice if somebody who knew had told me I was making a mistake, but then I should have checked harder myself. But I wasn't helping set it up, Detective. Not willingly. I'm a prosecutor. That means you and I are on the same side."

He snorted. "You're a lawyer," he said. "Lawyers protect their own. I've seen it before."

Padilla hadn't been able to resist saying that. He *should* have resisted, if he'd wanted to go on convincingly pretending there was no cover-up. He'd just implicitly admitted he knew of one.

"It's not just lawyers protecting this one, is it? You don't have to worry about lawyers."

He didn't say anything. I felt anger creeping up me, up my back, over the tops of my shoulders. "Let's cut the crap, okay? I don't care why you wouldn't tell me, because of me or you or whoever you suspect. Just tell me the name now."

"I'm still working on it," he said. He was asking me for time, maybe for time to check me out himself. But too much time had already been wasted.

"You've run into a wall, haven't you?" I asked. "You've run into this wall before and you think you're about to hit it again."

"No, sir. This time I'm not."

His face was stony, but he kept giving himself away. He couldn't help it.

"Every day you stall me is another day he's still out there," I said. Padilla's face told me he knew that. He might even have been thinking of doing something about it, but not what I wanted him to do. "Just breathe the name to me," I almost begged. "I'll work up the cases from there. I'll fade the heat from whoever's trying to ruin this case. No one will know I got the name from you. I just want to see if I'm on the right track."

I saw him waver and I saw him fall back. He had no reason to trust me and I had no way to convince him he should.

"All right," I said. "Then I'll tell you the name." He shrugged. He didn't care. I moved around in front of him. "Austin Paley," I said distinctly.

Detective Padilla's face changed as if a spell had been broken. But he still didn't look happy.

"If you already knew, why're you bugging me?" he growled.

"Because we've got work to do," I said. "And I need your help."

"You said all you wanted from me was the name," he said.

"I lied."

McCloskey and Padilla had their suspicions, and they coincided with my own, but they didn't know. They had some pretty good evidence, but they couldn't be positive. There were at least a couple of people, though, who did know for sure. It was time to return to the source.

"Do you really think this is going to help?" Becky asked. "Billy's already positively identified Chris Davis. And now he's not even saying Davis fondled him. He's just talking about a sort of lingering tucking-in. I'm not even sure it's a kidnapping case. He seems to have—"

"Billy's five years old," I said. "Some grown-up asks him, 'Is this the man?' he says yes. He says what he thinks adults want him to say. The first time somebody showed him a photo spread they thought Chris Davis was the one, and maybe they somehow subtly tipped off Billy which picture was the right answer. I don't mean to shock you, but it happens sometimes."

Becky in the passenger seat beside me was wearing a thin blouse over a casual blue skirt. It was a Thursday afternoon, her court work was done for the week, and she hadn't worn a suit to the office. She hadn't expected to be making this surprise trip with the boss. She looked a little uncomfortable. And of course she didn't want to challenge what I was saying. I was pressing her, trying to make her think I thought her naïve and inexperienced, so she'd come back at me harder. I wanted someone to tell me if I was acting crazy, and there was no one else I trusted at the moment. I hadn't had a good sounding board since Linda left the office. I thought Becky could fill that role, if she'd get over her deference toward me. I'd been thinking about her since Eliot had told me it was easy to know the real prosecutors in one's employ. That was true. I knew Becky was one of the good ones.

But I tried to put myself in her position. Fifteen or twenty years ago if Eliot had plucked me out of the felony section to sit second on a big case with him, and he'd spun wild theories about cover-ups and years-old conspiracies, would I have had the nerve to tell him he sounded like he was full of shit? Sure. I couldn't tell him even now.

"That's why you're coming along," I said. "You can show him the pictures, so we know it'll be a fair test." Because I hadn't told Becky who my real suspect was. "I threw a couple of surprises into the lineup," I went on. "Why don't you look at them now, so you don't look startled when you're showing them to Billy?"

I passed her my six photos. Five of them were police mug shots with the identifying marks excised, so they'd more closely match the sixth, the one of Austin I'd gotten from the bar association directory. The six pictures were pretty close matches in appearance—maybe *too* close, I was afraid Billy wouldn't be able to pick one out, but I wanted the test to be fair—but I'd had trouble finding five ringers of about the right age. Most mug shots are of young men. They get arrested early. Only a very rare criminal gets away with his crimes as long as this man had.

"Why, who did—" Becky said as she started sorting through the pictures, then came to a dead halt. She looked up at me, eyes wide, her expression asking what sort of vengeful quest I was embarked on.

"Remember, that's who Kevin identified on the videotape."

"But that—"

"No, we didn't take him seriously. But I've done some more checking. Other people have suspected Austin in the past."

"Other people?" Becky said. "Police? Then why have we never heard about it? Have we?"

"Maybe there's nothing to it. We'll see what Billy has to say," I said, as if speaking of going to have a chat with an adult witness.

We didn't go to Billy's house, we found him at the daycare center where he spent afternoons after kindergarten. His father had given us permission over the phone to see him, but neither of the parents left work early to meet us there. "Just see Mrs. Kelly," the father had said. I pictured my third-grade teacher, a sweet-faced grandmotherly old Irishwoman who'd come over from the old sod about the time of the potato famine. But this Mrs. Kelly turned out to be maybe twenty-two, wearing shorts against the lingering heat of early September. She seemed to have more energy than the five-year-olds in her charge, which probably made her good at her job but was a little frightening to see.

When I offered her identification she said, "Oh, that's okay. Mr. Reynolds called. You'll want a private room, won't you?" Maybe Becky made me look respectable. She was close at my side, like a military attaché. Becky stood very straight and held her purse at her side, and had the alert, cold look of a secret service agent checking out where the President was going to be spending the night. She gave Mrs. Kelly a tight little smile doled out by the millimeter.

We were in a big carpeted room with windows on three sides, filling the room with light even through the half-closed blinds. There were four or five little tables, several bookshelves, and plastic laundry baskets full of toys: stuffed animals and puzzles and things on wheels. Most of the kids were staring at us. One boy asked, "Is that your daddy?" and the three-year-old beside him glanced up at me, said, "Yes," and looked back down at the important coloring that occupied him.

Mrs. Kelly deftly cut Billy out of the herd and delivered him to me. "There's nobody in the office," she volunteered, and plunged back into the melee, clapping her hands to stir her charges from their group lethargy. "Who wants to play kickball?" she shouted.

Billy Reynolds looked up at me timidly but prepared to do whatever he was supposed to do.

"Hi, Billy. Remember me?"

He nodded unconvincingly. Becky took his hand. In the hall she explained to him that we just wanted him to look at some pictures. He nodded. He was an old hand at the routine.

The office had an unoccupied desk, a couch, and a couple of chairs, which we took. Becky pulled a small end table close to the couch in front of Billy. I tried to distance myself from the proceeding. I let her do the talking.

"Billy, I'm going to show you six pictures. They're pictures of men. Some of these pictures are just here because they look like the man you described. The real man might not even be here in these pictures. You don't have to tell me one is the right one. Just look at them very closely and tell me if one of them does look like the man who kidnapped you. Can you do that?"

He nodded, already studying the top picture curiously. He had a canny little expression, as if he were playing a game that involved secrets. He didn't give anything away as he looked closely at the first two photos in the small stack Becky had handed him. By the third one I thought he was growing bored. His study of it was more desultory.

But when he saw the fourth picture he dropped the one he'd been lifting out of the way. It fluttered to the floor. Billy was staring at the fourth photo. After a long moment he pushed back from the table and pulled his hands back against his chest.

"Turn it away," he said.

We didn't. "Why?" Becky said. "Is there something about that one you don't like?"

"It's him."

Billy's voice was tiny. He shrank back farther against the back of the couch. I'd seen him identify Chris Davis's picture before, but I hadn't seen a reaction like this.

"Don't be scared, Billy." Becky put her arm around him. He huddled against her. I tried to be invisible. I didn't want to be there, I didn't want to be a man in the room with him. "No one's going to hurt you," Becky said. "But you said he *didn't* hurt you," she went on. "You said you didn't remember anything except the man leaning over you right before you went to sleep. Remember, Billy? Is that all that happened?"

Billy started crying. We didn't ask any more questions. Becky turned the pictures over.

At the last ID session, Billy had been as composed as an expert who'd testified a hundred times. After picking out Chris Davis's picture he'd told us his revised story, that he didn't remember anything bad happening. He was successfully repressing it, Karen had said. I was glad the child advocate wasn't in the room with us now. I think she would have slapped both Becky and me.

Becky was rocking back and forth with Billy. He was still crying, but more softly. He was telling her something in mutters. "It's all right," Becky kept saying. Her voice was calming, but there was tragedy in her eyes. She was looking up at me.

We had thought Kevin had gone completely unreliable when he'd identified what we thought was the wrong man on the videotape. But it explained Kevin's behavior that day in court. He'd been terrified not by Chris Davis, in custody, but by the real molester in the courtroom with him, unconfined, unsuspected, free to walk out into the same world to which Kevin had to return after court. When both Detectives McCloskey and Padilla named the same man as their suspect, and then Billy identified him as well as Kevin, I was convinced. The identity of the molester made everything else make sense—the way the cases had come to me to begin with, and the skewed course of the investigations, reaching years into the past.

I went to the grand jury the next day and described the identifications I'd seen. Indictments can be based on hearsay, on descriptions from people who never witnessed the crime. Usually grand juries just hear a bored assistant DA read from police reports and victim statements. I was a livelier witness than they were accustomed to; perhaps in appreciation, they gave me the indictments I wanted. I used the indictments to obtain an arrest warrant.

This all happened very quickly. It can, if you walk it through. The only hitch was finding police to serve the warrants. Padilla refused, and I didn't blame him. Finally two patrolmen were assigned. No one of higher rank cared to participate in the arrest.

I led the patrolmen into the office building. The uniformed officers hung back, confused about their status, maybe. They weren't used to being led by a civilian. We rode the elevator in silence.

The receptionist seemed unfazed by the cops, but she admitted me deeper into the offices without squawking. Down two hallways I found the private secretary, who was already standing. "Is he in?" I asked.

"It will be a few minutes," she said. "He's occupied at the moment."

A light on the telephone on her desk went off. Both of us glanced down at it, then I looked back at her. "If you'd care to have a seat—" she began.

"I wouldn't." I walked past her and opened the door at her back. It was a big office inside, it took me ten steps to reach the desk. Austin Paley looked up from the other side of it.

"Mark, you should have called," he said easily. "I would have had something prepared."

He'd practiced enough criminal law to recognize the arrest warrant I held in my hands. "Don't tell me another of my clients has done something naughty," he said.

"No, Austin. This is for you. You're the one who needs a lawyer. You're under arrest for kidnapping and aggravated sexual assault, in three separate cases."

6

By the time I arrested Austin, Tommy Algren was on his way to me. After identifying Austin Paley on the television news he'd made his way through the layers of his parents, teacher, school nurse, doctor, and cops by his quiet, stubborn refusal to back down from his story that the lawyer on TV had molested him—two years ago. The news of Austin's arrest breaking publicly eased Tommy's way.

Tommy was ten years old. He looked like a little adult to me; by now I was used to dealing with younger children. He sat straight in his chair as he told his story. His voice didn't get away from him. But as he talked he seemed to slip back through the years to the young boy he'd been when his involvement with Austin had started. His carefully combed light brown hair dried and loosened and fell onto his forehead. He started swinging his legs more freely. His feet didn't quite reach the floor.

"At first we just talked. For a long time. We'd go for walks. He'd pick me up from soccer practice and take me to get ice cream and we'd walk around. There were a few other boys at first, but later on it was just me."

"We knew nothing about this," Tommy's mother interjected. She was a too-heavy woman who could have been in her thirties or forties. She looked like the former but spoke and dressed like the latter. For her formal appearance in the district attorney's office she wore a dark but patterned dress and a choker of pearls she kept fingering, especially when she spoke of her absent husband. "Mr. Algren and I thought Tommy was getting a ride home with another boy's parents. That's what he told us."

Tommy kept looking at me, as if his mother were inconsequential. I nodded at him and he continued.

"Then we'd—" He swallowed. I could see him rearranging the story. "In the summer I was supposed to be in daycare all day."

"His father and I both work," Mrs. Algren said, moving a hand like a shrug.

"Of course," I said consolingly.

"It was so boring," Tommy continued. "What were we supposed to do, push the little kids on the swings? Sometimes Waldo would come and get me—"

"Waldo?" I said. I was hiding half my face behind my hand, showing no reaction. I can do that for days on end.

"That's what he told me his name was," Tommy said. He smiled slyly. "But I knew it wasn't."

"How did you know that?"

"Sometimes he left me alone in the car. I looked in that box between the front seats. I found envelopes and things with his name on them."

"What was his name?"

"Austin Paley." He waited for reaction. I just nodded.

"Anyway, summers, that was better, because we had all day. Sometimes we'd go swimming. At first in pools, but Waldo knew other places we could go swimming when he'd forgotten to bring swimsuits for us. He said that was okay 'cause there were no girls around.

"We did that lots of times—I mean and other things too, going for walks or riding horses in Brackenridge Park. And just talking, you know. Waldo wouldn't ever say we shouldn't talk about something, or, you know, try to act like I was too little."

Mrs. Algren stared away toward a corner of the ceiling, looking stoical.

"The first time something happened—is this what you want to hear about?"

"Whatever you want to tell me, Tommy. Whatever happened."

He nodded and went on, unembarrassed.

"We'd gone swimming in the river he knew. No one else was around. It was way out in the country. After we got tired we laid down on an old quilt Waldo had brought. It was in the shade but it wasn't cool. It was August, I think. Waldo said we'd just let the air dry us. We laid there and talked a little, but not for long. Waldo closed his eyes and was breathing louder. I started getting sleepy too."

It was easy to picture. I could feel it: the deadened air of summer, bugs droning, the scratchiness of the quilt, long stems of grass tickling, water droplets evaporating off the skin. The imagined warmth made me drowsy in the cool of my air-conditioned office. I could put Tommy in the picture because he was right in front of me, but the man was just an anonymous length of shaded flesh, until I remembered with a shock that it was Austin Paley I was hearing described. The man in my imagination became harder to picture when I remembered who it was. "What happened?" I asked.

"Waldo turned over and his arm landed on me. It was hot, but I didn't move it because I was sleepy too. His arm just laid on my stomach for a long time like he was asleep, but then it moved down to my, my crotch."

"You know they never said one thing to us?" his mother suddenly said loudly. "Mr. Algren and I are thinking about suing that daycare center. Of course we didn't give any permission for these day trips. We didn't know anything about them. This man told them he was Tommy's uncle and Tommy didn't tell them any different."

Tommy was watching me. I tried to let him see that I knew there are some things you don't tell parents. "I understand," I said. "You couldn't be blamed." I looked at his mother, but I was speaking to Tommy. "Go on, Tommy."

"Well, he was touching me, my legs and stomach and—everything. I didn't stop him, but it woke me up. Then he opened his eyes too. He talked to me real seriously, the way he had before about other things. He said there was nothing wrong with it, it was just something some people did, and he thought I was ready and he asked if I thought so too. I didn't say anything."

"Were you scared?" I asked.

"Sure. But it wasn't awful or anything. After a minute he

took my hand and put it on him, too. On his leg, up at the top. Did I say we still didn't have any clothes on?"

Color had crept up his mother's neck into her face. Even the pearls weren't cool enough to stop it. "Must we go into all this now?" she said suddenly. "Tommy's given a statement to the police. A very detailed statement, I might add." She didn't look at me as she asked.

I had the written statement. "No," I said. "We needn't continue today. I just needed to know enough to know what kind of charges to file, what the exact offense was." I'd also wanted to get a glimpse of the kind of witness Tommy would make. Telling his tale in a courtroom wouldn't be as cozy as in my office, but the way he'd held his composure in front of me, a stranger, as well as Becky, Karen Rivera the child advocate, and his own mother made me hopeful.

"Of course," I continued, "when we start preparing the case for trial Tommy and I will have to go over this again and again. Or Tommy and another prosecutor."

"Trial?" his mother said. "Do you think there will be a trial?"

"We have to prepare as if there will be. And I'd say at this point the chances are there will be a trial. Several trials. There are other children, you know." I thought it might comfort her to be part of a crowd, but that wasn't the crowd she wanted to belong to.

"I just thought—" She was fingering the pearls like mad, as if they could teleport her out of this sordid place. "Mr. Algren and I assumed the man would plead guilty once he was confronted with the evidence. Don't they usually?"

Yes, they do. But Austin wasn't a usual defendant. I couldn't picture him pleading guilty.

"Often they do, Mrs. Algren, but often they don't. And in order to induce someone to plead guilty, we have to offer them a lower sentence than we could get from a jury. I wouldn't want to do that in a case like this. We want to take this man out of circulation, don't we?"

She sat for a moment as if she hadn't realized the question was directed at her. Then she came awake with a little start. "Of course," she said. "He certainly won't get near Tommy again, I'll assure you of that. Tommy's father has threatened to shoot the man."

Out of the corner of my eye I thought I saw a quiet smile cross Tommy's face, but when I looked at him directly he wore the same calm, serious expression with which he'd recited his story. He looked heartbreakingly old, as if he could endure anything.

"You see why I prefer children?" Karen Rivera said after she'd shut the door on Tommy and his mother.

"Think he'd make a good witness?" I asked Becky.

For once she didn't wait to hear my opinion first. Becky was standing with her arms folded, staring after the departed child. "He's *too* good," she said. I nodded.

The cases against Austin continued to pile into the office. Some of them came to us, after his picture appeared in the newspapers. Some we sought out. After I obtained the first indictments, Lou Padilla went back to some of the children he'd interviewed over the last few years, showed them new photo spreads. For some of them it had been too long, they couldn't remember the face. In at least a couple of cases the parents, or parent, wouldn't let the detective in the door. But one child, then two, three, looked at Austin Paley's photograph and picked it out. They, too, appeared in my office. It began to be a horrible, normal facet of life, this parade of broken children. Some of them hadn't seen their molester for two years, but they still wore the haunted expressions they'd carry into old age. They bore secret knowledge that had turned them from average children into something else. One boy wouldn't let his father near him, hadn't for two years. One five-year-old girl was horribly flirtatious, standing so close I could feel the warmth of her skin, and smiling at me with an expression that would only have been appropriate on the face of an old whore.

One boy was an aberration. When he waddled into my office the first thing I wondered was why Austin had suffered such a lapse in taste. The other children had been cute as a litter of puppies. Their skins glowed, their eyes showed quickness, their little faces could have sold Kodak film. This boy, though, was on the revolting side. He must have been sixty pounds overweight, which is a lot of fat for a four-and-a-half-foot-tall nine-year-old to carry. His skin was mottled. A candy bar stayed in his stubby fingers. He looked dirty.

I kept catching whiffs of him. To hear this creature give his saga of intimate contact while looking at him and smelling him was enough to put one off the idea of any form of sex. I didn't believe him. Austin Paley was nothing if not fastidious. He wouldn't have stayed in the same room with this child.

After he left I just cleared my throat, and Dr. McLaren knew exactly what I was thinking. She opened her file and put it on the desk in front of me. "Here's a picture of Peter taken two years ago."

"You're kidding. This is his little brother, this isn't him."

"Cute as a button, wasn't he? He was *too* cute. That's what Peter thinks. He's spent two years turning himself into something no one would want to touch. He's destroyed the thing that made him vulnerable. This is what we call effective response. He's protected himself very well."

So well I wouldn't think of putting him in front of a jury, I thought.

Janet McLaren was a psychiatrist who specialized in the treatment of children, particularly children who had been sexually abused. The chief of my sex crimes unit had suggested I talk to her, and after one meeting the doctor had attached herself to the cases as an unpaid consultant. I think she saw in me someone desperately in need of education.

"I haven't seen them all, of course," I said. "But Detective Padilla tells me some of the children seem to have recovered without any damage at all. Why are some okay and some are so—" I didn't want to say "twisted," but I didn't need to finish the sentence.

Dr. McLaren nodded. "I'm not sure I'd put much reliance on the detective's professional psychological opinion after one meeting with an abused child—"

That remark sounded gentler than one would think. Dr. Janet McLaren was about my age, late forties. At that age there is a wide variety in feminine appearance. Some women still look like Joan Collins. Others have already turned into everyone's memory of Grandmother. Dr. McLaren was somewhere in the midrange; she could probably go either way to suit the occasion. She was a bit too heavy and looked as if she didn't fight it too hard. The extra weight softened her face, and the flowered dress she was wearing didn't try to hide it. She had blue eyes and a full-lipped mouth that broke easily into smiles. Her hair was mostly gray, blending easily into the original blond; it was twisted atop her head into a neat but indifferent mass. Her voice was melodiously kind even when criticizing, or explaining psychological concepts. The kindness didn't disguise her apparent feeling that she was sometimes speaking over my head.

"—but it's true, many of the children seem to display no bad effects. Some have adjusted so well that, if they were my patients, I wouldn't let you put them through this pain of recalling it."

"You wouldn't want them to suppress it, would you?"

She smiled at me, at my attempt at psychoanalysis. "Suppression isn't necessarily a bad thing. They can remember what happened to them without dwelling on it every day. If we think they've managed to resolve the conflict, that it's not just festering inside them waiting to explode later, such as at puberty or after they're married, then that's fine. What's wrong with forgetting something terrible that happened but that doesn't affect your life any more?"

I was more interested in the children as witnesses. "You've seen all the children I've seen, Dr. McLaren. Are they all telling the truth?"

"I'm not a lie detector, Mark. There are indications. Peter, whom you just saw, of course demonstrates the symptoms. Peter was molested, I'm quite sure. Whether it was your suspect who did it, that's another question."

Her voice deepened, indicating a shift from the particular to the general, to a renewal of my education in child psychology. "Children want desperately to please us, Mark. Nothing is as important to them as adult approval. That's what we try to teach them, isn't it? We love them and reward them when they do what we want, ignore them or punish them when they don't. Do the same thing to a dog and you'll get the same result. When you start questioning these children, particularly *these* children, who've been hurt, who may feel rejected by their parents, when you bring them in here to this very adult, formal place, and look at them seriously and try to be their friend and then ask them important questions, they don't start searching their memories to try to find the true answers. They try to figure out what you want to hear. And if they can give it to you they will. The same is true when a police officer brings them photographs to look at.

"I'm not saying they lie. Certainly they do try to tell the truth, because that's what the grown-up says he wants. But if that grown-up drops any clues as to what *he* thinks the truth is—" She shrugged. "There's no better detective than an abused child."

I sat and digested that. She wasn't helping. The inevitable next question occurred to me: "Then *are* they all abused? If they think someone wants to hear that they were—"

The psychiatrist nodded at me approvingly. I felt some pleasure myself at having pleased her. *Stop that.* I frowned, seriously. This was a conversation between adults, not a session between teacher and pupil.

"You'd like medical evidence, wouldn't you?" she asked.

"Well, of course. I assume we have some." I hadn't delved into that aspect yet.

She gave me that smile, that knowing, pitying smile, only a flicker of it this time, because we were talking seriously about something important to both of us, and she did want to help. "Sometimes," she said softly, "a child is brought to me right away after reporting the assault, within a day or two. When I get that opportunity I do a physical exam. I'm looking for evidence of sexual assault, of course, but it's also a way of gaining the child's confidence. And of reassuring the child. Sometimes I do it even if the reported assault isn't recent. Then I can reassure the child there's been no permanent damage. They're often worried there's something wrong with them, with their bodies. I can assure them there's not.

"And usually it's even better than that. Or worse, from your point of view. In most cases I find no physical evidence of assault at all."

"None?" I asked, startled, wondering for a moment about the competence of this my supposed expert.

"None," she repeated, and perhaps she'd caught my thought. "Check with your doctor who does the initial exams and you'll find the same thing. I find definitive evidence of assault in maybe fifteen percent of the exams I perform. In approximately another thirty percent there's something I can spot that indicates abuse to me, but it's subjective, it's not definite. And these are only in the recent cases. If a child is brought to me well after the fact there's almost never any physical evidence."

I sat digesting this blow to my court cases.

"I have my own opinions, of course. Look at Peter. That boy was abused. There's no question about it, even though he doesn't have any scar tissue. His whole life is a scar. And Katrina, the flirtatious little girl." The five-year-old who'd stood so close and looked at me so knowingly. "Katrina didn't get that way from watching cable TV."

"Is that just a phase?" I asked.

Dr. McLaren sighed. She was sitting in one of the visitor chairs in front of my desk, which I knew from experience weren't comfortable for long sitting. She leaned back and stretched her legs in front of her. Long legs, I noticed. "No," she said sadly. "It may get better, if someone handles Katrina just right—which her parents aren't. They're afraid of her and Katrina knows it." She frowned at herself. "I shouldn't have said that, forget it, please. But these kids—they're sexual beings from now on. They're not going to forget what they know. They've been exposed to this world of adult knowledge long before they can handle it. Which of us can? But these children certainly aren't ready. Look at Katrina. She gets no pleasure out of the way she behaves. She's not really trying to seduce you when she acts that way. She'd be terrified if you touched her intimately. But it's a way of behaving she knows, it's a way she found approval once. She can't forget it."

She shifted to the general again. "None of them can. It sets them apart from other children. It's very hard for them to fit in at school after that, or find friends their own age. They have this dirty secret they think everyone can see in their faces."

She made it sound like a horrible, isolated world of never-ending pain. She spoke with a certain urgency, because we both knew I wasn't a real student of that world. I was just here to reach into it and pluck out one or two of the inmates for my own purposes. For those purposes a child like Peter or Katrina was of no use to me. Dr. McLaren knew how badly wounded they were; she'd made me see it a little. But you can't count on juries for imagination. I wasn't going to put some grubby fat boy or leering little monster in front of them. No, I needed a child obviously and conventionally damaged. One in pain and embarrassed and needing the protection of the adult community. Sorting through them, I felt like a pitchman for a charity. *Find me a pitiful one. Don't you have any with scars?*

"What kind of man," I asked, "can look at a four-year-old girl and think of her as a sexual object?"

"It's not about sex, Mark, it's about control. Just like a rapist of adult women is trying to assert control, not achieve sexual gratification. A raper of children is looking for *absolute* control. Who could you control more completely than a child?" She held up a hand, open fingers upward, enclosing a small soul. "These children's whole lives can be his, Mark. Everything they think, the way they react to everything they see, it can all be a reflection of him. You probably know this: Many of these children go on to become abusers themselves. After they're grown they molest children. They're still emulating him, a generation later."

"Let's talk about him," I asked. "This man, what would he be like?"

"He's not my area of specialization," Dr. McLaren said. "But I can tell you some things." She paused to get her thoughts in order, looking up over my head. She seemed to be sorting through a lineup in her mind, wondering which one to have step forward as an example.

"We divide these men—some of them are women, but usually it's men—into two types. The rapist and the molester. The rapist wants to hurt kids." She dismissed him. "The molester—your man is a molester—he likes children. He seduces them. Each one may take a long time. Because he wants so much more, you see. He doesn't just want the child's body, he wants to be loved."

"And power," I said, being the bright pupil.

"Love *is* power," she confided.

"But he—" I was frowning. "Most of the cases we have are against live-ins. Father or stepfather or boyfriend. I understand that. There's access. But this man, he's found victims all over. How does he get close to them?"

"With their help," Dr. McLaren replied without hesitation. "You'll find, if you haven't noticed already, that these children come from poorly organized families." Nice phrase, I thought. So much more descriptive than the currently fashionable "dysfunctional." "Single parents," she went on, "divorced parents, or just ones where the parents don't have much time for the child. The molester"—she spoke of him almost admiringly—"fills a need in the child's life. He gives them the nurturing they need and haven't found. The child loves him. The child needs him."

I remembered Tommy Algren's abetting of his own abduction from the daycare center, repeatedly. And again of the damage to my own cases.

"I hope you're not saying the child then is willing to cooperate—I mean willingly—"

"Has sex with him?" She shook her head adamantly. "These are young children. When a strange man starts treating them kindly and getting close to them and acting affectionate, they don't know he's after sex. They don't know sex exists until he exposes them to it. And they hate that part of it. It scares them; it ruins them."

Janet moved her head slightly, as if easing a neck growing stiff. She was still watching me. There was strength in her gaze, holding me, making me think for a moment that she was exercising some psychological technique on me.

I thought about Austin Paley. We weren't talking about an anonymous case study, we were talking about a man I'd known most of my adult life, with no suspicion of his real life.

"We haven't found nearly all his victims, have we?"

She shook her head. "A man his age, who probably started in his teens: Hundreds. Hundreds of attempts, anyway, and as careful as he seems to have been, most of them were probably successful. Even if it was only half—"

Started in his teens, I thought. That meant there was already an adult generation of Austin's victims—his spores, many of them already embarked on child-molesting careers of their own. Austin had already left his mark on generations.

I suddenly thought of Chris Davis. Maybe it wasn't blackmail that had made him step forward to own up falsely to Austin's crimes. Maybe it was love.

We sat in silence. I felt oddly close to Dr. McLaren after only a few minutes, maybe because we were collaborating on a common cause. Her manner contributed too. She acted as if she knew me, or had in a past life. I hadn't enough experience to know if all psychiatrists treated everyone like that. I had a childish urge to disrupt her assumptions about me, to prove myself better or worse than she thought.

"Will I need to repeat all this to the prosecutor who'll be trying the case?" she asked. "Of course, I've worked with most of the sex crimes prosecutors enough to—"

"I think I can pass it on to anyone trying the case with me," I said confidently.

She gave me that look. I returned a reassuring one. Thorough professional, master of a thousand arcane details.

"I didn't see you making any notes," she said.

"I didn't know there was going to be a test."

She arched her back to sit up straighter in the chair, and gathered her feet under her. But before she rose she said, "Trying the case with you? You're going to be trying one of these cases yourself?"

My campaign advisers wouldn't like it, but if I convicted Austin myself, putting an end to the menace to San Antonio's children, nothing would be better for my reelection chances. And I had my own reasons for wanting to prosecute Austin Paley personally.

"I think so. You'll help me, won't you?"

"Oh yes," she answered, as if to say I'd need it.

While I was making my preparations for trial, Austin wasn't sitting idly by. His war opened on two fronts. Publicly his implacable nonchalance remained untouched. He was free on bond, of course. He didn't go cowering into seclusion as most defendants would. On the contrary, he seemed more publicly active than ever. He gave interviews, and made them count. He appeared not to be bitter about his indictments. Instead he affected sympathy for me.

"The district attorney found himself in a tight spot. There was a growing public fear he had to play to, for the sake of his hopes of reelection. He had a suspect in hand, he saw himself getting the kind of favorable publicity he so desperately needs, then it all fell apart. He had to find another scapegoat, quickly. I was available."

"Do you think there was any personal animosity involved?" the television reporter asked, falling into Austin's scenario.

Austin reluctantly concluded that the reporter might be on to something. "Well, I *was* the attorney who brought forward the suspect who then refused to plead guilty, throwing a wrench into the district attorney's plans. And of course the district attorney and I have opposed each other on cases in the past," he went on. "But I doubt any of that affected his decision, consciously. I was just the most readily available suspect. I think this will all blow over after it's no longer a political necessity. Don't look for this case to be tried before the election. He wouldn't risk that."

To a newspaper columnist who followed up on this last line, Austin expanded: "There's no case against me. Mark Blackwell just wants the public to think he's put a stop to the threat against the city's children by arresting me. By arresting anyone—anyone would have served. But he doesn't have the evidence to actually try me, because he knows that would end in acquittal, because I'm innocent. I expect the cases will be quietly dismissed after the election. It's really rather a cynical manipulation of the system."

The columnist, who wasn't as gullible as his television counterpart and had done more research, asked, "What about reports that at least two of the abused children have identified you?"

I could picture Austin looking deeply troubled. That's how the columnist described him. "I wouldn't be at all surprised," was Austin's answer. "As anyone knows who has tried this kind of case, a child can be made to say anything, if someone works at him hard enough. I feel sorry for those children."

I didn't know what the public thought. Surely the small percentage of citizens who would vote in the district attorney's race was following the story. I couldn't help wondering how I was perceived. Austin, it seemed to me, was beginning to appear rather victimized himself, and I was his persecutor.

But Austin was no victim. He held a lot of strings, and he was pulling them behind the scenes.

*　　*　　*

"Blackie! Hey, hoss, if you're gonna go crazy, why don't you give your friends some warning, so we could steer you the right way?"

"Well, Harry, that's how craziness is, you know, it sort of sneaks up on you."

"Yeah, I've seen that happen." Harry's eyes shrewdly took me in. Those penetrating blue eyes looked out of place in the hearty bonhomie of his expression as he leaned toward me, one hand over my shoulder, the other pumping my hand.

There is an underground tunnel that connects the new Justice Center with the old courthouse. It was there Harry accosted me. I was on my way to his bailiwick, he had just entered mine. Lawyers have business in both court buildings; there is always a wealth of foot traffic through the tunnel. People hurrying by slowed to look at us curiously, the two elected officials having a very public conversation. Because Harry didn't lower his voice a decibel. Harry was of the old school of public figure, who thought a hearty manner and vaguely rural expressions made him seem a man of the people, though he'd never forked a load of hay in his life.

"Well, you sure could've picked on somebody more guilty than ol' Austin Paley, son. I think that case can stand some more investigation, you know what I mean? I mean, I can't believe it, myself. I *don't* believe it. And if Austin calls me as a witness, I'll have to get up and tell a jury that."

Harry was a much better politician than he was a lawyer, but he knew enough law to know that his personal opinion of a defendant's guilt or innocence would never be admitted in court. There in the public hallway, though, his opinion was perfectly admissible to everyone within earshot, which at Harry's volume took in two or three city blocks.

"You're certainly entitled to your opinion, Harry," I said calmly, "but you haven't talked to those children the way I have. You haven't seen them point out Austin Paley as the man who molested them."

"Well, I know most of us look pretty much the same to little kids. Hell, if somebody else went home wearing my suit tonight, my kids wouldn't even notice, long as he doled out the allowances like he was supposed to."

I happened to know that Harry's youngest child was a

sophomore at SMU. We were deep in the realm of metaphor, which is no place to prosecute a case. Neither is a public hallway. I didn't respond.

"Well, look for my name appearing on Austin's witness list as a character witness," Harry boomed anyway. "That man's done more for this county than"—*Than any one-term district attorney,* I heard—"than any ten other people," Harry concluded. But his little ice-chip eyes confirmed what I'd heard. I stared back to let him know I understood what this was all about.

"Whyn't you come see me?" he said in his lowest tone, the one a secretary sitting on his lap wouldn't overhear if he didn't want her to. For public consumption he repeated loudly, "Better find some better investigators, Blackie!" He clapped me on the back and went on down the hallway, shaking every hand, whether offered or not.

I hate that nickname. And the people who use it on me. But I could ignore Harry only at my peril. He was a county commissioner, one of five who run the county government: awarding contracts, setting salaries. Among other duties, they oversee my budget.

The next week I wanted to investigate my speculative insight into Chris Davis's motivation. This time I had no qualms about interrogating him without his lawyer present, since he and the lawyer had conflicting interests, but I discovered Austin had taken Davis out of my reach. He'd made his bonds. Chris Davis was no longer in custody.

That made sense. Once Austin's first scheme had failed because his substitute's nerve had, it was dangerous for Austin for Davis to remain in custody, where he might decide to talk at any time. In fact, it occurred to me, Chris Davis was a continuing danger to Austin, because of what he knew. I assigned an investigator to find Davis, but he had no luck. Chris Davis never returned to the apartment he'd given his bail bondsman as his address.

Well, I hadn't expected Davis to help me much even if I did talk to him. Even things that should have been important to me, that *were* important, began to seem nuisances, such as the calls from my campaign manager, Tim Scheuless.

"I had a booking fall through," Tim said in a puzzled

tone. He called my speeches bookings, as if I were a rock band playing the Ramada Inn. "You know, that south side what was it?"

"Yeah," I said, holding up a hand to tell Becky to stay in the room. She went back to her reading. "The Concerned whatevers for something-or-other."

"Yeah, them. They said they're canceling their Meet the Candidates series. They already had Leo Mendoza speak to them, though. I think they're going to endorse him."

"Well, that's not a surprise."

"Yeah, but still. I thought— Well, anyway." He must have remembered he wasn't supposed to discourage the candidate. "Say, aren't you going to try something soon? Remember what I told you? I still think that's our best chance for good coverage. Don't you have somebody really horrible who's got a lousy lawyer and no chance of—"

"As a matter of fact I'm preparing a case for trial now." I winked at Becky, who was pretending not to listen.

"It's not Austin Paley, is it?" Tim asked quietly.

"Why do you ask that?"

"Jesus, Mark, you need to stay away from that one. That's the hottest potato in town right now. I've gotten a couple of calls—"

"You too?"

He went on as if I hadn't interrupted. "I think it'll be okay if you treat it like it's just another case, you know, let it fall wherever it falls, have some assistant handle it, that'd be okay. But if people start thinking it's some personal vendetta of your own, there's going to be some fallout. The man's got friends. I mean—"

"He's a criminal, Tim."

"Well, nobody's convinced of that. Until they are, people are going to stand up for him. I've already had somebody tell me he's not going to send in the contribution he'd promised because of your false accusation of his old buddy Austin."

"I'm sorry to hear that, Tim, I really am, but what do you want me to do?"

His hesitation told me he knew perfectly well how much weight whatever he said would carry with me. "At least tell me you're not going to try it yourself," he begged.

"Don't you think voters will be happy for me to send a serial child molester to prison, Tim, no matter how many fat cats are offended by it?"

"Well, yeah. But it's not even that good a case, is it? I said a laydown, Mark, not something risky. Hand it off, all right?"

"I'll think about it," I said, and hung up.

He was right. I knew he was right. There was no reason to put my career at risk over this one case. I had a staff of competent prosecutors, some of them better than that. My sex crimes chief had already volunteered, and she had an impressive record in cases like this. I should take Eliot's advice: Talk tough, then let my staff do the work. I'd be shirking what I felt to be a personal responsibility—I'd brought the case into the office, I was the one who'd been duped by Austin's initial scheme—but no one expected the DA to try every case personally. No one would look askance if I let an assistant try the case.

What about Becky? I certainly trusted her. But when I looked at her and thought of handing these cases—*my* cases—over to her, I couldn't bring myself to do it. Why not? Because I saw a torturous path through a tangle of hazards to reach a conviction in this case. Isn't that terrible? I trusted only myself to negotiate it.

There must have been another reason for my reluctance to hand over the cases to someone else, someone as able a prosecutor as I. I sensed that reason lurking in the back of my mind, but I hadn't poked at it enough to goad it into revealing itself.

"So what do you think?" I said. "Pick your victim."

"I like little girls," Becky said. Once upon a time I would have made a joke from that line, but by this time I was so immersed in the world of child sexual assault that I barely saw the opening as it passed me by. "Little girls look more vulnerable and precious. You can drive fathers of daughters absolutely over the edge with the idea it could have been *their* babies instead. Juries want to protect girls. Boys, though—"

"They're supposed to look out for themselves," I said.

"Exactly."

"The trouble is," I pointed out, "our cases with the little

girls are lousy. They're the youngest, I don't know if they can even identify him. Plus, he didn't—"

"Yes," Becky said, already ahead of me. "So if it has to be a boy it has to be Kevin, obviously. He's a good age, he looks good." She looked up at me. "When he tells his story *I* want to run up and hold him, and I'm not a pushover for kids."

"No. And that's good right now. But for trial you'll need a rapport with them. Have you spent much time with children, Becky? Are you interested in them?"

"Of course," she said, but that was just a defensive response.

"It's no disgrace if you're not. Not everyone has to be interested in children. Do you want— Never mind. It's none of my business."

She answered me anyway. "No, I do. But you can't just decide to have children. You need some help, I understand." She cleared her throat. She was actually blushing a little.

"Come on, Becky, I don't believe that. A woman like you, with your—advantages. You must be hounded by men."

"Hah," she said. The blush was fading. "Besides, you're not going to pick just anybody and say, 'Hey, you wanta have a kid?' It's— Well, you're a parent. You know."

"Yes. When you first have a child you think this is the most important thing you've ever done, this is the one part of you that will live on. Then time goes by and you get caught up in your work again and the child grows up just a little. Just a tiny bit and already he's so changed you wouldn't recognize him if you went away for a week. You start to wonder if you're really a part of him at all." I lapsed into thought, and I would have stopped talking then, but Becky was watching me expectantly. "Then years go by and you think maybe that was the most important thing in your life after all and you realized it too late."

"Why is it too late?"

I just let the question float by. "So you think Kevin? I think you're right, the others—"

"I have this—friend," Becky said. It was odd the way her face changed, from one word to the next. Sometimes I thought she looked like a child herself, but then, without her even moving, a shadow dropped down her forehead and she seemed to be speaking from a perspective of long years; lost years. "Donny. I knew him from law school, and that goes back a long way now. Sometimes I think if things had been just slightly different, if one weekend had turned out different, or one job interview, we'd be married now, with kids or talking about it. But it didn't. And now we're both so caught up in work it doesn't seem to matter. But I think some day, maybe in years, he'll realize what you said, that something important passed him by."

"You still see him?"

She smiled. "Yes, definitely Kevin," she said. "Maybe we can get some parents of boys on the jury. If we do it right it might be even more heartbreaking than having a little girl up there on the stand."

I pushed aside the other files, opened the one, and Becky came and leaned over my shoulder as we went through it again.

7

Why Kevin? Why does it have to be him?"

I'm not the one who singled him out, I wanted to say. I'm not the one who made him a victim.

"Because Kevin's is the best case," I said. "Kevin can identify the man positively, and I'm convinced Kevin would make the best witness."

I didn't tell them all the reasons. Tommy Algren was the most articulate of the child victims, but he was too old and too controlled. Becky and I had decided that Kevin Pollard would look more pitiful.

Technically I didn't need his parents' agreement. I could just subpoena Kevin and he would have to testify. But I needed a cooperative witness. I needed to rehearse with him before trial, needed his trust when he looked at me from the witness stand. I needed his damned parents.

I'd done too good a job of informing the Pollards what the odds were in this kind of case. They read the papers, too; they reminded me that a man had been acquitted of a similar charge in federal court the month before. Jurors are reluctant to accept a child's story if an adult vehemently denies it. After all, we can imagine ourselves being unjustly accused by a child too young to understand the consequences.

Mr. Pollard said, "If Kevin testifies, he'll be marked. All the other kids will make fun of him."

And the guys at the bowling alley will look at you funny,
I thought.

"No," I said. "The media won't identify him. They don't
report the names of child victims."

He and his wife looked at me hopefully. "Really?" he
asked. "Is that the law?"

"No, it's just a journalistic tradition. But it's very strictly
followed."

They kept looking at me. "Uh-huh," Mr. Pollard finally
said.

I wondered if it would help to have Kevin in the room
with us. He was playing in the back yard so we could discuss
his future freely. Kevin would be willing, I thought. I
stopped pleading and just stared at them, as if I knew they
were good folks who would do the right thing.

Mrs. Pollard grew embarrassed by their slowness. "It'll be
okay, honey," she said to her husband. "When the jury hears
all those other children say he's done the same thing to
them . . ."

I cleared my throat. I thought about not correcting her.
Becky saved me the trouble of deciding.

"We won't be able to do that," she said. "Unless the
defense slips up, the jury won't be allowed to hear about
the other cases. We can only try them one at a time."

And the defense won't slip up, I thought. Whoever Austin
hired would be too good for that.

"No one will ever be safe," I said abruptly.

"What?"

"If I can't send this man to prison, no child in this city
will ever be safe again. Including Kevin. Do you think he's
safe just because we've caught the man who molested him?
That doesn't count for anything unless we can convict him.
And we can't do that by ourselves. People complain about
crime, but they have to help put a stop to it. Victims have
to fight back. They can't back down."

I thought this was language that would appeal to Mr. Pollard. But all he said was, "Mind if we talk about it alone
for a few minutes?"

"Okay," I said shortly, and strode past them, across their
brown shag carpet and through the sliding glass patio door
into their back yard.

"I have seen more public-spirited citizens," Becky said outside. "What do you think they'll say?"

"I don't care what they say. To hell with him. If he says no I'll come back after he's gone. Two can play at intimidating that wispy wife of his. Absentee fathers don't get to dictate what's best for their sons. I'll get her to give us the go-ahead. Or you can."

"Gee, thanks," Becky said.

"Kevin," I called.

He was alone on a swing set, on one end of one of those gliders made for two children. I wished I were small enough to take the other seat.

It was dusk, magic hour, when the day arrays all its previously hidden possibilities just before opening into night. It was early September, Kevin would be back in school. I remembered schoolday afternoons as precious, and twilight most precious of all, the air growing so still and clear it could carry a mother's voice calling you home for blocks and blocks. Dusk made every activity the most wonderful of the day, the one we could least abide giving up. But Kevin looked like a boy who didn't mind school, who probably had already done his homework.

"How are you?" I asked.

"Fine," he said placidly, not bored, a boy used to being alone. *What are you worried about?* I wanted to ask his father. *This boy's got no friends to lose anyway.*

"We arrested him, Kevin. The man you told me touched you. I didn't understand that day in the courtroom, did I? We had the wrong man. But when you told me the right one I had police officers go and take him to jail."

"I know," Kevin said. I tried to detect some reaction in his voice, eased fear, or even pride that he'd made such a big thing happen in the adult world, but I couldn't hear anything from Kevin. He might have been waiting to learn from me how he should react.

"But I can't keep him there," I said, "unless you help me. You have to tell your story to other people. Not just me, not just in my office. You need to tell it in front of a lot of people in a big room. Do you think you can do that?"

"We'll be there with you," Becky added helpfully. She knelt to his level, awkwardly in her skirt and heels.

"Will you help me?" Kevin asked. Promise of mere presence wasn't enough for him.

"Oh, yes," Becky said, reaching out and hugging him in what appeared a perfectly spontaneous response. "I'll help you, Kevin," she said. "All you'll have to do is watch me and answer the questions I ask. All right?"

He nodded. Very docile boy. He'd show more animation in court, though, after we'd rehearsed. And Austin would be there then. If Kevin had anything like the reaction to his presence he'd had that other day in the courtroom, the jury could have no doubt of his sincerity.

"Mr. Blackwell?"

It was that twilight voice, calling me home. A thrill ran along my arms, and I realized I'd been expecting the call, waiting for it. Time to go in. Becky and I trudged up the gentle slope of the yard to the back door, Kevin with us. Mrs. Pollard looked down at my hand on his shoulder.

"We've decided," she said.

"Yeah," Pollard said gruffly. "Can't let the bastard get away with this, can we? Sorry, hon," he apologized for the obscenity, then dropped into a squat in front of Kevin, his black pants stretching tight enough to create an embarrassing moment if the material was as thin as it looked. "How about it, Kevin, is it all right with you? Do you want to testify about what happened to you?"

"I already said I would," Kevin said.

Pollard gave me a funny look. "We've discussed it," I said. Pollard kept his stare on me for a long moment. I returned it blandly.

The next day I was making my usual rove through the courts, looking for Becky but in no hurry to find her. The sights of confrontations and deals being made raised my energy level, as usual, but also made me feel left out. It was with this soft jangle of emotions that I reached Judge Hernandez's courtroom and found Becky deep in conference with Linda Alaniz.

I went up the aisle faster. I was smiling. Linda was not, as she turned away from Becky. I knew the intensity of her expression. Someone's life was in her hands.

"Linda! I'm glad to see you. You know, I've tried to call you a couple of times lately, but you're never at home."

Linda smiled at me, too, but hesitantly, as if afraid a smile would convey too much. "Hello, Mark. You need to warn your prosecutor against being too harsh. She might make me try the case."

I certainly wasn't going to intervene. I barely glanced at Becky. But I wasn't done with Linda. "Are you through here? Do you have time for lunch?"

"There you are," someone interrupted, in a hearty lawyer's tone, so I thought it was aimed at me, but the thirty-somethingish man with the sculpted nose and wide forehead and dark-rimmed glasses came up to Linda instead. "Listen, I'm having a little trouble in the 175th. You think you could come— Oh, I'm sorry."

Linda's face was blank, an unusual expression for her, one she had to work to achieve. "Mark, do you know Roger Guerra? Roger and I are officing together now."

"Oh," I said. "No, I didn't know. Yes, Roger and I've met."

Roger smiled enough for all of us. "Yes, Linda's retraining me, telling me everything I learned wrong. She's the best." He laid his hand on her forearm. His look spoke of devotion. Linda was watching me, still blankly, still working hard. She patted his hand, and he removed it. "But I don't need to tell you that, do I?" Roger said to me.

I said that he didn't. To Linda I added, "I just wanted to thank you again for what you said about me to my campaign manager."

Her eyes warmed a little. No, they'd been warm all along, but carefully restrained. "It was all true."

"Gee, Linda, I thought you were just buttering me up, hoping for favors."

She finally smiled, because we both knew her tongue would stick to the roof of her mouth before she could make it say something insincere. Then her new partner hustled her away to deal with his problem in another court. Linda never looked back, maybe because she knew I was watching her, all the way out.

"You know, she wasn't a very good first assistant." Becky was standing with me. I barely heard her. "But then, she's a great defense lawyer." Brief silence. "On the other hand," Becky concluded, "my opinion of her probably isn't all that important to you."

It was a big chunk of my past that had just walked out of the courtroom, one that I'd thought might just possibly be in my future, as well, but I'd been wrong.

"What?" I said.

Later that afternoon I left the office early and went home. Becky was coming in my office door as I went out it, and she seemed confused by my early departure. "Where are you going?" she asked. "It's just personal," I said. That made her confusion turn to concern. "Really?" she said.

"Family personal." I wondered why I felt compelled to explain, and Becky must have realized it was strange, too. "Oh, sorry," she said. "Well . . ."

It seemed eerie to be home before dark, as if I might surprise the daytime owner. I sorted through my clothes, trying to decide what to wear to my own house. I was going by invitation, but I wasn't supposed to appear a guest.

"Listen," Lois had said, on the phone. "I have a favor to ask."

"Sure," I'd said automatically.

"I'd like you to come to the house next Friday night, for dinner. And stay after dinner," Lois hurried on. "I just want you to be here." She stopped and laughed at herself. When she started again she sounded more relaxed. "Here's what it is, Mark—Dinah has a date."

"A date?"

"Yes, her first date. I would have spared you the anxiety of knowing about it, but I'd like you to be here. The boy's coming to pick her up and I thought it would be nice if her father were here to meet him."

"Want me to put the fear of God into him, eh? All right, I'll get Muggsy and the boys together and we'll all be lined up at the door when the little terrorist shows up." Lois endured this stoically. "Okay, Lois. I'm sure we can pull this off. After all, the kid's only, what, thirteen? Want me to bring some of my dirty clothes and scatter them around? It'll be all right as long as Dinah doesn't trip over me and say, 'Dad! What are you doing here?' "

Lois ignored my attempts at humor. "Come for dinner early," she said. "I want the remains of dinner on the table when the boy arrives."

So it was that I found myself dressing for dinner at my old house, trying to strike the proper casually-at-home-but-formally-receiving-a-visitor tone. The silliness of it improved my mood, but the occasion disturbed me. My baby's first date. Date. She was much too young. Only a little jerk with too much self-confidence would ask a thirteen-year-old girl out on a date, especially so early in the school year. What did the little thug think he was after, anyway?

"You're not going to make me regret inviting you, are you?" Lois asked patiently, as I explained these concerns later in her kitchen. "Just meet the boy and don't say anything."

The doorbell rang. "Awfully early, isn't he?" I asked. Lois was just taking a roast out of the oven. "No, that's probably—" she began, but I was already heading for the front door. It opened before I reached it.

"Oh," I said. "David. We *are* going to present a united front, aren't we?"

I started to hug my son, thought that was a bit much, and ended up sort of grasping his shoulders like some dopey variety of French Foreign Legion officer. "How are you?"

"Fine," David said. "Fine. I invited myself. Couldn't miss this."

I pulled the front door farther open and peeked around it. "Where's Vicky?"

"She didn't come. Hi, Mom."

David crossed the dining room to hug Lois. He looked like a boy doing it, though he towered over her. David is twenty-six, my height or taller, but very slender. He looks too tall for his size, in constant danger of breaking, or tripping.

"Well," he said, stepping back, "where's the dream date?" and went down the hall to find her. I heard Dinah's door open, heard her greet her brother happily. I was surprised to hear that they sounded like such good friends. They had grown up separately, David already a high school boy by the time Dinah was aware of him, a married man with a home of his own before she was old enough to be of any interest to him. I was glad to think they'd found the time to become real brother and sister after David was already grown and gone. Lois and I looked at each other. She knew I was wondering if this had been a secret part of her arrangement, inviting David without telling me.

When Dinah emerged from her room she came shyly to greet me. She didn't overtly ask for my approval, but the request was in her approach. She wore a cream-colored dress with a sort of cowl covering her shoulders. It was fairly casual, by no means a prom dress. Wearing it, Dinah looked like a pretty little girl, not a miniature adult.

"You look beautiful, darling," I told her. She smiled, and in the next moment busied herself helping Lois carry dishes to the table. I filled the drink requests, iced tea and water and Coke. For a few minutes we were all busy between the kitchen and dining room; there was a pleasant bustle that sounded like conversation.

But when we found ourselves sitting at the table together, I turned to David and fell silent. Whenever I saw David now I remembered talking to him with bars between us. It had been three years, but I could never forget my son in jail, his bewilderment, the helplessness I'd felt. I still felt it when I saw him, that guilty certainty that there was something I'd neglected that had kept him imprisoned. I don't know if David felt that way too, but I felt it *from* him, and it still made me uncomfortable to be near him.

He looked all right, though. He had none of the haunted look one might have expected. Here with his family he seemed perfectly at ease. He looked older, of course, than he had before his jailing. There were moments when he frowned, or leaned solicitously toward Dinah, or paused before answering a question, when he could have been the man of the house. Lois leaned toward David just as Dinah did, waiting for his answers.

"So who is this boy?" I asked. They all turned toward me. I understood at once that I was the only one uninformed. David gave Dinah a sly sidelong look she acknowledged by slapping his hand without looking at him.

"His name's Steve," she said. "He's very nice."

"Steve? What happened to Jeff and—what was the other one's name?"

"Mutt." David laughed. Dinah regally ignored him.

"What about them?" she asked me, as if I were Barbara Walters getting a little too personal.

"I thought Jeff was the one you liked, but Danny'd been calling. Does this mean you like Steve better, or is he—"

"I'm not going to *marry* him," Dinah said, overly exasperated.

David leaned toward me confidentially. "Jeff's just a little slow."

"You mean," I said in the same tone, gesturing toward my head, "not the brightest boy in class?"

"Not slow like that," Dinah said. "Slow to *phone.*"

Dinah was even prettier when being teased. "I hope we're not going to be talking abut Jeff when Steve arrives," Lois said.

"Maybe these two shouldn't even *be* here when Steve comes," Dinah said. David and I grinned at each other.

Banter made us a family again. We fell easily into our roles. It was easy after that to talk about other things, Dinah's school, David's job. I tried to follow what he said about computer software. He'd had a good job before his arrest, with a small company through which he seemed to be rising rapidly. They'd taken him back after he was free again, but neither of them was the same any more. The company had expanded into other areas than the software for small businesses, in which David was expert. His degree was in accounting, he'd written a couple of the computer programs himself. But he was no longer as important to the company as he'd been before the interruption in his career. He told us this only by implication. What I really wanted to ask was, if after the tragedy of his arrest for rape he'd grown dissatisfied with his old job and old friends, then what about his marriage? How did he continue with Vicky, to whom he'd never seemed very attached even before the crisis? That was the question I might never ask.

I felt myself settling in now, comfortable, as if we were still what we appeared to be, an unbroken family. But it hadn't been like this when Lois and I were married, not in the last years of our marriage. I wouldn't have sat there extending dinner for the sake of its society. I would have been up and pacing, reading cases or on the phone, rehashing the day at the office or preparing for the next one. I don't mean I would have devoted the whole evening to work; just a few precious minutes snatched from family obligations. I hadn't thought of myself as a workaholic. But work was where my *interest* lay. I could see now that while work hadn't filled all my time at home, I'd devoted just enough important minutes to it that my family could see that's where my heart was. I was killing time with them until I could get back to the office or the courthouse.

Starting the affair with Linda had been secondary. I had already betrayed my home long before that. Now sitting among them, one of them but only as a visitor, the family life I'd neglected seemed terribly sweet to me. If I had kept just a fraction more of my life among them I could have saved my home, saved us all. We'd be here now just as we seemed, without the aura of temporariness.

"Yipes," Dinah said, having turned David's wrist so she could see his watch.

"You're already gorgeous!" I called after her as she bolted from the table. "I'll help," I added, as Lois stood and picked up plates.

"Sit, sit," she said.

"I thought you wanted the boy to see the family dinner still on the table when he got here," I reminded her.

"We don't want him to think we're pigs, do we?" she answered, disappearing into the kitchen.

David and I were left alone, rather artfully, if one chose to look at it that way. "Want to go in the front room and peer out the curtains?" he asked. I followed him. We remained standing in the living room. The early American furniture in that room was designed for appearance.

"What's Vicky doing tonight?" I asked casually.

David answered casually as well, but I thought I felt a tension that hadn't been there before. "Went to a movie. I wasn't interested in seeing it, and she thinks I'm silly for wanting to be here for this."

I didn't remember ever having been to a movie without Lois while we were married. I saw quite a few movies I wasn't interested in seeing. So did she. And I wondered if being married to a woman who thought family milestones like first dates "silly" made David question their future together. I wondered if David went meekly along to Vicky's family occasions and only she balked at attending ours, or was it mutual? Lois and I would never have thought of having such separate lives. It wouldn't have seemed an option.

All this speculation left me silent long enough, probably, to let David in on my thoughts. That's how we'd always communicated, by reading each other's minds. I remembered Lois's telling me that David seemed troubled, and that she hoped he'd confide his worries to me.

I said, "It sounds as if you do most of your work alone."

He answered as if he'd never thought of that before. "I guess I do."

"Did you plan that? Do people at the job make you uncomfortable?"

He laughed, humorlessly. David looked older now than the lighthearted boy who'd entertained us at dinner. "More like the other way around," he said.

"Well ... But you can't just withdraw from everybody, David. Nothing that happened was your fault. I know it will take even longer than this to feel your life back to normal, but you have to—"

"No." He was shaking his head, cutting me off, and he gave that dry chuckle again. "That's not it. I wasn't embarrassed. When I said I made them uncomfortable, I don't mean just people studying me when they thought I wasn't looking. Everything was fine, I slipped right back into my job. But—"

He dropped onto a wooden love seat that looked as spindly as he. "I mean I *deliberately* make them uncomfortable. Sometimes I'll give them this look." He stared at me, head slightly lowered, eyes very deep and direct, sizing me up as if deciding to slash my tires on his way out or do it to me instead. I'd seen that expression before, always on the face of someone charged with a terrible crime.

David laughed and looked boyish again. "I *use* it, Dad. I *want* to be this scary thing in their midst. I didn't want everything just to revert to normal. And if they were going to look at me I was going to give them something to look at.

"I still do it. I think." Now he did look embarrassed. He was looking away from me, out the curtains, down at the floor. "When I meet somebody new I wonder if they know my story. And you know what? I'd be disappointed if they *didn't*. And once in a while I've been negotiating with someone, and it's been pretty tough, real give-and-take, you know, and all of a sudden they give in. And I have to wonder, Did I just do it without knowing it? Or did they suddenly remember about me? Either way—" He laughed again. "I can't tell this so you'd understand."

"Maybe you couldn't if I didn't understand already," I said. His eyes stopped wandering around the room. "I know just what it's like, David. I think I do. You know, there are a lot of people who think they know the whole story of what happened in your case, but they don't all know the same thing. And a lot still wonder. They wonder what *I* did. Who I got to, or threatened, and how. And I've never yet claimed innocence. I just let them look at me. And sometimes I look back."

David was studying me, wondering if we really had this secret in common or if I was just trying to convince him we did. "Be a shame to have something awful happen to you and not be able to use it afterwards," I said.

Slowly, not the quick, false reactions he'd made during his speech, David smiled at me. I realized again how much he looked like both me and Lois. He probably didn't realize it. I think you have to look backward to see those things. But I'm sure he felt kinship in that moment.

The doorbell rang.

"Yipes," I half-shouted, "the kid sneaked up on us."

We were on our feet, milling toward the door as if we were a crowd. I put a hand on David's arm.

"Now don't terrify him, David." He looked at me as if I were making fun of him, as if it had been a mistake to tell me. "Unless it seems called for," I finished. He grinned.

"Hello," I said, before I even had the door fully open. I had to lower my gaze a little. Young master Robbins stood on our doorstep. He was less formally dressed than I'd expected, no tie, no jacket, but he wore conservative navy trousers and a plaid long-sleeved shirt.

"You must be Steve."

"Yes sir."

I brought him inside. David nodded to him and said, "I'll see how Dinah's doing."

I settled into a chair. Young Steve remained standing. He looked more composed than I would have been. I suppose he was a handsome boy. Hard to tell about a thirteen-year-old. He had a few freckles across his nose, no acne, straight white teeth. His dark hair was rather short on the sides but longer in the back.

"They always keep you waiting," I confided to him, by which I meant to ask whether this was his first date.

"I guess so," he answered.

David returned, with Lois, who made small talk with Steve about school, even calling a couple of teachers by name. I just stood by, trying to look like someone only a fool would cross.

Dinah entered, with a shy, measured step. Her home had become a theater. Steve turned and saw her. Dinah was obviously aware that she and Steve were the observed of all observers. It made her very stiff. Not so her date. He smiled unselfconsciously.

"Hello, Dinah," he said. "You look lovely." It sounded like a line he'd heard on TV, but he said it well.

Dinah and Steve didn't sit down with us. After only a minute or two they were walking toward the door. I stopped Dinah to give her a hug. "Have a good time," I said to her.

"Be careful," I told Steve, by which I meant to say, If you ever do anything to hurt her, I'll pinch your head off and beat you to death with it. I hoped he was as perceptive as he seemed, but if he had been he would have drawn back from me in fright instead of giving me the manly little handshake he did.

When they were gone I asked, "Someone did tell him I'm the district attorney, didn't they? I didn't want to say it myself, but he knows, right?"

David and Lois both laughed. "Come on in, Dad," Lois said. "Is your past coming back to haunt you?"

"I never did anything to be ashamed of on a date. Certainly not in the eighth grade."

We passed through the formal living room and went on into the den. "I remember some dates of ours that would have scared the wits out of *my* father if he'd known," Lois said.

"Hush, you'll shock the boy."

The phone rang, and Lois slipped out of the room to answer it. Realtors, I remembered, get calls at all hours, like lawyers.

"How are things at home?" I asked David, knowing I couldn't keep my tone casual enough to prevent his resenting the inquiry.

"Fine," he said. That was all. I had a flood of follow-up questions: Any chance of divorce? Am I ever going to have grandchildren? Is Vicky always as cold as she seems? Are you happy?

"Really?" I pressed.

David seemed ready to pounce on anything I said. "I know you never liked Vicky," he said suddenly.

"I don't dislike Vicky." I was genuinely shocked. "I hardly even know her. She seems very nice. It's just that I wonder—"

"She thinks you don't," David said.

"Is that why she's not here? I don't know how she could think that. I don't disapprove of people."

He laughed, harshly.

"I just want to know if you're happy with her, David. That's my only interest in Vicky." That sounded much too mean. I moderated it. "I like her just fine, but that doesn't matter if she doesn't make you happy."

"It's not her job to make me happy."

"That's not how I meant it. I mean if you're happy together."

"We are," he snapped. "I said we are, didn't I?"

Had he? "Well, good," I said mildly.

David cooled. He had heard the uncalled-for anger in his voice. "How's the campaign going?" he asked. And that was the end of the personal conversation. I was left where I usually was left with David, hoping I could fix things the next time.

8

... Because our campaign has convinced the people of this county that it is time for a change in the office of the district attorney. That is why the incumbent has concocted this case against an upstanding, and I might also say *outstanding*, public citizen. Trust me, there is no evidence behind these accusations. There is only the desperation of a public official who knows ..."

"He's bought the whole Paley party line," Tim Scheuless said.

"Leo doesn't buy. He sells," I answered.

"TV just slurps this drool up, don't they? Are they ever going to ask him anything?" Tim asked angrily.

"Wait." I turned up the sound on the tiny TV on my desk.

"But there haven't been any more children molested since Austin Paley was arrested for the crimes," the television interviewer said.

Leo Mendoza dismissed that fact. "The real molester isn't an idiot," he sniffed. "He's just lying low, happy that someone else is being made to suffer for his crimes. Once I am the district attorney, believe me, I will uncover the true offender."

Leo had chosen to conduct the interview on a street outside the courthouse. He was an imposing but oddly shaped figure. His stomach was oversized, but his legs and chest were very thin. This gave him a wedge-shaped appearance, the point of the wedge thrusting toward anyone standing in

122

front of him. He seemed to be leaning backward, his head withdrawing as he talked. He wore a white hat that further obscured his face.

Leo was a longtime defense lawyer who had paid his dues to the party without ever asking anything in return, until now, so he had the solid backing of his party in his race for district attorney. Years ago, half my lifetime ago, he had been an assistant district attorney for a while, so he claimed the background for the job. Since then he had prospered in a small way, handling low-profile misdemeanors and minor felonies, almost never drawing the public's attention. He had no record to attack. He could say what he liked about mine, with impunity. He knew how to run a campaign, paying proper subservience to the power groups, giving fierce interviews without saying much, courting the organizations that would encourage their members to vote.

"The cases will not be tried in court," he assured his interviewer. "The incumbent district attorney will never risk allowing his victim to prove his innocence. The arrest was just a campaign ploy."

"Aren't they giving Leo a lot of time?" I asked. "What is this, an endorsement?"

"They always have long features on the noon news," Tim said. "Wait, here's the big wrap-up."

"Crime is more rampant in this city than it's ever been," Leo was saying soberly, talking directly to the camera.

"No shit," I said.

"... while my opponent spends all his time sitting in his office spinning plots against innocents. Once I hold the office, all that will stop. Then we will see nothing but the impartial administration of justice."

Tim snapped off the television. "You see," he said at once. "He's gonna kill you with this. He's finally—"

"You don't think anybody's going to buy this crap, do you?"

"I *know* they are," Tim said emphatically. "Let me tell you what happened yesterday. I got a call from the North Side Civic Betterment Council. They're endorsing Leo."

"What?" I said, coming out of my chair.

Tim nodded. The North Side Civic Betterment Council was one of the groups that had first encouraged me to run for district attorney. Their support for my reelection was supposed to be a given. "Why on earth?" I asked. "They must know I'm the better candidate."

"It's Austin Paley," Tim said, indignant but calm. He'd had time to absorb his outrage. "I don't mean he's behind it, but it's about him. John Lyman called me himself to say that he was the one who'd insisted his group support Mendoza, and he wanted me to know it. He said, 'I told 'em flat out, anybody who trumps up charges against an innocent man doesn't care who he hurts. Any of us could be next.' And he was sincere as a nun, too. He absolutely believes—"

"Austin got to him," I said quietly, but not believing it. What Tim said next was true.

"No sir," he said emphatically. "How do you get to John Lyman? He doesn't give a damn what anybody thinks. But he believes Austin." Tim leaned toward me. "Everybody doesn't just dance to Austin's tune, you know, Mark. The man has genuine friends. He's given a lot of money to charities over the years, he's worked for the right causes, he goes to church, he's—" Tim spread his hands, delivering the blackest condemnation of all. "He's *charming*, for God's sake. *I* like him. My *mother* likes him. Think of people who've known him for years, think how they—"

"I'm one of them, Tim."

"Well, there you go. Look. I'm not asking you to ditch the case—"

"Cases," I said. Tim gave me a stern look: Don't get technical.

"Just let it cool off. It'll fade to background after a while if you don't do anything on it."

"No. I have to disprove what Austin and now Leo are saying. I have to show that I personally believe in Austin's guilt, that it's not just a politically expedient charge I've trumped up. Besides, didn't you say I need the exposure? Or are you going to buy TV spots for me out of your own pocket? You have any more speaking engagements lined up for me?"

"One or two," Tim mumbled. But they were dying, and my campaign treasury had sunk below empty into red.

I could still get news coverage, though. If I prosecuted

Austin personally, I'd get myself on TV and in print, for good or ill.

"It's not personal," I said. I was lying. "It's something I have to do."

"Well ..." Tim said. "At least for God's sake ..." Suddenly wondering why I was seeking his approval anyway, I tuned out his admonitions.

"Why don't you take his advice?" Becky Schirhart asked later. "I'll prosecute Austin Paley, and I won't let it get postponed. You can have it both ways."

I didn't answer, and not because I didn't think Becky deserved an answer. While I remained aware of the difference in our ages, I no longer thought of her as a kid, or as an underling. When we talked it was to plan our trial strategy, and that partnership demanded an equal footing, if she was to be of use to me at all. I didn't answer because my answer sounded sappy, even to me.

"It's the smart thing to do," Becky added.

"I know that."

I was looking out a window of my office. Becky was on the couch behind me. From the corner of my eye I saw her come toward me, hesitate, then take another seat from which she could see me better. I turned toward her.

"Why *is* it personal, Mark?" she asked. "It's obvious it is."

I decided to be sappy. I owed her that, because I'd drawn Becky into the case, too.

"I feel like he's stolen my past." I didn't have to identify "he." "This has been going on so long. Some of it must have happened while I was an assistant DA, fifteen years ago. Austin molesting children and having people quash the cases for him. While I—"

I leaned closer to her. Becky hadn't changed expression. There was no way she could understand this. "I believed in what I was doing," I told her. "I believed in Eliot. I listened to those speeches Eliot gave us about how every case was the same, you didn't hold back because you liked the defense lawyer, and how all the defendants were the same, it didn't matter if it was somebody's son or a nobody, and I believed it. I listened to other people making jokes under their breath—I even made some myself—but I believed in what we did in that office. I believed we were the law's last guardians, and that we could make a difference, and all that crap."

Even as I ended on a note of ridicule I remembered the feeling, one Becky couldn't share. I had believed that I'd chosen a life's work that made a difference in the world; that I served an ideal higher than money or power. Years of watching the outcomes of cases skewed by corruption or just laziness or stupidity had taught me better, but it hadn't touched the pride of those first years as a prosecutor. My cynicism about the system was deeply engrained and hard-earned, but the only true cynics are burned believers. I could admit it now: I believed in justice. I believed I personally could wrest it from an unfair world. I had once believed that.

And even as I'd changed, grown a coarser layer of protection, I still believed far in the back of my mind that I'd once been part of something noble. Austin had stepped on that bit of cherished pride. While I'd been relishing my role as a player on a team with an almost sacred mission, Eliot Quinn had quietly been killing cases against his political ally. It made me feel dirty to think of it now. It had rewritten my whole past. I hated to think of Austin oozing through the courthouse, being charming, expecting a certain deference and being accorded it. Confident of his power and his standing; perhaps thinking that more people were willing parts of his protection than actually had been. How many knowing looks had he given me in the past that I'd missed, that I'd just interpreted as expressions of general camaraderie?

"He's tainted everything," I said. "I'd thought I was part of something important, something uncorrupted."

"I know what you mean," Becky said, the kind of remark you make offhandedly to keep someone talking.

"Remember what I told you Ben Dowling, the old reporter, told me about the gentlemen's agreements they used to have, how they—"

"—would cover up for everybody from the President on down just because it was unseemly not to?" Becky said.

I nodded. "That had an effect, you know. I grew up thinking there really were noble institutions in this country, people who were genuinely heroes. I looked for them when I went to find a life's work. Your generation, you never heard anything from the time you were children but scandal and corruption and lies, and *that* became your norm. You can't be disappointed because you don't expect anything better of anyone."

"Don't assume too much," Becky said. "You can't explain everybody's personalities just by the times they grew up in. I understand what you mean about feeling part of something important."

I gave her some attention. She looked serious. But she was giving me the kind of scrutiny I'd never given Eliot years ago, and I knew she couldn't possibly share the illusions I'd had.

"Really?" I said. "You mean you're not just here for the money?"

She smiled back at me.

I supposed it was still possible, even in this latter age, for someone to idealize prosecution work. In a way, I did myself. Why else had I returned to the district attorney's office? I had made more money in private practice. But in my ten years as a defense lawyer I'd never defended anyone with half the fervor with which I'd prosecuted some of my cases in the DA's office.

"Just because there was one thing going on you didn't know about doesn't mean you were wrong about everything," Becky said.

I made a disgusted sound. "I was an idiot."

"And now you're going to do something about it," she said, once again drawing me out of my contemplation of the changeable past. Of the two of us, Becky looked like the hard-edged one now.

Suddenly I had a strong desire to win reelection. I wanted to regain my sense of purpose. In these cases against Austin Paley, I had.

"Let's go to work," Becky said. "Unless you wanted to go on whining about your childhood a while longer?"

I made a sound as if testing an empty tank. "No, I think I bottomed out, thanks."

She laid her hand briefly on mine, in sympathy.

* * *

"Let me ask it this way, Kevin. Was it your idea to go camping, or was it Austin's? Did you suggest it? Did you say, 'I know what, let's camp out'?"

Kevin studied Becky's face, searching for the answer. When she remained impassive, only smiled gently at him, he glanced away, seemed to search his memory.

"It must've been his idea," he said quietly. "I'd never been camping out."

Becky and I glanced at each other, and she turned back to the boy on the makeshift witness stand in his room. We'd brought a big chair in from the living room and ensconced Kevin in it, where he looked like a young prince suddenly elevated unwillingly to the kingship. I was letting Becky take a turn questioning him. She was getting better at it. Kevin watched her as she moved about the room, thinking of her next question.

"Did you ask your parents if you could go?" Becky asked.

"Yes."

Becky nodded. She smiled at Kevin. He didn't smile back. He sat waiting tensely for the next question. He had a stuffed elephant he was holding against his side, his arm so tight around the elephant's neck he would have choked it if it required breath. Nice touch. It might be overplaying if we let him bring it to court, but it was something to think about.

"Did you tell them who you were going with?" Becky asked. She'd stopped looking to me after every question. She was following her own train of thought. Becky was wearing a loose white blouse that left most of her arms bare. Occasionally, at a certain angle, she looked to me closer to Kevin's age than to mine. She could have been the older sister pretending to be a grown-up questioner. But there was an essential adult sternness about her, as well. Once in a while, turning away from Kevin, she clenched her fist.

"I told them I was going with some other boys," Kevin said. Again Becky nodded for his benefit.

"Let's look at the dolls again," Becky said.

Kevin immediately got down on the floor and picked up the two dolls, which were anatomically complete. Not impressive, but complete. Both male, one larger than the other. Becky took Kevin through the whole story, joining him on the floor. If one watched them only peripherally they looked like children playing with dolls. One had to look closely, and listen, to be aghast at the explicitness of the tale. The dolls started out side by side, sleeping. They wore no clothes. "It was hot," Kevin explained.

"And what was happening when you woke up?" Becky asked. A nice neutral question. But it wasn't the first time Kevin had been asked.

Kevin brought the man doll close to the smaller one. The man doll's penis touched the boy doll's shoulder, then his neck.

"Did you touch it?" Becky asked softly. "Why? Was it your idea, or did he ask you to?"

With every telling Kevin had brought the larger doll's penis closer to the smaller one's mouth. In two or three more sessions, I was sure, he would insert it. But I didn't know if I would believe him when that happened. I didn't know if Kevin was edging closer to the truth, because he was beginning to trust us and overcome his embarrassment, or if he was trying harder and harder to please. He knew what we wanted, I was sure. Kevin was six years old, but he was older than his peers. He was adept at pleasing adults.

When I'd ferreted my way through the years of stalled investigations, rumor, and reined-in suspicions, I'd become convinced of Austin Paley's guilt. It fit so well. I'd heard the children identify Austin with complete credulity. But as I began preparing one specific case, doubt crept in. Children *aren't* very reliable. They say what they think is expected of them. I know how investigations work, too. Once a man is accused, it's easier to bring other charges against him as well. Clearing cases, the cops call it. They can empty a file drawer of unsolved cases at a suspect's feet and turn it into a bonfire. Once the accusations begin to pile up, it's almost impossible to keep a clear view of the real man behind them.

I shouldn't harbor these doubts. That wasn't my part of the system. Eliot could have stilled my doubts, when I was working for him.

"Mark?" Becky asked.

"Well, that's enough for today," I said. "It's not a very fun way to spend a day, is it?"

Kevin answered my smile.

I put my hand on his shoulder. "You know we just want

you to tell the truth, don't you, Kevin? Whatever you say happened, we believe you."

He nodded soberly, then asked, "Can I play now?"

"Sure."

"With the dolls?"

Becky and I looked at each other. The kid kept throwing us loops. She shrugged at me. We weren't damned psychiatrists. Should we let Kevin keep the dolls, with their vacant eyes, slightly slack-jawed mouths, and their anatomical completeness hanging out? Maybe it would be good for him to familiarize himself with them. Maybe they'd scare him if he woke in the middle of the night to find them in his bed. And maybe when his mother found them on the floor she'd wonder what kind of perverts she'd let into her house.

"Why don't you play with them while we talk to your mom, if you want?" I stalled.

As we passed through the doorway I leaned close to Becky to ask, "Shouldn't we take them with us?"

"Not for me," she whispered back. "I've got my own at home."

I gave her the startled look she wanted. Becky looked slightly aghast herself—not, I thought, at the joke itself, but at the fact she'd told me a joke, as if I wouldn't think her sufficiently serious for the solemn occasion.

The dolls were back in my briefcase when we hit the sidewalk. We were in the middle of a northern suburb, far, far from the courthouse, it seemed. The day seemed both late and timeless.

"Do we have to—" Becky began.

"Go back?" I looked around. "Let's get a drink," I said. "But for God's sake don't say anything to make them search my briefcase."

All the courtrooms look alike in the new Justice Center. Small, functional, industrial beige. Some judges have found ways to customize their courtrooms with posters or other decoration, but it's futile. The walls seem to absorb adornments. But there are other distinctions. Courthouse regulars know they're in Judge Hernandez's court by the look of the staff. The judge seems to hire the same type of person, man or woman, armed bailiff, or clerk armed only with a lip.

They lounge around the court, talking idly to one another or otherwise loafing. If anyone approaches one of them, the court staffer turns the same knowing, disdainful look on the intruder. "Don't just tell me what you want," you can almost hear them say. "Tell me why I should do it for the likes of you." Their attitudes don't change when the judge enters the room. If anything, they intensify.

I've spent years looking for the good side of Bonita, Judge Hernandez's court coordinator, and decided it doesn't exist. Instead I've adopted an attitude of my own toward her, of distant professionalism as frosty as her own. Sometimes it works.

My elevation to eminence and power doesn't seem to have impressed her. "Mr. Blackwell," she said as I approached her desk. But she's always called me that. Anything less might imply something personal.

"Ms. Vargas," I returned. "Thank you for the special setting."

"We wouldn't want this mob messing up our regular docket," she replied. I shouldn't get the idea she'd done me a favor.

By "this mob" she meant the four reporters in the courtroom and the three cameramen in the hall, drawn to this quiet court on a Thursday afternoon for nothing more than to see us wrangle over a trial date. I had already talked to them. My stern line was that the cases must be tried right away, to remove the danger to the children of San Antonio. "You mean the voters of San Antonio?" Jenny Lord, the newspaper reporter, asked slyly.

"Children don't vote," I said, snappishly, because she'd made a joke I might once have made myself, in carefree days gone by.

Since he was a free man on bond, Austin had to come through the public hallway, running the gauntlet of reporters like everyone else. Austin, of course, would not duck the opportunity. He came across well on television. He appeared mild and unthreatening but with an underlying confidence and a glint of humor. He should have had his own talk show.

Austin kept us waiting while he indulged in an impromptu press conference in the hall. Becky and I just sat, having nothing to discuss today. Our only strategy at this setting was obvious.

Austin was the soul of friendliness when he arrived. I had turned my back on the courtroom doors by then, but I couldn't miss his coming. He spoke to everyone in the room. Austin stood over me with a smile. I didn't rise or offer my hand. He didn't appear offended. He called me by name and said, "How are things going?" as if he genuinely cared for my welfare. Even I couldn't tell we'd ever had a trace of acrimony between us.

"Fine, Austin. And for you?" He had a way of forcing you to play the game his way, because he'd react the same affable way no matter how inappropriate his partner's response.

He wiggled one hand at waist level and said, *"Así así."* "So-so" in Spanish. He continued smiling as he said it.

"Haven't you hired an attorney?" Becky asked him.

Austin's only answer was a smile. Missing the cue by just a minute or two, the door behind the bench opened and Judge Hernandez entered, chuckling appreciatively. Buster Harmony leaned closer to add a secondary punch line, and they both laughed. The judge stood behind his chair and Buster, in as much of a scurry as a large man in his fifties could manage, came around the bench and stood beside his client. He leaned across to shake my hand and say, in as *sotto* a *voce* as he ever employed, "Hello, Blackie."

I felt a wave of satisfaction because Austin was being so true to form, but not for that reason alone. If I had had to guess the kind of lawyer Austin would hire, fat old blustery Buster would have headed my list. He'd been around as long as any criminal lawyer in town, had made a lot of money over the years and lavished much of it on campaign contributions, was best friends with every judge, knew their children's names, had known every public official for years and years, since they were children together. As a lawyer he didn't do much any more and didn't have to do much, having won a few big civil judgments in the previous high-spending decade. He had a reputation as a fierce trial lawyer, but he hadn't been tested in a long time. Even in his prime, when I was an assistant DA, he'd had three shots at me and never won. He would be easy to anticipate, I thought.

After greeting me, Buster riveted his attention on the bench. Judge Hernandez slipped him a wink as he took his seat. The judge was in his late fifties, had been on the bench more than a decade—long enough, in his case, to forget any previous life. He was heavy but not extravagantly so, not enough to make the robe bulge. His dark complexion looked healthy, his eyes were sharp behind his dark, heavy glasses. His hair was thick, iron gray on top and white at the temples. He looked every inch a judge. He was the only person in the room who believed his own facade.

"Well, Buster, Blackie. Young lady. What a formidable assemblage of legal talent. You quite intimidate me."

While Buster chuckled extravagantly, I rose to say, "Good morning, Your Honor. We're here to obtain a trial setting for the State of Texas versus Austin Paley."

"Of course," the judge said grumpily, as if I'd interrupted him. "Well—are both sides ready?"

"The State is ready," I answered crisply.

"Well, Your Honor, if we can slow down just long enough for me to catch up," Buster drawled. "Which case are we announcing on? There's more than one with that style."

Judge Hernandez hated being told something wasn't simple. "Of course," he said by rote, and shot a look at his coordinator, Bonita. Bonita leaned over to push the folders on his bench toward him. The judge nodded sharply and pushed her hand away. Bonita sat down, visibly rolling her eyes. Judge Hernandez did not, of course, hire exclusively surly, disrespectful staff members. He created them.

"Yes, there are three cases," he said. "No, four." He read off the numbers at tedious length. "What is your announcement on each case?"

"The State is ready on number 4221," I said, and sat down. Fortuitously, the first indicted case had been the one in which Kevin Pollard was the victim, the one Becky and I had chosen to try first.

"We're not ready on that one," Buster Harmony said, shaking his ponderous head. "The defense is ready to try number 4222 or 4223. On the others we need more time for investigation."

The numbers he named were the cases involving the girls who couldn't quite identify their attacker. I'd kept them alive only for bargaining chips. The fourth case was the one in which ten-year-old Tommy Algren was the victim. There were other cases waiting in the wings, but I hadn't obtained indictments in them yet. I was going to try my best case first. Buster, of course, had other ideas. If he forced me to try one of my weak cases first, and Austin was found not guilty, it would make any later prosecution less credible—and less likely.

"State?" the judge asked.

"Not ready on 4222 or 4223," I replied blandly.

"Not ready?" The judge scowled at me.

"No, Your Honor, those cases are still being investigated," I said. "We are ready on the first case on the court's docket, and the State requests the earliest possible trial setting. This defendant remains free on bond, and the number of cases against him demonstrates clearly the danger to the community in allowing that situation to continue through many trial settings. The State requests an immediate trial." There are reporters in the room, I was as good as saying. It won't be me who has to fade the heat from the public for letting a serial child molester pass freely among them, Judge: it will be you. I had no doubt Judge Hernandez understood that. His scowl deepened.

"How can I force him to try a case he isn't prepared to try?" he asked me, waving his hand at Buster, who nodded politely in acknowledgment of the judge's courtesy. "Why aren't *you* ready on the others?" Judge Hernandez continued.

"The State is prepared to try number 4221, the first case," I said doggedly. "To answer Your Honor's first question, the way to force the defense to try the case is to set a trial date."

No one could force me to try a case I wasn't ready for. I could if I chose to dismiss every case except the one I wanted to try. Such a dismissal on the State's motion would allow me to refile the cases later. Nor could the defense escape trial indefinitely simply by announcing they weren't ready. At some point, when the judge insisted, the case would be tried no matter what the defense announced.

We all knew these things. Buster and I weren't arguing legal issues. We were sparring for control of the judge's will.

Judge Hernandez was a ditherer. As with most judges, he would do what he thought was right and what he thought was expedient, hoping like hell the two coincided. Judge Hernandez was known to go back and forth, often responding not to the force of the law but to the lawyer who could best wheedle him into something.

The judge didn't like to be confronted with this kind of stalemate. He preferred, by being blustery and unreadable, to bully the parties themselves into reaching a compromise. Situations that called for decision rather than compromise upset him.

And in a stalemate, I expected the judge to side with his old friend—who along with his client brokered more political weight than any other two people in the county.

"If all the state wants is speedy prosecution," Buster said helpfully, "we'd be willing to try the two middle cases together. That would dispose of half the cases at once."

"Thank you for the suggestion, Mr. Harmony," I said, turning to him. Buster smiled at me, just trying to help. "But I'm sure Judge Hernandez is quite capable of managing his own docket without—"

"It is not at all a bad idea," the judge said slowly.

There was a slight tug at my sleeve. I had forgotten Becky was there. When I looked down, annoyed at her interruption in this crucial moment, she handed me two sheets of paper: dismissal motions, already filled out with the names of the cases and the case numbers of the two indictments involving the little girls.

I glanced at Buster. For a moment I felt I was being maneuvered. But Becky was right. Drop the distractions.

"Your Honor, the State tenders motions to dismiss in cause numbers 4222 and 4223. In hopes of wasting no more of the court's time."

"Mr. Harmony?" the judge asked.

Buster spread his hands as if graciously accepting defeat. "I can't hardly object to the dismissal of half the cases against my client, Your Honor."

"Good, then," Judge Hernandez said decisively. "Then I shall set the other case for trial in, um, thirty days. October fourth. Can you be ready then?"

"I'll make my announcement that day," Buster hedged.

The judge stood up, and his naturally grumpy tone returned. "You had better be ready. Both sides. Or I will hold you in contempt." But before he turned away the judge pointed at Buster, making a gun of his finger and thumb. Buster pointed back. He shook his head, still the jolly old friend even after Judge Hernandez left the courtroom.

Early October was a fine trial setting for my purposes. Still a month before the election, and the trial should last not much longer than a week, if that. But I couldn't afford a reset past that setting.

"Smooth move, Blackie," Buster Harmony was saying. "Slid my cases right out from under me. Maybe I'm getting too old for this business." His smile shifted focus. "Or maybe I need a pretty young assistant, too."

Becky smiled back as if he were tolerable. "If I were flattered enough to take that for a job offer, Mr. Harmony, I'd have to say that I'm very happy where I am."

"Well, who wouldn't be? Prosecutor's always in the catbird seat, right, Blackie? Isn't that why you went back? Come on, Austin, let's get away while they let us."

Austin shrugged apologetically, as if he'd been caught cheating, as he followed his lawyer up the aisle. "Look forward to the trial," Buster's voice came floating back.

"Is he for real?" Becky asked. She was standing close at my shoulder.

"Before your time, he was considered a real terror in trial."

Becky's smile returned, this time for real. "Oh, good," she said.

In two weeks Becky and I had Kevin primed. He would tell his story to either of us, in detail. Sometimes it wasn't until Becky and I were talking about it after practicing with him that we'd realize *what* detail. While we listened to him we were clinically detached, no matter how much we smiled at him and patted his back and praised his sincerity; mentally we were consulting checklists as he talked. Now we have this element of the crime. Now that one. Good, he just raised the punishment range to life. It wouldn't be until later, in the Kevinless quiet of the car or a restaurant, that Becky and I would realize what he'd just told us, what a real memory it was for him. Only then would we picture the scene, picturing Kevin as he relived it for us.

"I think I can get him to cry again," I said. "Just by pausing a little between questions. Letting him dwell on it."

Becky nodded. We fell silent.

I stopped the rehearsals, afraid of Kevin's losing his naturalness for trial. Becky went back to her regular court docket. I was left with an occasional campaign appearance, with making humiliating calls asking for contributions, and with sizing up Buster Harmony. He wasn't the fool he projected. No matter what he might have owed Austin or what Austin might have paid him, Buster wouldn't have taken on the defense unless he saw a prospect of victory. I wondered what strategy he had in mind. I wondered how I would have run the defense myself.

As it turned out, I should have devoted more thought to Austin than to Buster. Buster wasn't the only one working on the defense case.

It was late in September when Becky and I went to Kevin's house to pick him up for our last rehearsal. This one was going to be in a courtroom. Mrs. Pollard opened the door, but not very wide. "Kevin's not going to come with you," she said.

"What?" I pushed the door open, gently; it didn't require much force to overcome Mrs. Pollard's resistance. "Is he sick?"

"No," she said quietly. I didn't ask her any more, because I'd seen Kevin. He was standing in the open doorway that led to the living room. He looked very young today. He was clutching a plastic soldier.

"Are you all right, pal?" I knelt in front of him.

"I made it all up," he blurted. "It didn't happen, Austin didn't do anything to me."

"Kevin," I began. Becky was kneeling beside me. She touched my side and shook her head slightly. I let her lead him back to his room. He'd tell Becky what was wrong.

But I already knew. Austin would do anything. He wouldn't confine his efforts to preparing for trial; he'd much rather ensure that there'd *be* no trial.

How do you bribe a six-year-old boy? Easily, as I recall:

with candy, balsa wood airplanes, the promise of a trip to the zoo. But how do you make sure he'll stay bribed?

"We just don't want to put Kevin through this," I heard an offensively familiar voice say. When I looked up, *Mr.* Pollard was there, standing behind his wife, his hands on her shoulders as if he were thrusting her toward me. She looked embarrassed.

"Through what?" I asked quietly. I was going to make them earn their money.

"The trial," Pollard said. "And everything that goes with it, the teasing, the name-calling at school . . ."

"I told you we'd keep his name out of the papers."

"Well, kids have a way of finding out," Pollard said defiantly. "Somebody hears a teacher talking to another one . . . The kids figure it out. We'd have to leave town."

I had come up close to them. Mrs. Pollard reached up and touched her husband's hand. They were united. One hears about crises pulling families together.

"I don't need your permission," I told them. "I can call Kevin as a witness whether you like it or not. I'll have him subpoenaed."

"Try it," Pollard said pugnaciously, looking like the schoolyard bully I'll bet he once was. Thrusting his chin forward looked oddly comic, since he was still standing behind his wife. "You'll have to find him first."

Mrs. Pollard patted his hand. "What good would that do, Mr. Blackwell?" she asked. "You heard what Kevin said. Nothing really happened between them. It was all just make-believe."

In answer to that I just stared at her. She kept her eyes resolutely on mine, but her eyelids fluttered. "He changed his story once," I said. "He'll change it back when I question him during trial."

But I couldn't be sure of that. I might get only one shot at Austin. I couldn't take it with a witness I was unsure of.

But they didn't know that. And Pollard was an angry man. A man's man, the kind who couldn't bear what had happened to his son. My best bet was to stir that anger.

"You're going to let him get away with this? The man who kidnapped your son and took his clothes off and touched him and put his penis in Kevin's mouth?" I made it as brutal as I could. I saw Pollard swallow hard. "You're going to take Austin Paley's money and let him get away with what he did to your boy?"

"Nobody took any money," Mrs. Pollard said, but that time she couldn't look at me.

I kept my eyes on her husband. "Don't you want to see him punished for what he did to Kevin?"

Pollard's pride was hurt. I had managed to humiliate him. But this humiliation wasn't a public one. He swallowed again, and when he answered me he was no longer blustering. He sounded like a reasonable man. He was asking me to be reasonable too. "We're more concerned with the rest of his life," he said.

That was probably what they'd convinced themselves of. It would require comfort like that to allow them to do something so despicable. I strongly doubted they'd dealt with Austin himself. He would have sent an emissary. The emissary would have spoken softly and reasonably, pointing out the uncertainties of trial, but the certainty of its outcome: the public humiliation for Kevin and for them. He would have weighed that against what money could provide: therapy for Kevin now, a college education later on. The benefit was tangible. And after all, what good would a conviction do Kevin?

"Becky," I called, and heard her voice answer me from the back of the house. I heard her footsteps. The Pollards looked relieved. In a minute the officials would be out of their house and they'd have their lives to themselves again.

"Whatever you do," I said, "don't you dare spend the money on yourselves. It's Kevin's. He earned it."

I took some satisfaction in the redness of their faces, in the silence of the house, as I took Becky's arm and escorted her out, but that satisfaction dissipated quickly once we were outside. The neighborhood, which we'd grown to know so well, looked completely alien. So did my car. Nothing looked familiar, because we were nowhere. We had a trial date in five days, but we had no case.

9

It's all right, Judge," I said to the sputtering Judge Hernandez. It was October 4, our special trial setting, and I had just handed him another motion to dismiss. I was tubing the case involving Kevin. I turned from the bench to look at the defense table.

"This comes as no surprise to the defendant," I continued. "In fact, it's at the instigation of the defense that I'm dismissing the case that was set for trial today."

The judge went from blustery to confused and back to blustery by the time he spoke. "The court should have been informed—" he began.

"We haven't been negotiating with the State," Buster said. "I don't know what the DA's talking about."

"No. Nonetheless, the defendant knew I would come into court today without a case, because I have no witness."

Buster sounded baffled. "If the State is having some problem, we'd consider—"

"My witness has been bribed," I told him. "How are you going to fix that?"

Buster went immediately to full court bluster. "That's an outrageous allegation! Unless you're—"

"That's why I said it quietly."

"Address the court," Judge Hernandez said peremptorily.

I wheeled to him. "Yes, Your Honor. The state offers its motion to dismiss in cause number 4221 and announces ready in the last remaining case styled State of Texas versus

Austin Paley. The State is prepared to try that case today, Your Honor."

That was a lie. I counted on Buster to help me out. He came in as if I'd written his lines.

"Well, the defense is *not* ready," he said. "That case wasn't even set for trial today."

"I believe both cases are on today's docket, aren't they, Your Honor?" As a matter of course they were, in case we reached a settlement on both before trial.

"Indeed," Judge Hernandez said portentously, staring at the docket sheet in his hand.

"That may be," Buster said loudly, "but we all agreed that the first case was to be tried today. The defense was prepared to go to trial today in the case the district attorney has just dismissed, not in the other."

Judge Hernandez pointed a finger at both of us. "The two of you are interfering with my docket. First one of you isn't ready, then the other. Do you think you are privileged characters, that you don't have to answer to the court? This time," he continued sternly, "I give you only three weeks. And I warn you—I warn you both—the case *will* be tried that day."

Buster and I stood for his departure, so it was easy to turn toward each other immediately afterward. "Mark, you're wrong. I have never been accused—"

"You still haven't," I said shortly, and stepped around him to where Austin still sat, with an air of baffled curiosity as if he were some rube to whom everything that happened in a courtroom was too complex to follow.

"I'm not forgetting Kevin Pollard," I told him. "I'll revive his case, too, maybe by the next setting. People who'll take a bribe will cave in to a threat, too. Once I find out how you got to them—"

I had been putting on an act, but the act overtook me as I stood over Austin. The muscles in the arm I was leaning on locked up. His bland face begged to be punched. A memory picture replaced the scene before my eyes, the picture of Kevin Pollard alone on his swing set, the hostage of the adult world, of not only his abuser but of the parents who wouldn't protect him, and wouldn't let me.

The memory had the effect of calming me. I couldn't give

in to anger. I had to be crafty, not explosive, because my adversary was the craftiest man I'd ever known.

But Austin Paley had seen murder in the way I stood over him. He had the good sense to speak quietly to me.

"Mark, I didn't do it. I don't know what those people told you, but if they decided the case shouldn't go forward it was because of their own doubts, not because of something I did. They know their son better than you. They know better than to believe his lie."

I wouldn't be drawn into discussion. Buster must have given some sign to his client, because Austin stood suddenly. Buster said he'd get back to me, then took Austin's arm and walked out.

Becky was standing slightly behind me, patting my back so gently, so discreetly I had no idea how long it had been going on. "I've never had a handler before," I said to her.

"Who knows how long you've needed one." Her gaze was troubled, and it was on me. "It's just a case," she added, echoing me.

My anger had receded, but it hadn't been replaced. I felt no sense of triumph. I'd only staved off disaster for a few weeks. Now reporters were coming toward me up the aisle, and I had to explain to them that I had indeed dismissed three-fourths of the cases against Austin Paley, just as he'd predicted I'd be forced to do, but that he was still guilty as sin and I'd prove it soon.

"Hell of an ugly way to practice law," I said.

I was in disguise by the time I reached the elementary school, dressed like a real person rather than a lawyer. The first time I'd come in a suit, of course, looking official as hell, but they knew me now, even in my khakis and open-necked shirt. One of the supervisors waved to me as I opened the gate to the playground. The children looked up, not in fright, in anticipation—any novelty a distraction.

Tommy Algren was standing apart, under a tree, watching two younger boys rolling cars down the slide, trying to aim them to crash into plastic soldiers standing unsuspectingly in the sand at the bottom. I stood beside Tommy and we both watched. His only acknowledgment of me was to nod toward the boys and say, "Psychopaths."

"Definitely prison material," I agreed.

Tommy smiled. We began walking away. This time the two high school students in charge, a boy and a girl, didn't notice me. They were sitting on a concrete bench very close, comparing the notes on their clipboards, leaning into each other, pointing out items of interest on the papers.

Tommy's parents no longer sent him after school to the daycare center from which Austin Paley had so often and casually abducted him, but they couldn't possibly have thought he was more secure now, if they'd spent ten minutes checking out the program. Tommy's elementary school allowed children of working parents to stay after school, on the playground or in the cafeteria, "supervised" by the two teenagers. The kids were left pretty much to create their own amusement. There were fewer of them than I would have supposed, maybe thirty. Other children of working parents were picked up after school by daycare centers or maids or, if they were older—ten or eleven—walked home and spent an hour or two alone until Mom and Dad got home.

"Anything you need to do today?" I asked Tommy as we left the playground.

He shrugged. "Not really."

"Done your homework?" I asked as we got into the car, and we both laughed. It was one of our jokes.

After Kevin fell through I'd felt paralyzed. I'd tried to think how to force him to testify for me anyway. Becky felt confident of opening him up on the stand if we got him there, but I didn't discount his father's threat to take Kevin out of our reach. I quickly discarded him and decided to move on to the one case I had left, the one involving Tommy Algren.

Tommy'd been slick as vinyl in my office, recounting his relationship with Austin. That was the main reason Becky and I hadn't liked him as a witness. He'd healed too thoroughly, he sounded unruffled about the abuse he'd suffered. And of course, he was older than I would have wanted. At ten years old he was on the cusp of adolescence. His experiences with Austin dated back two and three and four years, but Tommy was no longer the little boy to whom those things had happened.

But Tommy was all I had left. I'd begun cultivating him

the day after the Pollards told me Kevin wouldn't testify. I wasn't going to make the same mistake with Tommy I'd made with Kevin: I wasn't going to let the parents stand between us. I would make Tommy my own, I'd decided, so that he'd do what I asked no matter what his parents said.

Of course, Austin would try to get to him too, but he'd have to do it surreptitiously and cautiously, while I could do it openly.

Austin didn't have to win. He just had to delay. I needed to prosecute him before the election—now little more than a month away. If I failed, and if Leo Mendoza was elected in my place, Austin would never be tried. Leo'd already announced as much. Austin just had to stall me until I was off the stage. He'd done it successfully with Kevin. I was determined he wouldn't with Tommy.

"Want to hit a few?" I asked.

I parked the car at Batter-Up. Tommy followed me to the counter, hanging back a little. I'd already decided that little Tommy was no athlete, but I didn't want to make a major league slugger of him, I just wanted to find things to do with him, put in the time.

Tommy put his hands in his pockets while I judiciously ran my fingers over the bats, selected one, and took a couple of practice swings. Tommy was of about average height for his age, but thin. His arms were thinner than the bat I was holding. He looked good in his clothes, like a little model. He always seemed to have had more grooming than other kids, and he had an air of cool sophistication, but it evaporated when he tried to do something physical, when his limbs and body seemed barely connected. I know about playing cool.

"I was always one of the tallest kids in my class," I said as I selected a smaller bat for Tommy and handed it to him. He leaned on it like a cane. "But for years I was also the clumsiest," I went on. "My arms and legs were just too long for me, you know, they were so far out there I didn't even know where they were half the time."

I demonstrated, stretching my arms, rotating my hands on their wrists. Tommy laughed. He looked cool as Reggie Jackson leaning on his bat.

"So after a while I just said the hell with sports, you

know? It's no fun having everybody think you should be the best at something and instead you trip going after a ball and throw like a girl. So I retired. I acted like I was just too good for everything, like it wouldn't even be fair if I played. You know? And that was okay, except I really did want to play. Sometimes my dad and I would shoot baskets and that wasn't so bad because he never made fun of me. He even gave me a few tips."

"Like what?" Tommy asked. He swung his bat a couple of times in a swing that started behind his head above the level of his shoulders and ended up down around his ankles.

"Simple stuff," I said. I traded dollars for tokens and we headed for an empty batting cage. There was one gang of kids, probably a team, but they were down at the fast-pitch end and I chose the slow-pitch machines for Tommy and me. We were out of earshot of everyone else when we stepped into a cage. "Like paying attention. You know, I'd be trying to throw the ball toward the hoop and start running to get my own rebound at the same time. My dad just told me to concentrate on the one thing I was doing. Something you could figure out for yourself but never do, you know?"

"Yeah," Tommy said. He had stepped up to the plate. I casually adjusted his bat. "Straight across," I said offhandedly, as if reminding him of something we'd already talked about. He took a more level practice swing and I fed a token into the machine. Fifty feet in front of us the metal arm attached to the metal box of softballs stirred, revolved, lifted a ball, and hurled it toward the plate, toward Tommy, who swung and missed.

"You think it's coming fast but it's not," I said. "Watch it. You can see right where it's coming. Keep your eye on the ball, don't worry about the bat, it'll go where you're looking."

Another ball came in, fat and slow, so slow it bounced on the plate as it crossed in front of Tommy. He just watched it. "Good eye," I said.

"Then in junior high the basketball coach spotted me," I went on. "I mean, you couldn't miss me, I was already almost six feet tall. I didn't grow much more after I got to high school, but in junior high I was a real freak. You could see me coming from one end of the hall to the other."

The next pitch from the machine was perfect, just at shoulder level for Tommy. His bat met the ball, not a very good cut, he was under it, so the ball leaped up in what would have been an easy pop-up, but in the fielderless confines of Batter-Up its arc looked spectacular. "Good shot," I said. Tommy hunkered down and raised the bat again. I pulled it back a little farther. The metal pitching arm quivered and started around again.

"So the coach saw you," Tommy said.

"Concentrate," I said. The pitch came in, about waist high, but Tommy was crouched low enough to get it. He hit a line drive that would surely have been foul outside the first-base line. "A little slow," I said. "See, I pulled the bat back so you'd have more power, but that means you've got to bring it around faster. Watch for the pitch." He nodded.

"Yeah, so this big dumb basketball coach saw me in the hall and he made me go out for the basketball team. I mean I didn't even have any choice, he called my parents, he'd be waiting in the hall after my last class to take me to practice. I didn't get to decide at all. It was nice."

Tommy nodded, understanding how attractive it would be to be forced to do something one secretly wanted to do but didn't have the nerve to try. Another pitch came toward him and he swung ferociously. The ball slammed untouched into the netting behind us.

"That time you closed your eyes," I said. "That's the first thing, to watch the ball. That's all you have to remember."

"And to keep my swing level and to bring the bat around faster and to lean back instead of forward," Tommy said grumpily.

"Yeah, it's tough. This is the hardest thing in sports. Want to go shoot baskets somewhere instead?"

"Let me try a couple more times first."

I fed another token into the coin box.

The next pitch came toward his head. I was already darting toward it, trying to deflect the ball just enough that it would miss him, but long before I got there Tommy had jerked his head back out of harm's way.

"Dropped my bat," I said casually, picking it up again. "That was good watching, Tommy."

He might not have heard me. He was gritting his teeth, glaring as if the machine were a human rival who had just tried to take his head off. "Keep your eyes open," I muttered.

The next pitch was a good one and Tommy met it dead square. It leaped straight off his bat along the same line it had come in on, and smashed into the metal box of balls, making the whole thing quiver.

"That'll teach him," I said.

When the machine had given me my token's worth again, Tommy turned to me and said, "And by the end of the season you were the MVP, right?"

"It's not that kind of story, Tom. We didn't get into the playoffs and I wasn't the star of the team. But I got to play, and I liked it. Got to travel with the team, you know, made a few friends. By high school I even was pretty good. And it was fun. Beat the hell out of acting like I was too good to play. You know? You ready to go?"

"Let me take another couple of cuts," he said.

During the second batch of pitches Tommy hit one that arced high over the machine, almost brushing the top of the netting, hitting the high fence thirty yards away. It might have been a long fly out in a real ballpark, but it might have been a home run, too, and I acted as if it were. "Man," I kept saying. "Man, what a hit. You weren't aiming for that spot, were you? You didn't even know you'd hit it, did you? You just closed your eyes and swung."

"I was watching," Tommy insisted. "I watched it all the way in."

"Man," I said, and whistled through my teeth.

It was five o'clock, late, but Tommy's parents wouldn't be home yet. I drove slowly. "How did you meet Austin?" I asked, without emphasis, discussing a mutual friend.

"He had a house in my neighborhood," Tommy said. "I thought he lived there, but I guess it was a rent house, because when I went inside, later on, it was empty. But he showed up there one day, working outside like he'd just moved in and was fixing up the place, and we started talking. Just, you know, about the neighborhood, who lived where and where there was to go to the store and like that. There were other kids around too."

"And he was there again the next day."

"Yeah, or the day after, or some time. He was always outside. After a while he asked if I could do some work for him. I was only seven, you know, I couldn't mow the yard or anything, but I picked up trash and raked leaves and stuff like that, and he paid me two dollars. He said I really helped him out."

"Were there still other kids around then?"

"Some. We kept hanging around him. It's not a real exciting neighborhood, you know? One day he had to go to the store, and a couple of us rode with him, and the next day he asked us if we wanted to go on a picnic."

Tommy told the story with an admirable completeness of detail and not much prompting. He knew by now the significant aspects. He looked out the car windshield as he talked, his eye catching on points of landscape. His voice was calm. He seemed to remain emotionally level. This wasn't the first time we'd talked about Austin. Tommy knew I wasn't spending time with him just because I liked him. He knew we'd get to Austin eventually. He didn't seem to mind. He had told me more intimate details than these, but always in the same bright, reminiscent tone. It was just a story, one he knew interested his audience.

"Any more problems at school?" I asked him abruptly.

Tommy looked at me, put off his stride. We were stopped at a stop sign on a trafficless side street, so I could look back. After a moment's perusal of my face he shrugged. "No," he said, but he'd lost that cool, self-sufficient air.

"No? Has anybody found out you're going to testify?"

"I don't think so," he said, uncertainly, like a child. "I sure haven't told anybody," he added. I was certain of that. This was my fourth meeting with Tommy. I'd usually picked him up at school, but I hadn't seen or heard him mention a friend. I hadn't tried to explain that it was his friend Austin who'd set him apart from the other kids. Tommy was a smart boy, I'd rather he realize that for himself. But I could raise the subject.

"What about Brian?"

"That moron," Tommy said.

"Is he still picking on you? More than he was?"

Tommy shrugged again. He was leaning against the passenger door, not looking at me any more.

"There's always guys like that, Tommy, believe me. You can handle him."

He stirred. "Did you ever have to?" he asked.

"Me? No. No, I usually *was* the bully."

He laughed. "I'll bet."

It was my turn to shrug. "Not something I'm proud of, but it did give me a certain insight, you know?"

"I guess. So what d'I do with him?"

"Threaten him with a bigger bully, for one thing. If things get too tough, tell him your friend the district attorney is going to come see him and his parents."

From the look on his face I knew Tommy would never resort to that. It would single him out as a freak even more. "First I'd have to explain to him what an attorney is," he said morosely.

I laughed. At first it was a surprised response, but I kept laughing, more than the joke was worth, until Tommy joined me. We were still laughing when we pulled up to his house, a nice brick home in an upper-middle-class neighborhood, the yard mowed, the hedges trimmed. I could tell by looking at it that it was empty.

"It's okay," Tommy said. "They'll be home in a little while."

"I'll come in and wait, if that's all right with you. Maybe I could use your phone."

"Sure."

As we walked up the driveway my hand dropped casually toward his shoulder, but I stopped it. Tommy took his key from his pocket and let us into the big empty house.

"You can touch him, it's okay," Janet McLaren said. "He's got to learn somehow that people do touch each other just out of fondness, it's not necessarily sexual."

"I think I'll let somebody else try that experiment," I said. "I don't want to spook him. I'm not trying to rehabilitate him, Doctor, I just need to be sure of his testimony."

"Is there some reason why you couldn't help with his therapy at the same time?"

"Yeah, there's some reason. I don't know what the hell I'm doing. I don't want to go blundering around in his psyche like some half-assed amateur psychologist and risk giving him a breakdown two weeks before trial."

"You've seen too much TV. You're not going to send Tommy into a coma by putting your hand on his arm. As a fully assed professional psychiatrist, I assure you of that."

Dr. McLaren was wearing beige slacks and a short matching jacket over a striped blouse that showed a little more cleavage than she would normally have displayed in a professional appointment, I thought. When we'd shaken hands I'd noticed her quietly shining fingernails and that her blue, almost purple eyes were somehow more prominent than at our first meeting. I flattered myself that she'd taken extra care preparing for our appointment today. I know I'd looked forward to seeing her again. But almost as soon as we started talking about Tommy we were at odds.

I fetched her can of Diet Coke from the table and poured the remainder into Janet's glass, smiling as I did, hoping to restore socialness to the occasion. She nodded thanks.

"I've tried to get into the story almost without mentioning Austin to him," I said quietly. Janet's expression grew alert to match the concern in my voice. "I have to hear the details but I'm afraid to remind him. I'm also—unsure. No, I'm afraid, that's what it is, afraid of how he feels about Austin."

She nodded. "Yes. You're wise to be concerned about that. Children hate what happened to them but still love the molester. If you think he's going to be vindictive toward Austin Paley, you're dangerously oversimplifying Tommy's reaction."

"I know. But—love? Isn't that putting it a little too strongly?"

"No." Dr. McLaren had this knack of focusing all her attention on me. Her voice lowered, as if we were discussing secrets, which made me lean toward her. Her eyes held me the way a good teacher's voice holds students. "Who else does Tommy love?" she asked. "He has no friends, you're right about that. He used to have, but no more. No siblings. Until he found his abuser he was all alone in the world."

She paused, still watching me. I said, "You want me to say, 'But, Doctor, what about his parents?' "

She smiled sadly. We were comrades again, the only ones who understood the world.

"If Tommy were really sure of his parents' love, he would never have fallen into this man's trap," she said. "Has he told you how they met? Well, you see. There were other children in the initial group, but Tommy was the one who kept returning, day after day. Austin Paley knew Tommy was the one he wanted, the one looking for someone.

"The Algrens don't think they're bad parents," she went on. "They're *not* bad parents. They've put Tommy in a good school, given him a nice home, bought him everything he needs. They take him to the zoo or the museum, when they can manage. They buy him a book or a computer game at least once a week. They conscientiously remind themselves to do that for him."

"Like another appointment in their Filofax."

"It's not their fault they don't have time for him. Maybe they could get by on one salary, maybe they could both work shorter hours. But even if they did, it would be out of obligation, not desire. They're committed to work, that's the most important thing in their lives, and Tommy knows it."

"Then he met Austin Paley, who always had time for him."

Janet nodded. She put a hand on my knee, which was intriguing, but I couldn't escape the feeling that she was giving me a demonstration of the appropriateness of touching. "There was a void there not just of affection," she said. "There was a training gap. Tommy doesn't see his father enough to know what he's like. Tommy's getting old for a child, he needs to see how to act like a man."

"Austin was a role model for him."

She nodded.

"That's scary," I said.

I could see the truth of her observation. That's what had put me off about Tommy, not just that he was too cool to display his hurts to a jury, but that he was like Austin himself—charming, imperturbable. A dapper little socialite in a child's body and a child's confusing world.

I sat thinking about Tommy's future. But after a moment I shook off that concern. He wasn't my child, he was my witness. "There's something else that worries me. We're sitting here talking as if we're sure at least we've got the facts straight, but I'm not so sure. Tommy scares me. He didn't report he was molested and then we found a suspect and Tommy picked him out of a lineup. He saw Austin on TV and that was the first time he'd ever reported what happened to him. He told his parents."

Janet understood. "It sounds like a grab for attention."

"Even his parents didn't believe him at first. Why should I?"

"I don't always believe the children who come to see me," she said. "I tend to believe boys more, because—and this would explain too why Tommy didn't tell anyone he was being molested—boys are afraid to tell, more than girls. They're afraid of being called fags."

"Ten-year-old boys? Nine-year-olds?"

She was almost amused with me again. "Is that too dim a memory for you? Trying to be a manly little ten-year-old, playing catch with the boys instead of house with the girls?"

"Well, yes, but I don't think I even knew what homosexuality was then. We weren't so sophisticated back—"

"You'd have known there was something queer about touching a man's penis. Would you have been friends with a boy you'd heard stories like that about?"

She was sitting on the small couch in my office, I was sitting in the armchair just in front of her, facing her. I tried to be very adult as we discussed this, but being a psychiatrist she could probably read my body language. "I see your point," I said. "But do you see mine? I've got a trial. I've got to make people believe Tommy, over the vehement denial of an adult. There's no physical evidence, not this long after the fact. If I gave him a lie detector test, I couldn't get the result before a jury. Is there anything, some kind of objective evidence, that what Tommy says happened happened? Not that it was Austin, just that it happened at all. Something Tommy—"

"I have my own little test," Janet said. "I ask them to describe semen. Kids can pick up the outlines of seduction from TV or other places, but in the normal course of childhood they haven't come across semen. Without telling them what I'm looking for I ask them what happened, and if they finally say something came out of the man's penis I ask them what it looked like, what it smelled like. What it tasted like, if that seems appropriate."

I was sitting very still. Janet was talking quietly, watching me. She'd grown more clinical. "Did Tommy describe it?" I asked.

"Yes."

I nodded slightly, as if it weren't much. I didn't want her to see how happy the news made me. It was tragic for Tommy but good for me. Janet kept watching me. She knew just what I was thinking. She was the savior of children; I was only using them.

She wouldn't let me get away with anything, even within the supposed privacy of my mind. Janet put her hand on my arm and looked into my eyes.

"You know what you're doing with Tommy is dangerous," she said. "You could hurt him as badly as Paley has."

"I do understand that," I said. But I didn't make any promises.

She was still looking at me. "I think I need to work on you some more."

"Professionally?"

She nodded. "But so subtly you won't even know what's happening. It's best to start in a relaxing setting, like lunch. Or is it dinnertime yet?"

"Of the day, or in our relationship?" I asked.

The corners of her eyes crinkled, but whether in a small smile or in continued study it was hard to say. "You see?" she said. "I've already done wonders for your self-esteem."

"Austin's a licensed realtor, did you know that?"

I nodded, not to say I'd known it, just that it made sense.

"He's very elaborate, Mark," Becky continued. "He doesn't seem to have ever done anything on impulse. He has these systems. His neighbors are shocked that he's been arrested. The people at his church are outraged. He taught children's Sunday school, Mark. And he's never been anything but perfectly proper with the kids he comes into contact with."

"The ones that people know he's been in contact with." Not to my surprise, Austin lived by the code that says, Don't shit where you eat.

153

"That's right," Becky said. We were in her office, and she seemed more in charge in that setting. She leaned toward me across her desk as if I were a recalcitrant witness she had to bring into line. "But meanwhile he has this secret life. We'll never track down all his lairs. There's only a couple of rent houses he owns himself, I think, but being a realtor gives him access to empty houses all over town. He can just appear, start acting like he's moved in, and there he is, the new neighbor. But nobody knows his name or where he really lives. He must've had several of these going at once, in different stages of cultivating children."

Becky had a plant atop her filing cabinet, a sad lost cause beneath the slit window of her office. It was an ivy of some kind that had crept across the top of the metal cabinet and started down the side, searching. The plant had only a few leaves, it was mostly just thin vine, but it was green, it gave Becky's office slightly more homelike an atmosphere than most, which was rather sad in itself.

"It's kind of creepy, isn't it?" she said. "We can show some of this elaborate preparation he put into the seduction. The stalking."

I stood up. "You're doing good work, Becky. I'm sorry you're getting stuck with all the crud work, but that's how it falls out on this one. Meanwhile, I have to go cultivate the victim some more."

Becky stood up and already had her purse strap over her shoulder. "Okay," she said.

I shook my head at her. "I'll go by myself again this time."

Becky looked concerned. "Mark, don't you think I need to get to know him too? Even if you're going to do the examination at trial, two of us talking to him might draw more out of him. Maybe he's different with men."

"I do want that," I said. "But first I want him very dependent on me. That's not strong enough to dilute, yet. Next time, I promise."

As I turned in her doorway to wave goodbye Becky was still standing, looking at me worriedly. No one trusted me any more.

* * *

As I drove to Tommy's house that evening I thought about something else Janet McLaren had told me about him that might or might not be true. "If he's so afraid of how the story will make him look," I'd asked, "then why *did* he tell?"

"Maybe it *was* to get attention," she'd answered. "I don't discount that idea. But it was probably jealousy." She could see she'd surprised me. "I'm sure Austin Paley didn't brag about his other conquests to Tommy," she'd sensibly explained. "Tommy thought it was something new for both of them. He thought he was special to Austin. Then he saw him on TV, part of a case involving several children, and he knew immediately Austin was behind it. He felt betrayed. That's probably what undercut his loyalty to Austin enough to tell his parents what had happened."

It was, to use Becky's phrase, a little creepy. It wouldn't be the first time I'd used a jealous lover to testify against a defendant. But I wanted Tommy to have a more reliable reason for testifying, too.

This time his parents were home. Mrs. Algren answered the door, dressed like a sitcom mom on old TV, wearing a dress and necklace and stockings even at home after work. When she took me into the living room I expected her husband still to be wearing his tie and suit, but he was in sweat pants and T-shirt.

"Sorry," he said about the sweat as he shook my hand. "I've been riding the exercycle."

The living room was very big, high-vaulted. Through an archway the room blended into the dining room, making it appear even bigger. The carpet was white, and unstained. The fireplace was made of white brick. Beside it glass shelves held a variety of fragile knickknacks and one family portrait in a silver frame.

"I need to talk to you," I said. Mr. and Mrs. Algren looked uneasy, until I started talking, when they visibly relaxed. He ducked his head a little, keeping his eyes on me, and nodded in rhythm to what I was saying. His receding hairline gave him a serious air. He was very trim but not particularly muscular, as if too much exercise wasn't worth his time. Mr. Algren was a young man, by my standards, no later than midthirties, but he already looked like someone who'd come far in the business world, and had done it by shucking nonessentials like humor.

Mrs. Algren was the one who could have profited by time on the exercycle. That's why she looked older than her husband. She lacked his intensity, too. She had the look of a woman who wants to help you out but always hears something more urgent going on in another room.

What I said to them was, "You know I wasn't planning on Tommy's case going to trial this soon. I was forced to move it up because I lost my witness in the other case. I believe the defendant managed to bribe his parents."

"Bribe?" Mr. Algren said. I nodded sadly. The Algrens shook their heads in sympathy, appalled at the idea of parents who would take money for ignoring the best interests of their child.

"You see what will happen next," I said.

"He'll come to us."

"I don't want that man near this house," Mrs. Algren said. She drew closer to her husband.

"It won't be him, honey." He looked at me and I shook my head. "It will be some lowlife creep he's hired to approach us. Some lawyer, probably."

No one seemed to think I might be offended by this analysis, which I suppose was complimentary. There were lowlife creep lawyers and then there were ones like me.

"You don't have to be worried about us, Mr. Blackwell," Algren said. "I'll show that son of a bitch the door so fast he'll think he got hit by a train. I may put him *through* the door. Unless—"

He really was very quick. "Now you understand," I said.

"Understand what?" his wife said. She was looking past my shoulder.

"You want us to play along when we're contacted," Mr. Algren said.

"Exactly."

He nodded. I nodded. If Joe Friday had been there, he would have nodded. "And maybe we can lay another indictment on Mr. Paley's doorstep," Algren said.

"But won't he know you've warned us?" Mrs. Algren asked.

"It doesn't matter. He *has* to try to get to you. He's so afraid of trial he's desperate."

"Then mightn't he try to do something to Tommy?"

"That's something for me to worry about," I said. "I don't think Paley's the type to try something violent, but we've got the possibility covered. I'm seeing Tommy almost every day after school anyway, preparing for his testimony. The days I don't, I'll have an investigator with him. That only leaves school and home."

"And we'll take care of him here," Mr. Algren said.

"Excellent," I said.

What had passed unspoken in our conversation was any suspicion that the Algrens might actually accept a bribe—not the kind that came in cold sordid cash, but the promise of job opportunities, contacts, and, best of all, keeping Tommy—and themselves—out of the public spotlight. I didn't think they'd be susceptible even to that, but I had another way of protecting myself against that possibility.

"Let's just keep this to ourselves," I warned them. "I'm going to go talk to Tommy for a few minutes so he won't know why I came."

They nodded, ready to conspire in the deception of their son.

"What were you talking to Mom and Dad about?" Tommy asked when I found him in what the Algrens called the study, which contained a high techish metal-and-blond-wood desk, a computer at its own desk, and one tall bookshelf holding mostly bound manuals. Tommy was at the computer. He pressed a button and the words on the screen disappeared.

"Just telling them you're going to be all right. They're worried about you." He looked pleased to hear that. I continued. "Listen, Tom, I came by to talk to you because I got an idea."

This "Tom" business was a deliberate ploy of mine. I figured I was the first person in his life to call him by his name without diminution. I wanted him to appreciate me for seeing his maturity. Tommy'd been in therapy for weeks now, and he understood the implication of therapy, understood that everyone thought he was damaged. Tommy was going to drag this extra shadow at his heels for the rest of his life. When he was sixty he would still be the abused boy. But he could have something else, too: an early understanding that everyone was as fragile as he, that adults are only scared children too. He need never be afraid of anyone again. I could show him that.

"I've been thinking about this Brian business," I said, frowning. Tommy's own face opened. He'd looked resigned to going over details of the case again. But no, I was here because I'd been thinking about his problem at school.

"I was all wet when I told you to threaten him with me. That was stupid."

"Yeah," Tommy agreed.

"I know, I know. You'd just make it a bigger challenge for him. He'd eat that up." Tommy looked relieved at my enlightenment. He'd thought I'd lost touch with reality. "But you know the worst thing you can do to a guy like that? Give him something to think about. Because he can't do it; it hurts him to try. It'll burn out his circuitry. Whenever he sees you from then on he gets this pain between his ears. He starts avoiding you. It hurts to look at you."

Tommy had a little of that look himself. "You think so?" he asked doubtfully.

"Look, Tom, you think Brian's the only Brian in the world? I prosecute stupid jerks for a living, remember? I see Brian every day, sitting there in handcuffs and jail slippers, on his way to prison. These guys are morons." I touched the tips of both index fingers to my temples, like electrodes. "You can't outrun him, you can't beat him up. But up here, you're about eight feet taller than he is."

"So what do I do, tell him math problems every time he comes close to me?"

He was perking up and he was talking like a kid. I liked it. I said, "First off, tell him you've always admired him."

Tommy's face twisted. "That greasewad?"

"I said tell him, I didn't say mean it. Hey, *are* you smarter than this guy, or am I wasting my time? Put it to him like this. Tell him you saw him doing something nice once, taking up for somebody else, and it made you realize he's a better person than anybody else realizes."

Tommy had to set me straight. "This guy never took up

for anybody in his life. If ten guys were kicking a girl who was down, he'd come and take *their* side."

"I know that. *You* know that. But you think this idiot remembers every day of his life? Tell him it happened, make it sound good enough, and he'll be saying, 'What? No. Well ... Oh yeah, I remember that.' Believe me, you tell somebody they did something noble, they'll believe you."

"Maybe," Tommy said. He still sounded doubtful, but he was thinking.

"If this works, you're golden. When he sees you he's going to remember what a hero he is, and he isn't going to sully his reputation by being a jerk to you. Maybe to everybody else, but not to you, the one guy in America who looks up to him."

"I don't know," Tommy said. "Do I have to keep this up just 'til I puke, or for the rest of my life?"

"After a while it's automatic. Look, Tom, you're acting like this is a chore. It's fun. You take a guy who hates you and you turn him to your side, and he's sweet to you from then on while you're laughing up your sleeve about what an idiot he is; believe me, that's why God created the planet. There's nothing more fun in this world."

I hadn't meant to deliver a paean to the joys of manipulation, that was a little too close to giving myself away, but you get caught up in these things.

"Is it worth trying?" I asked. "Or are you having a better time eating dirt every time he catches you on the playground?"

"It's not bad," Tommy said slowly. He didn't want to come around too fast. "What's your other idea?" he asked.

"What makes you think I have another idea?"

He smiled at me.

"Okay, if this first brilliant idea doesn't work, if he comes around and starts picking on you again, its because he's managed to get over having to think about how much you admire him. But it's still in the back of his mind. He wants to reduce it to something simple, like you're a fag, but you don't let it be simple. Give him something else to think about."

I'd passed quickly over the "fag" aspect, as if only an idiot like Brian would entertain that thought.

"Like?" Tommy said.

I spread my hands. "You know the situation better than I do, Tom. Use something at school. Use what he says to you. If he says he hears you've been seeing a shrink, tell him, Yeah, and now you understand *his* problem. The shrink explained why Brian has to keep hanging around you. Don't tell him why, just tell him you understand, and it's okay."

Tommy was nodding. I went on offhandedly. "I'm going to have an investigator from my office picking you up from school the days I don't see you. If Brian gets wind of that and says something to you about it, just look real alarmed and say, 'You haven't said anything to anyone, have you?' Let *him* worry what he's done wrong. Or if you think it would work better, confide in him. Confide a lie, of course."

"Sure," Tommy said. He was as quick as his father.

"Just remember, the thing a guy like Brian hates worst is thinking. Keep it complicated, keep him off balance. He'll either wind up being your pal or he'll start staying away."

"And either one's fine with me," Tommy said. He sounded very adult, he had the mannerisms, too. He swept his hand in front of him in a worldly gesture I'd seen before. But it was a child's hand making the gesture, a small hand with fingers thin almost to the point of translucence.

"That's the best I can do," I said, wondering, *Did Austin Paley ever give you swell advice like this? Did he concern himself with your problems?* "If all else fails, tell me and I'll have my investigator pound him into oatmeal."

"You'd get sued," Tommy said.

He followed me out into the living room, which had the effect of making everyone furtive. We closed as if it had been a business call. I let myself out. When I looked back from the doorway the Algrens were standing as if for another family portrait, Mrs. Algren beside her husband, Algren's arm draped across Tommy's shoulder. Father and son both wanted to wink at me. I returned their waves with a significant nod and look at each of them in turn. I had them all well in hand, I thought.

"Well, it's happened," Tim Scheuless said on the phone. "I guess you've already seen it, haven't you?"

The latest poll, he meant. Leo Mendoza had just passed

me in supposed voter popularity. "It looks like I lost more to 'undecided' than I did to Leo," I said.

"Yeah, that's the good part," Tim said, but his tone of voice needed work. It sounded as gloomy as November. "What we've lost," he said, "is the advantage of incumbency. But we could get it back. Don't you have anything ready for trial?"

"I'll see," I said shortly. "Meanwhile, let's plunge into debt. Put up some billboards. Let's run those radio spots again. Is there time to make some new ones?"

"Maybe. I don't know if I can buy the time. Or the signs. Things are pretty well booked up already. But I'll see what I can do."

As usual when I hung up from talking to my campaign manager, I was depressed. I put on a brave front for the benefit of the troops.

"See if anybody's got a really ugly, easy case going to trial this week," I said, "so I can take it over from them."

"I'll pass the word," Becky said. She was responding in kind to what I'd said, but I couldn't tell if she thought I was serious or joking.

"And, Jack," I said to my chief investigator, "see if you can find any evidence Austin Paley got to the Pollards. Sudden deposit in their bank account, you know the kind of thing."

"Sure."

"Oh, and assign somebody to pick up Tommy Algren after school. Some days—"

"Already done," Jack said, and left my office with the busy air that was perpetual with him.

Becky Schirhart was studying me quite frankly. I remembered the air of uneasiness that pervaded the district attorney's office during close election times when the chief's job was on the line, which meant everyone else's was too. Maybe a new broom would sweep the place clean. People would be busy brightening their resumés and having lunch with lawyers they knew in the outside world. I'm sure I wasn't the only one in the office who'd seen the new poll. I attributed Becky's concern to that.

But she said, "The trouble with Tommy is—?" prompting

me to complete the sentence that had been interrupted by the ringing of the telephone.

"The trouble with Tommy is he's modeled himself on Austin," I said tiredly, my enthusiasm for rehashing the case at a low ebb. "The most worldly man on the planet. Everything's an amusement for him. I need to break through that to the pain if I have any hope of convincing a jury that this boy's been hurt."

"Maybe—this would be tougher, but maybe what you could show them is how deadened Tommy's been made by this, how all his reactions now are inappropriate. I'm sure you could get psychiatric testimony to that effect. What always strikes me about that little boy is how empty the whole rest of his life is going to be. That's just as frightening as him crying all the time, isn't it?"

"Maybe," I said.

"Let me talk to him this afternoon." Becky was leaning toward me. If I were an energy vampire, if I could absorb her enthusiasm, I could lift myself out of this paralysis. But I intended only to deflate her.

"Becky," I said, "I think I can take it from here by myself."

She looked at me as if she couldn't think what I meant by "it." "This really isn't a two-person prosecution," I elaborated. "I appreciate all your work on it, but I won't need a second chair at trial."

I expected her to think I wanted only to grab for myself whatever glory was to be had. I was prepared for her to think that. But if she had thought that, she wouldn't have argued. She would have just left, offended.

"You'll need me," she said.

"It's best if I do it alone."

She sat there. I hadn't the heart to dismiss her, but that was the effect of my silence. We'd grown closer while working on the case, but I was still the boss. In a moment, when I had the energy, I'd stand up, and the interview would be over. Becky understood. Her shoulders hunched inward, as if she were lowering her center of gravity, anchoring herself in the chair, defying me to pull her out of it.

"I know why," she said.

"There's no why, it's just—"

162

"You think it would be bad for my career to be associated with you so publicly if this turns out to be your last case. You think I need to pull back in case Leo Mendoza wins the election."

"As it looks like he's going to," I said.

"You don't think I'd stay here anyway if he wins, do you?"

I smiled slightly in gratitude. "That's nice to say, Becky, but it's tough out there in the real world. There's a recession going on. Some of the big firms are laying off lawyers, not hiring new ones."

"It doesn't matter, I wouldn't work here," she said. "I've heard what this place would be like without you. Having to worry about who you're dealing with, whether he's connected, having to make better offers to lawyers who helped out Leo in the campaign."

"That's just talk," I said. "There's always talk like that. This place is a machine, it runs itself, no matter who's at the top."

"No," Becky said, with some ferocity. She still had her head lowered slightly. Her determined air made her look even younger than she was, but that didn't make the determination ring false. On the contrary, she looked young enough never to have been disappointed, to believe that what she thought must happen would happen. "I was here before you came," she said. "I saw who got promoted, and why. You had to hang out with the section chiefs after work and go to meetings for causes the boss believed in. What you did in the courtroom didn't matter so much."

Becky was probably right that the character of the office would change if Leo was elected. Leo wasn't a bad man, I didn't suspect him of harboring one evil intention. But he believed in the system of favors and personal loyalty. If he did win the election it would be because he'd been faithful to that system. He wouldn't forget the favors. That wouldn't make much difference in the day-to-day running of the office, though. As Eliot had said, murderers don't wield much influence. Any district attorney has to go after criminals as hard as he can.

"I'd never have made first chair under the old system,"

Becky continued. "And I won't go back to it after I've seen how the office should be run."

Her loyalty was flattering. But I felt the lure of private life. It would be so easy to let go, just give up the office gracefully. Give up the hard decisions and the badgering by citizens, the phone calls from angry cops, the endless stupid meetings with other public officials. I'd been curious about what it was like to run the district attorney's office, I'd found out, and it stunk. It would be a relief to let go.

Before Becky's comments I couldn't remember the last time I'd been praised for my job performance. Criticism was the only constant. No one was ever satisfied with the results that emerged from the criminal courts. I didn't blame them, I wasn't satisfied either. True justice was a possibility so faint that it wasn't even a day-to-day goal. Every day was a compromise. I was tired of compromise, deathly tired of the burdens of the office.

"All right," I said to Becky. "It's your head. But you know, there's a good possibility we could lose the trial *and* the election. Then your prospects would really be dim."

"We can't lose the trial," Becky protested. Quickly she realized I might question her priorities, and added, "*Or* the election."

"Trials like this—" I began instructively.

I was discussing reality, but Becky—she *was* as naïve as I'd suspected—was telling me what *had* to happen. She interrupted me. "He can't get away with what he's done to these children. We can't let him go on doing it."

I hadn't realized she was so caught up in the facts. I hadn't seen Becky evince that much sympathy for the children, and when we'd talked about the case we'd talked about the practical aspects of it. I'd forgotten what had impressed me about Becky to begin with: her passion for the victim.

She was no longer sunken into herself. She was leaning slightly forward, eyes shining. I'm sure that would have disturbed her; I'd seen Becky make efforts to look as blasé as the rest of us. But she couldn't pull that off. She could have been one of the child victims herself.

I gestured toward my office door. Becky took it for dismissal and stood up. But, "Do you think," I asked her, "if we barricaded that door and locked the windows I could stay here even after January?"

Because I *wasn't* ready to let it go. To hell with private life. I *liked* making the decisions. No one could run that office better than I could. The compromises hurt me, the injustices gnawed at me. I didn't want to see the place taken over by someone who could take them in stride.

"We'll try it if we have to." Becky smiled.

At least I sent her on her way more cheerily. I was left looking around my office with a premature case of nostalgia.

10

I appreciate that, sir. I hope you can appreciate *my* position as well. I can't—"

I felt like a shnook for having called him "sir," but it certainly wasn't a discussion between friends.

"You may be right," I inserted into a lull in his speech, waited for him to interrupt me with the inevitable assertion that he *was* right, and continued, "But that's not for me to say. That's going to be up to a jury."

"Don't give me that," my phone caller said. "You know more than any jury will know. *You* decide who to prosecute."

I let him go on haranguing me. I was polite. I was deferential. But finally I felt compelled to ask, "May I ask, sir, what your interest in the case is?"

After a moment I put my hand over the mouthpiece of the phone and whispered, "He's just interested in justice." Becky smiled.

"I'll give that a lot of thought," I finally said, sounding painfully sincere, I thought. It wasn't my tone that convinced him, though, it was my caller's assurance of his own importance. He couldn't be ignored.

"That was the mayor," I said after I hung up. Becky raised her eyebrows. "He'd appreciate it if I could postpone Austin Paley's trial long enough for more investigation."

It had been my first conversation of any substance with the mayor of San Antonio. Theoretically he had no influence over my decisions. He was city, I was county; he oversaw city departments, I prosecuted criminals: our functions didn't overlap. But the mayor's real authority derived from being the acknowledged local leader of my political party. That gave him control over campaign funds, endorsements, any number of tidbits he could throw to local officeholders.

I stared at the phone. "I swear, the last few days politicians have been swarming over me like I'd stepped in an antbed. I've never known a man with so many friends."

"You were his friend, too," Becky said.

I didn't deny it. "But I wouldn't do this kind of thing for him. What are they all so worried about?"

She shrugged. If I couldn't answer that question, Becky certainly couldn't. "Are you thinking about agreeing to a continuance?" she asked quietly.

"Of course not. If you and I don't try it next week, nobody ever will. Don't they think I know that?"

"This is a lot of—pressure," Becky said carefully.

I shrugged. "What are they going to do to me?"

Becky wasn't that naïve, even as uninterested in politics as she seemed to be. It wasn't a question of what local leaders could do *to* me; it was what they could refuse to do *for* me, in the closing days of a campaign I was beginning to lose. They were starting to make me feel pigheaded. Maybe there was something to Austin's claim of innocence, when it was supported by so many people. Maybe I should accede to their demands, or at least appear to do so: delay the trial, win back my campaign support, have a chance of retaining my office. Then I'd have four more years in which to decide whether to prosecute Austin.

But being pigheaded was not entirely a bad feeling. Having a host of politicians arrayed against me tended to make me think I was right.

"Well, I've got to get out of here anyway," I said. "Ugly duty calls."

"I'd like to go with you," Becky said.

I frowned at her. "You're kidding."

"You must have had something better to do than this," I said to her half an hour later.

"No," she said quickly, then realized the answer was

something of an embarrassment to her. "Insider politics," she added, "it should be fascinating."

I made a noise. She felt comfortable enough with me to be sarcastic, and by now I knew her well enough to recognize it. Becky and I had grown quite accidentally close in the last month or so. As my life outside the case fell away in large chunks I found myself talking to her more. Our intense trial preparation meant there were days when we saw almost no one but each other, when we ate all our meals together. Though she was still making appearances in her regular court, Becky had turned over most of her responsibilities to the other two prosecutors there. I knew, from things she didn't say, from seeing her in the halls when she didn't know I was watching, that our isolation was telling on her, too. She felt set apart, even from other people in the office. We'd imposed such tight secrecy on our case that we could talk to no one but each other. Inevitably, during little breaks, over sandwiches, we'd talked about things other than the case, as well. She'd seen Linda definitively walk out of my life, and I hadn't seen anyone else *in* Becky's life.

"Why don't you call up that guy"—I'd almost said boy— "Donny and do something with him? Surely—"

"You don't intrude on Donny," Becky said, "you wait for him to come to you." Her tone was so neutral, almost amused, she seemed to be reciting a poem she'd learned through hours of repetition. "And please," she added in a more lively voice, "if you ever meet him, don't call him Donny. That's our little secret. He goes by Don now."

"Did you consciously deepen your voice when you said that, or—?"

"That's how you say the name," Becky said, lowering her chin toward her neck to say it deeply again: "Don."

"That's how the announcer will say it when introducing our next governor," I suggested.

"Oh, Donny'd never have anything to do with politics," Becky said quickly. "He—"

And stopped abruptly. She'd embarrassed herself again. Actually I was flattered that she'd forgotten she was in the company of a politician. To cover her discomfiture I said, "You're not afraid to call him because you don't want to appear forward or something stupid like that, is it? Because let me tell you, guys love that. Smart ones, anyway. Every girl who ever pursued me, I fell in love with."

Becky grinned at "every." These lawyers, you can't slip one word by them. "The whole crowd, huh?" she said mockingly.

I grew lost in thought. Literally lost: it took me minutes to find my way out. When I did I realized Becky had fallen silent for that long too. I was embarrassed at brooding in front of her.

"This will be humiliating," I said, pulling into the brewery parking lot. The lot should have been filled. It wasn't half so. This was my big fund-raiser, the last gasp of my campaign. There'd be at least a small crowd here no matter what. Lawyers hedging their bets in case I did stage a come-from-behind win; other candidates using my event to make appearances of their own; small contributors not enough in the know to have heard what a political pariah I'd become. From the looks of the parking lot there were few of those.

Becky was staring at the low blocky building, looking far away in the gloom of twilight. "You should let people know," she said quietly, "about what they're doing to you on this case. About the calls you're getting and the pressure you've had to resist. If people knew what you're fighting on this case—"

"It probably wouldn't matter."

We stepped out of the car. The interior lights illuminated our bodies briefly but our heads were shadowed. Becky must have liked it that way. "Can I tell you something?" she asked.

"Sure." I closed the car door and started walking. She caught up and stopped me. She didn't want to say it on the fly.

"You know, you give the impression of playing no politics and no favorites, and that's how the office seemed to run," she said hurriedly, "but I was never close enough to know if it was true. I figured you had to do the crummy little things that politicians do to keep their jobs. We all figured that. But now I have gotten close enough. And I know it hasn't been just an act. You know I'm not political at all, I try hard to avoid all that stuff, but I've been telling everyone

I know to vote for you. I'll bet everyone who really knows you is doing the same thing. Maybe if—"

"Becky," I said, feeling rather pained and flattered at the same time, "thank you. But let me tell *you* something. Don't have heroes. Heroes are bad for you."

"I didn't say you were my hero," she said snippily.

"Good. Because there aren't any heroes."

The impetus for my speech had been the sight of someone going in the doorway we were approaching. He'd reminded me of someone. Someone who wouldn't be here.

But he was. "Eliot!" I said happily. It *had* been him. And in spite of what I'd said to Becky, I was delighted to see him. He clasped my arms warmly. "It's great of you to come. Hello, Mamie." Eliot's wife of about forty years was standing back just a step or two from our reunion, wearing the hat she'd worn to every political function I'd ever seen them at. I'd have recognized the hat if it had come on its own. Mamie beamed at me. She looked so much like my grandmother that I felt myself shrinking to the size of an eight-year-old boy.

There was a crowd of fifty or sixty people, enough to stave off absolute political embarrassment. There were quite a few other candidates, desperately looking for civilians to glad-hand. In this crowd of insiders Eliot drew more favorable attention than I did. I would have had to wait my turn if he hadn't drawn me aside. I wasn't going to take this public occasion to ask him what I was curious about, I just wanted to tell him I was glad he'd come. Eliot Quinn's appearance at my rally carried some weight. Not enough, unfortunately, but that made his coming even nicer.

He cut off my expressions of gratitude. "How bad has it gotten?" he asked.

"Worse than I expected," I said jokingly. The way I towered over my old boss embarrassed me, like a gawdy bid for attention. I lowered my head toward him.

"Are they being subtle about it, or have they come right out and threatened what they'll do to you if you prosecute Austin?" Eliot asked. He sounded as if he were joking, too, and anyone seeing us from across the room would have thought he was, from his smile, but his eyes were dead serious.

"Increasingly less subtle," I said. These men were Eliot's old friends. He knew them, even if he wasn't in active conspiracy with them. So I asked, "Haven't these people bothered to learn anything about me? Don't they know the best way to ensure I'll prosecute Austin Paley is to tell me I can't?"

Eliot smiled slightly, rather wistfully. He must have been thinking of the years when he'd shared power with these old pols, when he'd had to deal with them, help them out or seek their help.

"These men don't think that subtly," he said. "They're used to telling people what to do and having it done."

"What are they afraid of, Eliot? Because this is starting to sound like fear, not like favors for a friend. What does Austin have on everyone?"

"I wish I could tell you, Mark. If I find out, I will."

We stood quietly. I wanted to believe that Eliot didn't know. Eliot had a lifetime's experience of reading people. He knew I *didn't* believe, not quite.

I made my speech, the audience applauded politely and immediately headed for the doors. Becky was waiting for me when I'd shaken the last hand. We drove back to the Justice Center in silence that seemed to be imposed by the night. It was after eight, our end of downtown was cleared out. Anyone on the street had nowhere at all to go.

"Mark?"

"I'm okay." The failed rally had made me mournful, but I didn't feel like sharing the reasons with anyone.

I found Becky's car and saw her safely into it, then drove away as if I had somewhere to go, but instead found a parking space of my own.

The Justice Center loomed bulky and ugly, almost as wide as it was tall, a plaid block. The soft light that made the old courthouse next door look romantic didn't soften the hard edges of the new building. I didn't stop to gaze on it fondly, I just went in. The corridor was dark. A few of my ambitious assistants would have worked late, but not this late. The elevator seemed to lift off with a groan, protesting that it was off duty.

The DA's offices were empty, I was thankful to find. There were enough lights to find my way to my office; I

171

didn't light more. Once the door closed behind me I began breathing more deeply, the way a man does who is happy to be home after a weary day.

No thoughts. The site did away with thinking about my life. That's why I'd come. The papers were already laid out on my desk. I didn't have to look for a thing. I sat down and put hands on them and my personal life went away. I wanted only to immerse myself in the abstract problems of the case. I checked the indictment for the thousandth time, making sure Austin's victimization of Tommy was set out with sufficient exactness. I let the picture of the act described in the document form in my mind, filling in details, hoping the scene would be as vivid for the jury.

My thoughts returned to Tommy instead. He scared me. I wasn't sure what the jury would think of him: a boy mature beyond his age, calm as he told his tale, with that little twist to his mouth. A miniature Austin Paley, in fact.

David flashed across my mind. Tommy'd reacted to his father's distance by seeking love elsewhere. David had reacted by giving up on it, settling for a loveless marriage. I didn't want to feel responsible for him—he was a grown man—but I was. I always would be, no matter how old he grew.

Night had stolen over the city, cool and dark, and over these offices as well, because I hadn't turned on any lights. I wanted dimness, quiet. I wanted sleep, but I knew sleep wouldn't come tonight.

I could no longer keep my mind on the case. In the lonely dark the shambles of my personal life seemed to surround me. Linda and I would never recover. She had started to put together a life free of our differences. I wondered if it would take as long to see her without pain as the years we'd been together.

My family had dissolved in my wake, as well. David and I might develop an uneasy truce, but anything warmer seemed unlikely. Lois had quite rightly made a new life for herself. Dinah had given up her endearing efforts to keep me close. The most recent weekend I'd kept her what she'd talked about was school, which obliquely meant boys. Now a veteran of three dates with two different boys, Dinah was eagerly examining the future, not brooding over the past where

I lay. I would never figure very prominently in her thoughts again.

Even old friends like Eliot had grown distant. There was no one I trusted any more.

Which left nothing. No human heart held me first. There was no one to whom I'd be the first person to run, with good news or tragedy. I didn't know where *I* would go, for a celebration or commiseration.

I found myself outside on the tiny fifth-floor balcony, where I was arrested by the rising of the moon. It rode a hand's breadth above the horizon, low and huge and orange, its color diffused beyond its outline, as if colored by a young child. It rose in flame like a phoenix. I stood and watched. The moon was not quite full, which made it look lopsided, tilted like the head of a questioning person. I forgot it for a few minutes and when I looked again there was a different moon, smaller and tightly contained and dead white. I remembered nights in my youth when the full moon called me outside, called me away, told me other people, women, were staring up at that same moon that warmed the night, dreaming of a man like me. The world was full of romance and I could be part of any one I could find. I had limitless possibilities. The moon of my youth was close enough for me to mount and ride.

But this wasn't that moon. This was a cold stone that blocked the stars.

I was quite self-consciously aware of my mood. After a while it grew almost laughable. But I wasn't ready to be amused. What I did achieve was a certain coldness of my own. I could be hard as stone, too. If all I had left was my work, I would throw myself into it. I would be the finest prosecutor this world had seen. If I had only one case left to prosecute, I'd prosecute it in a way people would talk about for years.

I returned to my office and stood at the desk, trying to decide whether to gather up the case file or go home completely alone, when I heard steps in the outer office.

My first thought was that I was all alone, and Austin Paley was a desperate man. But I had nowhere to retreat. The steps began slowing before they reached my door, as if the walker had faltered in his resolution.

But the door flew open, banging back against the wall, startling me even though I'd been expecting it. The visitor stopped in the doorway, where dim light rendered her a charcoal sketch. "I knew it," she said.

It took me a long moment to recognize her. I was expecting someone more ominous, and at first she did look ominous, with her face shadowed. She looked tall and slender and the slow way she moved spoke of purpose. She came toward me, adding, "I didn't even have to follow you, I knew this was where you'd come."

"Becky," I said. "This is a surprise."

"Not yet," she said. She walked straight up to me. In her heels she was tall enough to put her palms on my cheeks and pull my face down only slightly, to reach hers. But her lips didn't quite hit mine, she had to slide them an inch or so across my face before our mouths met. Mine was already open from surprise. Becky's was open too, with a purposefulness I'd only seen in her when pursuing a prosecution. I bent to her willingly, put my arms around her automatically. Her hands stayed on my face, then slipped to my neck, my shoulders.

Becky drew back from me as if to make certain I knew who she was. The night's light through my windows illumined the side of her face. By moonlight she looked untouched, skin as smooth as a child's. I wanted to put my palm on her cheek, just to feel something so warm and soft. Becky no longer looked sinister. In the gentle light she looked completely guileless.

We kissed again. Her lips were softer than the first time. But there was determination behind them. Her teeth lightly clenched on my lower lip. I could feel her individual fingers on my shoulders.

After a long time she drew back. "This has crossed your mind, hasn't it?"

She talked tough, but she was too close to me for disguise. I could feel her trembling. She'd really had to work her nerve up to come here.

"My God," I said, "are you real? You're like something I conjured out of the moon, because I needed you so bad."

Her face lit up as if she were indeed moon-wrought. She stepped into me and we encircled each other with our arms.

The hug was better than the kiss, because it wasn't startling and it covered more ground. It warmed me. I hadn't realized how chilled I'd grown in the lonely dark.

We held each other until it began to feel awkward to stand so still. Her fingers moved softly, making me suddenly sad, because they forced thinking on me, driving away the lovely thoughtless reveling in sensations we'd had for a minute or two.

I desired her the way anyone desires sweet young flesh, firm and yielding, that can be molded into any shape desire asks. I felt her mind, too, the way we'd come to know each other without meaning to, so that she'd known where I'd gone and what I was feeling. She'd felt the same, I knew, consumed with one passion that seemed like another, because it had to fill all the empty spaces in her life.

But there was a gulf between us of years and of experience, and of authority. I knew that if I followed the flow of this lonely, inviting night, by the next day I'd feel I had taken advantage of her, because I hadn't thought of her this way until I needed someone and she was the closest person.

I was still holding her. "Damn," she said against my neck, quietly and emphatically, telling me in one word that she knew me as well as I knew her, that she knew exactly what I was thinking, and how I regarded her.

"It's not that way," she said, looking up. "I was thinking about it long before tonight. Look." She pointed at what she'd set down on the table beside my couch. "I brought a bottle of wine. It's been in my desk for a week. I thought some night after we'd worked late . . ."

She had broken our contact with the gesture, and I kept it broken by stepping back, subtly, I hoped.

"Becky, I'm very flattered, and I'm enormously attracted to you, but I can't take the chance, because I need your help more than I need—the comfort you want to give me."

She laughed softly, derisively, at my word choice. She looked flushed, but in laughing she was recovering herself. When she spoke she sounded very sure of herself, but she had folded her arms across her chest self-possessively, acknowledging that our contact was over. "Why can't we have both?"

I spoke flatly, looking at her, not being evasive. "I put

you on this case because I could trust you, because you were a nobody. Everybody I trusted had failed me. If I sleep with you now you'll be connected to me, you'll have an in. I won't be able to trust you any more."

Her expression grew concerned. "Is that how things work in your world?" she asked.

"It is lately."

But this wasn't true. This wasn't my reason. The main reason, probably, was that I was an idiot. I had no doubt I'd regret rejecting what Becky offered. But I'd have regrets either way. I'd feel deceitful if I let her close to me, because as lonely as I'd been, Becky hadn't crossed my mind. I'd be using her. And some day when we inevitably broke apart, she'd find that I had wasted part of her precious youth. Worse, she might end up the way I was now, with only work to sustain her. And if she didn't hate me for that, I'd hate myself.

There'd been a few moments of silence. Becky was looking up toward the ceiling, hugging herself. "Can I just creep back out under cover of darkness and we pretend I was never here?" she asked. The jaunty tone she sought sounded more like her voice was on the edge of breaking.

I took her hand. "I'm glad you came," I said. "I do need you. This case is giving me fits. You're the only one I can talk to about it. Be my partner."

I said the last sentence quietly, and as quietly she answered, "Okay." I walked across the office and turned on a light. Becky still looked beautiful. She was wearing a dress, not a fancy one, but not one of the suits I was used to, either. She probably felt uncomfortable. And I was probably selfish to keep her there, but I did want her. I did want to talk. And as soon as we began, as soon as I drew her attention to the papers on my desk and took up the conversation we'd broken off that afternoon, Becky lost her self-consciousness and immersed herself in argument. She even, as she reached for a notepad, brushed my arm with hers without seeming to notice. We were such lawyers, it was embarrassing when I thought about it later. Romance is a nice little diversion, but a case is a case.

"Just ask the question," Becky was saying animatedly. "We can't lose. If the defense objects, they've told the jury the answer. If they let us get into it, explore his romantic history. The jury will be interested, I guarantee. A forty-three-year-old man with no serious involvement with an adult woman, ever?"

"Maybe he'll show up at trial with a girl friend," I suggested.

"If he does we'll call *her* as a witness," Becky said eagerly.

I laughed, touched her hand without thinking, then turned quickly away before she could react. We'd made a pot of coffee. The cup I poured was the last of it. Becky's unopened bottle of wine still stood on the end table, a reproach to our seriousness.

The truth was, I was more attracted to her during our brainstorming session than I'd been when holding her. It reminded me of old times with Linda. I wanted to touch Becky more intimately, to ask if her offer was revivable. Only my strict self-discipline stopped me. That and that I would have looked like an idiot.

"We have to talk," Austin Paley said on the phone.

"Fine. Your lawyer's office? Or mine?"

"No. This has to be very private." He spoke quietly, even furtively, utterly without his usual offhand air.

Then he surprised me by giving me directions to an address I'd never been, in a south side neighborhood I might have trouble finding. "What's this place?" I asked.

"It's just a house, that no one else knows."

"Austin. Tell me why I should come."

The line was silent for several seconds. Austin seemed to be fading from me. "Mark, do you really think I'll have a gunman waiting for you? Or a naked whore? Tell your assistant where you've gone, or anyone else you trust. But don't let it go any further. And come alone."

"You haven't told me why I should."

"Because you want to know the truth," he said.

As always, leaving the courthouse during daylight hours was a guilty pleasure. The courthouse is my home, more than any other building of my life, but my responsibilities there are constant. I drove away with the thrill of a boy skipping school. That Wednesday the weather had finally turned, south Texas's version of autumn at last appearing. The air hadn't lost its morning chill, but the sun was warm. By afternoon it would feel like summer in a normal climate. The kind of weather in which kids wore sweaters to school, then left them lying in tangles on the playground.

I got turned around trying to find the house, in a tangle of streets such as seems peculiarly indigenous to San Antonio, where a street would change names at the end of a block, or run parallel to another street for blocks only to meet it perpendicularly. Dead ends abounded. One of those dead ends turned out to be my destination, a narrow street so short it held only eight houses, four on each side. My address was one near the closed end of the street, a tiny woodframe house with a sagging porch the size of a welcome mat. The house was no better kept than the ones around it. It needed paint; the windows were so dirty they were obscured without being curtained.

I assumed this was one of Austin's many hideaways, the lairs he'd scattered around town as child traps. I couldn't picture him in it.

But he was. Before I could knock the door was pulled open, jerkily, because it dragged on the floor. There was Austin, looking as I'd never seen him: underdressed. He wore slacks, an open-necked yellow shirt, and brown loafers without socks. Yellow wasn't a good color for Austin. His skin seemed to absorb it, making him look sickly. Even his smile wasn't as hearty as I'd always known it. His manner was a diminished version of itself.

"Mark. Come in. Please excuse the dreadful surroundings. Don't touch anything, you'd catch a disease."

He didn't offer to shake hands, but otherwise he was hostly, ushering me into a dim living room made smaller by a clutter of old-fashioned furniture, scratchy love seat, wooden-armed chairs with doilies. We had left daylight behind. Inside the little parlor it could have been midnight. Austin turned on a floor lamp, which accented his paleness.

It didn't cross my mind that Austin might actually be sick or scared. I had grown used to thinking of his life as a facade. This was only a new facade for a new situation. I was impressed, though, at being given a peek behind his veil, even if all I glimpsed was another veil.

Austin was more solemn than I had ever seen him. "Let's speak quickly," he said. "I know you don't want to be here any longer than you have to be. But, Mark. Promise me you'll keep an open mind. I tell you this not just because I need your help, but because I'm tired of carrying it alone. So listen, please. Even if you decide not to give me the time I need, promise you'll look into what I'm about to tell you. Something has to be done."

I nodded skeptically. Austin leaned forward and began talking in a rapid voice. He rubbed his hands together as he spoke, rubbing each finger in turn as if desperately trying to get warm, or clean. His story quickly became familiar.

"About four years ago a man named George Pendrake had plans to build an office tower. With shops on the ground floor, a bank, fountain. Beautiful little white model of the place he had. He schlepped that thing all over town, trying to interest backers. He found the land—close to here, as a matter of fact. Poor neighborhood, but close to downtown. George's center could have revived the whole area. That's what he said. He raised the money fairly quickly."

"From you among others?" I asked.

"No." Austin shook his head ruefully. "He didn't need as small an investor as me. The project went ahead very quickly. Pendrake got the permits he needed with amazingly little trouble. The lot he wanted was vacant, the county condemned it and sold it to him for virtually nothing. Construction began.

"Then everything went bust," Austin said—sadly, as if he *had* been afflicted personally by the loss. "The recession finally reached San Antonio, money dried up, construction costs began to overrun as they always do. Some people claim George Pendrake had underfinanced the place from the beginning, by siphoning off too much of the money he'd raised, but it doesn't matter, he went broke too. His creditors forced him toward bankruptcy. Which isn't a disgrace at all these days, it's a normal business move you pick up and go on from, but in this case George and his friends fought like hell to keep that from happening."

"Because?" I asked. Austin looked at me hopefully, glad of my attention.

"Because if Pendrake Plaza had been forced into bankruptcy, a receiver would have been appointed to untangle the debts and the assets and which of the partners owed what. And Pendrake had secret investors who didn't want their names coming to light."

"I know this story," I told Austin. "Pete Jonas resigned his county commissioner post. Alice Sylvester was defeated in the next city council elections."

"You know some of it," Austin said. "The fact is, Pete and Alice weren't even in as deeply as several others. I felt sorry for Alice especially. She was barely involved, but she went down. She had a future, too."

"So you did know about the project," I said.

"Not yet, I didn't. I'm sorry, I'm getting ahead of my story. At this point I was going my own merry way. But nobody knew anything yet, except the people on the inside."

"Politicians who'd helped smooth the way for Pendrake because he'd cut them in for shares of the profits on the tower," I said. "And they didn't want it leaking out in bankruptcy proceedings because it made them look sleazy."

I was surprised that Austin didn't protest such a judgmental word, because I had a feeling the secret investors we were discussing were going to turn out to be Austin's friends, the people who'd been pressuring me to forego prosecuting him.

"But then hope gleamed," he continued. "Pendrake found another speculator, someone from Houston, who'd buy the unfinished project. Nobody'd make any money, but they could all get out from under. You could almost hear the sighs of relief.

"But the buyer had a condition. He'd only buy the tower if he could also buy the property adjacent to it, which would give him access to the expressway. He said the project was a loser without that adjacent property included.

"But no problem." Austin smiled. "The city owned the adjacent property. The same people who'd cut through the red tape to obtain building permits for George could help the new buyer buy the adjoining land too. Because the city owned it and they *were* the city. But they ran into a hitch."

"Because there was a community center on the adjacent property," I said.

Austin grimaced. "A lousy community center. Ever see

it? One little wooden building, one story and a basement, a couple of meeting rooms not much bigger than this living room, no use to anybody. Basketball court with the hoops perpetually in ruins. Nobody used the place. It would have been no loss to the neighborhood."

"But."

"But there was a technical problem. The land had been willed to the city, with a clause requiring the city to build and maintain a community center on the property. If the community center were ever removed, or if the city tried to sell the property to a private owner, the property would revert to the grantor's alternate heirs."

Austin paused, kindly, but, also kindly, didn't ask. "I'm keeping up," I volunteered. "I remember these terms from law school. It comes back to you."

Austin smiled. "Yes," he said. And returned to his story. "But again, no problem. The heirs would have been glad to sell. They'd love to inherit this land out of the blue and have a buyer all ready to take it off their hands. But there were too many threads, you see. The city couldn't sell while the community center stood on the property, and the heirs couldn't sell either. The buyer was on the verge of saying it was too complicated and walking away. Too many inquiries had been made, word was starting to leak out that this little tract was important to somebody important. The community activists got into the act and started trying to force a referendum to vote on a bond issue to improve the community center. The investors were getting frantic."

"That's when they turned to you," I said.

Austin shook his head. "They didn't need a lawyer. They already knew the legal problems. They needed an *extra*legal solution. So one night—"

"One night the community center burned to the ground," I said.

"Everybody knows that part, don't they?" Austin said.

Yes, that was the event that had nudged the scandal into the light. The fire had obviously been arson, though no one ever determined who had given the order. Pendrake Plaza's corrupt foundation couldn't bear its weight any more. The project collapsed under public scrutiny. A couple of the secret investors were uncovered; but not, as I'd now been told by both Eliot Quinn and Austin, all of them.

"Why did a couple of the conspirators allow themselves to be exposed without exposing all the rest, too?" I asked. "It seems overly noble."

Austin had gradually stripped himself of mannerisms. He'd grown calm, lost in recollection of the story. "Because there was another aspect of the story that *never* came to light," he said. "I told you, the community center had a basement. The night of the fire, it was occupied."

I blinked. I sat there picturing a family, or a crowd of children, scrambling through the dark, frantically searching for a way out through the smoke until the burning roof collapsed on them. "That's horrible," I said.

Austin nodded. "The body was discovered during the cleanup. A fire department investigator found it, and by that time the scandal had started breaking enough that he realized the news might be worth something to someone. Instead of including it in his report the way he should have, he thought he'd try to supplement his income."

"Who was he?" I asked.

Austin shook his head. That was one of the secrets he was holding. But I could find out. The inspector's identity would be a matter of public record.

"*This* was when you were brought into it," I said.

It wasn't a question. Austin nodded. "I helped smooth things away," he said. "Then we all sat tensely for weeks, waiting for someone to report that their brother or husband or father was missing. But no one ever did. Apparently it was a homeless vagrant who broke into the center to spend a warm night. Or looking for something to steal."

Which didn't diminish the crime, which was murder. Knowingly or not, the arsonist had murdered the man in the basement. Under the law of parties, so had whoever ordered the arson. It hadn't been just a financial scandal or the loss of an election that had been at stake. It had been criminal charges and the prospect of life in prison.

"Who knew?" I asked.

"The secret investors," Austin said.

I couldn't be sure who they were. Maybe some of the people who'd been calling me the last few weeks to ask for

clemency for their old friend Austin Paley. But maybe the
callers were just unwitting pawns of the real conspirators,
doing favors for friends. There was a wide web of friends.

"The arson inspector," Austin continued, "who's now retired and living in—another state. And me."

My mind spun with the plot. I'd be able to find the fire
inspector; I might be able to coerce him to talk. Doubtful:
the story implicated him as well. But if I could make him
think I already knew . . .

It could have been a minute that passed while I was beginning to put together a case. It may have been only seconds.
I remembered who was telling me the story, and I realized
how far afield we were from the case that had brought us
together.

"I'm not going to bargain away the cases against you to
get these people," I said. "If that's what you were hoping,
I might as well leave."

He shook his head slowly. "No, Mark, you don't understand. I am innocent of the charges you've brought."

We seemed to have changed subjects. Austin's face was
drawn. He was beginning to look like the portrait in Dorian
Gray's attic; still handsome, but with his paint peeling off
in spots.

"I've been set up," he said. "I was planning to come forward with the story I've just told you. I couldn't keep it to
myself any more. That body in its anonymous grave, it was
starting to haunt me, Mark. Two or three nights I even
dreamed of him, standing at my door, shuffling up to my
bed."

Austin shuddered. He did look like a haunted man. If he
was lying he was a hell of an actor.

"You may think my conscience isn't what it should be,"
he said soberly, "and I'll admit I've kept some ugly secrets.
That's why they trusted me to help hide this one. But not
murder. I balk at that. I couldn't live with it."

So? I was thinking, still trying to hold on to the thread
of the child sexual-abuse cases we had pending. Austin saw
my doubt.

"I decided to break my silence," he said. "And I made
the mistake of telling people. I tried to get someone to come
forward with me. I didn't have enough evidence of what had

happened by myself. I hoped someone else was as troubled by it as I. But they have more to lose. No one would agree to corroborate my story. One of them seemed susceptible to persuasion, though. He kept me talking until suddenly I found out I was the subject of a police investigation. That I was the prime suspect in these child abductions." He stretched a hand toward me. I remained immobile. "You see what happened, Mark. They struck first. They stalled me to keep me quiet and then they saw to it that no one would believe me when I did come forward. They've tarred me with the worst crime a man can be accused of. If I accuse *them* now, it will just look like I'm blowing smoke, trying to cover up my own guilt."

"Yes," I said.

Austin stared at me. "I swear, I've never touched a child improperly in my life. The thought is disgusting."

"So the children are lying. Every one of them."

Austin looked more sure of himself. "What's the lie? I'm sure they're telling the truth about what happened to them. Their only mistake is in identifying me. And they were led into that. A policeman or someone acting like a policeman comes to them with a photograph, in some instances long after the fact, and tells them, This is the man. You know they'd believe. They'd pick that picture out again even from a later lineup."

"Like they picked Chris Davis," I said.

"Yes." Austin was unapologetic. "That was my doing, I admit that. Once I found out what they were doing I tried to protect myself. But then Chris couldn't bring himself to go through with it. And the delay gave you time to uncover *my* deception, but not my enemies'. I know, Mark, you thought you were doing the right thing when you had me indicted. I trust you. I know you're not in with them."

When I didn't acknowledge the compliment he hurried on. "You know how these cases are. The little girls can't identify anyone. They're no evidence against me. The boy Kevin Pollard, he's so unsure he couldn't bring himself to testify. Mark, you've had to dismiss three of your four cases. Don't you see, all the cases are weak because they're fabricated."

"But there are other cases that haven't been indicted yet."

"And so haven't been tested," Austin said quickly. "Besides, you know why there are so many. You know when police have one suspect they think they can close every open case they have even if—"

"I know."

He looked at me very openly. "Well, then?"

"What proof do you have of this community center business?"

"Not much, unfortunately," Austin admitted. "I have this." He handed me a much-folded piece of paper. "That's a copy of the original arson report, that describes finding the body. The inspector prepared it to show he was ready to file it."

The document was as Austin had described it, an official report on an official form, with a date four years ago. The box for the name of the report-maker was blank.

I didn't even have to tell Austin the slight value this had. Anyone could have obtained the blank form and filled it out.

"A person, Austin," I said patiently. "Tell me who we suspect. Who were the secret investors?"

His expression didn't flicker. He was looking at me politely, waiting for my question, as if I hadn't spoken.

"Damn it, you expect me to give you a continuance on a trial set less than a week away but you won't give me a crumb of information? Tell me."

"This is why we need the time," Austin said. Now we were a team. "You can imagine how hard this will be to uncover. But I know the guilty parties. I can trap them, perhaps even bargain with them."

"The way you break a conspiracy like this," I said, "is to make the conspirators think the conspiracy's already breaking up. Set them against each other, make each one think the others are setting him up to take the fall. That's when they start talking."

"Yes," Austin said, "and with your help that's what I intend to do."

I sat and thought. I didn't believe Austin's story. I didn't disbelieve it. There were elements of the story that made some things make sense. But there were flaws, too. I pointed one out.

"Why have I been getting all these calls from politicians speaking up for you? If they're all plotting against you—?"

Austin turned a casual hand. The question gave him no trouble. "We're negotiating. They've managed to put me in an even worse position than they're in, and they've offered to free me from the false charges in exchange for my silence. They assume that now I've seen their power I won't dare cross them. And," he continued smoothly, watching me the whole time, "not to put too fine a point on it, but I do have my supporters. Not everyone who's called you knows anything about Pendrake Plaza. Some of them are just old friends genuinely convinced of my innocence. And rightfully so." He sat with his hands folded, waiting for my next question, opening himself to interrogation.

"Tell me the name of just one of the investors," I said. "Give me a starting point." Into the ensuing silence I added, "It will enrich your credibility."

The silence continued. Just as I was about to rise, Austin said, "The mayor."

I raised my eyebrows. "Now that's odd. He called me to plead on your behalf just this week."

"That's because I've been talking to him," Austin said. "I've almost got him believing the others are going to turn on him. He wants to buy us time."

I doubted I could raise a question Austin couldn't answer. Just for practice, I tried.

"Maybe everything you say is true," I said. "Except when you were brought into the scheme. Maybe you were the one who gave the order to burn down the center."

Austin only smiled, in his old self-deprecating way. "I don't give orders. If I did, who would listen? Yes, I make suggestions occasionally. Sometimes they're even followed. But do you think with my training I would suggest a crime? This obvious and unsubtle a crime? No, I was strictly the maid on this occasion. I just tidied up."

He made sense. There was no need for Austin to have been a *secret* investor. He didn't hold public office; there'd have been nothing wrong with his participation in the project. If he'd been involved in the scheme it would have been ahead of time; he would have been a perfectly public investor. I could find that out easily enough.

I stood up. "I can't give you an answer now," I said. "You'd better assume we're still going to trial next week. But I'll start digging into this. If I find anything to corroborate the story, I'll agree to a continuance while we investigate. That's all I can tell you now."

"I'll tell you where to start," Austin said. "Eliot Quinn."

He threw me off stride, as he'd planned.

"Eliot? Was he—?"

"No," Austin said reassuringly. "Eliot wasn't in on the plot. But he knows what happened, he knows what they're trying to do to me now. That's why he tried to help me by bringing Chris Davis to you.

"Eliot knows I'm innocent. Ask him."

He returned my stare as guilelessly as a child.

PART TWO

It is the nature of man to feel as much bound
by the favors they do as by those they receive.

Niccolò Machiavelli

11

If he's telling the truth," Becky said, "then the children are lying."

I'd told Becky the story immediately, without giving much thought to whether I should. She was the only confidante I had. There was unresolved tension between us, but when we were working—and we were always working—it expressed itself only in a closer ability to read each other's thoughts.

She added, "And if Kevin Pollard was lying, he's the most convincing liar I've ever seen."

"I know," was all I said. Becky kept watching me as if I were slipping away from her, which in a sense I was. I was falling into the past, into a still-real world where Becky couldn't follow, where my guides were near-strangers to her, but had once been my intimates.

In confirmation that she knew what I was thinking, Becky said, "And if you go see Eliot Quinn like he told you, you can't believe anything Mr. Quinn tells you. I'm sorry, Mark, but you can't."

"I know," I said again. That was why I hadn't run to Eliot immediately after hearing Austin's story. I hated to give Eliot another chance to lie to me. I hated to think he'd use it.

"Why do we have to decide?" Becky said. "Let's just go to trial and let all this come out. See who a jury believes."

When I hesitated she continued, "I don't think a jury would believe his cockamamie story. It's too complicated."

"It's not designed to convince a jury. It's designed to convince me."

"And has it?" Becky asked. She sounded curious. She hadn't seen Austin, she couldn't judge his credibility. Or maybe she was curious about me.

"I don't know," I said.

A month earlier, I would have dismissed the story out of hand. Now, through Eliot's stories and the pressure I'd felt myself, I had glimpsed the furtive world of backstage politics. I believed in *it*. Whether Austin was a victim of that kind of maneuvering was another question.

"You don't have much time to get sure," Becky pointed out.

If conspirators had actually framed Austin, they'd picked a hell of a crime. The victims were children, which made it the ugliest crime of all, the one with the longest repercussions, the most pain. But child sexual abuse was also the easiest charge for an innocent man to be caught in. Because children don't know. Adults are an alien race to them. Don't we all look alike?

"Let's just forget it," I said to Becky, as if dismissing the issue.

She stood her ground. "When are you going to see him?" she asked.

"Tonight."

"Hello, Mark. Nice to see you."

A lie, born out of habitual politeness. I'd given Eliot the choice of meeting places and he'd said he'd come to my home. I think Eliot didn't want his own house tainted with the memory of the meeting we were about to have.

"Come in, Eliot. I appreciate you coming. What can I get you? I've got bourbon, club—"

"Do you have tea?" he asked. In Texas tea means iced tea; he made the request more specific. "Hot tea?"

Maybe I looked surprised. He followed me into the kitchen to explain.

"I used to be hot all the time. Well, who isn't, down here? But I must be getting old. Now as soon as the sunlight grows slanted I start feeling chilled. I understand now why all those retired Yankees move down here in the winter."

Indeed, Eliot was wearing a three-piece suit, with the vest tightly buttoned, and a hat, which he'd already removed. He looked dapper as a caricature. He had a gold watch chain dangling across his stomach atop the vest. I know Eliot. He started wearing outfits like this as a costume. He'd made himself into a portrait people embraced, of an elder states-man who hadn't quite let go the reins, who had three times the style of anyone who'd followed. Now he'd become the portrait. Dressing this way to come to our private meeting proved that. Or maybe he expected me to embrace the image too. I always had.

It was six o'clock, the cusp of afternoon and evening. The slanted sunlight was almost gone. It threw a last shaft across my balcony, at the end of the white living room. I let the room grow dim as we talked and waited for his tea water to boil. After a few minutes we crossed into the living room. Eliot carried his cup right beneath his nose, letting the steam perform a facial on him.

"My one sense that's grown stronger with age," he said.

"Well, good," I said. "I need your nose." I sat in an armchair, Eliot settled himself beside me, at right angles, in the end of the sofa. I picked up two remote controls, snapped on the TV; the red power light came on on the VCR. Eliot looked at them as if I were going to show him a modern marvel. "I never knew anyone with a better nose for who was lying than you. Would you mind watching something for me and telling me what you think? It's not long."

"Of course," Eliot said.

Darkness had fallen completely, making my living room a theater. I hit another button and the snow on the screen was replaced by a picture that took a moment to sharpen. It was a young boy, sitting in a big chair that made him look even smaller. It was Kevin Pollard. Karen Rivera's offscreen voice asked him, so kindly, to tell again what had happened to him. Kevin obliged, at first with little feeling as he de-scribed a car trip, streets he didn't know, houses disap-pearing. As he grew lost in the story he grew lost in time. His face changed from that of an uncomfortable but restrained little boy into that of a much younger boy, frightened by darkness and all the unknowns the darkness harbored. When the car reached its destination it was a frightening wood, of shadows and trees both like clutching fingers. Kevin would not be comforted, and the man with him grew impatient. His need was too urgent for him to keep being soft with the boy.

Then Kevin jerked, memories of pain and fright still real in his face. He started crying. He cried throughout the rest of the narrative, though he grew less frantic. "We drove away," he finally said. "He kept saying he was sorry. He bought me an ice cream."

I let the tape run out, stopped it, ran it back to the beginning, as if raising a club to strike again. Instead I turned off the TV, let it die in the silence. The silence built. I was staring at the dead screen. I didn't look at Eliot until I turned to snap on a lamp. He looked suddenly captured in the lamplight. His face was crumpled, as Kevin's had grown. Eliot's eyes were wet. His tea was on the coffee table, no longer steaming.

"That's one of Austin's victims," I said unnecessarily. "What do you think? Is he telling the truth?"

Eliot didn't move to wipe his eyes. "What do you want?" he asked. It was the answer to my question.

"I want to tell you another story, and see if you can tell me secondhand whether somebody's lying. You already know the story, but I just heard more of the details yesterday."

I described briefly the meeting with Austin, how Austin had looked, and then relayed to Eliot Austin's explanation of the charges against him. Eliot showed little reaction. A time or two he made a rolling gesture with his hand, telling me to get on with the story, he knew this part. "So that's how Austin became the accused," I concluded. "That's why boys like Kevin and Tommy were induced to make these accusations against him. So the boy you just saw was wrong, or lying, about who raped him."

Eliot jerked his head minutely at my verb, as if he'd argue. I waited, but he didn't.

"So tell me, Eliot. Was Austin telling me the truth?"

In the spaces between my sentences Eliot was forgetting

me. His mind was far away. He made an effort to rejoin me. "About the razed community center and the body in the rubble?" he said. "Oh yes, I believe that happened. I'd heard hints. This explains them."

I was surprised. The story was true. I had a lot to do. Austin would cooperate, that was clear. If we hurried we could—

"But it's just a smokescreen," Eliot continued. "It has nothing to do with the cases against Austin."

Eliot was sharp-eyed again, watching me.

"But you tried to help him set up a substitute to take the fall for him. You tried to save him."

"Yes," Eliot said. "I'm very sorry about that. I won't lie to you again. But I still have to save Austin. I'm asking you, Mark. Let him go."

It had been a long time since Eliot was my boss. He didn't speak as if he had any residual authority over me. It was a request. I looked at him sympathetically, but that's all I did.

"Offer him probation, then," Eliot said. "I think he'd take it. He knows he needs help, he hates what he does."

He started to say more about Austin, but I interrupted. "I can't agree to anything without hearing the reason, Eliot. And I can't imagine a reason compelling enough to let him remain free."

Eliot looked at me, glanced over my head, looked back. He'd already decided what he was going to do, but he hated his decision. Finally he forced himself.

"I'm responsible for Austin," he said. "I should be on trial, not him."

"Nothing's going to come out about the old cases against Austin that never reached indictment," I said. "He certainly won't want to bring them up, and I have no reason to, either. I don't see how you'll be mentioned. These are new."

He shook his head. I shut up. Eliot knew he had to tell me or leave, and he couldn't leave.

"This is the hardest thing I've ever had to tell anyone," he finally said. "No one knows, not Mamie, not anyone."

I'd seen Eliot tell many a story. He was Irish, he always took some joy in the telling even when it was a terrible story, even when it was on himself. But in this one there wasn't a trace of pleasure. He spoke woodenly at first, doing his best to be absent while he told the story.

"My best friend in law school was Austin's father," he said. "Pendleton, his name was. Pen and I had met here at St. Mary's. We were nothing alike, I was studious and Pen was casual. He was easygoing, I was intense. So of course we became friends. Which was very flattering to me.

"Did you ever meet Pen?" Eliot asked suddenly. "No, of course not. You're not much older than Austin, are you? And Austin was just a boy when I knew his father. Sometimes—" He shook his head. His eyes were hooded, then brightened. "Pen was something special. Everybody liked him. He'd gotten on with the professors at law school as if he'd been their friend instead of their student. My standing in school was improved just because he took up with me. Pen had money, and connections. After school he went with the oldest-money private firm, while I went into the district attorney's office.

"Now this seems like such a brief period of my life," Eliot said. He would look sharply at me, gauging me, then let his eyes slide away, almost as if forgetting I was there. "It's easy to forget it. But at the time it seemed to have such permanence. Pen and me, best friends. We'd get together and tell each other what we were discovering the world was like. I was newly married to Mamie, but Pen had married young and already had a young son. Austin," he repeated, but not for my benefit. Eliot said the name softly to himself, as if just then remembering that the story he was telling was about that young boy, or for his sake.

"At first we socialized together, Pen and his wife, Julie, and Mamie and me. We'd have dinner at least once a week. Then that stopped, abruptly, and Pen became a little hard to reach. I'd call him at the office to see if he wanted to meet for a drink and he'd be gone already, but when I'd call him at home he wasn't there, either.

"So it was no great surprise when I learned that he and Julie were divorcing. Pen and I had known each other for four years by then, I suppose I was the best friend he had, so of course I saw it through his eyes. But Mamie and I were family friends, too. His son called me Uncle Eliot."

Eliot picked up his cup of tea but didn't sip from it, just

held it in his hands, as if warming them, though the cup couldn't have held much warmth by then.

"Was it a messy divorce?" I asked.

"Very. Pen had some family money, like I say. Julie had nothing, but she liked the life, and she didn't plan to work. His parents had given them the house in Olmos Park, but Julie loved it, too, and every stick of furniture in it. His parents even thought of intervening in the case to reclaim family heirlooms they'd given the couple as gifts. Of course, I was hearing all this filtered through Pen. We were having lunch often. Some days he'd come from just having met Julie and her lawyer and he'd still be red-faced, calling her the vilest names he could think of. Saying he'd see that she never got a dime of his, or the boy either."

"They fought about custody?" I asked, realizing I didn't know a thing about Austin's parents. I'd assumed he came from a moneyed background, he had that air, but the air could have been as false as so much else about Austin. I also thought about myself, growing up in another part of San Antonio. I would have been about ten then, no wonder I knew nothing about all this. But Austin, five years younger, had already been the center of a legal controversy.

"They fought about everything," Eliot said. "The divorce colored all our lives for months. Mamie and I tried to stay neutral, we still met Julie, too, occasionally. If I mentioned Pen to her she would just say I didn't understand, I didn't really know Pen. Of course a bitter woman would say that, but I could have said the same thing back to her with equal justification. Some people live such compartmented lives. I realized Pen had been like that. I knew him well, and his family, but I didn't know his friends, what he did nights after he'd moved out of Julie's house."

"And so?" I asked. Eliot's eyes jerked back to me as if I'd interrupted a private conversation. There was a pause after my question, until Eliot's eyes returned to the carpet, the walls, and my blank TV screen.

"And one day," Eliot said quietly, "all the screaming stopped. Pen grew dead quiet. He tried to concentrate on his law practice again. He wouldn't talk about the divorce at all. But it was still taking its toll on him. He suddenly looked years older—meaning he looked his age. He'd always had that boyish carefreeness, but it was completely extinguished. He started looking nervous. He'd jump if you came up beside him. I kept asking him what was wrong, but he wouldn't tell me."

I was watching Eliot, waiting for him to enter the story. It was a story he'd told no one, he said, not even his wife. I hadn't gotten the impression that was because it was someone else's secret. It was a shameful story for Eliot himself. His eyes studying my carpet reinforced the thought.

He broke his brief silence. "Until one day Pen came into my office in the courthouse with no steam at all, no anger, barely enough strength to walk, it seemed. He came straight into my office and closed the door. I asked him what was wrong, but he wouldn't say anything at first. He walked completely around the room, more than once, running his hands along the walls as if judging how thick they were. I thought he had lost his mind. Maybe he had.

" 'She's going to ruin me,' he finally said. That was how he started, no greeting, no introduction. Of course I knew whom he meant. I could see he was distraught, I tried to tell him it would be okay, he'd make more money, he could remarry and have another family.... But Pen just shook his head and glared at me as if I were talking nonsense. 'You don't know what she's going to say,' he finally said.

"He sat in front of me and just stared at me. I asked what his lawyer thought about the latest development, and Pen said no one else knew yet, that Julie had called him, Pen, at home the night before to tell him what she was going to do if he didn't stop fighting her."

"What did she threaten?"

Eliot looked up at me. "Exactly what I asked," he said. "But Pen didn't want to answer me and I was starting to think I didn't want to hear. But finally he said, 'I need your help, Eliot.' Of course I offered to do whatever I could. 'I need to talk to Austin,' he said. 'She won't let me get near him right now. But if I can talk to Austin I can straighten this out. He won't go along with her if I can talk to him first.'

" 'Go along with what?' I asked him. He didn't want to tell me, but he saw he had to if he wanted my help. He stood up and he walked away from me and he laughed, the way a man would laugh just before he shoots himself, and he said, 'She's going to say that I sexually molested my own son.' "

"My God," I said, and Eliot said it along with me, still in his story, quoting himself.

" 'Has she gone crazy?' I asked him. Pen said he thought she had. She'd reached the point where she would say anything to get what she wanted, and this was the worst thing she could think of. Well, I agreed. Wouldn't you, Mark? Can you think of a worse thing a man could be accused of? You must remember, this was the early 1950s. We never even read about such things. I was— It made my skin crawl just to hear Pen say such a thing. All I could think was that Julie must be clinically mad. The divorce had been so bitter already, it had escalated to the point that she would do anything. You see, I didn't even get my mind around the accusation itself. It was like a thick, horrible dose of poison, you'd spit it out the instant it touched your lips. Do you understand?"

"Yes," I said, because he had to hear me say it. I was thinking of Austin.

"When Pen saw I didn't believe it for a second, it didn't even cross my mind to believe it, he was relieved, and he hurried on. He said Austin had been alone with Julie for months by this time, there was no telling what she had filled the boy's head with. No telling what he might say. I told him just to let her make the crazy accusation, no one would believe her. But Pen said he couldn't let Austin be caught in the middle. If Julie convinced the boy to lie for her, it would dog him for the rest of his life. Austin's life. Understand? He was concerned about his son. And he said he couldn't let his parents even hear such a thing. They'd never be able to look at their grandson again."

Eliot stopped talking again. When I'd first turned on the single lamp it had seemed terribly bright, but now the room had grown dim again. There was nothing to be seen through my balcony doors, just the blackness of night. Anyone could be peopling that darkness, any decade. Eliot and I were completely alone, but there seemed to be any number of ghosts just outside the ring of lamplight, an arm's length away.

"What did he convince you to do?" I asked.

I'd said it to allow Eliot to skip that part of the story where he justified what he'd done, to tell him I understood, but Eliot winced momentarily, taking it like a blow.

"To go to Austin's school," he said. "Julie had said she had already told the school authorities not to let Pen see Austin, and had probably convinced Austin to run from him, too. But *I* could pick up Austin from school. I was a friend of the family. I told Pen it was a bad idea, but he said he knew his son wouldn't betray him if he could only talk to him. His eyes were so tragic I didn't know what he might do if I didn't help him. He kept saying if only he could talk to the boy. So finally I agreed to help."

"How old was Austin?"

"He was six. Just six. This was November, so he'd just begun first grade. I didn't even think much about Austin himself, to tell you the truth. I was only thinking how awful it was of Julie to be using him as a gambit this way. I'd lost sight of Julie, too, by this time. I had forgotten that I'd ever known her. She had just become this horrible, calculating witch in Pen's stories. It was almost a shock to see Austin again, to see him in the flesh, just a normal-looking, handsome little boy. They brought him to me in the principal's office. I wasn't just a family friend, you see, I was an assistant district attorney. I showed them my identification. I told them there was a family crisis, which was true enough, and that I'd been sent to bring the boy home. Austin believed me, too, when they brought him in. He was glad to see me," Eliot said quietly.

"We got into my car and drove away from school and I was talking to Austin the way I always had—"

"What was he like?" I asked.

Eliot shrugged. "He was a six-year-old boy. He was quiet, polite. I'd always liked him, but he didn't occupy much of my thoughts. This was before I had children of my own, and children didn't interest me much. The best thing about Austin was that he didn't get in the way. You could take him to dinner with adults and not even know he was there. But I suppose I'd always been nice to him. I suppose he liked me."

Now the story was disturbing me as well. My eyes were following Eliot's, to the carpet, to the darkness outside.

"A few blocks from the school I stopped the car and Pen

got into the back seat beside Austin. The boy didn't say a word. He didn't even greet his father. He slid to the far side of the seat, directly behind me, so I could no longer see him in the rear view mirror. I thought how horrible it was that his mother had done this to him, made him afraid of his own father. Pen just smiled and nodded to me in the mirror."

"Where did you go?"

"A motor lodge. Not a hotel, where we'd have to cross the lobby. A motel, where you could park your car right at the door of your room. Pen had already rented one. There was a string of the places along the Austin Highway then."

There still was, but now the interstate had turned the old Austin Highway into just a wide, decaying road, where the old motels advertised kitchenettes and weekly rates, or water beds and adult movies in the rooms. It was hard to picture the dreary old places when they'd been new, inviting.

"We went into the room, all three of us. Austin stayed as far from his father as possible, but he shrank from me, too. I was talking to him, quietly, telling him it was all right, but he wouldn't even look at me. Pen hadn't said a word. He'd taken off his coat and dropped it over a chair back and sat on the only bed in the room, and after a few minutes he said, 'Why don't you leave us alone now, Eliot, so Austin and I can talk?' "

"And you did," I said, after a long quiet spell.

"Austin was looking at me," Eliot said hoarsely, but he was talking in a rush now, and didn't stop to clear his throat. "He hadn't been before, he wouldn't look at either of us, but when he heard his father say I should leave, his eyes came up and latched on me so hard I could feel them, like hands. They were brimming with tears. His face was white, just white, almost transparent. My God, Mark, I looked at him and I thought—I still didn't think it was true, I couldn't think that, not of Pen—but I thought that Austin believed it. I thought, My God, the woman has hypnotized him."

"Don't tell me you walked out of the room," I said. It was jerked out of me, I hadn't meant to say it. I was thinking, *Don't tell me you left that boy alone with his father.*

"I said—" Eliot was almost mumbling, the way he must have mumbled what he'd said more than thirty-five years earlier, in that room on Austin Highway. "I said I thought

I should stay, in case someone tried to make something of the story later. But Pen just smiled. He'd regained his composure so completely it was as if I'd given him a tonic. He said, 'That won't be necessary, old friend.'

"And I couldn't," Eliot continued, "I couldn't stay in that room and let him see I suspected it was true, I couldn't let him believe I suspected him of something so unnatural. He was my friend. I owed him some loyalty. I tore myself away from his son's stare and went outside. I said I'd be nearby, and I left the door ajar, but it closed behind me.

"I walked up and down outside that door, making as much noise as I could. I walked around the whole motor court, to the back window of the room, but it was just a bathroom window, frosted. It was open a fraction, and I could hear a boy crying. And heard Pen say, 'Give me a hug, son.'"

"So finally," I said, and my voice was much harsher than I'd intended.

"So I hurried around and knocked and went in. Nothing had happened, Mark, I'm sure of that. Pen had removed his tie, but he was still fully dressed other than that, and the boy still had his jacket on. There was nothing—in the air, you know what I mean. Pen just smiled at me.

"But Austin wouldn't look at me at all. He didn't run to the door when I came in. I wasn't his savior, you see. I was his kidnapper. I was one of the conspirators."

"But nothing happened," I said.

Eliot was finally looking at me. "Something very important happened. I had helped Pen demonstrate to the boy that there was nowhere Austin could hide from him. That no matter who was protecting him or whom he trusted to keep him safe, his father could always get to him again."

Eliot stopped, the confession ended. "What happened?" I asked.

He sat up straighter on the sofa. "Julie withdrew her threat. You understand why, of course."

Because she couldn't rely on her six-year-old son's testimony any more. Pendleton Paley had taken that from her, with the help of my old boss. Austin would have been too afraid to accuse his father, when he'd learned he couldn't trust anyone in the adult world to believe him or protect him.

"The divorce was settled without trial after that. Both sides grew less demanding. Everyone calmed down."

"Visitation?" I asked. I'd caught Eliot's hoarseness.

"The usual arrangement," Eliot said, staring across the room. "Every other weekend, some holidays. I heard that Julie contrived as often as possible to avoid letting Pen take him, or to see that he went to his grandparents' instead. And Pen didn't press it. But I lost touch. I didn't want—Something—" He shrugged. "The next time I saw Austin Paley was when he was graduating from college. He needed law school recommendations. I was the district attorney by then and he came to see me. You know how Austin is, always friendly, polite to a fault. He was that way to me, too, but he turned away from my handshake to look at the pictures on my wall, and just before he left he looked at me perfectly levelly and unshaken and said, 'It was true, you know.' That was all he said. And he smiled and he nodded and walked out. I gave him his recommendation, of course, and saw that he got others."

But he came to you for a recommendation, I thought. *He wouldn't let you touch him, but he used the connection.*

"And what about his father?" I asked. If Pendleton Paley were still practicing law in San Antonio I would have heard of him. Even if he'd been practicing twenty years ago, when Austin was of law school age and I was a new assistant to Eliot.

"Long dead," Eliot said. "Only a few years after the story I just told you. I saw him very seldom by then. In the back of my mind I think it was a relief to hear—"

"How?"

"By his own hand," Eliot said. An old-fashioned turn of phrase that reminded me how old Eliot was. How old the story was. "He didn't leave a note, but the fact of his suicide itself told me that my suspicion had been true."

I stood up, walked stiffly into the dimness. "Did Austin's mother get Austin some help?" I asked.

Eliot looked pained by the question. "No one went to child psychologists back then. No one specialized in treating cases like this. No one acknowledged that such things happened."

"You never talked to Austin about it," I guessed. Eliot gave me a look as if I were stupid even to ask.

"But you tried to make it up to him."

"Of course I followed his career," Eliot said. "When he graduated from law school I would have given him a job, but he never applied. He didn't try to trade on what had happened. But I did what I could for him. I introduced him to judges, saw that he got some appointments."

After Austin became a defense lawyer, Eliot, the district attorney, would have been in a position to do him any number of favors. "You helped him out," I suggested.

"Once or twice," Eliot said, "I stepped into little cases and gave him a break. It helped his confidence, early on in his career. Little cases that didn't matter to anyone."

While otherwise doing away with the favor system he'd found when he first took office, Eliot had created one favored person. It made sense now, that aura of specialness Austin Paley had always carried. I'm sure Eliot hadn't intervened for him often—I would have heard if he had—but those few little favors had contributed to Austin's sense of himself. I remembered the way he always seemed to move more slowly than everyone else. People would wait for him.

"And later on he did ask you for help."

"A time or two," Eliot repeated. "It was nothing terrible, Mark. A little extra consideration when he had a special client. Just making sure the case got examined more closely."

Giving a case the kind of scrutiny few could bear. Exercising the discretion that was supposed to be for judges or juries alone.

"Until finally," I prompted.

I don't think Eliot had intended to tell me any more. He'd thought the years-old episode explained everything I was supposed to do now on the current cases. Further explanation made the story more sordid. It was in danger of turning ordinary, the old tale of favors growing bigger until the recipient owned the favor-giver.

"Finally he came to tell me he'd been arrested himself," Eliot said, after an audible intake of breath. "For indecency with a child. I think I explained to you before, we didn't—no one took those cases so seriously then as you do now. I investigated, I found the child hadn't been hurt at all. He'd been safe the whole time. It didn't amount to more than touching. I doubt we could even have gotten a conviction. But just an indictment would have ruined Austin. He came to me and cried. He wept like a baby, he swore he could control himself in the future. He was so terrified I was sure nothing like that would ever happen again.

"And he never said that I owed him. Neither of us said that I knew why he was the way he was. He didn't demand anything of me."

I hated to hear the tone that had crept into Eliot's voice. I wanted to turn away from his justifications. I didn't want to hear his implicit plea for my understanding.

Eliot probably understood how he was making me feel, or maybe he suddenly heard his own voice. "I made the case go away," he concluded simply. "I signed the dismissal myself, I didn't have anyone else do it for me."

"By the next time it happened," I said, "Austin could take care of it himself."

"He never asked me for help again," Eliot acknowledged.

This was just wrapping up, avoiding the issue, the request with which Eliot had begun his story, the reason for his confession. To understand all is to forgive all, and as district attorney I was the only person in a position to render Austin Paley concrete forgiveness.

I wondered if Eliot understood—I don't think he intended it—that implicit in his request that I let Austin off was the understanding that by doing so I would be sparing Eliot, too. Because the story of Austin and his father would certainly be brought out at the punishment phase of trial, if we got that far. And part of the story was that the district attorney of Bexar County—Eliot hadn't been that then, but that was how everyone remembered him—even the toughest DA everyone had ever known had failed to protect the boy Austin. And as a result had derailed child-abuse cases against that grown boy during Eliot's whole subsequent tenure as district attorney. It would change the way people remembered Eliot. It had already changed the way I thought of him, and Eliot realized that, from my outburst question a few minutes earlier. He didn't offer his hand again on his way out. And I didn't make him ask again. But it was not a simple request.

"Eliot," I said. "I'll think about it."

I did, all night, with only occasional interventions of sleep. When I'd wake, I'd find myself in the middle of imaginary conversations. "What do you want me to do, Eliot? Set him loose among the children of this city, assure him he's free to do whatever he wants? I don't hate him, I don't want to see him hurt. Tell me a way to deport him off the planet and I'll do that instead."

Or I'd wake to find myself very small, a boy, alone in the endless dark, listening, on the verge of tears, holding the thin sheet so tight it was in danger of tearing.

When morning finally came I was no longer tearing at the problem. Every answer seemed wrong, but the struggle had left me. The first thing that morning, I went to see Janet McLaren.

It was the first time I had. She had always come to me before, but when I called her at home early that morning she was already gone, and when she finally called me back from her office she said she couldn't get away, but she could squeeze me in between appointments.

Her office was in a twelve-story building out on the northwest Loop, near the medical center. Coming from downtown, I felt as if I'd passed into a different world, one built decades after my own, where the problems of dirt and poverty had been done away with. But in Janet's waiting room was a young girl, five or six, dressed in jeans, with a woman close beside her who glared at me in the fraction of a second before I looked away. I walked stiffly to the receptionist's window and she let me right in. The short hallway had the clinical look of a medical doctor's office, but not the right smells. It smelled of books and paper and the pine cleaner with which the janitors had mopped the linoleum floors overnight.

I found Dr. McLaren in a slightly jumbled office where framed diplomas hung on the wall beside bright, intricate posters of plants, and the heavy, somberly bound tomes on the shelves were bookended by stuffed Eeyores and Madelines. Janet was behind the desk, behind an opened file, but her eyes were closed. She was drinking black coffee as if it had been prescribed. When she opened her eyes she smiled, faintly.

"Hello, Mark. I'm sorry we couldn't have met for breakfast, but I had to rush in this morning. Someone had a bad night."

"Looks like it was you."

"Why, thanks. A child psychiatrist should know better than to stay up late watching a dumb old movie while her patients are having nightmares and waking up crying."

"What was the movie?"

She grimaced. *"The Ghost and Mrs. Muir.* And here you are, looking rather ghostly yourself, as a matter of fact."

I dropped into a chair. "I didn't have much of a night myself."

She looked at me tenderly. "Tell me all your problems. I can give you a minute and forty-eight seconds."

So I talked quickly. "I just wanted to ask you how effective all this is." I gestured around her office. "Take Tommy. Do you think you'll be able to turn Tommy aside, help him be normal?"

She didn't even correct the word. She said, "Psychiatry isn't fortune-telling. I know I can help Tommy. I don't know how much."

"What if you hadn't already started? What if he didn't start getting treatment until years later?"

The weariness had abruptly left Janet's eyes, if not the dark smudges beneath them. "How many years?"

"A man in his forties, who was molested as a young boy, who's been molesting children himself for twenty years, maybe more?"

Janet was watching me closely, obviously fitting each new detail I gave her into a pattern in her head. She realized I wasn't being abstract.

She said slowly, "A man like that, whose whole lifetime has been built around power over children, who doesn't question his values until late in life—I don't know. If he wanted to change—"

"What if he were forced to come see you, if he didn't seek treatment voluntarily?"

She just looked at me. My interjecting the question told

her I understood the importance of the detail. After a few seconds she drew a deep breath and said, "What if someone forced you into therapy to make you get over being sexually attracted to women?"

We were asking each other questions that didn't require answers, that *were* answers. I began, "But I—"

"And don't say but your orientation is normal and his is perverted, so it should be easier to change his. The sexual urge doesn't recognize convention."

"That's not what I was going to say. I was going to say I wanted to help him."

Janet looked at me the indulgent way a parent looks at a four-year-old who has offered to help fix the car. "Given what you do," she said, "the only ones you can help are the Tommys who haven't happened yet."

"You mean put this one away where he can't hurt anyone else. But suppose it *were* Tommy we were talking about? It might be, twenty years from now."

She dealt with children all day long, but childishness hadn't rubbed off on her. She was tougher than I. Janet gave me a long look that took only a second. "I'd say the same thing."

She stood up. "And that's all the time I can give you. Come back at lunch time, I'll buy you a tuna sandwich out of the machine." On her way out she squeezed my shoulder, which made me feel better for seconds after she was gone.

I thought about the task she'd given me, the only one I could perform. It was a thankless calling, being the champion of victims-yet-to-be. When I tried to picture them I pictured instead the boy Austin, alone in the dark, wondering if everyone in the house is asleep, if that small sound he hears is a footfall. His horror made unbearable because there was nowhere to turn. He couldn't run to his natural protector for shelter, because that footstep in the dark that made him shudder *was* Daddy's.

But I couldn't picture Austin *as* that boy. Emerging from that wounding helplessness, he had become a man who demanded control, whose whole character was obsessed by the need for it. I could picture the Austin I knew now in therapy, sent there as a condition of his probation: eager to learn, to confess, to change; wooing the therapist as he'd charmed everyone else in his life, but behind his tears and earnestness remaining utterly unchanged, a man who would rule others any way he could, and who viewed the entire world of children as a nation ripe for conquest.

It wasn't a question of blame. If anyone was to blame it might be Austin's father, but he probably had his own history to explain what he'd done. He was long dead, but the damage he'd done was alive in the world. Pain lives, like a radio signal continually received at farther and farther reaches, long after the transmitter has ceased operating.

I was as thoroughly sorry for Austin as I've ever been for anyone, but it wasn't in my power to help him. That he had been a victim didn't change the fact that he was a victimizer. And I was the only person who could stop him. If I didn't, if Austin managed to escape unscathed after I'd brought to bear on him all the heat I could generate, he would emerge assured of his invulnerability.

12

I owed Eliot a personal response. His office said he was gone for the day, though it was only early afternoon. Mamie told me yes, he was underfoot at home. I told her I'd drop by.

Eliot and Mamie had lived forever in Olmos Park, an old, expensive neighborhood, but theirs was one of the least grand houses. It was rock, one story, and not rambling at all. It must have bulged at the seams when their three children were teenagers. Now it looked like a grandmother's cottage, with well-tended flower beds bordering the house and an autumn wreath on the dark varnished front door. It made Eliot look rather gnomelike when he answered the door with his vest unbuttoned and his pipe in hand.

"Come in, come in," he said, and Mamie, passing through the hall behind him, called an invitation as well.

"I've just got a minute. Could you come out instead?"

As he passed through the doorway Eliot changed. He left the pipe behind and his face closed down into watchfulness.

"I've already informed his lawyer, but I thought you should know too. We'll be going ahead with Austin's trial Monday morning."

Eliot waited. Absence of expression made his face look hard.

"I can't take the chance, Eliot. My experts say someone like Austin will never change. He'll always be a threat to children. I can't—" *Neglect my responsibility,* I'd started to say, but I didn't want to sound critical of Eliot himself.

"He's not to blame," Eliot said softly, but he no longer sounded as if he were pleading, the way he had in my home. He sounded as if he were giving *me* my last chance. I didn't understand, but his tone stopped me from feeling apologetic. Eliot tried to continue: "He was just a boy—"

"He's not now. He's a grown man, he's responsible for what he does. It has to stop somewhere. Everybody can't be the victim in this. Somebody has to be the villain."

Eliot's voice was still quiet, and still hard. "I told you, I think with therapy—"

"Therapy wouldn't change him. He doesn't want to change, he just wants to get away with it. For as long as he wants." Eliot didn't offer any more argument. I felt suddenly deflated as I turned away. "I'm sorry, Eliot."

"I am too, Mark."

His voice stopped me. He'd known it would. I waited for his explanation. He didn't look away from me.

"I've agreed to represent him at trial," Eliot said.

If he had punched me I would have been no more immobilized. I don't know if Eliot thought he owed me more explanation or if my face demanded it. "Austin asked me and I agreed," he elaborated. "I hate to oppose you. And I hate like hell how it will look, what it might do to your reelection chances. But I owe that boy so much more.

"And there's one other thing, Mark." He had hold of my arm. "He's innocent. I wish I could show you the evidence, but . . ."

But we were on opposite sides now.

My car drove itself back to the Justice Center. In the DA's offices, I went straight to Jack Pfister's office. He and another investigator had a gin game laid out on a small typing table between their knees. When I went in, the other investigator swiveled away and became very busy with paperwork at his desk, but Jack just looked up at me, raising his eyebrows.

"Did you ever find out what happened to Chris Davis?" I asked.

"Dropped off the planet," Jack said.

Or into it. We knew of one buried body in Austin's past. He claimed not to be responsible for it, but he claimed lots of things.

"Put somebody in Tommy Algren's school," I said. "Don't wait until he gets out. I don't want him alone for a second."

"Already done," Jack said.

I gave him a look. "Why so skittish?" I asked.

"Just being careful. And I thought I'd stick with you."

"Not necessary," I said. "But thanks."

He shrugged.

"What else could he try?" I asked Becky Schirhart an hour later. I was hunched in the one uncomfortable visitor's chair in front of her desk, feeling hemmed in by her cubicle of an office. I was talking about Austin, but I was thinking about Eliot. That's how Becky answered.

She said, "He could get you so distracted with other thoughts that you won't be prepared for trial."

She was favoring me with the kind of warm personal regard one friend gives another while telling him he's being an idiot. "Did you ever see him try a case?" She shook her head. "He's the best, Becky. Everything I know about prosecution I learned from him, and I didn't learn everything *he* knows."

"But this time he's defending. And his defendant is guilty." I nodded, but Becky could see it didn't mean anything. "He's just another lawyer, Mark. Rusty at that."

"Oh, please don't let him make you think that. That's exactly how he'll act, until he sees his opening."

"Where are you going?" she asked.

"Away from here. You do, too. We're all set. Go have yourself a good weekend. Try not to think about the case."

She laughed.

"I know," I said. I touched her lightly on the arm. "See you Monday."

"Mark. Don't you want—?"

"No. Thanks."

I found my investigator in the kitchen, having a sandwich while waiting for Tommy's parents to get home and relieve him from duty. I dismissed him, but I let him take his sandwich with him. Tommy seemed glad to see him go. "What are we going to do?" I asked.

"Let's go outside," I said. "Got a football?" Tommy shook his head. We went out through French doors into the back yard. It was after five, late in October, a seasonless time of day and year. It could have been a summer morning or a winter noon. The sun had declined enough to lose its dominance. It left warmth behind but a chill was creeping in, around our ankles. A breeze encouraged it.

"Have you seen Steve lately?" I asked. Steve was a boy Tommy had mentioned, but only in the past tense. I figured they'd been friends.

My question took him by surprise, as I'd intended. "Steve? No."

"You don't see him at school?"

"We're in different classes," Tommy said.

"Maybe next year."

Tommy looked across his back yard as if it were a foreign place. There was a swing set in his line of vision, but it looked designed for a much younger child. "I'll be in middle school next year."

We talked about middle school, about the pleasure of not being trapped in one room all day. I hinted at the possibilities for change that middle school offered: different friends in different classes, different personality if you wanted. A whole new past and future every fifty minutes.

Tommy had greeted me in his little-man-host role. As we talked in the yard he turned back into himself, the self I knew, the serious boy who could talk about things to come in his life as if he'd already experienced them. I had helped give him that voice. In a few weeks we'd talked about many things—things that might happen in his life; not only about the past.

We didn't talk about the case. I wasn't there to rehearse, I was just fine-tuning the boy, his dependency on me. That's what I wanted, that's what I'd spent weeks trying to accomplish.

If Tommy was telling the truth, he was going to be twice a victim. Seduced and abandoned by Austin, seduced and to be abandoned by me. I wasn't going to spend the rest of my life being his tutor, his friend. Once the case was over he'd be on his own.

That's something prosecutors do sometimes: let the victim think he's their friend, their champion, when in fact the victim is only a necessary element of the case. I wouldn't let myself feel guilty about Tommy. He had to suffer this second victimization so there'd be no other victims.

This time, after what had happened with Kevin Pollard, I'd deliberately set out to bypass Tommy's parents. I wanted to replace them as the authority figure in Tommy's life. I'd put the full court press on Tommy—batting practices, walks in the park, talks about his life—as if to compress years of parenting into one brief month, and I'd succeeded so well that I'd been surprised by the ease of it. There was no one to replace. Tommy's father had abdicated the position years ago.

I didn't hate James Algren. I didn't even dislike him. I understood him perfectly. He was an up-and-coming man, already successful and on the verge of something even better. It didn't take imagination for me to put myself in his place. His work was important to him and he was good at it. It was effortless, compared to raising a son. I could see how easy it had been for Austin to insinuate himself into Tommy's life. I'd only followed the path Austin had blazed for me.

And I wasn't going to let Tommy slip away three days before I needed him.

"What's the matter?" I asked when we went back inside. Tommy shrugged.

"Nervous?" I asked.

He shook his head.

"You will be," I said. "When you walk into that courtroom and see all those people. But you only need to do one thing. Look at me."

He did. "What?" he said.

"That's it. Just look at me. When you walk in the courtroom I'll stand up. Just ignore everybody else. They're nobody anyway. They're people you'll never see again. They don't know you, they don't care about you two days later. They don't matter. You just look at me. When you get on the witness stand you'll just be talking to me, the way we've always talked. Understand?"

"Yes." He started crying. He looked away from me again. "But I don't want to be there."

"It'll be okay," I said patiently. "We can go practice right now if you want. You've already sat in the chair. You'll—"

"No, no." He shook his head violently. "I mean I don't want to testify. Against Waldo. I don't want to hurt him."

That son of a bitch, I thought. He'd managed to get to him after all. How? I seemed to see Austin Paley's softly smiling face in the room with us. He was inescapable.

"When did you talk to him?" I asked gently.

"I haven't!" Tommy shouted, as if I'd accused him. "I've just been thinking about him. He never hurt me. It wasn't only his fault, what happened. I don't want to hurt him back."

Janet McLaren had warned me to expect this reaction. Austin hadn't just molested the boy, he'd mentored him. Tommy loved him. And he felt a share in the guilt for what had happened.

"Tommy." I waited until he stopped sobbing. He looked at me, scared, understanding the authority he was defying.

"It will be years before you understand how much he hurt you," I said. "I think you're starting to feel it already. You sense it, don't you? Tommy, Austin Paley didn't become your friend and then realize how much he needed to touch you. He stalked you. From the first time you saw him, he was plotting how he could get you alone and get your clothes off. Nothing that happened was your fault. Nothing. Don't let him make you think that."

"I know." Tommy wiped his eyes with the back of his hand. His face looked blurred. "I know about that part. But I still don't want to hurt him."

"And he did the same thing to other boys, too," I continued. "And girls. And some of them *were* hurt. It's not just you. There're others we have to protect. You may think he didn't hurt you, but he might hurt the next boy, very badly. We can't take that chance, can we?"

He shook his head, halfheartedly. I continued talking gently, but now more confidingly. "I like Austin too, Tom. He's been my friend for years. I don't want to hurt him, either.

But it's not up to me. Or you. We don't get to decide whether what he did is a crime or not. Other people have already decided that. You and I have jobs we have to do. We can't get out of them, no matter what we think about them. There's a system for deciding these things, and we have to do what they tell us, like it or not."

What bullshit. I *am* the system. I decide whom to go after, and to what extent. I wouldn't let anyone take that decision away from me. Certainly not some damned defendant who'd managed to worm his way into his victim's heart.

"Do you understand, Tom?"

"Yes," he said. He'd stopped crying.

This was the payoff. I had to know now if I'd succeeded or failed. It hadn't just been Tommy's father I'd been struggling to supplant.

"But you can tell the system to go to hell," I said. "You can tell me, too. And I'll just have to go try to find somebody else to tell what Austin did to them."

I wished I could have seen my face. I'd given up sternness. I was trying to look brave but hurt, ready for the worst. Tommy studied me as if he could pluck out all the subtleties of expression, not only what I displayed but the intention behind it.

"No," he finally said. "I'll do it. You can count on me."

"Good boy," I said. I hugged him. It was a spontaneous gesture. I made it brief, then we went into the kitchen and made nachos out of Doritos and processed cheese spread. Tommy loved them. I stayed with him for half an hour after his parents came home. When I left I shook hands with him. He was so little I could have picked him up with one hand. I could have made him do whatever I wanted, but that way wouldn't work. He had to love me. I looked a question at him, and he nodded.

I am not a complete clod. I couldn't miss the comparison. Seeing Tommy with his father was, for me, like looking at old family pictures. Tommy was my son in miniature. His relationship with his father was mine with David in embryo. His father was too busy for him, except in bursts of baffling closeness that were more alarming to the boy than reassuring. The month I'd spent talking with Tommy, taking walks with him, ball tossing, represented just about the same amount of time I'd spent with David during his childhood.

I didn't know whether to expect David to be at home on a Friday night, but he was, and he wasn't alone. Vicky answered the door. "Well, hello," she said, more hearty than I'd ever heard her, pushing wide the door for me.

She was stunning. She was wearing a long white dress that made her fair skin look tanned, and left lots of skin to inspect: shoulders, chest, arms. Her blond hair was loose to her shoulders. She had, I'd never noticed before, a sprinkling of freckles across her nose. Earrings glittered halfway down her neck, it seemed.

"Quiet evening at home?" I asked.

She laughed. "We're going to a *ball*."

In a horse-drawn carriage that had started life as a pumpkin and six white mice, from the looks of her. "I hope you're the guest of honor, because you're going to put everybody else in the shade."

She dimpled, the final touch. "Oh, I'm not even half ready," she said. "Come on in."

I remembered that I had seen Vicky vivacious a time or two before. Usually she was reserved to the point of iciness, as if she were only enduring whatever occasion brought us together. Tonight she looked so happy she made me hopeful for the whole world.

If David had looked happy too I would have made a few minutes of small talk and gone on my way. He was in his den, sitting on the edge of the coffee table, forearms on thighs, holding a drink. The television was on and he was staring in its direction, but he didn't look as if he could have passed a pop quiz on the contents of the show.

"Look who's here," Vicky announced, in a tone of voice I knew well from my own twenty-five years of marriage. It means, *Shape up, Jack, we're not alone any more.*

"Hey, Dad," David said, sounding more puzzled than anything.

I'd never seen him in a tux before. "You look almost handsome enough to be Victoria's escort," I said. I resisted the impulse to straighten his tie and brush off his lapels.

I had to say something else to get the ball rolling. "You're going to a ball?"

David smiled abashedly. "It's for this charity we've gotten involved in."

"I've dragged him into, he means," Vicky said. "I'm sorry, I've got to finish making up or we'll never get there. I'm sorry, Mark."

I turned in time to catch the tail end of a look she'd shot past my back. She smiled at me.

"That's okay, I just dropped by for a minute."

"Offer your father a drink," Vicky called in departure.

David smiled like a little boy, the way he'd been treated, and extended his glass to me. "Just one sip," he said. "It's mine."

I shook my head. "Thanks, I just had some nachos that're still settling.

"So, going out together," I said, in the way I'd speak to an acquaintance met in a theater lobby.

"We do that sometimes," David said. You couldn't put anything past the boy, he was always too alert.

"Glad to hear it," I said. I glanced around the room as if something would give me an idea. Now I was embarrassed I'd come. "I was wondering if you might have a chance to play golf some time," I said off the top of my head.

"Not this weekend, but maybe one day next week."

I had to cough. "Well, that'll be a problem for me, since I've got this trial starting Monday. But as soon as it's over, start looking—"

"And the election," David said. He had a bemused but superior expression, because though my appearance had been a surprise, I was now perfectly following his expectations.

"Oh, the hell with the election," I said. "It's probably over already anyway. But this trial's important."

David didn't take the opportunity to share my burdens. He just nodded as if he already knew everything.

I started shuffling toward the door. "You doing okay, except for the misfortune of having to attend this ball?"

"I don't mind," he said.

"Really? You look pretty tragic about it."

"Would you rather have found me alone?" he asked.

I was close to the wide doorway leading out to the entryway. "I just dropped by, I didn't have anything in mind.

I just wanted to see you." As usual, I was making my way out too quickly, fending off attack on the way. Whatever I'd wanted to accomplish, I hadn't. I stopped.

David provided a thin opening. "Why?" he asked, sounding, I'm sure, more vulnerable and hopeful than he would have wanted.

"Because I care about you, David. I love you, and I'm concerned about you. I don't dislike Vicky. But she's not my child. It's you I worry about. If you were happy I'd be happy. But every time I see you you're either alone or unhappy-looking."

"I'm fine," he insisted.

I just looked back at him. He grew angry under my gaze. He waved the hand holding the drink, sloshing it. "Do you care about what I want," he asked, "or just what you want me to be like?" I didn't answer. "I'm *happy*," he insisted.

It was only my expression he kept having to answer. "Look," he said. He waved me over, took my arm, and led me through the kitchen, out the back door onto the patio. There were two tall pecan trees in David's back yard, the shade of which had prematurely killed the grass. A scattering of leaves blew across the bare ground.

"I don't owe you an explanation," David said.

"I don't want one."

"Dad, I am happy. I have just the life I want. Maybe Vicky and I aren't in love, but we're comfortable. We don't pick at each other, we let each other go our own ways."

I was shocked. Not in love? They were too young to have fallen out of love. "But that's not marriage," I said.

David sighed. "Yes it is. It's our kind."

I continued, groping for words. "It's roommates. It's—it's business partners."

David's vulnerable look was gone. He had no trouble looking at me. "That's what I thought marriage was," he said. "People living in the same house, getting along with each other. Smiling over breakfast, then going their own ways."

I took it. I let him see I'd felt it. He looked a trifle scared, the way a boy looks who's punched his opponent and drawn blood, so he suddenly realizes how grim the fight is. I answered him quietly.

"David, you don't know. You don't have the perspective. Your mother and I were in love. My God, we were in love when we were eighteen years old, and there's no love like that. There's no *feeling* like that in this life. We couldn't—" I was struck dumb by images of Lois. Lois young. Her face, over and over, laughing, crying, gazing at me. Green fields, deep woods, the sea. Fighting to get each other's clothes off, buttons popping. Sitting beside each other silently for hours, studying, then looking up at the same moment. "You didn't exist then, David. For you to deny it now—to deny *yourself* that. You've shoved right on past life, David. Why are you in such a hurry? Where do you need to get so fast?"

"I saw you together, Dad. What good is all that wild youthful passion if it disappears so completely that you can spend a whole evening together without speaking to each other?"

"We spent half a lifetime together, David. Longer than you've been alive. Everything fades in that time. That doesn't mean there's nothing left, or that either of us regrets that time. I wouldn't give up those memories—"

"But you see," he said reasonably, "Vicky and I just came to that point sooner, easier, without any bitterness."

I stared at him, appalled. "Some day you'll be forty, David, and you'll explode."

He'd regained his composure and with it his superiority. "I don't think so," he said comfortably.

We went back inside the house, and straight on through the living room. I wasn't going to linger. It was best, when things had gone so badly, to withdraw quickly, not prolong the unpleasantness.

Wasn't that what I'd always thought?

I turned at the door. David almost bumped into me. "I'm going to be around," I told him. "You're going to find me underfoot. When you need me, let me know, okay?"

He didn't look quite so superior. I'd surprised him, which for the moment was about the best I could hope for. I hugged him, too abruptly. He was stiff as a scarecrow made of pipes.

"Tell Vicky I said goodbye," I said.

On the Saturday night of the last weekend before trial, I arrived at a house in Terrell Hills carrying a small, discreet bouquet of flowers. It was a stucco house, big and imposing, but with a friendly bay window. A circular driveway took up most of the front yard, leaving only a small, heavily land-scaped plot of earth bristling with flowers hanging on against October. I stood looking at the house, thinking about driving away again.

But at that moment the front door burst open, so I had to start walking as if I'd never been standing there staring. A girl was carrying a hanging bag of clothes. She stayed in the doorway, turned back to call inside. As I drew near she turned abruptly, almost in my face, and said, "Oh! Hi! I forgot Mom was having company."

Dr. McLaren said, "Don't believe it, she's been standing inside that doorway for five minutes, casually holding that bag, peeking out the window."

The girl laughed indulgently. She was about twenty, long-legged, thin—too thin, one would say, if she were a daughter rather than a model in a magazine—with dark hair to her shoulders and sparkling eyes and pale skin. She might have looked rather drab without her smile and her animation, but we would never know for sure.

"Besides which," Janet continued, "she was supposed to be gone this afternoon, until she heard I had—a visitor coming."

The girl stuck out her hand, making me shift the flowers. "I'm Eloise." She had a firm grip. "Mom, would you mind getting that other bag for me? Do you know how to put the top up on one of these?"

Janet smiled a greeting as she withdrew, as I said, "Not really," about the dark green convertible sports car in the circular driveway. Eloise dropped the hanging bag unceremoniously into its miniscule back seat. "Never mind, just pull when I say, okay?"

I set the flowers down, but she immediately snatched them up. "Oh no, not on the hood, they'll wilt. Flowers. That's so—"

"Please don't say sweet."

"—thoughtful. Nobody does that any more."

This was the interrogation I'd planned to do on Dinah's first date: small talk, friendly, but with a maximum of dis-comfort effect. I steeled myself not to put my hands in my pockets. "Really I'm just here on business. We need to talk about your mother's testimony."

Eloise stepped close to me to return the bouquet. "Right, you just brought the flowers to fool the neighbors."

Her look from under her brows invited confession. "You have your mother's mouth," I said instead.

It quirked into a broader smile. Janet came out of the house carrying a small suitcase. "Is that everything?"

"Ah, the endless parade of beaus," Eloise said. "You did get rid of that last one, didn't you? He's not still upstairs?"

"Get out of here," Janet said. "Go on." Then they flung themselves at each other as if gravity pulled them that way, as if all they had to do was stop resisting and they'd be drawn together from miles apart.

Feeling intrusive, I stepped into the house. I was in a white-tiled-floor entryway lighted by window panels around and above the front door. To my left was a living room with a bleached oak floor and cream-colored wallpaper with a tiny pale blue floral print. And flowers for miles: a large arrangement on a table in the entryway, three more arrangements I could see in the living room. I could have dropped my tiny bouquet into any of them and it would never have been seen again.

"Eloise is on her way back to Austin," Janet said. "She's my youngest, I spoiled her. What can I say? Everyone wonders what a child psychologist's children are like, but I think Eloise would have turned out the same way no matter how we'd raised her. She has a mind of her own."

"Then that must be how you raised her."

Janet smiled. She'd been wiping her cheek as she came inside and I'd given her a moment, standing as if still admiring the entryway. When I turned to look at her completely she said, "I'm not half ready, of course."

"Then I can't wait to see the final result." She was wearing a dark blue dress that displayed her without encasing her, with a thin gold necklace close around her throat. Her hair looked no color at all, the color of elegance, and her eyes were the shade of the dress. She looked even better when her cheeks flushed at my compliment.

"How nice," she said. "I love flowers."

"Gee, really?"

As she led me into that living room I said the obligatory. "Beautiful house."

"Yes. I got it, Ted got to keep his practice."

"He's a lawyer?"

"Doctor. Orthopedic surgeon."

"Ah. You met in medical school."

"No." Janet hesitated. "I didn't go to medical school until years later, sort of to find out what kept Ted so fascinated he could never get home before nine. Then it turned out his fascination wasn't strictly medical."

She realized there was very little I could say to that, so she kept talking. "I should have moved some place smaller years ago. But I wanted the kids to come home to the house they grew up in. Would you like the tour?"

I felt the house spreading around and above me, every foot of it saturated with her memories. The kids' bedrooms, the pictures either displayed or put away in cupboards, the scenes that had happened here, and here, and several here, years jumbled and overlapping, occasions happy and forlorn.

"No," I said.

"Good. Maybe some other time. Maybe one room at a time, over several visits. Or—"

"Maybe not," we both said. Janet continued, "Sit down. What would you like to drink? Scotch? Wine?"

She had the makings handy. We talked while she poured. We told each other our children's ages and occupations, then capped that conversation because any more of it would have led to talk of ex-spouses, and it was too early to expose each other to that. Janet sat beside me on the couch but not too close and clinked her glass quietly against mine but without offering a toast. I sipped and cleared my throat.

"We probably won't call you to testify the first day. It probably won't be until—"

"I know," Janet interrupted. "You told me." She hesitated. Hesitation and small talk had comprised our whole conversation so far. "Let's not talk business," she said.

"Right, you're right."

I had the sudden feeling Janet was going to ask me why I'd called her, and I didn't have an answer. A date seemed so juvenile. How could we approach it any way but awkwardly? Linda and I had never dated, we'd fallen into each other when we could no longer stop ourselves. Becky hadn't offered me a date, she'd offered herself.

That's why I was there. I'd grown into a perpetually mournful after-working-hours state, replaying to exhaustion my loss of Linda, of my family, of any personal life. If I'd been noble about Becky, then I needed to do something about the one new person in years who *had* interested me.

So I was there in Janet's lovely living room, feeling sixteen.

"I made a reservation at L'Etoile."

"Oh. Good," she said.

"What's wrong with that?"

"Nothing, it's one of my favorites. Well, it's just that it's almost my neighborhood tavern, I always see half a dozen people I know there—"

"Oh, I didn't realize we were skulking around. Well, I know this great little inn in Fredericksburg, they serve dinner right in your room."

She laughed and put her hand on mine. "It's not that. It's just that people would come up to our table, or I'd feel like I had to stop by theirs, and I don't want us to be interrupted."

No, we wouldn't want anything to sidetrack this scintillating conversation. "How about La Scala?"

"Oh, another favorite. But I happen to know the Tuckers are having a private party there tonight, and everyone—"

"Listen," I said. "On this flood of dates of yours, is there any place you find safe to go?"

"That was just Eloise being an idiot."

"But you go out."

She sized me up. "Is that important to you?"

"No. Why would I—"

"Listen. Mark." She sighed, but she didn't stop looking at me. "When Ted left, or I kicked him out, or whatever happened, I felt very, very low. I'd lost the only man I'd ever loved just because he found someone more—attractive. You know how that makes a woman feel?"

"I know how it feels to lose someone."

"But—" She clenched her fist in the effort to make me understand. "What I did was, after an appropriate interval spent in a vegetative state, I picked myself up, got myself together, and set out to dazzle every male I saw. This was ten years ago, when I worked at it I could still be—"

"Devastating."

She smiled. "Let's just say I was near the top of my form. And I wanted to know it. I don't mean I slept around, that wasn't what I was interested in, I just wanted to feel that response. And I mean, I got dolled up to go to the grocery store. I lowered my voice for waiters. No one was safe. My women friends stopped inviting me to their parties.

"But when I let myself get a little close to a couple of particular men, I found I just didn't want it to go any further. I thought, What's the point? In a few years either he finds somebody new or I get bored with him."

I found it very easy to follow her stories. I could say the punch lines along with her. "So you put away your sequined sheaths and ever since you've lived a life of quiet contemplation."

"Not quite. But this is the first date I've looked forward to in quite a while, and I'm wondering now if I want to try hard to make it work or if I want to deliberately screw it up."

I felt a great ease descend on me. "Ah. Yes."

Her face brightened. "That's how you feel too?"

"I didn't until you described it, but now I think I do. Did. Have been. So which should we do? Work at it, or—?" To cast my vote I stood up, slipped off my suit coat and laid it across a chair, then returned to the couch.

She considered. "I know a good pizza place near here that delivers."

"I know it too. I like their Don Corleone combo."

She widened her eyes at me. "Oh, the heart attack special. How are your arteries? Do you jog?"

"No. I pace."

"Their number's beside the phone in the kitchen," she said. "And I'll permit you to loosen your tie if I can take off this dress."

From my seat I could watch, through the entryway, her legs going up the stairs. I imagined her changing clothes in that room upstairs, and my imagination wasted no effort on what the room looked like.

* * *

"What?" she said later, brushing at the collar of the white blouse she'd changed into, along with jeans. "Did I spill?"

The remains of the pizza and salad were back in the kitchen. We were still working on the cabernet. We'd talked about our professions, dipped back into families, talked about books, movies, where we'd been students. We'd never again gotten as personal as Janet had to start the ball rolling, but I felt as if I knew her. She must have realized she'd been more giving in the conversation than I had. "So tell me something awful about yourself," she said abruptly.

And I found that as much as I'd laughed in the last hour, that subterranean river of melancholy was still flowing. Now it was red like the wine. "I've lost everyone I ever cared about," I said, "and I wonder sometimes if that's just the way life happens or if I did it."

Janet sat up straighter. "Whoa, what are you trying to do, top me? Not *every*body, that's just a cliché. Maybe a wife or girl friend or two, but not children. Friends?"

"Go ahead, I'll stop you when you hit one."

"Mark, seriously." She touched my hand again.

"No, not my last good friend," I said slowly. "I'll start that Wednesday."

"You don't lose a friend over every case you try, do you?"

"This is something special. If I ruin his client I'll be ruining Eliot too. Eliot will probably have to bring up Austin's childhood during punishment, what he helped do to him. That will start people wondering what Eliot did *for* Austin later to make it up. And if I don't ruin them both, if I lose, how will I ever forget that Eliot set loose a man who—"

I stopped. I was talking business.

"Mark?"

"This is one of those times when touching would be appropriate," I said.

She wasn't slow about it. She continued flowing toward me and put her arms around me. I clutched her, very tightly at first, then more loosely. We mumbled inarticulate syllables. That was how I found her mouth. After that I felt her fingers on my back. It was no longer a hug of comfort. It could have become painful, in fact, if it hadn't felt so good.

When we drew slightly apart, still holding hands, she smiled, then frowned and again brushed at the front of her blouse. "Are you sure I don't have a stain? You keep looking at my blouse."

"Not at the blouse," I said. She laughed and came to me again.

That part was effortless, thrilling, the touching and tasting and wondering if this skin would become more familiar and more exciting in time. But when my mind became as engaged as my hands, plotting what to do next, I slowed. Next week she would be my witness. I didn't want a closer connection with Janet until after that.

Thinking is a terrible thing.

We talked some more. Even when we stopped holding hands I could still feel her. That feeling was good enough, for both of us, for the time being.

When she walked me to the door I tried to warn her about the week ahead. "The next time you see me, I'll be very different. So will everybody else."

"What do you do, change personalities, like suits?" She laughed.

I found her so appealing I kissed her again, for the last time, before trial.

13

Lawyers have trial personalities. It's not strictly voluntary. I've seen the nicest man I know turn into a slavering werewolf every time the jury files into the box, then smack himself in the forehead when they were gone and ask himself, "What am I doing?" I've seen laughing, casual women turn into tight-mouthed statisticians. Quiet homebodies turn into shouting idiots. Good trial lawyers can turn it on and off. The best have several personalities they can slip into and out of as the occasion or the witness demands. I waited nervously for Eliot's appearance.

He wasn't on yet when he came in. The three of them entered together, Eliot and Buster Harmony flanking Austin, chatting as if they'd just finished a round of golf.

"He looks nervous," Becky said.

"That's just what he wants you to think. He's ready."

"How long has it been since either of them tried a case?"

"That doesn't matter."

Eliot took the lead defense counsel's chair, near me across the narrow space between the counsel tables. Before sitting he stood over me without offering a handshake.

"I can't wish you luck, Mark. But I wish we were both somewhere else."

"This is my favorite place in the world, Eliot."

Damn it, he'd already made me start sounding stupid. "Easy, big guy," Becky muttered.

*   *   *

When Judge Hernandez took the bench he looked unhappily at us, then motioned us forward with small movements of his fingers, a very subtle gesture for someone of the judge's expansive personality. He looked for the first time like a man who didn't enjoy the spotlight.

"I feel it is my duty," he said quietly when Eliot and Buster and I were at the bench in front of him, "to inquire if there is any chance of a settlement in this case. If a postponement would help you reach agreement, I am prepared to grant one."

He'd made this speech with his eyes downcast, shuffling their way around the objects on his bench. But when he finished he looked closely, almost imploringly, at me.

"We'd be happy to discuss—" Buster began heartily.

"No," I said. "There's no chance."

Judge Hernandez tried to regain his normal bluster. "All right, then," he said snappishly. "Let's get on with it." His hands did the duty of brooms, waving us away.

The judge was in a tight spot and could easily put me in one. He was undoubtedly under a lot of pressure, just as I'd been, from Austin's political cronies. Buster Harmony's presence at the defense table was a constant reminder of that pressure. And Judge Hernandez was in a position to accommodate them. He could wreck my case any number of ways, such as by ruling that my child witness was too young to be qualified to testify. He could cast subtlety to the winds and rule that my evidence wasn't enough to prove guilt, setting Austin free.

And destroying his own career. No matter how many powerful backstage men the judge might please with such a ruling, at the next election voters would remember the judge who so favored a child molester that he let him go without even giving a jury a chance to decide his guilt.

The judge's self-interest was as much on my side as on Austin's. And I thought Judge Hernandez had too much pride to appear so obviously in someone's pocket. From his grumpy, stiff-necked expression that morning I believed I was right.

But there were more subtle ways he could screw me in an attempt to please his friends. He would bear watching.

We were all still rather low-key. The seats behind us held

thirty or forty people, reporters and friends and mere spectators, but we were still essentially offstage. The jury panel
hadn't been called. I looked at Austin Paley, sitting at the
defense table. He turned to me, not offering the comradely
smile I knew so well. He just gazed at me rather sorrowfully.
He didn't look frightened, just sad, as at watching a friend
destroy himself. I returned his gaze for a long time, studying him.

When the prospective jurors entered the courtroom we
were facing them, with the judge behind us. I don't know
what kind of faces the others put on for the panel. A lot of
lawyers smile insipidly. I sat quietly myself, hands folded,
glancing neutrally at their faces as the prospective jurors
took their seats. They looked back at me nervously or intently or glanced away as if embarrassed to be there, as if
they were on trial themselves, which in a way they were.

Like all trial lawyers, I fear and mistrust juries. Who are
these strangers who come straggling in off the streets to
judge our work, knowing nothing about the law or the history behind the case? But jury *panels* are even more frightening, because of their potential: thirty-two or more people
out of whom we choose twelve to judge us. Somewhere
there, I knew, were twelve people who would convict anyone I showed them. Also scattered through the panel, the
defense hoped, were twelve people who would vote for acquittal if given the chance. But how were we to winnow
them out, when they sat there ready to lie to us and disguise
their feelings and try like hell to get off the jury or get on?
Jury selection is the worst part of trial, the part where you
can win your case or hopelessly fuck it up, with no idea
which until it's too late.

Becky and I wanted parents on the jury, people who
would fear that their own children could fall into the hands
of a monster such as we were going to portray. But it soon
became clear that the defense might want parents as well.

"How old is your daughter, Mrs. Paglia?" Eliot asked,
smiling but in a formal way, not trying to be insidious.

"She's seven," the prospective juror said quickly, the way
she'd answered every question, sure of herself.

Eliot tilted his head as if he could see the child in memory.
"Has she ever said something to you that you thought might

not be strictly true, but that she said just to get your attention?"

The woman appeared to think it over, but was already shaking her head before the question was done. "No, I don't think so."

"No?" Eliot asked incredulously.

And around the woman, other members of the panel were looking skeptical, or smiling in disbelief.

"She's never shaded the truth just a little, or said something for effect, or exaggerated? Goodness, what an honest girl. We need to have her testifying in this trial," Eliot said, drawing laughter.

Buster, beside him, was noting the other members of the panel who shook their heads in disbelief at the idea of a perpetually truthful child.

It's called poisoning the panel. Eliot's questions weren't aimed just at the one prospective juror he was questioning. They were aimed at the whole panel. And they weren't just eliciting information, they were conveying it. Through the questioning of one prospective juror Eliot had ferreted out others on the panel who might be of use, and he'd planted the idea in all their minds that children lie, they can't be trusted.

We did some poisoning of our own, of course. "How do you know when someone's lying to you, Mr. Hendricks?" Becky asked curiously.

"I don't know," the middle-aged service technician said uneasily, "watch his eyes, see how nervous he looks."

"Really? Does that work for you?" Becky asked as if she genuinely wanted to know.

The poor man shrugged. "I don't know. I guess not too many people lie to me."

People around him nodded. Becky nodded too. "Because I'll tell you," she said, "I can't ever tell. I believe everybody. I'm the easiest mark in Texas." Becky was the youngest of the four of us lawyers facing the jury. The jurors smiled at her, at her naïvete. They believed in it instinctively.

"I've made a rule for myself," she went on. "I never make a major purchase the first time I go look. Because when that salesman starts talking, my mouth just goes dry from hanging open. I believe every word he says. I'd buy anything. So

I make myself step back, and go home, and then I think, 'Wait a minute, this guy's trying to sell me something.' "

Jurors nodded again. Oh, sure, *salesmen* will lie. We thought you were talking about real people.

"And sometimes," Becky went on, "I've heard other prosecutors in our office talk to Mr. Blackwell here, who's our boss, and they tell him what a wonderful job they just did in a trial, how they asked great questions and argued brilliantly and really kicked some defense lawyer's— Well, you know how people will talk. And I just listen in admiration, hoping I can be that good some day.

"Then later I hear from other people who watched the trial and they say, 'You know, Eddie didn't really do such a hot job at trial, he just got lucky, he just stumbled around and somehow it worked out.' "

Jurors were nodding again. Oh sure, people with something to gain will lie. They'll lie like fiends.

"And what I've learned"—Becky no longer sounded so ingenuous; she appeared to have grown up before the jurors' eyes, grown older and wiser and harder to fool—"is that people with the strongest motive to lie sometimes sound the most sincere. Somebody who just comes forward to tell you his story because he thinks he should, without anything to gain from it, sometimes stumbles a little and seems unsure of himself, but somebody else who really has something to lose, who *has* to make you believe him, he's practiced and he's calm and his face just shines with sincerity. Because he *has* to convince you. Has that been your experience, Mr. Hendricks?"

Mr. Hendricks's answer didn't matter. It was just an opportunity for Becky to explain that if Austin Paley sounded believable when he testified it would be because he was on trial for his life. The jury panel was no longer smiling at Becky. They looked sobered. Several of them glanced at Austin. They knew what we were talking about.

The judge let the prospective jurors go to the bathroom and get drinks for a few minutes, and the opposing lawyers separated. Becky and I made our strikes. We couldn't make sure anyone we wanted would be on the jury, we could only keep off the ones we disliked. We got to strike ten and the defense got ten. The twelve who were left, the ones neither side was sure about, became the jury. I watched them take their seats, certain as I always am that I'd made mistakes in their selection.

". . . We expect the evidence to show that the defendant cultivated a group of children, that he gradually singled out one of them, deliberately got close to this boy. Until the boy came to rely on the defendant, to think Austin Paley was his friend. And when he'd finally won that trust, Austin Paley violated it in the worst way an adult can harm a child, by raping the boy."

I didn't shake with rage as I made my opening statement, or tremble on the brink of tears. I looked the jurors in their faces and kept the facts I expected to prove short and straightforward which, Becky and I agreed, was the kind of case we had. I sat back, letting Becky answer Judge Hernandez's order to call our first witness.

That was a nice, competent lady named Maria Alonzo, who testified that Austin Paley had been a licensed realtor for almost twenty years. In answer to Becky's further questions Ms. Alonzo explained to the jury that such a position would allow the defendant access to lockbox combinations on houses for sale.

"So the defendant would have free entry to a large number of vacant houses in San Antonio?" Becky asked.

"Yes."

When Becky passed the witness Eliot said something that troubled me slightly. "No questions," he said, glancing up to smile at our witness. Well, the defense could hardly deny that Austin held a realtor's license.

Next Becky called an officer of a real estate company to testify that a house at a certain address had been vacant during the whole month of May two years ago. Any jurors who had listened very carefully to my opening statement had a chance of understanding where this was leading, but the information was less than scintillating. Again, Eliot asked no questions on cross. Buster Harmony looked bored and impatient, and leaned across to whisper to Eliot.

We hadn't used up half an hour of trial time when Becky called Debby Wesley, a twelve-year-old girl who'd probably been cuter and more pliable two and a half years ago. I wanted to ask for a brief recess to approach the witness and slap the chewing gum out of her mouth.

"Where do you live, Debby?" Becky asked her, smiling.

"Here in San Antonio."

Like pulling teeth. It took another question to elicit the address, 814 Sparrowwood, which the jurors, if they had phenomenal memories, would realize was next door to the vacant house about which they'd just heard testimony.

"How long have you lived there?"

"Since I was little," Debby said, a little irritably, as if offended by the implication that she was one of those flighty types who move all the time.

"More than three years?" Becky asked, still smiling, as if little Debby were the sweetest thing she'd seen in a week.

"Oh yeah."

"Do you remember when the house next door, at 818, was vacant for several months two years ago?"

"Yeah. We didn't think anybody was ever gonna buy it."

Those little unelicited bursts of recollection are nice, they add authenticity. They also make the lawyer doing the questioning cringe with the fear the witness will rattle on and add something else, damaging to the case. Becky's voice grew a little tight.

"Specifically do you remember whether it was vacant in May of 1990?"

"I guess." The near-teen pushed her lank hair back off her cheek and cracked her gum.

"Don't guess, Debby. The jury has to know for sure. That last month of school two years ago, when you were in fourth grade, was the house next door empty?"

"Oh yeah. Yeah, I remember then. I had Miss Jennings, I couldn't wait to get out of her class."

So we had finally pinned down the date. Two or three of the jurors looked as relieved as I felt. A couple of the motherly ones looked as if they wanted to push our witness's face into a sink of soapy water. I scribbled a note to Becky.

"Did something happen with the house next door that month?" Becky asked.

"You mean when he came and started fixing it up?"

Becky used the natural occasion, standing and walking

slowly to stand behind Austin. "When you said 'he,' were you pointing at this man?"

"Yeah."

"Your Honor, may the record reflect that the witness has identified the defendant?" Becky took her seat. "Tell us about that," she said. While Debby did, Becky read my note and glanced at me with a small frown. I nodded for emphasis.

". . . we thought he was gonna move in."

"Sit up straight, please, Debby," Becky said, not harshly, but it was such a departure from her earlier tone that Debby looked startled and did indeed rise out of her slouch. One of the women on the jury nodded and one of the men looked satisfied. I crumpled my note. It's a mistake for a lawyer to think you have to treat every one of your witnesses as if she's your own dear child. Jurors understand that you don't pick your own witnesses. Some of them are criminals and some of them are not too bright and some of them need to be told to sit up straight and spit out their gum.

"How is it you remember the defendant?" Becky asked.

"Well, he was right next door, and he was outside a lot, working on the yard and fixing up the house, and I used to go over and talk to him."

Little flirt, I thought, then grimaced, wondering if anyone else was thinking the same thing.

"Were you the only one of the neighborhood kids who started hanging around the house where the defendant was working?"

"Oh, no, there was a bunch of us. Kids'd ride their bikes by and stop, stuff like that."

"Do you know Tommy Algren?" Becky asked neutrally.

"Yeah, he lives on my street. He's a little kid, though."

Bless you for that, Debby.

"Was he one of the children who started hanging around at the defendant's house?"

"Yeah."

Whew. I doubted that anyone realized how tough this short line of questioning had been, with our little darling continually veering outside the outlines of her testimony as we'd prepared it. It was a relief when she finally said what we needed and Becky could pass her. But Becky didn't relax. She couldn't, not with Eliot now doing the questioning.

Eliot smiled. Debby smiled back.

"You have a remarkable memory, Debby, to remember a man you only saw a few times two and a half years ago."

Debby shrugged, in that charming way she had.

"How many times did the prosecutors show you pictures of Mr. Paley before you identified him?" Eliot still smiled.

"Four or five times," Debby said.

I didn't wince, except internally. Becky rolled her eyes and made a note on the yellow pad in front of her.

"And when you practiced the testimony you were going to give today, did they tell you where Mr. Paley would be sitting in the courtroom?"

"Yeah," darling Debby agreed. Becky made another grimace and another note.

Eliot got down to business. "Now, this man at the house next door, what did you talk with him about?"

Debby frowned. Her remarkable memory took flight. "I don't really remember talking to him much. I'd just go over there 'cause there were other kids there, you know. Mostly I'd just talk to them."

Eliot nodded with a satisfaction that was probably apparent only to me. "So you don't remember him saying anything to you."

"Not really."

"Did he ever ask you to come inside the house?"

Debby wrinkled her nose to help herself think. "Nah, I don't remember going inside."

"There were always other children around?" Eliot emphasized.

"Yeah."

"The man didn't ever make you uncomfortable, did he, Debby? He didn't ever say anything bad to you or touch you in a way that bothered you, did he?"

Debby started shaking her head, then checked herself. "Once I was standing next to him and he was talking to all of us and I started talking to my girl friend and he reached down and squeezed my shoulder to make me shut up. It really hurt, too."

Hah, I thought. At least Debby's flighty memory could offer unpleasantries for the defense to step in, too.

Eliot looked unhurt. "Did he ever take you anywhere in his car?"

"Nah."

He decided to quit there. As soon as the witness was returned to her Becky began asking questions, not bothering to try to charm the witness with a smile first.

"Debby, you said you identified the defendant after we showed you pictures of him four or five times. How did we do that?"

Debby blinked. I was afraid she'd forgotten already. "His picture was mixed in with other people's pictures."

"Yes," Becky confirmed. "And every time we showed you a group of pictures, you picked out the defendant's picture, didn't you?"

"Yeah."

"So it didn't take you four or five times to pick out his picture," Becky made crystal clear. "You picked it out every time we showed you pictures. Isn't that right?"

Debby nodded. Becky had to tell her to answer aloud.

"You also," Becky went on rather grimly, "told Mr. Quinn that Mr. Blackwell and I told you where the defendant would be sitting in the courtroom. What did you mean by that?"

Debby demonstrated with her hands, as if moving doll furniture. "You know, you told me you and Mr. Blackwell would be sitting here, and the jury'd be over there, and the defense table here, and the judge up beside me." She smiled up at the judge, who couldn't decide whether it was more politic to beam at the little tyke or to glare sternly at her, so he gave free rein to his natural inclination and just stared at her as if she were a stain on his witness chair.

"And that there'd be people in the audience," Becky prompted her. Eliot didn't bother to object that she was leading the witness. He sat as if as curious as anyone why the prosecutor was having such trouble making her witness's testimony sound the way the prosecution wanted it to sound.

"Yeah," Debby said blankly.

"Did I ever say anything to you like, 'This is where the

man will be sitting you have to identify,' or, 'Be sure to point at the man sitting at the defense table'?"

"You didn't have to tell me, I know it's him."

"But did I? Or did Mr. Blackwell?"

Debby thought she'd already answered. "No."

"No," Becky said firmly. Having worked so hard to clean up two of Debby's answers, Becky didn't elicit any more. Eliot didn't have another go at her either. Debby went traipsing down the aisle and out of our lives.

We hadn't liked Debby much, but she'd been the surest of our child witnesses, because she was the oldest. We put on two more after that, including a boy who *had* gone for a ride to the store with Austin, but hadn't made the final cut. Austin hadn't even touched the boy, a fact Eliot was careful to emphasize on cross-examination. But we'd established that all three children remembered Austin as the friendly man who'd seemed to live in the vacant house on Tommy Algren's street for a month or so around the time of the offense named in the indictment.

Becky and I had debated whether to put on these children as part of our case in chief or hold them in reserve for rebuttal. The latter might have been better: let Austin testify that he'd never seen Tommy before, then bring on these children to say they remembered the two of them together. We'd decided instead to put them on first because our case would have been so brief otherwise. We had no medical evidence. Tommy showed no signs of scarring, and no medical exam could determine whether he was a virgin. We had no cops. There'd never been a police investigation of this particular accusation. We had essentially nothing but Tommy. We were afraid if we put them head to head, Tommy against Austin, the adult could leave such a strong impression of innocence that our attempts to bolster Tommy's testimony afterward would be hopeless. We wanted to make our case as strong as possible from the beginning, so the jury would already be convinced of Austin's guilt before he took the stand. The children, at least, had been able to corroborate part of Tommy's story. But the burden of our case still rested heavily on Tommy.

I rose to say, "The State calls Tommy Algren," and I

remained on my feet, looking back up the aisle, waiting for his entrance.

The defendant enjoys protections no one else in this free land does. Rightfully so, because he is the accused. He has to defend himself. But in trial one of these rights gives the defendant a certain advantage. He has the right to confront the witnesses against him, so he can sit through the whole trial, listening to everything, waiting until last to speak, so that he can tailor his own testimony to conform to everything that's gone before. Other witnesses, including the victim, are excluded from the courtroom except during their own appearances on the witness stand. So Tommy entered the room glancing around furtively, already a little embarrassed, not knowing what had been said about him already, what intimate details of his life these strangers knew before he ever spoke his name.

He was wearing khaki pants, brown loafers, and an open-necked, short-sleeved shirt with blue and white stripes. His blond hair had been slicked down so that the tracks of the comb's teeth were still visible. He looked quite the little man. I hadn't tried to dress him like a young boy, hoping instead that the very formality of his appearance would invite the jury to see through it to the hurt boy beneath.

After his glances around the room Tommy looked straight ahead, at me. I stood waiting for him, held the gate open when he arrived, and squeezed his shoulder as I directed him toward the witness stand.

"Tell us your name, please, Tommy." A bailiff crossed the front of the room and pushed the microphone down lower, into Tommy's face.

"Tommy Algren."

"How old are you, Tommy?"

"Ten."

"What grade are you in in school?"

"Fifth. Fifth grade."

He looked calm, but he sounded nervous. I continued asking him the easy questions to let him loosen up. "You'll be in middle school next year, is that right?"

"Yes sir."

"Where do you live, Tommy?"

"On Sparrowwood. Number 823."

"With your parents?"

"Yes."

He seemed to be settled down. He was watching me, waiting for my cues. He had, as I'd instructed him, shunted aside everyone else in the room. I was speaking to him as calmly and as reassuringly as I could, nodding occasionally to let him know he was fine.

"I'm going to ask you about some things that happened about two and a half years ago," I said. He looked alert. "Do you remember a house in your neighborhood that was vacant then?"

"Objection," Eliot said. "Leading."

He could have that objection sustained all day long. I'd already told Tommy with the question what we were talking about.

"Do you remember in May 1990, when a new man moved into a house on your block?"

He hesitated. I wondered if my phrasing had confused him. "Yes sir," Tommy finally said.

"Do you remember what he looked like?"

"Yes," he said softly.

"Tom. I want you to look around the courtroom very carefully. Look at people's faces. Take your time, you don't have to hurry. Do you see that man?"

Eliot was on his feet well before I finished. "Objection," he said. "Bolstering."

I rose too, genuinely puzzled. "How can it be bolstering, Your Honor? The witness hasn't even made an identification yet. You can't bolster testimony that hasn't happened."

"It's prebolstering," Eliot said calmly.

"*Pre*bolstering?" I said loudly. I was both irritated with Eliot for intruding this novel argument into my important questioning, and unconcerned, because it didn't matter how Judge Hernandez ruled on the silly question. It was just an interruption before Tommy could continue.

I looked at Tommy and saw that while Eliot and I argued, Tommy's gaze had settled on Austin Paley. Tommy didn't look revolted, frightened, or in fact emotionally involved at all. He was just watching. Austin was looking back at him in the same way. There was communication between them, not necessarily antagonistic communication. There in that mutual gaze was the relationship between them, perfectly visible for all to see. There was the hold Austin had had on Tommy. It hadn't just been molesting, it had been mentoring. Tommy's mouth moved a little, ironically. His eyes blinked slowly. He looked like what Austin had made him. He looked sophisticated far beyond his years. It was sad to see that look on the face of a child whose main worry in life should have been not losing his best comic book in a bad trade.

It was also terrifying, to me. Tommy was something more than a child, and Austin was not his enemy. I saw what I'd feared all along, that when the time came to tell his story in public, Tommy would balk. He wouldn't be able to bring himself to hurt his old friend, his hero, Austin. He would exonerate Austin Paley on the witness stand, winning Austin an acquittal when there would no longer be time before the election for me to prepare another case against Austin.

"May I approach the witness, Your Honor?" Without waiting for the judge's permission, I did so. I didn't need to be closer to Tommy, I just wanted to stand between him and Austin. I'd hoped the bond between them was broken, that Tommy hated Austin now, but Janet McLaren had told me otherwise: "The child hates what was done to him but loves the molester." I'd tried to establish my own bond with Tommy, to overcome Austin's power over him, but our friendship was newer and not remotely as deep. I had only a few minutes to win Tommy over in spite of his past. After all the pretrial maneuvering, that's what the case came down to: a direct tug-of-war between Austin and me over this boy.

And I was mad as hell. God damn Austin Paley, he wasn't going to steal this case away from me. Even if my own witness wanted to help him.

"Tommy," I said quietly. "You remember spending time with other children at the house where the defendant seemed to be living, on your block?"

Eliot objected to leading again, and was sustained again. I still didn't care. I couldn't tell Tommy the testimony we'd already heard that morning—Eliot would have properly objected before I'd gotten a sentence into it—but Tommy had known who else was going to testify before him, and what they were going to say. My phrase *other children* was to remind him of them. He'd look like a liar if he contradicted them. Even if he were prepared to lie on Austin's behalf, Tommy didn't want to look like a liar. He would want to be believed when he denied the essentials of the crime, the private acts only he and Austin knew about. He could tell the truth about this without hurting either of them.

"Yes," he said.

"Point out that man, please."

Tommy hesitated, but Austin even obliged by leaning to the side, so Tommy could see him past me. Thus prompted, Tommy said, "There."

I moved slightly. Tommy's eyes were on me again. His mouth was pursed, the tip of his tongue just visible. He looked a little scared of me.

"Who were some of the other children who played at the defendant's house?"

The question caught him off stride. "Peter," he said slowly. I wondered if Peter had been his rival for Austin's attentions. "Debby, and Jennifer, and Bobby and Dawson and Stevie. A bunch of kids."

"Where they your friends?"

"Some of them." He shrugged.

"Steve was your friend, wasn't he?"

"Yes." Tommy forgot for a moment to wonder why I was asking, as memory surged. "Sometimes Stevie would come over to my house, or I'd go over to his, and we'd get bored and go to Waldo's, because there was more to do there. Enough kids to have games with."

"Waldo is what you called the defendant?"

Uh-oh, he'd let that slip. Secret name. But again, no harm. "Yes," Tommy admitted.

I put him back on the memory track. "Do you still play with Steve?"

"Not so much," Tommy said.

"Could the prosecutor please take his seat?" Eliot asked behind me. "I can't see the witness."

In San Antonio one of our local rules requires lawyers to question witnesses from our seats at the counsel tables, unless there's some particular reason for standing close to the witness, such as to demonstrate a piece of physical evidence. I had no such legitimate excuse. I walked back to my seat.

"Why not?" I asked Tommy, about why he was no longer friends with Steve. I was just shooting in the dark. I didn't know what had come between Tommy and Steve, but there'd been only one major event in Tommy's life that I knew of. I was thinking of what Dr. McLaren had told me, and guessing that Austin had somehow come between Tommy and Steve. Either Tommy had gone along with Austin's scheme and Steve had balked, or Tommy'd no longer felt quite childish enough to have child friends, after what happened to him.

Tommy shrugged again. "We're in different classes this year."

But friendship could survive that, and Tommy's downcast eyes made me think there was something more.

"Remember May twenty-third nineteen-ninety, Tom?"

"I guess."

May 23 was the date alleged in the indictment. Tommy knew it very well, he'd helped us reconstruct just what day it had been. It had been the day of his first sexual encounter with Austin. We'd chosen that day to prosecute, the day Tommy'd been robbed of his virginity, and his childhood, rather than some later occasion when he might be thought a more willing participant. Tommy knew the day I meant. He knew the subject we were edging into. He looked at me with his mouth a thin line, looking defiant. *Go ahead, ask me*, his expression said.

"Do you remember when you came home that night?" I asked.

Eliot said, "Objection. Assumes facts not in evidence." From the corner of my eye I saw him giving me a curious look. I was taking a very roundabout approach.

More important, Tommy was caught a little off guard. He thought I'd asked the wrong question, too.

"Were you playing at Waldo's house that day after school?" I asked.

He hesitated, not sure what he should say, when he should start denying. "I think so," he finally hedged. I didn't care about his uncertainty.

"Do you remember when you came home from his house that night?" I asked.

This was what he didn't understand. I had skipped ahead to *after* the event. "Remember?" I asked quietly.

"Yes," he said.

"Did you tell your parents that anything unusual had happened to you?"

"No."

No, he hadn't. It had been Tommy's secret then—his and Waldo's, but mostly Tommy's. Not a happy secret, a shameful one. He'd still longed for his parents then, his love for them had been stronger than his love for Austin, but he couldn't tell them what had happened because it was something dirty that he'd done. He'd cried himself to sleep that night, not just because he was small and scared, but because he was alone.

I was asking my questions slowly, leaving Tommy time to fill in the gaps from memory.

"Do you remember going to school the next day?"

"Yes." Wondering if it had been a dream, if he could pretend it had never happened. Looking at the children around him and marveling at how young and carefree they were.

"Did you tell anyone there that anything unusual had happened to you the day before?"

"No," Tommy said quietly.

Eliot was openly staring at me now, because I seemed to be asking the questions he would ask, proving that Tommy hadn't made any outcry at the time of the supposed rape. But I wasn't concerned about Eliot. I was concerned with goading Tommy's memory of how he'd felt in the first hot, shameful aftermath of sex with Austin. It hadn't been a happy memory. He hadn't wanted to share it with anyone. Not because it was his special secret, but because telling would reveal to everyone how different he was, what a dirty little boy he was.

"Did you tell your friend Steve?"

"No," Tommy said quietly, remembering, I hoped, that he had still been friends with Steve that day, he did have a friend he could talk to. But not about this new friend in his life. That was when he'd begun losing Steve.

"At lunch and at recess that day, did you play with the other kids like always?"

"Yes," Tommy said, but he was lying. He'd walked apart, feeling unfit to mingle with the other children, as he'd still been walking alone on the days I'd picked him up after school. He had no friends left by then, except Austin. And possibly me.

"After school that next day did you go back to Waldo's house?"

"Yes." Tommy had stopped looking at me, but he wasn't looking at Austin, either. I thought I sensed motion at the defense table as Austin tried to recapture his attention, but Tommy was looking off beyond the jury, into the past.

"Was Waldo there?"

"No."

No. Austin had lain low for a few days, to make sure Tommy hadn't reported what had happened. The vacant house was just a trap that had been sprung. He could walk away from it leaving no trace if he wanted. That was the beauty of his design.

But Tommy had come to the house and found it as abandoned as he felt. After Tommy's long day of secret-keeping on his behalf, Waldo left him alone. If Tommy'd needed final proof that they'd done something shameful, he had it when he found the house empty. It told him something else, too: that his new friend didn't trust him.

"Did you go back the next day looking for him?"

"Yes."

"Was he there?"

"No." Tommy shot a look at Austin. Tommy's eyes looked hot. I couldn't see how Austin looked back at him.

"How did you feel, Tommy, when you kept going back to the house after that day and Waldo wasn't there?"

Tommy shrugged, an adult gesture for his narrow shoulders.

"Did you keep going back?"

He nodded.

"Was he there?"

"No," Tommy said bitterly.

"After you thought he was gone, did you tell your parents what had happened?"

Eliot objected: there'd been no testimony that *anything* had happened. Neither Tommy nor I paid attention to him.

Tommy shook his head while Eliot talked. I took that for my answer. Tommy looked very small in the oversized witness chair. I noticed a couple of the jurors were leaning toward him as if to see him better.

"Why didn't you talk to your parents?"

In a very small voice Tommy said, "I was afraid."

It seemed a small breakthrough. He hadn't admitted so far that anything had happened to make him afraid. I didn't press my advantage. "What *did* you do?" I asked.

He shrugged again, like a longtime prisoner describing his daily life. "Ate dinner with Mom and Dad, did my homework, went to bed."

"Did you play with the other kids after school?"

He shook his head.

"Did they miss Waldo too?"

"I don't know."

Idiot, I thought. *Stupid, stupid idiot.* It was suddenly a refrain beating like a pulse in my head. Tommy'd told me what I needed to know and I'd almost missed it, as I had missed it for weeks.

"Tommy. When you went to bed at night, would you go right to sleep?"

Tommy's stare was turned inward. He blinked hard. "Sometimes," he said.

"And sometimes you'd wake up during the night?" I was guessing, but guessing well. I could see it in Tommy's face.

"Yes," he said, softly as a boy not wanting to stir the creatures in his room.

"What would you do?"

"Just laid in bed," Tommy said. I could picture it. In the silence I knew he was picturing it too. That big white house turned dark, with Tommy so far at one end of it that he was completely alone.

"How did you feel?" I asked.

"It was cold," Tommy said, hunching his shoulders. *Cold?* I thought. *In May?* Maybe Tommy's father turned the air conditioning far down at night. Or maybe it had only been Tommy who was cold.

I looked at him in his dress shirt and his neat hair, a little boy all got up as a man. That was how I'd treated him all along, the way Austin had, appealing to the desire in him

246

to grow up fast; trying to seal pacts with a manly squeeze and a knowing look. I'd been wrong, God, all wrong.

"Why didn't you get up and tell your parents?" I asked.

Because the house was cold, and big and dark and what was at the end of it but a man, and Tommy didn't know if any man could be trusted any more.

He didn't answer.

"Did you think about what had happened?" I asked.

Tommy looked up, wildly, frightened. I jumped from my chair and was beside him in a second. I put one arm around his back and he clutched my other hand with both hands. I held them, strongly as I could. "It's all right," I said as he cried. "It's all right."

It was probably the first time he'd cried in front of another person, the first time he'd cried at all since those nights alone in the dark. He'd toughened amazingly since then, but not at the core. It wasn't a friend Tommy needed, it was a father. One who wouldn't betray him by asking him to be an adult too soon.

The image that flashed through my mind was not of Tommy alone in his room, but of David as I'd last seen him, a boy in a tuxedo, not brooding but longing, somewhere deep within him, so deep he probably didn't know it was there; longing to be held, comforted, protected.

I held Tommy against my chest, blocking him not only from Austin but from everyone in the room, shielding him until his sobs were trailing off. Tommy wasn't lost. I could still save him, but only with his help.

"Tommy," I said, squeezing his hand. He looked up at me, lips pressed together, still fearful. "Tell these people what happened," I told him.

"I have to object now, Your Honor," Eliot said quietly behind me. "We cannot see the witness because the prosecutor is blocking him, the defendant is being denied his right of confrontation. And it appears that the district attorney is coercing the witness."

Keen insight, Eliot. Under the cover his voice provided I squeezed Tommy's hand and said, "Tell them the truth." Then I took my seat.

Tommy looked scared still. He watched me, as I'd instructed him to do long ago, last week. I nodded reassuringly. "Was Waldo finally at the house again?"

"Yes," Tommy said clearly. His eyes stayed on me.

"How long later?"

"I don't know."

"A week?" I asked. "A month? A year?"

"Only a few days," Tommy said. But they'd been three or four or five days of painful anxiety, wondering if he was changed forever but also abandoned.

"Were you glad to see him again?"

"Yes." You could see that Tommy remembered the happiness of finding that his friend hadn't left him forever, but he didn't smile now, in the courtroom.

"What did you do together?" I asked.

They'd done the things friends do: gone for a drive, talked, laughed at private jokes. Austin had touched his arm or his leg, giving Tommy momentary scares, but the touches had been fleeting.

"Did anything else happen?"

"No." Tommy said that unthinkingly. It was the truth.

"Did you keep seeing the defendant?"

"Yes."

I took the plunge. "Now let's talk about that other day. You know the one I mean, Tommy. What day was it? The first time."

It didn't take Tommy long to decide. He gulped quietly, but that was only because his voice still wasn't quite steady. He was just watching me, answering my questions.

"May twenty-third," he said. "Nineteen ninety."

"Did you go to the house?"

"Yes."

"Was that the first day you'd gone?"

"Oh, no. I'd been there lots of times by then."

"You'd already talked to Austin alone?"

"Yes."

"Did you like him, Tommy?"

"Yes," he said. Answering that simple question made his voice give way again, a little.

"How did he treat you?"

Tommy thought. "He talked to me like he cared what I thought. And, and you could tell sometimes when another kid said something, Waldo'd look at me like, Boy, what a dummy. Sometimes we laughed when we were the only two laughing and everybody else wondered what was going on."

Tommy chattered this out like a little child telling you his latest enthusiasm.

"So that day, May twenty-third, when you went to the house, was Waldo outside?"

"No."

"Were there other kids there playing?"

"No." Tommy still sounded a little puzzled about the change in circumstances.

"What did you do?"

"I almost just went home again. But I knocked on the door, just for"—he shrugged—"and he was there, and he said he'd been waiting for me."

"Was anyone else inside the house?"

"No."

"What was it like inside the house?"

Tommy wrinkled his nose. "It wasn't like anybody really lived there. There was a couch and a couple of folding chairs and that was about it. I asked Waldo wasn't he going to get any more furniture and he just laughed."

"What did you do there?"

"We talked, and we played a couple of games. Some other kids knocked on the door but Waldo didn't let them in. We stayed by the door and said, 'Shh,' to each other and laughed about it."

"Why did he say he didn't want them in?"

"Just because we were having so much fun by ourselves."

"Did you go outside at all?"

"Waldo kept saying how hot it was, how it was too hot to do anything outside."

"Was it hot?"

"I guess."

"Do you remember what you were wearing?"

"Shorts, I guess, and a T-shirt. That's what I always wore after school."

"Where were your parents, Tommy?"

"They weren't home from work yet."

"But you were home."

"Usually I'd go to the daycare after school, but sometimes

back then we had a maid two days a week and she'd watch me until Mom and Dad got home."

"But she'd let you go outside to play?"

"Yeah."

Tommy's parents were in the audience. I didn't turn around to watch them squirm, and Tommy didn't look past me at them. There were probably any number of parents in the room who might have been having guilty thoughts, maybe some on the jury.

"What was Waldo wearing?" I asked.

"He was— It looked like a suit, I think, but without the coat or tie."

"Did you ever go outside, or anywhere else?"

"After a while Waldo said, 'I know what let's do,' and he jumped up, but he wouldn't tell me what. He went in to the other room and he changed clothes."

"Did you go in with him?"

"No, but it was just in the next room, and he left the door open." Tommy looked uneasy.

"What did he put on?"

"Shorts, and another shirt."

"And what happened?"

"We got in his car, and we drove, and Waldo knew another house, not too far away, and it had a swimming pool."

"Was there anybody else there?"

"No. It had a For Sale sign."

"Did it look like the other house inside?"

"Oh, no," Tommy said. No, Austin wouldn't have introduced him to their new intimacy in the sordid environs of the vacant house, with its bare walls and sagging couch. Tommy still seemed dazzled as he described the other house. "It was pretty. There were gold lamps and glass tables and curtains and the pool."

"Was it the defendant's house?"

"I don't think so. We never went back there again."

"But he knew his way around it."

"Oh yes. He made a drink and got me a Coke and showed me around a little."

Like a tour guide, which Austin was. "Then what did you do?"

Tommy hesitated. I didn't press him. His eyes moved past

me, but not toward Austin. Tommy chewed his lip. "He said we should go swimming. I said I didn't have my swim suit, but Waldo said that was okay, since it was just us there."

"And?"

"He went outside and he started taking off his clothes, then he stopped and looked at me like what was wrong?, so I took mine off too." He crossed his arms. "It felt funny to be naked outside like that."

"Weren't there any neighbors?"

"There was a tall fence."

I nodded. "Did you go swimming?"

"Yes."

"Was it fun?"

Tommy looked at me as if the question were unexpected or the answer awkward. I just gave him the same forthright stare I'd worn since resuming my seat. "Yes," he finally said, glancing down. "We swam and floated on air mattresses, and we played tag and submarine races and stuff like that."

"Did he touch you in the water?"

"Yes."

This wasn't the story Tommy had first told me in my office. That one had not been his first sexual encounter with Austin. This story of the first one was remarkably similar, though. Austin had had to reseduce Tommy every time they met. Maybe that was one of the attractions of child molesting. Once the child grew jaded and accepting, it was time to move on. By the time there was no more need for conquest, no fear to overcome, Austin *had* left Tommy behind.

"Did it scare you when he touched you?"

"It just seemed like accidents at first."

"What happened next?"

"I was just floating on an air mattress, resting."

"On your back or your front or your side?"

"On my back."

"Where was Austin?"

"He was swimming around me. He'd swim under my mattress and then come up on the other side. Then once he came up and he seemed real tired, so he put his head and his arms down on my mattress."

"Was it a very big mattress?" I asked. My voice was very level, as if there were no wrong answers and nothing surprised me. Tommy held up his hands about two feet apart. "So he touched you," I said.

Tommy nodded. "His head was right next to my leg and his arms were on top of me."

"On top of you where, Tommy?"

He swallowed. "One was across my legs and the other was sort of up to my waist."

"Were you still naked?"

"Yes."

"So his head and one of his arms were close to your penis," I said.

Eliot objected to leading. Judge Hernandez sustained him. I'd just wanted to be the one to say the word first, giving Tommy permission to do so. "What happened?" I asked.

I didn't think Tommy was going to answer. His mouth was compressed, his lips almost vanished. I could hear the little noises of his fingernails scratching at the rail in front of him. I was on the verge of asking him another question when his voice began:

"He turned his head so he was looking at me, and he smiled at me, and he said my name, and while I looked at his face I felt his hand moving up my leg and then he left it there, right at—right at the top of my leg."

"And then?"

"Then he said something like, 'Oh, what's this?' So I looked where he was looking—I thought there was a bug or something—and he was looking at my penis." Tommy didn't hesitate over the word, he said it in a rush, breathlessly. "Just staring at it, like he'd never seen one before."

I asked questions only when Tommy paused, and when I did he'd rush on, as if my voice released him. "Did he touch it?" I asked then.

"First he just stared, and I got very— I was embarrassed, I started to cover up with my hand, but he stopped me, and then he looked up at me and he stopped smiling, he looked very serious, and he said, 'It's all right. There's nothing to be ashamed of.' Something like that, and I said, 'What do you mean?' and he said, 'Getting excited. It's nothing to be ashamed of, it happens to everyone all the time.' "

"Did you know what he meant?"

"No, not then. But I— But, you know, I knew where he

was looking. So I guess I had some idea. Then he said, 'It's perfectly nice.' Not just all right, he said perfectly nice. Then he said ...'"

He stopped. Tommy wasn't looking at anyone else, but he wasn't consistently watching me, either. His eyes would lock on my face, as if undetachable, then suddenly skitter away, drop to the floor, cruise across the legs of the furniture, then dart back to my face. "What?" I asked.

"He said, 'May I touch it?'"

"What did you say?"

"I don't think I said anything, but maybe I nodded or something, because he acted like I had. He held up his hand, very still, like he was trying to catch something, then he brought it down and covered my penis with it."

"Covered it?"

"So you couldn't even see it any more. His whole hand just hid it. Then he—"

"What, Tommy?"

"He just breathed. Just breathed. I could hear him breathing. That was all I could hear."

In Tommy's pauses, I couldn't hear even that much in the courtroom now. It was Becky's job to watch the jury and keep me apprised of their reactions, but I shot a glance at them as Tommy described listening to his attacker's breathing. One man was looking down at the floor, staring at it, as if concentrating on not being where he was. Two or three other jurors had their hands up to their mouths.

"What did he do next, Tommy?"

"He opened his hand, like he was just taking a peek, and he smiled again. He smiled at me. He told me it was okay again. Then he—he kissed it."

He'd said it so low I was afraid some of the jurors might not have heard. I didn't like to be overly dramatic, but I had to make sure they'd heard. "Kissed what, Tommy?"

"My penis."

Tommy looked down at the interesting twinings his fingers were performing among themselves. I prompted him again. "Then what happened?"

Tommy looked up, apparently glad to have gotten past the beginning. "Then he just stood up, and he smiled again, and he started pulling my air mattress toward the side of the pool."

"How did you feel then, Tommy?"

"I was glad that was over. It made me feel very strange."

"Strange how?"

"Like I didn't know what was going to happen next. I was glad when he stopped."

I couldn't get him to say he'd been afraid. I waited, but Tommy didn't add anything about his emotions. He continued his narrative. "He pulled my air mattress over to the shallow end of the pool, so I figured we were getting out, so I got out, and then Waldo came walking out, up the steps." Tommy paused. His face was a study: Overlaying his expression was the imposed maturity I'd seen so often, but underneath, crawling like a sudden rash spreading, was anxiety so deep it was fear. When he spoke, his voice sounded like an eerie child's impression of Austin's own casual drawl. "And he said, 'See? I told you it happens to everyone.' "

"What was he talking about, Tommy?"

I thought I'd have to prompt him again. But when he spoke the words came quickly: "His penis. It had gotten hard."

"What did he do?"

"He came over and put his arm around me and he said let's dry off. And we went over to where we'd left the towels. They'd been laying in the sun and they were very warm. Waldo picked up one of them and started drying me off. First he was standing next to me, right next to me, and he—"

"So that his penis touched you?" I asked. It was the first time I'd interrupted.

"Yes."

"Where?"

"Here," Tommy said immediately, touching his chest as if the spot were tattooed. "And here. And it ran down my back when he stooped down to dry off my legs."

"What did you do?"

"I just stood there. When I was dry I reached for my shorts and shirt, but he grabbed my arm and said, 'Let's get a little sun first.' And he had me lay down on this wide what-do-you-call-it, like a long beach chair but with a mattress on it. And he laid down next to me. And we just laid there for a while.

"Did Austin lay on his front or his back?"

"His back," Tommy said.

"Did he cover himself?"

"No."

"Did he say anything?"

"He started telling me," Tommy said, "that it was very secret, that only people that were very, very good friends could be together like this. And that he wouldn't ever tell anybody and I shouldn't either. He was holding my hand. And he hugged me, he put his arms around me and squeezed me against his chest."

And Tommy squeezed back, I had no doubt, because he'd never had enough hugs in his life. For a long moment he'd probably thought the worry was past and he finally had someone who loved him and would always be close when Tommy needed him.

"Then he touched me again," Tommy said abruptly. "He ran his hand down my back and he held my behind, and then with both hands. His cheek scraped my face. And he pulled back, and he was still holding me, and he said, 'Look.' "

"At?"

"At his penis. It was right there in front of me, and it was hard again, and it was right in front of me, and he said, 'Wouldn't you like to touch mine?' "

"Did you want to, Tommy?"

He shook his head, back and forth, back and forth. "No. It scared me. It was very red, and it was big, I didn't know it could get so big."

"Did you touch it?"

"Yes."

"Why?"

"Because he wanted me to."

Tommy's voice hadn't faltered very often as he talked. Generally he said things in a rush. He didn't appear on the verge of breaking down as he had earlier, so it may have been very belatedly that I noticed he was crying. There were two shining streaks down his cheeks, and as he talked another tear welled out and slid down the path. He kept talking as if he were somewhere else, watching what he described.

"How did you touch it, Tommy?"

He demonstrated, holding out his index finger, making it as long as he could. "I was just going to tap it, but when I touched it he put his hand around mine and mine was inside and he closed his eyes and I was afraid to move. He didn't move again for a long time, like he'd gone to sleep."

"Did he ever open his eyes?"

"Yes. Then he smiled at me and he said, 'I kissed yours.' "

The story flowed on. Tommy described the oral-genital contact Austin was accused of, and then ejaculation. When I had to intrude questions I did it with a voice so steady I became that voice, detached, nonjudgmental, sympathetic but uninvolved. Tommy sounded similar, but he kept crying, and when he described the shock of climax his head jerked backward and he looked frightened. He sobbed. I didn't return to the witness stand to comfort him. I gave him a moment's respite and a one-sentence reassurance, and he composed himself again. The courtroom was dead silent, as if Tommy's story were a sea that had covered us quietly, flowing in so silently it had taken us unawares, leaving us in a soundless undersea world.

When he was quite, quite done I had him tell about being taken back to his neighborhood and dropped off, left to go home and explain to his parents where he'd been, and to keep Waldo's and his secret that night and for many nights to come, even when Waldo wasn't there to reward his loyalty, when there was only Tommy alone in the dark, alone in the wide world. He was crying again at the end, and I did leave my chair and put my arm around him, and murmured softly to him in front of all those strangers. "I'm proud of you," I said too softly for the microphone to pick up. Tommy nodded and used my handkerchief to wipe his eyes and gradually recovered himself. He smiled at me weakly. I gave him one last warm touch and turned away. I looked at Eliot and said, "I pass the witness."

14

I felt an eerie nervousness as I took my seat. At first I thought it was the silence ringing in my ears, but it was part of me, it was something running on my skin like ants. Later I realized it was adrenaline, it was the urge to leap up and smash someone. My nerves were rising through my skin with the dread of handing Tommy over to Eliot.

I'd felt Eliot's eyes on me occasionally during my questioning, but as soon as the witness was his he focused on him entirely. Eliot sat straight but at ease, looking at Tommy without a trace of hostility. He looked nothing but compassionate, and disturbed by the story the boy had told.

"Would you like some water, Tommy?" he asked. Tommy shook his head. "Would you like us to stop for a few minutes? All right. My name is Eliot Quinn, Tommy. I'm the lawyer for Austin Paley. I'm helping him the way Mr. Blackwell has helped you. We're trying to find out the truth of what happened a long time ago. To do that, Mr. Blackwell asks you questions and then I do. If you don't understand one of my questions, tell me that, all right?, and I'll try to think of another way to ask it. And you can take your time to think about what you want to answer, all right, Tommy?"

My feet were beneath me. An urge to object kept me on edge, though I don't know what my objection would be. But he was taking too long to get to his questions, he was setting him up. Tommy nodded at him. He'd stopped crying.

"You didn't tell your parents when this happened, Tommy?"

"No."

"Why not?"

"I was afraid," he repeated.

"Afraid of your parents?" Eliot still looked troubled, but now his trouble was in understanding.

Tommy shifted in his seat. "No, I was afraid—because of what had happened."

"But I'm talking about your mother and father, Tommy, not the man. If you were afraid of him, why didn't you tell your parents, so they could protect you from him?"

Tommy struggled to make Eliot understand. "Because it was bad, what I did. I was afraid they'd be mad at me."

"Your own parents?" Eliot asked. "Did they get mad at you a lot?"

"No."

No, I could have explained. They were proud of Tommy, in a distant, abstracted way, and glad in the same way that he caused them so little trouble. Even at eight Tommy must have sensed that, that his parents wouldn't like problems.

"Did they punish you much?" Eliot asked.

"No," Tommy said, then hastened to add, "But I'd never done anything that bad before."

"But it wasn't your fault, was it?"

The language doesn't have enough tenses. I didn't know if Tommy could answer from the precise spot in the past Eliot was talking about. Tommy may have been thinking of the later times when he was Austin's willing accomplice. And those times had convinced him that he'd been at fault from the beginning. He had attracted the grown man. "No," Tommy said slowly, but that was a woefully incomplete answer.

I was still tense in my chair with the urge to intervene. I could feel Eliot closing in on Tommy, the way I'd seen him trap a hundred witnesses. *Restraint,* I thought, *restraint.* I had to let Eliot do his work. *But how,* I thought, *can you hurt this boy, when you're acting out of guilt over what you once helped do to the onetime boy beside you?*

"Then why didn't you tell your parents?" Eliot asked insistently.

Tommy sat silent. Eliot let him. When it seemed Tommy couldn't come up with an answer, he finally said, "I didn't want them to think I'd been bad."

Eliot regarded Tommy quietly. Eliot was a grandfatherly presence in the trial, and he knew it. He wasn't going to press too hard. Eliot spoke as if moving on to something else. "Who *was* the first person you told about what had happened?"

"Mom and Dad," Tommy said.

Eliot looked baffled. He even said aloud, "Hmf." Then asked, "You didn't tell anyone else?"

"No. Not at first."

"You didn't tell any of your friends?"

"No."

"All these children who used to hang around at Austin's house with you, you didn't warn any of them, you didn't tell them just a little bit of what had happened to you?"

"No."

"Not the whole thing, Tommy. I mean didn't you just say something like, 'I didn't like the way he touched me,' or, 'He made me feel funny,' or even just, 'I don't want to go play there any more'?"

"No," Tommy insisted.

"In fact, you *did* keep going back there to play, didn't you?"

"Yes," Tommy admitted.

"When did you tell your parents?" Eliot asked.

"This summer."

"*This* summer? Two months ago, three months ago?"

"Yes."

"How long was that after it had happened, Tommy?"

"Two years."

"*More* than two years, yes, from May nineteen-ninety to August or so of this year?"

Tommy shrugged.

"Why did you tell them then?" Eliot asked, adding before Tommy could answer, "Were they asking you if something like that had happened?"

"No," Tommy said.

"Had you been acting like something was wrong? Were your mom and dad worried about you?"

"Objection," I said, finally having found a spot for it. "He can't testify what was in someone else's mind."

Eliot was on his feet, too. "He would know if his parents acted worried about him, Your Honor."

"Phrase it that way," Judge Hernandez said neutrally.

"Tommy." Eliot was making his transition now. Not quite so kindly, a little more stern. He was leaning toward Tommy, a constant small frown shaping his features as he struggled to understand. "At the time you told your parents what had happened, were they acting concerned about you? Did they seem to be worried about the way you were acting?"

Tommy's eyes were downcast as he searched his memory for a time when his parents had seemed concerned about him. "No," he said.

"What was the occasion, what was happening, when you did tell them? Were they talking to you?"

"No. We were watching TV."

"TV. What were you watching?"

Bingo. *Say it, Tommy.* Eliot had read Tommy's written statement, he knew he'd picked out Austin from television news. I'd hoped Eliot would ask him about that, because it was such a fluky ID. Eliot had to broach it. And when he did, Tommy could say what *hadn't* been in his written statement:

"The news," Tommy said. "And I saw him, I saw Austin on TV. They said other children had been molested. So I knew he'd done it to other kids too," Tommy concluded.

Good boy. I couldn't offer evidence of the other child-molesting cases against Austin, but if Eliot accidentally elicited the information himself, well, that couldn't be helped, could it?

When I turned toward him Eliot was still looking at Tommy, showing no sign that he'd just been hurt.

"But Austin wasn't accused of those crimes, was he, Tommy? He was representing someone who was accused. Isn't that what the story on TV said?"

"I think. But I knew it was him who'd done it to them," Tommy said, true to the program. But I didn't like the way he looked as he made his accusation. He had lost the hurt-little-boy look; now he looked like a little man again. He even shot a look at Austin as he mentioned the other children, a look that spoke of very adult jealousy and sense of betrayal. Maybe there *is* nothing adult about our emotions. Maybe children feel them as strongly as we. But what was important at that moment was that Tommy no longer looked childish enough. Eliot sat silent for a few seconds, letting the jury study Tommy's expression before he asked another question.

"So what you told your parents—correct me if I don't have this right—was, 'Me, too. I was molested too.' Was that what you said, Tommy?"

"Yes." Tommy saw nothing wrong with that.

"And what did your parents do?" Eliot asked. "Did they call the police, did they take you to a doctor?"

"No. Not—"

"No?" Eliot stared at him. "Did they bring you the next day to see the district attorney?"

"No," Tommy tried to explain. "Not at first."

"Did they do anything at first?"

"Just talked to me," Tommy said.

"How *did* you get to see a doctor and the police and these prosecutors?"

"I told my teacher at school the next day."

"Your teacher. This was August," Eliot said.

"And the nurse," Tommy added, nodding.

"The nurse. Had you talked to her very often?"

"I think I saw her in third grade," Tommy said, "when my stomach hurt and I had to go home."

Eliot nodded at the recollection. I saw exactly where Eliot had led him. I assumed everyone else did, too.

"I have no more questions," Eliot said.

Which startled me. I'd expected Eliot to challenge Tommy's identification of Austin, which would have allowed me on cross-examination to expand my inquiry in order to show the jury how long Tommy and Austin had known each other, therefore how sure Tommy must be of his molester's identity. Eliot hadn't given me that opening. Without it, I wasn't sure I'd even be allowed to introduce Austin's subsequent continuing sexual assaults on Tommy. They would be considered extraneous offenses, irrelevant to the one assault that was the subject of this trial.

I felt Eliot close beside me as the witness was mine again.

"Tommy," I said, speaking slowly, "why did you tell your parents about this man molesting you?"

"Because I thought he'd done it to other kids, too," Tommy said earnestly. "And I thought—"

"Objection," Eliot said, on his feet at once. "This is pure speculation on this boy's part, based on nothing. It introduces the idea of extraneous offenses, to the defendant's extreme prejudice, and is completely unfounded."

"Your Honor, the defense inquired into the witness's motive for his accusation. That makes my question—"

"Motive?" Eliot said to me, throwing up one hand. "All I asked was when he finally told someone, after years of silence. What does that—?"

"Now *I* object to this speaking objection," I said. "Defense counsel can make a speech when the time comes—"

"Stop arguing with each other," Judge Hernandez snapped. "The objection is sustained. Ladies and gentlemen," he added to the jury, "ignore that last answer. As defense counsel said, it has no basis in the evidence at all. You are concerned with only one accusation in this case."

I shook my head and sat down, not as displeased as I appeared. The jurors understood, I hoped, that if they had a question about Tommy's motive it wasn't my fault that it wouldn't be answered for them. It was the defense that was determined to cut off any mention of those other children. The jurors wouldn't forget.

"Tommy," I continued. "Was that day that he took you to the swimming pool the last time you saw Austin Paley?"

Tommy shook his head.

"Did he come back to the vacant house in your neighborhood?"

"Yes," Tommy said softly. He appeared a little frightened by the exchange Eliot and I had had over his testimony. I liked the effect on him. He looked small and scared again. I wasn't going to waste that emotion.

"Did the defendant come to find you?"

Now it was Eliot who was tense, ready to object. I could feel him coiled beside me. I tried to ask questions that would keep him poised just that way, anxious to spring to his feet but with no objection to make.

"Yes," Tommy said.

"More than once?"

He nodded.

"Speak up, please, Tommy. Did he come find you more than once after that day by the pool?"

"Yes."

"Twice, three times?"

"More," Tommy said. "Lots more."

"Total, Tommy. Between that day by the pool and the day you saw Austin on television and said, 'That's him,' how much time did you spend with him, total? A few minutes?"

"Hours," Tommy said.

I think Eliot was going to object then, that my questions and Tommy's answers were implying other crimes his client had committed. But I was the one who rose to my feet. I walked behind Eliot, inches from his back. He ignored me. Buster Harmony looked up, his mouth falling open.

I stood behind Austin Paley. He didn't turn to me. I couldn't tell from his posture if he was even nervous.

"Forget television, Tommy," I said loudly. "Look here, now. Think about those times, and particularly that first day beside the swimming pool. Is this the man who was with you that day?"

Tommy was staring at him as instructed. He looked sad, sorry, a victim of violated trust. "Yes," he said.

"Is this the man who put his penis in your mouth?"

"Objection," Eliot said. "This has been asked and answered. The district attorney is just straining for effect."

I don't think anyone was listening to him. Because I had achieved my effect. Tommy's face was closing in on itself. His eyes turned wet again.

"Sustained," said the judge.

"Do you have any doubts?" I asked Tommy.

He shook his head. The movement started a tear down his cheek.

Eliot was still on his feet, right beside me. He was looking at me without hostility. I felt a strange intimacy in his almost-blank expression.

"Your witness," I said.

Tommy, on the witness stand, had his hand in front of his mouth. He was no longer looking directly at Austin. He was trying to stop crying but couldn't. His crying was soft and undemonstrative, but that only made him more pitiful. Eliot looked at him and saw only damage to be done to the defense case. "No more questions," he said.

I walked to the witness stand to help Tommy down. "Don't worry," I said softly, and put my arm around him. He kept his head down as I walked him to the railing. "You did fine."

"We reserve the right to recall the witness," Eliot was saying.

Karen Rivera was waiting at the railing to take Tommy off my hands. She frowned at me before she led Tommy out of the room. Mrs. Algren, halfway back among the spectators, struggled out to the aisle to join them. Mr. Algren remained where he was, watching me.

"Call your next witness," Judge Hernandez said.

I didn't let him hurry me. I resumed my seat and leaned close to Becky. "Do we need somebody now?" I asked softly.

"We need everybody we can get," she said.

"Yeah. You're right." I reflected that it was the first conversation I'd had with Becky since the trial had begun. It seemed like days. She looked at me seriously, offering her best advice, not a smile of encouragement or intimacy. I nodded and stood up. Judge Hernandez was regarding me as if I were an inept waiter too slow to take his order.

I said, "The State calls—"

And stopped. I looked down at Eliot, in the chair on my left. He was leaning the other way to confer quietly with his client and co-counsel, but when my voice stopped he glanced up at me. I had a sudden fear that I was doing something wrong. My case was essentially done, only the filigree work left. But anything I added gave Eliot another chance to hurt me. I'd planned to save this witness for rebuttal. This last-minute rearrangement made me feel I was being pushed into making a mistake.

"Who?" the judge asked ironically.

But Becky had agreed, and she was watching the trial from the side, less emotionally involved than I. She thought our case needed help now.

"Dr. Janet McLaren," I said.

Judge Hernandez nodded to one of the bailiffs, who started toward the gate in the railing that opened to the courtroom's aisle. I stopped him.

"Dr. McLaren isn't here," I told the judge. "We need a few minutes to bring her from her office."

He frowned at me. "You didn't know you were going to need her testimony?" he asked loudly.

"Your Honor, maybe a doctor will spend all afternoon waiting in *your* waiting room, but I can't get any to do it for me. We'll need a few minutes."

Judge Hernandez didn't like the knowing chuckles my explanation received. He looked at his watch, an ornate gold affair heavy on his wrist. "We'll take fifteen minutes," he decided. "Be back at four-thirty. Sharp. Bailiff, see if the jurors need anything." He wouldn't let them escape his benevolence. They were voters.

I was surprised by the time. It was almost the end of the first day, and we were about to call our last witness. I couldn't believe it had gone so fast.

"I'll go call her office," Becky said, and was gone. I sat alone at the State's table with no notes to peruse, nothing to do but worry. I had an urge to turn to Eliot and discuss the case with him. It wouldn't be unprecedented. Prosecutors and defense lawyers often chat together during breaks in trials, each more interested in his opponent's opinion of his performance than in the feelings of laymen such as the jury and the defendant. But when I turned toward Eliot he was deep in quiet conversation with Austin and Buster. Buster was the one doing the talking, animatedly. The few words I picked up were angry: ". . . hit him harder . . ." I couldn't hear Eliot.

It was Wednesday, October 30. Election day was Tuesday, six days away. Three days should be enough to finish the trial. By the weekend I'd know whether I still had a career. No: I'd know if I *didn't*. Losing the trial would almost certainly lose me the election. I'd look as if I'd engaged in malicious prosecution for devious reasons, and induced children to lie, to try to convict an innocent man. I wasn't sure that winning the trial would win me the election. Maybe I was too far behind. I was sure only that losing the trial would set Austin free, and leave him so sure of his power that he would never restrain himself again.

I looked at him across the narrow space of the front of the courtroom. He was facing my direction, head inclined toward Eliot beside him, nodding at his instructions. Then Austin began speaking, in an intimate undertone, but he looked not at his lawyers but at me. In Austin's eye was his familiar sparkle and I swear his mouth shaped itself into a wry smile as he spoke. It was the same look he'd given me a hundred times in the past. Now it seemed to say, *I'm not worth all this trouble.*

What I thought in return, staring back at him, was, *I may have to kill you, Austin, my old friend.* If I lost this trial, and lost my office as well, how could I retire to private life with the picture of Austin unbridled, no one to check him? How could I sleep at night knowing he was out in the same night, planning, stalking, perhaps with his hand at that moment on a child's shoulder, smiling charmingly?

I came to myself with a start, as if awakening from a nightmare of falling. Austin was no longer looking at me, but I thought I detected the residue of a satisfied smile on his face, as if he knew what I'd been imagining, because he'd been picturing the same scene himself, with relish.

I looked in his face for traces of the boy who had been molested by his father. Eliot must have seen them; if he didn't see Austin as a victim he could never have agreed to defend him. But all I saw was the man who had used Eliot Quinn's guilt feelings to cover his own crimes. All I saw was the victimizer. It was strange I had never seen that in Austin's face all these years. It seemed so plain now.

"I wish there were some land mines we could lay in your testimony, but I don't know of any—unless there's something you haven't told me, like you once happened to stumble upon Austin Paley fondling Tommy?"

Janet McLaren shook her head.

"Too bad. Then we're just going to ask you questions until they stop us. We're just going to pound you as far as we can."

"Like a battering ram," she said.

"Exactly. And when they do cut us off I want you to look

like there's lots more juicy stuff you could tell the jury if not for these darned rules."

She nodded, accepting her instructions without demur, but with an ironic cast to her mouth. Janet looked like a completely professional woman, but not one trying to be a man. She wore a dark green suit that made me aware of the flash of her eyes, and the silky blouse beneath the jacket made it clear she was flesh, not animated fabric. I had greeted her with pleasure, but while instructing her made sure not to touch her or smile.

"Tommy's telling the truth, and there are damned good reasons why he didn't speak up sooner. He's a frightened little boy, abused by a man who took advantage of him. By that particular man." I pointed downward, to the courtroom two floors below my office, where the three of us stood. Janet looked poised and ready. Becky stood beside her, arms folded, head bent slightly, staring at me as if she too were accepting instructions. "Right?" I asked.

Janet McLaren nodded, but too slowly; too judiciously, I thought. "You have to come across as a detached professional," I said, "who has coolly evaluated the evidence and come to conclusions. But I hope that's not what you are. I hope you don't feel neutral and impartial about this case." She started to speak and I stopped her. "Don't answer that, Eliot might ask you if you've ever expressed a personal opinion about this case. But we understand each other?"

She nodded.

"Good. And, Doctor? They're going to hit back. You have to take whatever Eliot hits you with and shrug it off, as if he's just not bright enough to understand. Don't let him get to you. Your personal feelings aren't involved. If he makes you testy, or flustered, you'll be that much less use to me. And to Tommy. Just sit quietly and let the questions roll off you. Take your time to think about your answer; don't blurt anything out in the heat of the moment. And never, ever, ever give him one word more than he asks for. Don't give him even that if you can avoid it."

She began to let her exasperation show. "This isn't my first time to testify."

I laughed harshly. "Tell me that again in an hour. *I* just made you visibly annoyed in less than a minute. And you

267

are going to wear some expression other than that supercilious smirk you have on now, aren't you?"

Janet turned to Becky. "Is he always like this during trial?"

"We all are," Becky said.

"How many children have you examined, Dr. McLaren, during your ten years working in this field?"

"Hundreds. Perhaps as many as a thousand."

"All boys, all girls, or a mix?"

Janet took her time answering. The jurors were to her left, within a few feet of her. I looked in their direction. Janet showed no reaction to my glance. "I'd say a slight majority have been girls," she said.

"But you've examined hundreds of boys who had been sexually abused?"

Now she turned toward the jurors. She looked them over swiftly but individually, as if under other circumstances she'd like to get to know them better. "Yes," she said.

"Have your examinations been limited to verbal interviews?"

"No. I also examine the children physically."

"You are a medical doctor, I believe you testified?" We had already established Janet's professional qualifications. She explained for the jury's benefit that she insisted on doing physical exams of the children before starting her psychological evaluations, in order to gain the children's confidence, to reassure them they were still physically normal. She didn't tell the jury, as she'd told me weeks ago, in what a small percentage of cases she found physical evidence of abuse.

"Do you continue treating these children for some time, Dr. McLaren?"

"In most cases, yes. On the average I treat a child for three or four years."

Good answer. It told the jury not only that Janet knew what she was talking about, from long examination of abused children, but that such children *required* lengthy treatment to recover from the effects of sexual abuse.

"Do you have a pretty good cure rate?"

She smiled, slightly and sadly. "I'll never know. We make

progress, the children and I. I help them reconcile what happened to them with how they feel about themselves. Often when they leave my care I feel their self-esteem has recovered enough to allow them to find happiness—or at least to give them as good a chance as anyone else has. But the literature tells us that in children who've been sexually abused problems recur years later, sometimes decades later. So I can't use a word like *cured.*"

I paused as if I were absorbing this sad truth. Then, "What are some of the long-term effects on children who have been sexually assaulted by adults?" I asked.

Again Janet paused for reflection. She was taking my advice seriously. She appeared both knowledgeable and thoughtful. But this time her pause gave Eliot time to stand.

"Objection, Your Honor. This is irrelevant. There is only one alleged victim in this case. Case studies on other children are irrelevant."

I started to rise too, but Judge Hernandez said, "Sustained," before I could even push back my chair.

"Then let's just talk about Tommy Algren," I said. "Have you treated him professionally, Doctor?"

"Yes. But only for the last two months, since he came forward with what happened to him."

"Have you had enough sessions with him to form professional opinions about him?"

"Oh, yes," Janet said. Careful. A little too eager.

"He's told you what happened to him?"

"Yes."

"Do you have an opinion about the psychological effect on him?"

"Yes."

"Has he been damaged?"

"Quite definitely." Janet glanced at me, she didn't want to jump the gun, but when I nodded slightly she began speaking quickly, to the jury. "Tommy Algren is ten years old. I had to keep reminding myself of that while treating him, because he gives an appearance of much greater maturity. He comes across as a little man. I can tell Tommy's modeled himself after his abuser, who must be a man of some—"

She had turned to look directly at Austin, who stared

back at her as if she were a faintly amusing movie but he was about to go to the lobby for popcorn.

"Objection," Eliot said exasperatedly. "It strains credulity to believe that Dr. McLaren can give a profile of someone based on her examination of someone *else.*"

"I believe that's a question for the jury, Your Honor," I interjected quickly, hoping I could nudge the judge aside from his ruling.

"Not when it's a question of law," Eliot said. "The doctor hasn't been qualified as an expert on anyone except children."

"Sustained," the judge said laconically.

"What about Tommy, Doctor?" I asked.

She lifted her stare from Austin. She pursed her lips. "Sometimes," she began slowly, then spoke with increasing urgency, "a child comes to me just shattered. We have to start from zero to build a personality. The child has retreated so far inside in response to the abuse that there's nothing left, no visible signs of responsiveness. In other cases, I learn from questioning others that the child has undergone a complete change in personality—has become, perhaps, more aggressive. Constantly acts out inappropriate behavior."

Janet wasn't glancing at Eliot as if putting one over on him, but it was patently obvious that she was now giving the testimony to which Eliot had successfully objected: detailing the various reactions of child rape victims. *I* looked at Eliot, who was watching my witness closely, not at all caught napping. I frowned. Something— I tried to put myself in Eliot's position. Why was he letting this happen?

"A case like Tommy's is the most difficult, in many ways," Janet was continuing. She was talking directly to the jury and they were watching her with absorption. "Because he seems at first untouched. But what I've discovered is that his maturity is a thin shell, over a personality much too young for its age. Once you pierce that shell—once you make him question whether he's really found the right way to behave—you break through to a very, very young boy who has no idea *how* to act. He doesn't know how to be a child and he doesn't know how to be an adult. Tommy is ten years old, he'll be an adolescent soon. But he's not ready. He's hopelessly muddled about sex, of course, but it goes deeper than that. He's only passing as a child, and not very successfully. For example, he has no friends. He's cut himself off from the few he had, because it's too difficult for him to try to behave normally with them. He doesn't know what normal is. He's a very isolated, very troubled little boy."

I did not nod in sympathy. "It sounds, Doctor, as if you're describing a typically confused boy on the verge of being a teenager. Aren't even normal kids 'hopelessly muddled' at Tommy's stage of life?"

She shook her head emphatically. "Not to this degree. Normal children—we don't use that word, so let's say untraumatized children—have *some* place where they can be themselves. School may scare them but they're all right with their families. Or with their friends. Or they *like* school, and they're okay there. Or in church, or with me—often it's with me. But Tommy has no place to be himself comfortably. He *has* no self. He's putting up a front for everyone, and inside he's just scared to death. I'm very concerned about him."

I expected that expression of personal feeling to draw another objection from Eliot, but again there was only ominous silence from the defense table.

"Dr. McLaren, Tommy didn't report this sexual assault on him for a long time, two years or more. And then he blurted it out while watching television with his parents. Doesn't that sound to you like a story he might have just made up on the spot to draw attention?"

"Objection, Your Honor. No matter how expert the witness is, she can't testify whether someone else is telling the truth. The jurors must decide that for themselves."

I almost stepped on the end of Eliot's last sentence in my eagerness to dissuade the judge from ruling in his favor. "I'm sure the court understands," I said smoothly, "that I'm not asking the witness to tell the jury whether Tommy was telling the truth. I'm asking her whether his behavior is consistent or inconsistent with the many hundreds of patients she's examined. Of course," I added, in a tone that said the judge and I understood this well, I was only speaking for the benefit of less astute minds, "that's what being an expert witness is all about."

Judge Hernandez nodded. "Overruled," he said.

I hurried on with my questioning. "Doesn't it sound like a lie, Doctor?"

Janet spoke as if I were the one who needed educating; or as if I were trying to trip her up with subtle questions. "Of course it could be a lie," she said, "from the bare facts you've given me. But it's also consistent with Tommy's telling the truth. Again, children react differently. Many of them do make an immediate outcry right after the abuse. But many others conceal it, sometimes for years. They feel guilty. And of course the child is afraid of what people will think about him when they find out.

"The way Tommy told what had happened, when he sees the man again after some time, but he's safe at home with his parents at the time, and finally he can't suppress his anger and his hurt any more, I find that consistent with the behavior of a sexually abused child."

Janet turned from the jury to me. It was probably my imagination—I'm sure I was the only person who saw it—that her expression seemed to challenge me. *See? I told you I could do this.* From the corner of my eye I saw Eliot watching her intently.

Janet continued, "The way Tommy's behaved since his revelation also convinces me he was telling the truth. A lying child will break down any number of times, change the story, back off from it. The way Tommy's persisted through telling the story to teachers, police officers, people in your office, and of course me, over the course of weeks of treatment, makes me very much doubt he's lying."

That seemed a good assertion with which to stop. "Thank you, Doctor. I"—Becky was scribbling me a note—"pass the witness."

Becky moved the note toward me. It said, "medical evidence."

"I'll clean that up on redirect," I whispered.

There are so many subtleties to questioning a witness, and everyone has a different style. I had meant to bring up the subject of what Janet's medical exam of Tommy had uncovered. But her answers had led me away from the subject, and I thought it more important to stop when I had, rather than return to, and end with, the weakest feature of my case. I try to hand a witness over to the opposition just when the witness has made her strongest statement on my behalf, when she sounds most credible and, I hope, the jury is most in sympathy with her. Janet had made a very good impression. Let Eliot start attacking her while the jurors were still nodding to themselves over Janet's sincerity and professionalism.

Eliot didn't shy away from the job. "Dr. McLaren," he said, without introduction or preamble. "You said you also gave Tommy a medical examination. What was the result of that exam?"

Shit. This is why *I* should have broached the subject first, to take the sting out of it. By neglecting it I'd given Eliot a weapon.

"The physical exam was consistent with a child who has been sexually abused," Janet said calmly.

Oh, no, no, no. Janet thought she was being clever, but she was giving Eliot exactly the answer he wanted, the one I would have wanted if I'd been on the defense team.

"Let me be more specific," Eliot said. "Did you find physical evidence of sexual abuse?"

"Not definitive evidence," Janet said, "but indications that told me—"

"Any scarring in the anal area?"

"No."

"Or redness?"

"Of course, redness wouldn't have persisted long enough for me—"

"Yes or no, Doctor, redness."

"No."

"Any enlargement of the rectum?"

"No," Janet said coldly. "Of course, from Tommy's descriptions of the sexual assaults, there wouldn't have been."

I caught the plurals. Janet was fighting back. I wanted to call a time out to tell her to calm down. This was my fault. I'd handed my witness over to Eliot with a target plastered on her chest.

"Was there any scarring in the mouth, then?" Eliot asked reasonably. "Or the genitals?"

"No," Janet said. "There wouldn't necessarily—"

"In other words," Eliot concluded, "you found *no* physical evidence of sexual abuse; yet you conclude that that is consistent with sexual assault. Wasn't that your testimony?"

"What I *found,*" Janet said firmly, "was that Tommy was familiar with male sexual physiology in a way no ten-year-old, physically immature boy could be without having experienced—"

"What I asked, Doctor, was whether you had found any *physical* evidence. I didn't ask for your psychological conclusions."

"It's not psychology—" Janet began.

I interrupted. "Objection, Your Honor. This is argumentative. Defense counsel is badgering the witness."

And very effectively. I was speaking more to Janet than to the judge. *Don't argue with him. I'll straighten this out when I get you back.* Janet drew a deep breath while Judge Hernandez overruled my objection. She looked at the jury again, gave them a tight smile.

Eliot had changed personalities like putting on a new hat. Janet wasn't a child. He treated her as if he were as professionally qualified as she, and had no faith in Janet's diagnoses.

"Let's discuss the various reactions you said abused children have. I believe you said if a child is very withdrawn, overly shy with strangers, that tends to indicate the child has been abused."

"I don't believe I said overly shy, but yes, those are common symptoms of sexual abuse. Having been molested by one, of course the child withdraws from other strangers, or even from family members."

Eliot nodded. "And if a child is overly aggressive, that can be a sign as well. What did you call it?"

" 'Acting out.' Meaning a child acting aggressively toward other children, especially sexually aggressive." Janet seemed to want to say more, but perhaps she remembered my advice to give Eliot nothing extra.

Eliot seemed satisfied. "Then you have a case like Tommy's, where he seems perfectly normal, even mature for his age, but that's only a mask for deep insecurity."

"It can be," Janet said carefully, with perhaps an inkling of where Eliot was going. "Of course, there are some perfectly happy-seeming children who actually *are*—"

"So in other words," Eliot said again. I hated that phrase so much that I stood to object to it.

"He's putting words in the witness's mouth, Your Honor."

"Not so far," Eliot answered. "I haven't even finished my sentence yet."

Judge Hernandez motioned for him to continue.

"So," Eliot continued, "if a child is shy, that can be a sign of sexual abuse. If a child is *not* shy, is in fact outgoing, *that* can be a sign of sexual abuse. Or a child who is neither too shy nor too aggressive lights up a signal in your mind that he has been sexually abused."

Janet didn't let Eliot get to her. "There is a wide range of reactions," she said.

"I'm afraid you're going to scare the parents on this jury to death," Eliot said calmly. "Every one of them can go home after hearing your testimony and find signs that their own children have been sexually abused."

"Objection, objection," I was saying well before he finished. "He's not questioning the witness, he's making an argument."

"You have a question?" Judge Hernandez asked Eliot mildly.

"Yes, I have a question. Doctor"—Eliot used the title in a tone that made clear he extended it to the witness only out of politeness—"you said you've examined hundreds of sexually abused children. Have you ever examined any who *haven't* been sexually abused?"

Janet didn't understand. "Of course I treat children who have other problems. My field of specialization is sexually abused children, but I have other types of patients."

Eliot was shaking his head. "I mean, out of the thousand children who've come to you claiming to be sexually abused, have you ever concluded that *any* of them was lying?"

"Of course," Janet said.

"How many?" Eliot asked. "Out of the thousand you've interviewed, how many did you not believe?"

"Objection," I said, with no idea what I was going to say next. I fell back on the standard. "This is irrelevant. We're only concerned here with one child."

Eliot turned to me with a look of surprise, because my objection sounded so familiar. "I believe we talked about a great many children during the witness's *direct* examination," he said innocently.

"Overruled," Judge Hernandez agreed. He looked at me as he would have at a virgin trial lawyer appearing in his court for the first time, making rookie mistakes. "You opened the door, counsel," he added to me, gratuitously.

"How many?" Eliot urged my witness.

"Several," Janet said, and immediately corrected herself. "Quite a few. I can't give you a number—"

"Several?" Eliot said unbelievingly. "Out of a thousand children? What does 'several' mean? Five, six?"

"Many more than that," Janet said hastily. "But you have to understand, the children aren't brought to me until they've convinced other people that something actually happened to them. I'm not—"

"Particularly their parents, who would naturally be very concerned if their children said they'd been sexually attacked by a stranger," Eliot said. He appeared very cool. It was Janet who seemed nervous, or at least pressed, eager to explain everything she said.

"Yes, of course," she said, "but usually they've convinced other people, too. Teachers, their pediatricians, sometimes police officers."

"But you're the professional, Doctor. You're the one who evaluates the children based on your years of experience"—his tone gently mocked the phrase—"and you believe them *all,* don't you, Doctor? You *never* think a child is lying when he claims to have been sexually abused, do you?"

"That's not true," Janet insisted.

"How often? In what percentage of your cases do you decide the child is lying?"

"A small percentage," Janet admitted.

"Very small, wouldn't that be more accurate?"

Janet was straining. She wanted very much to be understood.

"Children come to me very, very hurt. Very troubled. It would be hard to say, 'No, this child isn't damaged. This child is just making up stories.' "

"Well," Eliot responded, " 'troubles' can arise for any number of reasons, can't they? A child could have been damaged in many other ways than by being sexually abused. Ways that could result in lying, couldn't they, Doctor?"

"Yes. Certainly."

"Some children lie every time they open their mouths, isn't that true, Doctor? Have you encountered any pathological liars in your practice, Doctor?"

"Yes. One or two. Genuine pathological liars, rather than the way laypersons throw the term around, are very rare."

"At least *you* don't uncover any very often, do you, Dr. McLaren?" There was no good answer for that. Janet made none. Eliot continued, "If a child immediately reports the sexual attack, that's evidence of truthfulness, isn't it? If the child is still in the immediate grip of the pain and the fear, he or she is believable, isn't he?"

"Yes. Most of us—"

"But if he puts off telling anyone for a week or two, struggling with guilt, or the fear the stranger will return, that's consistent with truthfulness in your evaluation too, isn't it, Doctor?"

"That *is* the way some children react."

"And if he waits more than *two years,* passing up many, many good opportunities, many occasions when he's alone with his parents, safe as he can be, but he doesn't tell them until they're all sitting in front of the television, with a news announcer talking about other children, and the boy's parents paying more attention to those children's stories than to him, and *that's* when the boy tells his story, you find *that* consistent with truthfulness too," Eliot said harshly, almost out of breath from the length of his statement.

"In this case, yes," Janet said, having regained her composure. "I've treated many children who kept silent for months or longer without telling anyone they'd been abused. It's consistent."

"Is there *any* possibility in the timing of when Tommy told his story that would arouse your suspicion?" Eliot asked, as if on the verge of giving up.

Janet struggled to come up with an answer. Eliot let her struggle. So did I, because I couldn't think of any way to help. Long seconds passed. "Many children don't tell for a long time," Janet finally reiterated weakly.

Eliot sat for a moment, tapping a pencil. Buster was tugging at his sleeve, but Eliot ignored him. "Dr. McLaren, you testified that you're concerned about Tommy."

"Yes."

Eliot nodded. "And of course you're trying to help him. You believe what he's told you, don't you?"

This was a question I couldn't have asked without objection. Whether Tommy was telling the truth was, as Eliot had pointed out, for the jury to decide, not any other witness. It worried me that Eliot was asking the question.

"Yes, I believe him," Janet told the jury.

"In spite of the delay, in spite of the complete absence of physical evidence to corroborate his story."

"As I said, those are explainable."

"Yes," Eliot said, "because you believe him you can excuse any inconsistencies."

"Objection. Argumentative."

"Sustained," Judge Hernandez said. "Don't argue with the witness. Disregard that last remark," he added to the jury. As if they could.

"Let's help the *jury* decide how to evaluate Tommy's testimony," Eliot said. Feeling me stir, he added quickly, "Based on your years of experience and hundreds of patients. What did you say are some of the things that would make you think a child was lying?"

"Well, changing his story, for example. Not sticking by it when challenged."

"Like Tommy," Eliot said suddenly.

Janet frowned. "No," she said.

"I mean," Eliot said earnestly, as if just trying to jog the doctor's memory, "there *have* been occasions when he's backed off his story, said it wasn't true."

Janet shook her head, still frowning.

"He's *never* denied the story to you, even once? Never said it was all a lie, nothing actually happened between Austin Paley and him?"

"Never," Janet said firmly.

Eliot sat staring at Janet, with a puzzled look. The back of my neck went cold. Eliot did not ask questions at random. He knew something.

After letting the jury see his surprise, Eliot seemed to

recover himself. "What else, then?" he asked. "What else would indicate to you that the child was lying?"

Janet thought carefully. I wanted to help her, but I couldn't object. This followed exactly my own line of questioning to her.

"Inconsistencies," she said finally. "If the child couldn't keep significant aspects of the story straight, that would certainly be some indication that it wasn't true."

"Changing the story," Eliot said helpfully. "Forgetting details."

"Well, of course, no one's memory is perfect, and often children repress—"

"Doctor," Eliot said gently, "you're making excuses for him again."

"Objection."

"Sustained. Please disregard."

"I mean major details, Doctor," Eliot continued. "Where the assault happened, when, that sort of thing. The identity of the attacker. A child who says this person assaulted me, no, that person did it, no, the first one again, tends to invite suspicion, doesn't he, Doctor?"

"Yes. Of course. But children do get confused about details more easily than adults," Janet said.

"And sometimes they lie, don't they, Doctor?"

She had to say yes. If she said no, children never lie, she'd destroy her own believability. But if she said yes she was admitting the possibility that Tommy had lied. "Yes," Dr. McLaren said.

Eliot didn't give her right up to me. He sat silently for several beats, letting us all think about lying children and the damage they can do. When he finally passed the witness I spoke quickly.

"But you don't think Tommy is lying, do you, Dr. McLaren?"

"No."

"This lack of physical evidence," I asked, frowning as if it troubled me, too. "Is that rare?"

"No, it's common. It's the norm." Janet became more authoritative again as she described how seldom she found physical evidence that children had been raped. I let her speak at some length, until the subject was thoroughly exhausted.

I think my next question surprised her. "Are children naturally suspicious of adults, Doctor?"

"Not in my experience," she said. I didn't like to hear her equivocate that way. I think she heard the doubt in her voice herself, and continued more surely, "Children tend to equate all adults with their parents. They look up to them, literally and figuratively. When he's frightened or hurt, a child looks around to any adult for comfort. That trust seems to be instinctive, until someone violates it."

"Which would confuse the child?"

"It can wreck his entire view of the world," Janet said simply.

"So once that child's trust has been abused, he no longer knows whom he *can* trust, is that right?"

"Yes. Exactly. He has nowhere to turn."

I had no more questions. Neither did Eliot. It was after five-thirty, the jurors looked tired. I was surprised when Janet was excused and Judge Hernandez looked at me inquiringly. I leaned over to Becky. "What have I messed up?"

She showed me her copy of the indictment, on which she'd checked off all the elements of the crime as we'd elicited testimony covering them. We had proven our case, if the jury believed us. That "if" made me very reluctant to rise and say what I had to say.

"The State rests, Your Honor."

The judge nodded briskly as he turned to Eliot. "You'll be prepared to begin in the morning, Mr. Quinn? That is, if you have any witnesses to offer?"

"I do, Your Honor. And we will be ready."

"I'm going to excuse you now...." Judge Hernandez droned his instructions at length before letting the jurors file out. "Well, shit," I said. Becky shot her eyes sidelong at Eliot. As if I were telling a secret, as if Eliot didn't know the damage he'd done.

"I need to apologize to the doctor," I added.

Janet was still in the courtroom. I swept her up with a word and a hand on her arm. There were reporters to get past, of course, but their eyes began to glaze over after only a minute or two of my variation of "This guy's gonna be sorry he ever pulled this nastiness in *this* God-fearing county, by golly," and we were on our way, Becky and the good doctor and I.

"I'm sorry," I said to Janet on our way up the stairs. *"I* should have asked you about the physical evidence first. And I should have given you a better idea how he was going to come at you."

"Hey," she said casually, "I told you this wasn't my first time. I didn't expect him to take it easy on me."

Oh, right. I gave her a look that said it was easy to act nonchalant about the ordeal of cross-examination now, but I'd seen her sweating on the stand. I put my arm around her and she touched my hand. Just for a moment, as we went professionally side by side up the stairs. Just a touch.

We were in my office before I turned to Becky. "He knows something," I said of Eliot. Becky didn't have to ask. "But what?" I added.

"What *can* he know?" Becky answered. "What *is* there to know?"

"What are you talking about?" Janet asked.

"Tommy's denied the story to me," I said. "Who else has he told it didn't happen?"

Becky shrugged. "His parents, probably? Teacher, maybe someone at the daycare center?"

I addressed the doctor: "Tommy's never told you it was someone else who molested him, not Austin?"

Janet shook her head. "I swear," she said, which may have been ironic, since I was asking her in effect if she'd just lied under oath. She smiled at me.

"That was just smoke," Becky opined. "He just wants the jury to start wondering."

"Maybe," I said. "But I hate to leave it at that." Eliot was perfectly capable of that, in fact it was almost required—scatter-shooting doubt through our witnesses' testimony—but I'd be very surprised if he didn't have some evidence to back up at least some of the questions he'd asked. He'd as good as told me so, when he'd claimed Austin was innocent. He must have some proof.

"There's not much we can do about it tonight," Becky said, but when I looked at her her stance belied her expression of resignation. She looked eager to do something, question somebody. I realized how little Becky had done in the trial so far, and what a disappointment that must have been to her, a good trial lawyer. But I couldn't stand to give up any of the weight of the trial. I didn't believe its outcome could be as important to anyone in the world as it was to me.

"How was Tommy?" Janet asked. The rule that excludes witnesses from the courtroom had kept her from watching his testimony.

"He was fine," I said briefly.

But Becky contradicted me. "Not at first. He was so weak when he first took the stand I thought we'd lost him."

"You thought so too?" I said with relief, as Janet asked, "What do you mean?"

"Mark broke him down," Becky said admiringly. "If he hadn't started with how Tommy felt about what had happened, if he hadn't reminded him of how scared he'd been, the rest of his testimony would have been terribly bland. You know how Tommy talks, like he's talking about something that happened to someone else. But he was a sobbing little boy by the time he finished today."

Janet was looking at me with something other than the admiration Becky was expressing. "I hope it didn't look contrived," I said.

"*I* believed him," Becky said. That's all we can ever know. Jurors, if they talk to us at all after trials, tell us such bizarre details on which their decisions turned, things we never noticed, that we've learned not to try to predict them.

"We almost didn't call you today," Becky continued to Janet. "We thought we needed to explain Tommy's delay. But from the way Eliot went after you"—Becky turned to me—"you would have thought Dr. McLaren was our main witness."

Whenever Eliot's name came up they both turned to me, as if I knew everything our opponent was thinking. "Yes," I said slowly. "Because Janet *was* bolstering Tommy's testimony. So if Eliot demolished Janet it would leave Tommy standing alone."

"But he hardly went after Tommy at all," Becky said.

Yes. Eliot had avoided the problem I had seen in his path.

I had laid the trap for him and he had sidestepped it, as casually as if he hadn't known it was there.

Janet was looking back and forth between Becky and me, left out. She turned to me alone.

"Will you need to recall me, do you think? If so, perhaps we should go some place where we can—"

I felt Becky watching us. "I'll call you," I said to Janet. "But first, I have another appointment." I resisted their questions.

It was late for my surprised hosts, but they let me in. I answered their questions, which they interrupted each other to ask, but I didn't stop walking, through the elegant foyer, into the white living room, and through it. "May I?" I asked. They nodded. Mrs. Algren reached for her husband's hand and he looked down at hers, with a surprised expression, as I turned my back on them and went into Tommy's room.

It was dark, except for light through the miniblinds that threw a railroad-track pattern on the carpet leading toward the bed. Tommy wasn't asleep. As I stopped in the center of the room I realized he'd been waiting for me.

"I came to tell you you did fine today."

There was enough light that I could see his head turning back and forth on the pillow in denial.

"Yes you were," I said. There was a desk across the room, with a straight-backed chair. I took it and sat beside the narrow bed, right next to Tommy. He made such a short mound under his covers that he looked like an amputee.

He stopped shaking his head, but not because I'd convinced him. "I'm sorry," he whispered.

"You don't have anything to be sorry for. Anything."

"I wasn't going to—" Tommy said. "I almost didn't—"

"That wasn't your fault either," I told him. I put my hand on his arm that was lying atop the covers. He sighed. "Did Austin ask you to?" I asked quietly.

Tommy nodded. "He called me."

"While my investigator was here with you?"

He nodded again. "But I answered the phone and I told him it was somebody else."

Austin needed Tommy's help to get to him, and Tommy had provided it. "It's all right," I said.

Tommy's voice was so faint I knew he'd lost control of it. "He told me he'd go to prison. He told me what they'd do to him in prison."

"Whatever happens to Austin, he's brought on himself," I said. "You were too young, Tommy, you had nothing to do with it. He planned it all. And with lots of other children. We had to stop him."

There was no response. I wondered how long Tommy had been lying in the dark waiting for me to come, and how long he'd lie there awake after I left. I squeezed his arm again. "He won't bother you any more, ever," I said.

Tommy started crying. Maybe from relief, maybe from the thought of never seeing Austin again, never having a private moment with him.

I hugged him, half-lifting him from the bed. He felt like a much younger boy than he was, like a long-ago memory of my own tiny children, years ago when I'd felt I could encompass their whole lives in my arms. I held him tightly, because the hug had to last Tommy a long, long time. All night.

His tears were wetting my shoulder. After a while he said, "Mr. Quinn knows."

"Don't worry about him," I said. "He's done with you. You're done. You don't even have to go back to the court."

Tommy shook his head against my neck. "He knows," he said again.

I let him back down on the pillow. "What does he know?"

He just shook his head.

"That you wanted to help Austin? That doesn't matter. He won't tell anyone that."

We talked in the dark a while longer. I led our conversation from the past, through today, to tomorrow, to school, to the long future when other things would capture all his concern, and he'd forget all this as surely as we all forget how it is to be a child, guilty but helpless. When Tommy's answers grew short and the silences long, I covered him and pushed aside the hair on his forehead and kissed him there.

"Good night," I said from the doorway, and there was only a faint murmur in reply.

15

Coming back into the courtroom after having rested his case racks a prosecutor's nerves. I've spent my case, put on everything, but then have to walk back in and sit in front of that jury and wait for what the defense will do. The first part of trial is not so tense for the defense, because the State's case is not a surprise. The prosecution lists its witnesses on the indictment, and the defense lawyer has had access to the State's file. Perhaps the defense doesn't know everything a prosecution witness will say, but for the most part the State's case is straightforward and unsurprising.

The prosecutors, by contrast, do not get to review the defense case. That *will* be a surprise. You just have to sit there and take it, hoping you'll have material for cross-examination, hoping inspiration will come when you need it.

One opportunity I felt sure of was that of cross-examining Austin. Eliot and I know what the presumption of innocence is worth. A defendant who sits mum in front of the jury, offering no alternative to the State's story, is just asking to be convicted. Eliot would have to call Austin to testify in his own defense.

When Eliot entered the courtroom he was in close conference with Austin and Buster. Buster was doing the talking. That had often been the case during breaks in the trial. Buster must have been frustrated at being allowed to do so little in such a highly publicized trial, but Eliot would not have let him take over the defense, and Austin would have supported Eliot: he knew who was the better trial lawyer. But Buster was getting his licks in among the three of them. Today he seemed to be upsetting Eliot, and Austin was nodding sober agreement to whatever Buster was saying.

I took my seat. Becky was beside me, but we didn't speak. There was nothing to say. We didn't know what we had to be ready for.

A few minutes later, the jury in the box and the judge on the bench, Eliot still seemed to be in charge of the defense. He rose to say, "The defense calls Martin Reese."

Becky and I gave each other raised eyebrows. Martin Reese was a stranger to us. I turned and saw him coming up the aisle, a pudgy man who'd bought his suit when he was fifteen pounds lighter. He had heavy cheeks, a thick black mustache, and several strands of brown hair combed from one ear to the other. He glared at me as if I were the one who'd made him out of breath.

Becky shook her head when I looked back at her. She didn't know him. "Me," she said softly.

I was the lead prosecutor. Normally that would mean I'd question our victim and cross-examine the defendant if he testified, and the second chair prosecutor could handle the lesser witnesses. But this wasn't a normal case. I'd taken almost everyone during our case in chief. And as I stared at this stranger taking the oath and the witness stand I was already studying him for weaknesses.

"Me," Becky said more emphatically, still too softly for anyone but me to hear.

I looked down at her hand on my wrist. I took a breath. I let my own grip relax slightly. "Yours," I muttered.

She turned away from me at once, pulling a pad toward her, uncapping her pen, and staring at the witness, as did I. Who was Martin Reese?

He didn't want to let us know. Eliot's second question to him, after he'd stated his name, was, "Where do you live, Mr. Reese?"

"I'd rather not say," the witness said. And again he glared at me.

"Do you live in Texas?" Eliot asked.

It appeared he wasn't going to answer. After a few beats

he burst out, "I don't want anyone involved in this trial to know where I live. I've already been harassed enough."

By whom? As some members of the jury followed Mr. Reese's glare to me, I strove to look innocent and perplexed. It wasn't hard.

"Let's put it this way, then," Eliot said consolingly. "Where did you live two years ago?"

"I lived on Sparrowwood Drive, here in San Antonio."

Ping. The first blip of distant alarm sounded in my mind. Martin Reese had been Tommy's neighbor. But how could he refute Tommy's story? Had he stared through his window and seen something *not* happen between Austin and Tommy? I turned and saw that Mr. and Mrs. Algren were again in the audience. Mrs. Algren was pressed as far back against her bench as she could be, as if she were trying to leave the room without moving. Her face was white.

"I'll be right back," I whispered to Becky, and stepped quickly to the gate and through. As I approached the Algrens I gestured to them, restrained but in a way that would not brook refusal. They turned guilty eyes toward me and followed me out of the courtroom.

I ushered Tommy's parents into one of the small conference rooms by the entrance to the courtroom and closed the door behind us. "Who is he?" I asked.

Mrs. Algren was clutching her husband's hand again. He edged subtly between us, but if he was trying to look like his wife's fierce defender, he was failing.

"He was our neighbor," he said. "He moved away about a year ago."

"And?" I didn't want the slow buildup.

"This is why we didn't believe Tommy at first," Mrs. Algren said, imploring me to understand.

I felt cold all over. It was hard for me to move. I turned only my eyes, to her husband.

"Tommy accused Mr. Reese of molesting him," he confirmed.

"Oh, Jesus." I put a hand to my forehead.

"It wasn't true," Mrs. Algren said hastily, as if this news were helpful. "We looked into it and it just wasn't so. Tommy admitted after a while that he'd made it up."

"We were damned lucky the man didn't sue us," Mr. Algren said. "He *would* have, if we hadn't managed to keep the whole thing quiet."

"Even from me," I said quietly. My mind was racing.

"We didn't think anyone else could have known," Algren was saying. "And we didn't dare let a peep of it leak out. He still could have—"

"Go up to my office," I said quietly, disagreement not to be tolerated.

"What are you going to do about it? Can't we—?"

"I don't know yet," I said very quietly. "Be in my office when I come. Whenever I get there."

I felt everyone staring at me as I walked back up the aisle. But they weren't. They were watching the witness.

I didn't have to ask Becky how it was going. She didn't glance at me. Her attention was divided between Martin Reese and the notes she was writing.

As I sat she stood. "Objection," she said. "Calls for hearsay."

Eliot said pedantically, "We're certainly not offering the statement as the truth. We intend to show, to the contrary, that it was not true. Mr. Reese is only going to testify that he heard it made."

"If he heard it," Becky insisted. "I thought he was about to testify that someone else told him the statement was made."

"We will show indicia—" Eliot began, but Judge Hernandez was tired of the argument, and he wasn't going to take the chance of excluding important defense evidence.

"Overruled," he said.

"What did Tommy Algren's parents tell you?" Eliot asked.

"That Tommy had told them I'd molested him," Reese said, in a quiet but fierce voice, a restrained bellow. He was so dark in the face I feared he'd have a stroke before Becky could cross-examine him.

"Could you be more specific?" Eliot asked.

I wrote quickly on my own pad, "It wasn't true. Tommy took it back." Becky glanced at the note with no reaction. She'd already figured that out.

"They said he said I'd lured him over into my yard one day before they got home from work and that I—I *did* things to him. Disgusting things. Made him take off his clothes. Made him do things."

"Was that true?" Eliot asked.

"No!" This time the bellow wasn't restrained. "It was a damned lie! I've got kids of my own. I never—*never*—did anything like that in my life. Never *thought* about it. I'd kill someone who did."

"What happened?"

"The Algrens said they were going to call the cops. I told them they'd better make goddamned sure what they were doing before they made a public fuss of it. I think that took them back a little."

"What did you do?"

"I told them I'd take a polygraph test, and they could get their lying kid to take one, too."

"Did you take such a test?" Eliot asked.

"Objection." Becky was on her feet quickly. "The results of polygraph tests are of course not admissible."

"I didn't ask him for the result," Eliot said easily, not even bothering to stand.

But even mention of having taken a polygraph test is objectionable. The judge sustained Becky's objection. But one of the nice things about being on the defense side is that there's no fear of asking improper questions. The defense doesn't fear a reversal.

"Did you take a lie detector test?" Eliot asked his witness.

"I did," he said, and everyone heard it, over Becky's objection. "And I passed it," he added vehemently, after the judge's ruling. He glared at Becky and she stared back. I was impressed by her coolness, knowing she had nothing to back it up.

Equally coolly, as if he and his witness had done nothing wrong, Eliot asked, "Were the police called?"

"Not after that," Reese said self-righteously, folding his arms.

"Did Tommy ever make this accusation to your face, Mr. Reese?"

"No. I said I wanted to talk to him, with his parents there, but they wouldn't let me near him. When I *would* see him he'd turn his head, he couldn't look at me."

"What finally happened?"

"I kept asking them if they'd made the kid take a lie detector test yet, but they never—"

"Objection," Becky said. "Hearsay." She was sustained, but the witness continued.

"They started avoiding me, but I wouldn't let it drop. I told them they owed me an apology or I was going to sue. Course, I probably wouldn't have, because *I* didn't want it all aired in public either, but I think it scared them when I said it. They finally admitted it'd all been a lie. They said—"

"Objection. Hearsay."

"Sustained."

"Did you get your apology, Mr. Reese?"

"Yeah."

"From Tommy's parents?"

"Yes sir. I told them they needed to make the boy come tell me himself he was sorry, but he never showed up. A few months later I was offered a transfer and I was glad to take it, since the neighborhood didn't appeal to me any more. It should've been them that had to move, though."

Eliot probably realized his witness was less than appealing, no matter how damaging his testimony was. He didn't keep him talking long. When he was passed to our side, Becky began without formalities.

"Mr. Reese," Becky said. "You never heard Tommy accuse you himself?"

"No. He wouldn't face me."

"So everything you've testified about that has just been something you heard from someone else." She shot a glance at the judge. He looked back at her imperturbably.

"I never heard him say it."

Becky nodded. She hesitated. I sensed her nervousness. That's the problem with cross-examining surprise defense witnesses. Too often you have to violate the rule that warns not to ask a question to which you don't know the answer.

"How long were you a neighbor of the Algrens, Mr. Reese?"

He exhaled rather noisily as he thought. "I don't know, five years. Six."

"What kind of relationship did you have with Tommy before this accusation you heard about?"

"What relationship? He was a kid. I didn't have anything

to do with him. Maybe he played with my kids, I don't know, but I hardly even noticed him."

"Never any unpleasantness between you?" I knew Becky was groping in the dark, but I admired her tone. She sounded as if she had something she was about to spring on the fat blowhard.

"He was a *kid*," Reese insisted. "What'm I going to do, get in a fight with him?"

"Did you?"

"No!"

"I don't mean a fistfight, Mr. Reese. Did you ever order Tommy out of your yard, or yell at him for doing something you didn't approve of?"

Reese looked baffled. "Who knows? Maybe."

Becky stared at him as if deciding whether to drop the bomb. Wisely—since there *was* no bomb—she withheld it. "I pass the witness."

Eliot efficiently cleared up the tiny stain Becky had sought to cast on his witness's motives. "Mr. Reese, did you agree to testify today because you have something against Tommy Algren?"

Reese's face darkened again. "You think I'd come here because I'm mad at some kid? You think I like being here? I didn't want to come at all. But when I heard that lying kid was wrecking somebody *else's* life, I knew I had to come."

"Thank you, Mr. Reese."

Good public citizen, he nodded to the jury before he left. We reserved the right to recall him to the stand, hoping we could dig up some dirt on him by the end of the day, but I doubted that. Eliot would have already checked him out thoroughly.

I was thinking of leaving the next witness to Becky as well, and going to confront the Algrens in my office, but when Judge Hernandez told Eliot to call his next witness he surprised me.

"The defense calls Austin Paley."

It seemed too soon. One other witness and then— boom!—the defendant on the stand. But I suppose it made sense. Eliot had already softened up the jury's faith in Tommy's story. Now Austin could kill it completely.

Austin was very formal taking the oath. He looked as if

he were being sworn into office. He held his right hand high and looked the bailiff in the eye as he swore. When he took his seat he relaxed slightly, looked at the jurors without smiling but without looking frightened of them, either.

He was, of course, the best-dressed person in the room, in a gray pinstripe suit, a pale yellow shirt, and a blue and gray patterned tie. Sometimes it was considered best for the defendant to dress down for trial, but there was no reason in this case. Austin wasn't charged with theft. Still, a man with a fashion sense is suspect, isn't he? A man who considers his appearance too carefully? I watched him as coldly as I could, trying to be objectively analytical. Austin was no longer my friend of many years. Nor was he the monster I'd come to picture him. He was a defendant about to testify. I had to destroy him.

"Austin Roberts Paley," he said clearly.

"What do you do for a living, Mr. Paley?"

"I'm a lawyer."

"Are you a native of San Antonio?"

"All my life," Austin said. He was answering the questions in a precise voice, louder than his normal, and without a trace of his usual irony.

"You understand what you're charged with?" Eliot asked.

"Yes," Austin said, with a hint of distaste, and growing more steely.

"Did you do it? Did you sexually molest Tommy Algren?"

"No," Austin said firmly.

Well, we were getting right into it. Austin didn't babble in faked outrage that he'd never touched a boy improperly. That would have allowed me to put on evidence of the other cases against him. He only made a simple denial of the crime with which he was charged in this trial. Austin was a lawyer, and in danger of having his carefully cultivated life stripped from him. He wouldn't misstep.

"Do you *know* Tommy?" Eliot asked next.

"Yes."

What? I thought the jurors stirred, but maybe it was me doing so. I'd expected Austin to deny ever meeting Tommy.

"How do you know him?" Eliot asked.

"Very slightly, and quite some time ago. In addition to

my law practice, I make some investments in real estate from time to time. I was looking over a house in Tommy Algren's neighborhood a couple of years ago, thinking about buying it. I spent a few hours there several different days, because I was afraid the house had some structural problems and couldn't be remodeled the way I wished. While I was working around the house, some neighborhood children took to dropping by. One of them was Tommy."

"You remember him in particular?" Eliot asked, dangerously.

Austin nodded. He looked troubled. "Because he was the one who came most frequently. Sometimes when I arrived Tommy was there waiting for me. He seemed—"

I rose. "Objection, Your Honor. He can't testify what was in someone else's mind."

Eliot was standing beside me, looking only at the judge. "He can certainly testify to his impressions, Your Honor. He was there, he can say what he saw."

"Objection is overruled." I sat down slowly, wondering if any of my objections would be sustained. Now that it was Austin himself on the stand, was the judge determined to cut him as many breaks as possible, to appease Austin's friends?

"How did Tommy seem, Mr. Paley?"

"He seemed like a lonely little boy. I wondered why he never stayed at home, or played with the other children."

"Did you talk to him?"

Austin shrugged. "No more than to any of the others. Well, that's not true. Necessarily I talked to him more, because he spent more time there. But not about anything consequential. It wasn't my place."

"Did you ever take him inside the house with you?"

"No. I never let any of the children inside. It wasn't my house. I didn't want them damaging anything."

"Did you ever take Tommy anywhere else with you?"

"Never."

Austin was looking at the jury, not at me. He was looking from face to face with absolute sincerity. I studied him as scientists study a virus. Was he convincing? Was he believable to strangers who knew nothing about him but what they'd heard in this trial? I saw him as the most careful of liars. It was almost as if he'd planned this day in court, years ago. He'd never been alone with Tommy when someone else could know it. Inside the house, they'd hidden and laughed when other children rang the doorbell. Then he'd driven Tommy to another empty house, and afterward let him out again, unseen, near Tommy's house. No one could deny what Austin was saying now except Tommy, whose testimony had suddenly been rendered suspect by the prior witness. I was coldly frightened as I watched Austin on the witness stand.

Eliot looked at his client sternly. "Austin, did you ever touch Tommy in a sexual way?"

"I don't remember ever touching him at all. *No,* to answer your question. I never felt sexual desire for Tommy. I never touched him that way."

"Did you have occasion?" Eliot asked.

Austin shook his head. "We were never alone together. We never had a private moment, except outdoors in front of the whole neighborhood. The boy and I were never alone."

Eliot looked at him with complete confidence. "Why would he accuse you like this?"

"Objection, Your Honor. He's testified he hardly knows Tommy, he's certainly not qualified to guess what he was thinking."

"He can testify to what he observed, Your Honor, and let the jurors draw their own conclusions." Judge Hernandez, I thought, appeared grateful to Eliot for giving him a good reason for overruling my objection, which he did.

"Why do you think Tommy brought this false charge against you?" Eliot put it this time.

Austin looked as if he'd given the question some thought. "As I said, he appeared to me a lonely little boy who didn't have much of a home life. I assumed it was a bid for his parents' attention."

Eliot nodded: that sounded reasonable to him. After a thoughtful pause he said the words a prosecutor eagerly waits to hear in that situation. "I pass the witness."

There is nothing sweeter for a prosecutor than having the defendant handed over for cross-examination. So many of them are such obvious liars. So many have criminal records that can be brought out on cross. So many have poorly-thought-out defenses, and contradict themselves with only slight aid from the questioner.

But Austin was far from an ordinary witness, and his lawyer was close to being the best in the business. They hadn't rambled while presenting their defense. They hadn't strayed into secondary material. They had not, in short, given me very much to work with. The legal pad before me was almost clean.

"Hello, Austin," I said.

He nodded politely. "Mark," he said.

"You and I have known each other for a long time, haven't we?"

"Yes. Quite a few years."

"I'd say we've been friends. Would you?"

Eliot stood to ask, "Could we get to something relevant, Your Honor?" Judge Hernandez sustained him, so I didn't get to hear how Austin would have answered the question.

"You've told us a little bit about your background," I hurried on. "Tell us a little more. Are you married?"

"No."

"Have you ever been?"

"I fail to see the relevance of anyone's marital history," Eliot said.

"You really can't understand why the jury would want to know that?" I asked him. Eliot didn't return my look. He scrupulously kept his eyes toward the bench.

"Sustained," said the judge.

"Any serious romantic involvements with grown women?" I returned quickly to Austin.

"Same objection."

"I'll answer that," Austin said. He was looking at me, not at the jury. "Of course I've been seriously involved in committed relationships with women. But I'm not going to drag those women up here so you can attack them. This isn't their problem, and I'm not going to embarrass them with it."

"How noble," I said. I thought it and I said it. There was no pause for reflection.

"Objection to the sidebar," Eliot said just as quickly.

"Sustained. Keep your remarks to yourself," Judge Hernandez ordered me. I didn't even glance at him.

I said to Austin, "So you knew Tommy Algren but not in the biblical sense."

"I knew him slightly," Austin said carefully. "Very slightly, for a very short period of time. But I never molested him."

"Not as short a time as most people would expect, under the circumstances. You spent quite a long time at that vacant house, didn't you? How many days did you go there?"

Austin shrugged. "Maybe seven times. Maybe eight."

"For several hours each time?"

"For one or two hours, perhaps. I'm very careful about my investments. I don't make many. I try not to make mistakes."

"Don't you find it surprising that these children remember you more than two years later, after you made only a few brief appearances in their neighborhood?"

"Three of the children *say* they remember," Austin said icily. "I'm sure their recollections have been assisted. After people started questioning them about it, it must have seemed important to them that they identify me, no matter how little importance they'd attached to my appearances at the time."

"But you remember *them,* too. At least, you remember Tommy."

There was ever so slight a pause, while Austin thought how to answer that, or perhaps swallowed the first answer that had sprung to his lips. "I've always had a good memory for faces," he said. "That helps, in my business."

I gave the jury a pause to consider that answer. Which of them would remember a child he'd seen a few times two years ago?

"Since you were there only a few times, the children must have started playing at the house—in its yard—as soon as you appeared."

"It was a vacant house," Austin said casually. "I'm sure they'd already been playing there, before I came and after I stopped coming. Children do like empty houses, don't they?"

"Do they? But they're usually frightened of strangers."

"Not—" Austin stopped himself. "Not in my experience,"

I'm sure he'd been about to say. "Always," he concluded smoothly.

"No," I said. "Certainly not in your case. They came to your house and they remember you playing with them."

"I didn't hear anyone say that," Austin said. He was shifting a bit in his seat. He made himself sit still. "I was inspecting the house. I stayed outside *with* them, sometimes, but I didn't join in the play."

"The children just gathered around you, without your doing anything to encourage them?"

"Children flock to me," Austin said, a trace of wonderment in his voice. "They always have. The Sunday school class I teach at St. Michael's—"

"Objection, Your Honor," I said harshly. "This is unresponsive and self-serving."

"You asked for explanation, counsel," the judge said. "Overruled."

"I was just going to say it's a popular class," Austin concluded with an offhand shrug.

"And I'm sure you enjoy teaching it. Are you a Cub Scout pack leader, as well?"

For a moment Austin forgot to be warm and poised. Then he remembered. His eyelids fell for a moment over the angry glare he'd directed at me. When he opened his eyes again he was looking at the jury, almost apologetically. He gave them again a few seconds of study, and the chance to study him, at ease and sincere. "No," he said quietly.

"You deny the story Tommy told this jury."

"I certainly do," Austin said firmly.

"How much of it did he get wrong? Did he go inside the house with you?"

"No. I already testified, I never let any of the children inside."

"Was the house furnished the way Tommy said, with an old sofa and some folding chairs?"

"No. It was completely vacant."

"With all the empty houses you've been inside with your realtor's license, you remember particularly that this one was completely empty?"

He blinked, but only for an instant. "I spent more time than usual in this one, because I was thinking of buying it."

"So you remember this particular house vividly. It stands out in your memory."

"I wouldn't say vividly."

"But Tommy remembers it vividly, doesn't he, Austin?"

"With Tommy it's his imagination that's vivid," Austin snapped.

I wanted to keep him talking about Tommy. It seemed to me that Austin's voice had an intimate quality when he mentioned the boy. "He remembers seeing you change clothes," I said. "Did that happen?"

Austin shook his head impatiently. "I didn't keep clothes at the house."

"So if anyone saw you arrive at the house wearing a suit and leave wearing casual clothes, they'd be wrong too?" I had no witness to this, but Austin didn't know that.

He frowned in memory. "I suppose once I might have taken a change of clothes, if I was going to play tennis or something after stopping at the house."

"So Tommy might have been right about that."

"Not about watching me change. I told you—"

"But he could have gotten that detail right. What about the drive? Did you ever take him anywhere in your car?"

"No."

"What kind of car did you drive then, Austin?"

His eyes flickered. He saw the trap. "I believe then I had a Continental." He glanced at the jury. "The economy was better back then," he told them. No one chuckled for his benefit.

"What color was it?"

"White. Maybe the children would remember it. It was a very gaudy machine." He rubbed his lips together briefly.

"What about the interior? What color was it?"

"Oh, I don't remember very well." That was a poor answer. He thought better of it. "Maroon. It was maroon leather inside."

"Bench seat or bucket seats in the front?"

"I think everything has bucket seats now, doesn't it?"

"So it had bucket seats."

"Yes."

"Anything distinctive about the interior?"

He blinked again. He'd lost a bit of his composure. No

matter how debonair you are, the witness stand makes you sweat. Especially if you're lying. "I don't think so," he said.

"What was between the front seats? A hand brake? A storage compartment?"

Austin leaned toward me. "If you plan to pass these details on to your complainant, in hopes of convincing this jury—"

"Don't you want to describe the car?" I shot back. "Or do you think Tommy will remember it better than you?"

"Objection," Eliot said sternly, as if putting a stop to a spat between children. He not only stood up, he moved out into the narrow space between us, toward his client. "I object to the prosecutor badgering the witness and arguing with him. This isn't a duel."

Eliot was only giving his client time to recover himself. Austin was quietly drawing a breath, regaining his calmness. I didn't want to give him any more time.

"I'll sustain the objection," Judge Hernandez said easily.

Eliot took his time taking his seat. I started speaking again before he did. "What was between the front seats of your car, Austin?"

"A storage compartment," he said.

"What did you keep inside it?"

"I object to this as irrelevant," Eliot ventured.

I stood to argue the point. "This is to test the witness's memory, Your Honor. As opposed to the victim's memory. That's precisely what's at issue here."

I stared at the judge. I needed this. He looked back at me with a stare that said he owed me nothing. "Test it on something more relevant, counsel. Objection sustained."

I sat down, with no time to seethe, and asked quickly, "So Tommy's wrong about the car. Is he wrong about the house you took him to?"

"Yes," Austin said.

"It didn't have a pool?"

"There was no house," Austin said calmly, not remotely falling for that.

"It didn't have white furnishings, and pastel prints on the walls? There wasn't a bar from which you made a drink, and gave him a Coke?"

"I never took him to any such house."

I sat back, staring at him. After a few moments I said, "You heard Mr. Reese's testimony."

"Yes," Austin said vigorously, nodding. It was nice of me to remind the jury of it.

"That Tommy falsely accused him of sexually assaulting him?"

"Yes. Just as he's falsely accused me."

"Then why didn't you settle the problem as easily as Mr. Reese did?"

"What?"

"Why didn't you take a lie detector test?"

"Objection," Eliot said. "The prosecutor knows this is a completely improper question, Your Honor."

"So the defense has learned some law between this witness and the previous one," I said. "It was the defense who opened this door, Your Honor."

Judge Hernandez hesitated. Austin, who had had a few moments to think, saved him from making a ruling. "I don't mind answering that, Your Honor," Austin said easily. And just as easily, he turned back to me confidently and said, "I *did* offer to take a polygraph exam."

"What?" I was outraged. "To *whom* did you make such an offer?" Austin had cornered himself. He must have known that whatever name he said next, I'd find that person and put him or her on the witness stand to contradict him.

"I told my attorney I'd take one, if it would clear this thing up," Austin said. He looked directly at Eliot.

If Eliot was surprised, he didn't show it. He looked straight back at his client. His eyes didn't widen. His mouth, perhaps, hardened slightly. I know lawyers who, in that situation, would nod in support of their client, or turn to the jury or opposing counsel with a knowing look and smile of assurance. Eliot didn't do that. He sat stock still, giving nothing away. But I knew. I knew, from his lack of response either way, that Austin was lying. But there was nothing I could do about it. He had picked the one person I couldn't call as a witness to refute him. The attorney-client privilege wouldn't let me.

"But Eliot said there was no point," Austin continued smoothly, looking at him. "He said since the result couldn't be admitted in court anyway, it wouldn't solve anything. I decided—"

"Oh, stop it!" I snapped. "This is self-serving hearsay, and you know very well I can't call him to contradict you."

"Objection, Your Honor," Eliot said. His voice was cool as iced tea. "Counsel should address his objections to the court, not the witness."

"Don't argue," the judge said noncommittally.

I hadn't let my attention stray from Austin. "Go take one now," I told him. "We'll take a recess. I won't—"

"Objection," Eliot said again, exasperation creeping into his tone. "Counsel isn't even asking questions. And he knows this is an irrelevant line of inquiry."

"I won't object," I said, holding out my hands in a gesture of reasonableness.

"Move along, counselor," the judge ruled.

I sat for a long time, as if his ruling had defeated me. I was trying to project my entire mistrust of the defendant. I glanced at Becky. On the legal pad in front of her were a series of questions she'd thought of, then crossed out as I'd asked them on my own. Only two sentences remained.

I looked back at Austin, who waited for me, more warily than when he'd first sat down. "Did you buy the house on Sparrowwood?" I asked.

He shook his head. "It wasn't suitable."

"After you'd used the house to spring your trap," I continued, "after you'd found Tommy and raped him, you wanted to stay well clear of the neighborhood, didn't you?"

Austin sighed, unreasonably maligned. "After I'd decided the house wouldn't do, I had no reason to go back."

"Did you ever contact Tommy again?"

"No. I never contacted him at all."

I nodded. I held Austin's stare. He didn't drop his eyes. "No more questions," I said.

Eliot had a few, mainly reiteration of Austin's claim of complete innocence where Tommy was concerned. His redirect examination was brief and offered nothing new. I didn't take up the witness again. Austin stood and walked back to the defense table, walking a little stiffly in his desire to appear unruffled. I had shaken him, but that was only a personal satisfaction. It didn't help the case. It was hard for me to evaluate his performance. There was no way he could have appeared credible to me. I'd have to wait for the jury's reaction. I was afraid of what their answer would be. For a jury to take a child's word over a grown man's, the disparity in their honesty has to be obvious. Austin hadn't been an obvious liar by any means. And the defense had Martin Reese on their side. Two grown men against Tommy.

"Call your next witness," Judge Hernandez said. He was sitting up alertly, expecting Eliot to rest his case. Traditionally the defendant is the last defense witness, the one who will leave the strongest impression on the jury. But it wasn't Eliot who stood in response to the judge's order. It was Buster Harmony, looking self-satisfied at finally getting an official word in.

"The defense calls Mamie Quinn," he said.

I turned to stare at Eliot. He sat with his eyes downcast as if he hadn't heard. But then he stood too, along with Austin, and I looked up the aisle and saw Mamie Quinn, Eliot's wife of forty years, walking serenely toward us. Mamie was a lady of grandmotherly proportions, today wearing a flowered dress and without, for once, her traditional campaign-function hat. I stood, automatically, as she neared us. She smiled at me in greeting. The round lenses of her glasses magnified her blue eyes, making her appear a wide-eyed innocent. There was nothing troubled in her expression.

I turned toward Eliot as I sat down, but he had already reseated himself and didn't look up. Buster Harmony made harumphy noises of greeting as Mamie was sworn in.

So Mamie did know. She knew the old story—she and Eliot had already been married then—of when Eliot had failed to protect Austin, and she felt the family obligation toward him extended to her, too.

I looked at Austin. He didn't look smug, or even relieved. He sat stiffly, his mouth compressed, like a ventriloquist being very careful not to move his lips.

Since sitting down again I'd remained stock still. I hadn't even drawn a legal pad toward me as Buster began questioning Mamie about her name and background. Becky touched my wrist. When I looked at her she mouthed, "Me."

I shook my head, and did reach for a pad. "I have to do it," I whispered.

Becky shook her head minutely but more urgently than I had. "I'll take her," she said, very quietly. "I don't owe her anything."

I looked at Mamie, listening intently to Buster's routine question, then returned my gaze to Becky. "Very, *very* gently," I said. "She's mistaken, not lying."

Becky nodded at once. She turned her attention to the witness. I looked again at Eliot. He was aware of my gaze, I was sure, but he just stared straight ahead, making notes, watching the witness as if she were a stranger to him. I chewed my knuckle and watched Mamie's performance, wondering if anyone could possibly disbelieve her.

"Mrs. Quinn, do you know this man beside me?" Buster was asking her.

"Of course. Austin Paley. Hello, Austin."

"What is your relationship to him?" Buster asked.

"He's a longtime family friend," Mamie said, smiling at him, "of Eliot's and mine."

"So you see him socially."

"Oh, more than that. We rely on him."

Buster smiled in satisfaction, but he didn't want to lay on the friendship angle so thick that people might think Mamie would lie to save Austin. So Buster cut to the facts. "Do you remember what you were doing May twenty-third, nineteen-ninety, Mrs. Quinn?" Naming the date Tommy had testified he'd spent the afternoon with Austin.

"Yes."

"Where were you?"

"I was at home, all day."

"Was your husband home with you?"

"No. Eliot was working."

"He was retired by that time, wasn't he?" Buster asked officiously.

"He was retired from public office," Mamie corrected him gently. "But he still maintains a private practice. He was in his office that day, I believe."

In those few words Mamie left Eliot out of the picture. She was protecting him from perjury as well as from his past. I looked at him again and whispered to Becky, "Eliot

won't testify either way, I'm pretty sure. Play it that way."
Becky nodded. She might need the information for her
cross-examination, and I knew Eliot much better than she.
He wouldn't commit perjury, even for this. But he sat there
condoning it.

"Were you alone all day?" Buster asked Mamie. Buster
had fallen into his own trial personality, in which he sat up
very straight in his chair, frowning slightly with each question, and speaking in a loud, overenunciated voice as if he
were addressing a crowd of foreigners.

"No. At about noon I received a call from Austin. He
called to confirm another appointment we had, and then we
just chatted, as we often did."

"How did you feel that day?" Buster asked.

"I was not at my best," Mamie said slowly. "I'd awakened
that morning feeling rather oppressed by the heaviness of
the air. It was hard for me to catch my breath. By lunchtime
I had a cough."

"Did Austin notice that when you were talking on the
phone to him?"

"Yes. He acted very concerned, of course. When he heard
me having trouble drawing a breath he said I should call
my doctor. But I said I'd be fine. He said then he was going
to come and sit with me. I told him don't be silly, that
wouldn't be necessary, but before I could say any more he'd
hung up.

"Well." Mamie laughed gently, rolling her eyes at the
jury. "I felt like a silly old woman. But I was happy when
Austin arrived at my door a little while later. He was very
sweet, made me tea and made sure I was comfortable, and
we just sat like old friends in a nursing home for the rest
of the afternoon, talking and laughing and watching some
of the silly shows on the television."

Did this sound believable? It did to me. I could picture
it: Mamie the gracious old lady from another era, who
missed the tea parties she'd once had and was glad to host
another; Austin rather time-displaced himself, happy to play
the gentleman caller. I could see them gabbing away the
afternoon, sometimes laughing and leaning forward to touch
each other's knees, gossiping about everyone they knew with
that friendly maliciousness of small town southern ladies.

"Did he stay late?" Buster asked.

Mamie nodded. "Until after seven. Eliot was running late, and Austin stayed until Eliot called to say he was on his way home. I kept telling Austin he shouldn't waste his whole day on me, but he wouldn't hear of leaving me alone. He insisted he had nothing better to do—which I didn't believe for a minute," Mamie added, smiling, as if speaking fondly of a nephew she knew got into mischief when she didn't have her eye on him.

Buster asked, "Did he ever leave, even for a few minutes?"

"Leave the house?" Mamie asked. "No. I don't believe he even made any phone calls. He was keeping rather a close eye on me, as if I were a critical case."

I looked at Eliot. Mamie Quinn was throwing herself into her role, acting as if she'd never been asked these questions before and as if she didn't understand the significance of her answers. She sounded quite sincere. Eliot was doing his own job, making notes, nodding along with the testimony. But his face was rather lifeless.

"Thank you, Mrs. Quinn," Buster said, with a valedictory lighter-toned flourish. "I pass the witness."

Mamie turned to me. She'd seen many trials, she knew what happened next. She gave me a disarming smile but settled herself for my attack. I looked back at her, not angrily, but not with any sympathy, either. Mamie looked surprised when it was the girl next to me who spoke up.

"Mrs. Quinn, my name is Rebecca Schirhart. I'm going to ask you a few questions now, all right?"

"Certainly."

"Please, if I don't make myself clear, just ask me to rephrase. Now, you said Austin Paley has been your friend for many years."

"Yes."

"And he must be a very good friend, to have rushed to your side the way you've described."

"He is," Mamie said. She was more subdued than she'd been under Buster's questioning. She was watchful.

"Have you spent many social occasions with him?" Becky asked.

"Very many."

Becky nodded. "Mrs. Quinn, we've been talking about a day more than two years ago. Not a particularly eventful day, from what you've said. Nothing out of the ordinary, just one of many visits from your good friend. How can you be so sure of the date?"

Mamie smiled at her, prepared for the question. "I probably wouldn't have," she said, "but I keep a medical diary. I've had a few problems over the years, and my doctor suggested I keep a diary, so we could trace my symptoms that recur. As I said, I was very short of breath that day in May. I kept a record of that, and that helped me place the date exactly."

Becky smiled at her admiringly. "Do you have the diary with you? Or could you bring it for us to see?"

No, Mamie wasn't going to provide us with documentary evidence with which to impeach her. She laughed lightly. "Oh, my dear, I threw it away some time ago. It's not a personal diary, just a medical one. There's no need to keep it long after each doctor visit. I usually start anew each year."

"So you threw that one away at the end of nineteen-ninety?" Becky asked. "But that's been almost two years. So you *haven't* been able to consult it recently to be sure of the date."

Mamie had been ad-libbing about the medical diary, I was sure, and as extemporizing witnesses usually do, she'd messed up. She looked flustered. "No, I kept it past the end of the year," she said, contradicting herself. "I came across it again recently, and it was only then I threw it away."

"After first leafing through it to see which afternoon you'd spent with the defendant," Becky said gently. Mamie frowned but didn't answer. "If you *could* bring us the diary," Becky continued, "wouldn't it show that May twenty-first of nineteen-ninety wasn't the only day you were short of breath? Wasn't that a common symptom of yours, if you kept a diary to record it?"

"Of course it did happen now and again," Mamie said. "But not often as severely as that day. And of course, I remember the day for other reasons."

"Such as the TV shows you watched with the defendant?" Becky asked.

Mamie laughed again. "Oh, they were nothing memorable. Just silly things, you know, old reruns and game shows. Nothing that would stick in my mind for two years."

"You can't tell us one television show you watched and enjoyed with Austin on May twenty-fifth?" Becky asked. I winced at the question, but then, I had the indictment in front of me. Mamie didn't seem to notice anything amiss.

"Andy Griffith, I think," she said, concentrating. "And what's that ridiculous one about the people lost on the island?"

"Do you remember the particular episode you saw on May sixth?"

"Could anyone?" Mamie asked the jury, reasonably. None of them responded even by gesture. Jurors have a way of keeping their feelings to themselves, as if it would be cheating to nod or smile.

"Have you talked to Austin Paley about what date it was?" Becky asked gently.

"No," Mamie said quickly, then realized that was unbelievable. "Well, of course we discussed it, to be sure I was right. But *I* was the one who remembered the day. I came to him to tell him I could"—she didn't want to use the word *alibi*, which sounded like something a criminal needed—"vouch for where he'd been that day."

"So the date of May twenty-fourth, nineteen-ninety, was pretty firmly fixed in your mind by the time you talked to him?"

"Yes." Mamie nodded, sure of herself. Eliot stirred, finally, pulled his file toward him and found a document, then hastily leaned over and whispered to Buster, who looked back at him blankly. Eliot whispered again, more urgently.

Becky was asking, "And when your good friend needed help to place himself somewhere other than in a house where a young boy was being raped on that day, you came forward?"

Mamie looked at her interrogator with conviction. "I knew he was innocent as soon as I heard. I was very glad later when I realized I could help."

Becky let her get away with the testimonial. The jury could see the bias behind it. "Help him by establishing an alibi for him on the date of the crime," Becky said. "Which was that?" she asked suddenly, as if she'd forgotten herself. "What day have we been talking about?"

"May twenty-fourth," Mamie said confidently. Silence greeted her answer. She heard it. "Of nineteen-ninety," she added, "not this year." More silence. Mamie looked at the jury.

"Are you sure?" Becky finally asked.

"Objection, Your Honor," Buster said, standing and leaning forward on the defense table. "The prosecutor has obscured the date by injecting incorrect ones into her questions, without foundation in the evidence. The witness has already testified that the date was May—"

"Objection to counsel leading the witness!" Becky shouted quickly. "Especially as he's not even examining the witness at the moment."

I think Buster had said the correct date, but I hadn't heard him over Becky's raised voice, so I'm sure Mamie hadn't either, so much farther away. She looked puzzled to the point of fright. She shot a helpless glance at Austin, but he could do nothing to help. I watched him, as I'm sure did at least a couple of the jurors, to see if he was giving his witness a signal. Austin sat with his hands in his lap, looking sad for Mamie. His mouth still didn't move.

"Overruled," Judge Hernandez snapped. "Both objections overruled. Take your seats."

As she did, Becky asked immediately, "What date was it, Mrs. Quinn?"

"The same date you've been talking about," Mamie said. She pointed toward us, toward the notes and documents on the table in front of us. "The date the boy says—says . . ."

"But what date was that?" Becky asked gently.

Mamie stared at her, not glaring, but very intently, as if Becky's face would give her a clue if Mamie watched it hard enough.

"May," she said slowly, then quietly took her shot: "twenty-first. Nineteen-ninety."

At the defense table, Austin winced, but by now Mamie wasn't watching him. She was looking to Becky for reaction, to see if she'd gotten it right.

"Are you sure?" Becky asked quietly.

"I think so. I'm sure it was the same day. I made sure of that."

"Then what you're sure of is the date your old friend Austin Paley needed help with, not the date you actually saw him."

"No." Mamie shook her head vigorously. "I told you, I came to him. I was sure before I talked to him."

"Perhaps your husband could confirm the date," Becky said. "Perhaps he kept his business appointment book."

"I told you, Eliot wasn't there," Mamie said firmly. She was probably glad to shift away from the subject of dates.

"That's right," Becky said as if she'd just remembered. "Austin Paley came to your house when you were alone and he left before your husband returned, even though he didn't want you to be alone."

"He'd been there a long time by then," Mamie said, "and he knew Eliot would be home momentarily."

"But the timing was such that only you can say he was there that day," Becky said, an unnecessary remark. Sometimes we say unnecessary things to make sure everyone in the courtroom is thinking them at the same time.

"Yes," Mamie said.

Becky looked at her indulgently. "I pass the witness," she said.

Buster gave Mamie the chance to repeat again her certainty of the date Austin had been at her house, and offered Mamie the chance to say that she hadn't been confused about the date at all until the prosecutor's misleading questions. When Buster passed the witness again Mamie turned her staunch gaze on Becky, ready, but Becky, as if forbearing to mistreat an old woman, simply smiled at her and said she had no more questions. This time Austin rose to assist Mamie through the gate as she made her way past us. She favored him with a smile and a touch on the arm. Her concern and affection for him were obvious, and unfeigned.

Eliot was on his feet in response to Judge Hernandez's command to call his next witness. There was a pause. I knew that pause, the fearful one when the defense lawyer is certain he hasn't fully done his job, that there is some obvious witness he's forgotten to call.

"The defense rests," Eliot said.

Judge Hernandez's eyes went up to the clock above the courtroom entrance. It was after eleven-thirty. "Both sides approach," he said, drawing us with his fingers.

When Eliot and I stood before him he leaned forward, hand covering his microphone, and asked me, "You have rebuttal witnesses?"

"Yes."

"Who are they?" he asked.

I scowled. He was being too blatant. "I don't have to tell you that. Certainly not in the presence of the defense."

The judge sighed as if I'd wronged him. "Don't get your back up, Blackie. I'm simply thinking of my schedule. How soon can you have them here, and how long will you take?"

"Soon. We should take the afternoon."

He nodded. "Step back."

He released the jury, and all of us, for lunch. That gave me about an hour and a half to take apart Eliot's well-constructed defense. I started by taking apart the parents of my victim.

"Why the hell did we first hear about this in the middle of trial and not before?" Becky was already interrogating Mr. and Mrs. Algren when I walked into my office. I stayed to the side and let her.

Again Mr. Algren was the one who spoke up. "We didn't think anyone else knew. We wanted it kept quiet."

"Mr. Algren, you try to keep things quiet from the other side, not from your own lawyers," Becky explained. "Did you think we'd pass the news on to the media if you shared it with us? Did you think we'd want *any*one to know?"

"He almost sued us," Algren explained quietly. "If word had gotten out about what Tommy'd said about him, he probably *would* have sued us. This is a big office, we didn't want anyone to know. Besides, we didn't think it would hurt your case. No one knew except the Reeses and us. We didn't think anyone would find out."

"Well, they did," I said, stepping forward. "The defense in this case is very, very thorough. There were probably rumors around the neighborhood. They tracked them down."

As we should have done. *I* should have learned this long

before trial. I'd spent my investigational resources on the defendant; I hadn't investigated my own primary witness closely enough. I hadn't realized his damned parents would try to hide information from me.

"What can we do now?" James Algren said. "How can we make up for it?"

That's what I'd been thinking about, ever since Reese had testified. What I'd realized was not only what had to be done, but how I could again lead my opponent to the edge of the pitfall he'd avoided once.

Becky was waiting for my answer too. She saw that I had one. "We need your wife's help," I said to James Algren. Mrs. Algren tilted her head, surprised to be singled out.

"And Tommy's," I said sadly.

16

I had found in my mind a plan. It had formed there without conscious effort, but with a certainty that it was the only thing to be done. In fact, I marveled at the beauty of it: an opportunity to betray both my "client"—for if a prosecutor has a client in a case it is the victim—and my old mentor.

Then, sitting at this intersection of my life, a spectator to the imminent collision, I saw my son.

The Algrens had left when Becky and I emerged from my office, and David was sitting there, his legs jutting out from the plastic visitor's chair, quietly waiting his turn to see me. I said his name, with the surprise I felt. He stood and was introduced to Becky, who quickly left us alone.

"I came to watch a little," David said. He must have realized the inadequacy of that explanation; he hadn't come to watch me in trial since he was thirteen. He smiled awkwardly. "I know you don't have time for lunch. Want me to get you a sandwich or something?"

"I have time," I said. Judge Hernandez did not skimp on lunch breaks, and I had nothing else to do before trial resumed.

David and I walked across Main Plaza, past the *raspa* vendor and through the noise of the five-man band in the square, to a Mexican restaurant dense with smells and close-packed tables populated by courthouse regulars. Judge Hernandez occupied one, with a courtier or two. There were even a few jurors, wearing the bright blue badges that identified them as unapproachables to the participants in the trial.

David and I got a booth, as private as lunch got that close to the courthouse. I ordered light, flautas and rice, but David got the special that came on two plates. He seemed to absorb the food without filling his mouth, because he still did most of the talking.

"How's it going?" he asked. "The papers make your case sound airtight."

"Wait 'til you read about this morning's developments."

He asked what they'd been, but I dismissed the subject briefly. I found David's presence touching. And, as always, touchy. He knew the importance of this case to me, but I didn't believe he'd come to offer his support. But with David I couldn't question him openly.

"Were you in the neighborhood?" I asked instead.

"Sort of. Well, really I was just wandering." He took a breath. "I'm leaving the company."

It didn't sound like good news to me, after what he'd told me of his corporate life. Had he grown too uncomfortable working with people, or had they finally found him too hard to work with? I didn't know how David got along at work, except by his own account, which hadn't made the workday sound like fun for anyone.

"Really?" I said, concerned. "You think maybe the company's not doing well?"

"The company's doing great," he said, around a mouthful of *chalupa compuesta*. "I think I can do better."

I nodded. "You're responsible for a larger share of the company's success than you're getting paid for," I guessed, smiling as I said it.

He shook his head impatiently. "It's not just that. I'm tired of running everything I think through three layers of foot-draggers. By the time we get around to doing it it's not worth doing any more."

"Tired of having bosses. I understand that."

There was a pause, for me to express an opinion or question his loss of security or nervously ask about his other prospects. I didn't. David looked up at me, waited, then went on with a note of relief. "I'm going into business for myself."

313

I smiled again. "That's the only thing to do if you don't want bosses. Are you looking for backers?"

Lines appeared above his nose as he shook his head quickly. "I'd rather lose a bank's money."

"I know you're a good risk," was all I said. Modest as his accounts of his working life were, I thought I'd detected that most of the computer software company's new product ideas were David's.

He was still waiting, as if he'd be plagued by his own doubts until he'd fended off mine. I was thinking of Tommy. The night before I'd tucked him in, something I would never do again for my own son. I had done it often, years ago. Often the tucking in was the first time I'd seen David that day. It didn't seem that long ago, and maybe David was here because it didn't seem very far in the past to him, either. He was still, I realized, waiting for me to play the coda of his day.

But I wouldn't do it. I wouldn't pick at his plans. As I'd realized that I must loosen my grip on the trial, set its participants free, I had realized the same thing about my son. "David," I said, putting my hand over his, "I hope it will be a great success. If there's any way I can help, just tell me. And if you need any advice, you know what mine will be worth. Because I haven't even figured out how to turn on a computer yet."

He looked at me suspiciously. My laissez-faire approach to his affairs was new. He was waiting for me to drop it and begin meddling.

I was still remembering him as a baby, maybe one year old. There'd been moments then, before he could talk, when David would look at me with such perfect comprehension that I was sure he would remember the moment for the rest of his life. I'd told myself to take note of them, so we could compare memories some day, but I had forgotten. Looking at David grown, I was sure he *had* remembered everything. He was giving me the same look of perfect understanding. I tried to remember the good moments of his childhood, the baseball advice, the walks. Had I forgotten some, good or bad, some moment so poignant for him it had shaped our whole relationship without my knowing? "David?"

"Uh-huh."

But it wasn't his burden, for me to ask for that interpretation. Maybe some day he'd have a son of his own who could ask him about those times he'd spent with his father, and David could pass on those important memories to *him*. That's how memories should pass, not *up* the generational stream.

I said, "Did you know it's considered good luck, after telling someone you're starting a new business, to buy his lunch?"

He grinned.

As I began my rebuttal case, a phrase from the war in Vietnam stayed in my mind: "We had to destroy the village in order to save it." That's what I was about to do to the family that was the centerpiece of my case. Because the case wasn't about them. They were only there to represent all of Austin Paley's victims, past and potential. As symbols they were necessary. As actual people, they were expendable.

"The State calls Pamela Algren." I'd had to ask her her first name in my office during the lunch break. Pamela. Pretty name. A girl's name. She'd probably been a pretty little girl, devoted to her parents. Her first name reminded me that Mrs. Algren had a life much larger and longer than the part this trial would touch. But she could be injured here in a fundamental aspect of her character, an injury she would reexamine for the rest of her life.

"You have a son?" I asked her before she was quite settled in the witness stand.

"Yes, Tommy. He's ten years old." Pamela Algren shifted, trying to make herself comfortable. She glanced at the judge and the jury and looked away again. I waited until she was looking at me, which she did with a little start, because she'd just remembered her instructions, which were to watch me. She'd failed already.

"The Tommy Algren who was sexually assaulted by this man here," I said, pointing.

All I wanted was to turn Mrs. Algren's attention toward Austin. She studied him with appalled curiosity. I don't think he'd been real to her until that moment.

"Yes," she said, looking down at her hands. I waited.

When she looked up at me I said, "Austin Paley isn't the first man Tommy's accused of sexually abusing him, is he?"

"No," Mrs. Algren said in a small voice.

"Who *was* the first?"

She was very quiet. She didn't want to say the name, even now. "Martin Reese," she said, "a neighbor of ours."

"Was he a friend, as well as a neighbor?"

"No. Just neighbors. You know, we'd wave. I don't think he was ever in our house."

"Did Tommy play at Mr. Reese's house?"

"Once in a while, I think," Mrs. Algren said, after hesitating. "The Reeses had a boy close to Tommy's age."

"Did Tommy like Mr. Reese?"

The question took her by surprise. "I don't suppose Tommy knew him any better than we did. At least before."

"Before Tommy accused him."

"Yes," she said softly.

"How did that happen? What did Tommy tell you?"

"He told us during dinner one night. He said he'd been playing in the back yard and Mr. Reese had leaned over the fence and called him over and asked Tommy to come help him with something, then he just lifted him right over the fence and Tommy saw that he wasn't wearing any pants."

"You must have been surprised," I offered.

"We were stunned," Pamela Algren said, forgetting her nervousness in front of the crowd in the courtroom as she fell back into that amazing scene. "We just—couldn't even move for a minute. We couldn't think what to do."

"Did Tommy say anything more?"

"Yes. He described it all. He said—" She stopped, self-conscious again. I nodded to her. "He said Mr. Reese made him take off his clothes, too. He said no one else was home, and they went inside, and Mr. Reese—abused him."

"Did you believe Tommy?" I asked.

"Of course."

"So what did you do?"

"We were going to call the police that night, but James— my husband—said we should confront Mr. Reese ourselves first. So we waited until the next day and James went to see him, but it turned out Mrs. Reese had been home too, inside the house, the day before when Tommy said Mr. Reese had

316

abused him. Well, of course, we figured she might say that anyway, but we did more checking—"

"You confronted Tommy."

"Well, that too, and it turned out not to be true. It just didn't—match up."

"Tommy lied," I said briskly.

"Yes."

"Did you ever call the police?"

"No. There was no need."

"Did you have Tommy examined?"

She looked surprised. "By a psychologist?"

"By a medical doctor."

"Oh. No. There was no point. It was over too quickly."

"The case never came to trial."

"Oh, no," she said in a horrified tone. "Nothing like that. It never went outside our two houses. We told Mr. Reese we were sorry and that was that. He moved away later, to our relief."

I paused to study her. So did everyone else in the courtroom. Finally I said, "You said Tommy told you Martin Reese had abused him. Is that how he said it?"

"No. I don't think he ever used that word."

"Did he say Mr. Reese had touched him in a bad way?"

Pamela Algren's denial came in a rush. "Oh, no. It was much more explicit than that. That's why we believed him." She appealed to us all to understand their mistake. "Tommy told us things he couldn't have just heard on TV, or at school. He described it in great detail."

"What did he say?"

She gave me a disapproving glance. Wasn't "great detail" enough for decent people? I returned her stare absolutely blankly. I wasn't pretending to be her friend.

"He described the man naked," she said.

"What, in particular, did he describe?"

She was blushing. "An erect penis," she said clearly, so she wouldn't have to repeat it.

"To your satisfaction? So you were convinced he'd seen it?"

"Yes," she said tightly, still red.

"And what else?"

She was speaking in a voice that tried for firmness but

didn't have much breath behind it. "He said Mr. Reese took off his clothes, Tommy's clothes, and ran his hands over him."

"Again, did he go into detail?"

"Yes, very much. He said he put his finger between Tommy's buttocks."

"And what else?" I asked relentlessly.

She was looking at me as if she hated me, which was neither here nor there. "He said the man kissed his penis. Tommy's penis. And made Tommy kiss his."

"Anything else?"

"And he said white fluid came out. Tommy said it looked like Elmer's Glue when it starts to dry."

I hoped the jury found that accurate. I thought it had the ring of authenticity. It had obviously made an impression on Mrs. Algren, because she'd remembered it.

"How long ago did this happen, Mrs. Algren?"

"About a year ago."

"No more than that?"

She did some calculating. "A year ago last month."

The questions about dates had given her a moment to recover her composure. She looked relieved. She was taking deeper breaths.

"Before that time, had Tommy ever seen you and your husband making love?"

She gasped. It was audible to me. Her blush returned instantly. "No."

"Are you certain?"

She turned her embarrassment to anger, glaring at me. "I absolutely am. We close our door."

"Had Tommy had any other occasion to see representations of sex? Have you or your husband ever had X-rated videocassettes in the house?"

"No," she almost shouted. "Not even *Playboy*. Never. Nothing like that at all."

I nodded. I paused for so long that she must have thought her ordeal was over. "Mrs. Algren," I asked softly, "what kind of relationship do you and your husband have with Tommy?"

She looked confused. "We're his parents. Tommy's our

only child, so I think we're closer than other parents and children."

I nodded as if I believed her. "Do you pick him up from school?"

"Yes."

"Immediately after school lets out?" I clarified.

"Oh. No, we can't do that. He used to go to a daycare after school. Now he stays right at the school until we come get him."

"Which is what time?"

"Five. Or as soon after that as we can make it."

"Sometimes later?"

"Yes," she said. She wasn't defensive. She was describing a normal life.

"Do you and your husband both work?"

"Yes. I'm a special accounts manager at First Security Trust. James is a vice president at Quantco Equipment Corporation."

"Vice president in charge of what?" I asked.

"Sales, basically. Quantco holds several smaller companies, and James is primarily in charge of sales for all of them. Particularly in expanding their markets."

I wondered if she was aware of the pride that had crept into her voice and posture. "Does that involve travel?" I asked, sounding suitably impressed.

"Yes. Usually a couple of trips a month."

"And your job, Mrs. Algren, what does it entail?"

"I help clients make investment decisions, particularly long-range investments."

"You're a stockbroker."

"It involves much more than that," she said, as if I'd insulted her. "Stocks are only a small part of what I deal with. Government bonds—of all kinds—mutual funds, real estate, sometimes more exotic opportunities such as motion pictures, or private companies that aren't listed on the stock exchanges."

"You put together movie deals?" I asked, glamour-struck.

"I have," she said. "I mean, the investor-package portion of the deal."

I asked, "Is that a nine-to-five, Monday-through-Friday sort of job?"

"Well, it can't be," Mrs. Algren said. She had completely recovered herself. She was assured again. She turned toward the jurors. "Many of my clients are busy people who can only meet on a weekend or an evening."

"So where's Tommy when you're meeting with a client and his father's out of town?"

The question jarred her. I hoped the jury could see that in the pleasure of describing her job she'd forgotten, momentarily, her son, the object of this trial.

"We have a couple of regular sitters," she said.

"When's Tommy's birthday, Mrs. Algren?"

"In March."

"Do you remember what you got him for his last birthday?"

She was ready for me. She took pride in her gifts. "His main present was a computer game he'd been wanting. It teaches geography while making a game. He goes all around the world trying to find stolen objects. He knows things now that I don't think I ever knew. He amazes me."

"Exactly how do you play the game?" I asked.

"Objection," Eliot said. "I question the relevance."

I stood. "It goes to the victim's motivation to lie, Your Honor, an issue the defense raised."

Eliot was looking at me oddly. He knew I must have a goal with this line of questioning, but he couldn't see it. Judge Hernandez overruled his objection, probably because he thought I was doing myself more harm than good.

"How do you play this computer game, Mrs. Algren?"

"You'd have to ask Tommy," she said indulgently. "He's the expert."

"He plays the game by himself."

"Yes," she said. "Usually."

"When was your last family vacation, Mrs. Algren?"

She looked puzzled. "James and I managed a weekend—was that this summer? No, it—"

"Family, Mrs. Algren. All three of you."

She hesitated. Then, realizing how it sounded that she didn't have a ready answer, she began explaining. "It's very hard for us to get our schedules together to get time off. James doesn't have a slack season, and I never know when I'm going to be able to take some time."

I waited patiently. She didn't have an answer.

"I suppose Tommy plays with his friends," I said. "Who's his best friend, Mrs. Algren?"

"Stevie," she said promptly. "Steve Petersen. He—"

"Tommy hasn't talked to Stevie in more than a year, Mrs. Algren," I said quietly. Eliot objected to my testifying, but it didn't matter, Pamela Algren was looking at me startled, assuming I was telling her the truth. "What's the name of Tommy's best friend *now?*" I asked her.

Her eyes scoured my face for the answer, didn't find it. "There's another boy in his class," she said slowly, improvising as much as remembering. "Tommy talks about him. Jason. He's mentioned him. I don't know if that's his *best* friend. I'm not sure he has one particular boy now. He plays with several."

"At your house?" I asked.

"Well, no. But there're neighborhood children. Sometimes I see Tommy with them, riding bicycles or . . ."

I let her wind down, and just sat watching her, a specimen I had studied long enough to label. I was sure everyone else could, too.

"I pass the witness," I finally said in the silence of the high-ceilinged, closely packed courtroom.

Eliot was studying Mrs. Algren too, but he didn't ask a question immediately. I doubted he knew what to do with her. She already seemed thoroughly demolished by *my* questions.

"You didn't believe Tommy when he accused Austin Paley of having molested him, did you, Mrs. Algren?" he finally asked, going right to the heart.

"Not at first," Mrs. Algren hedged.

"Not for a long time," Eliot insisted. "You didn't call the police, did you?"

"No."

"You didn't take him to a doctor."

"Not then."

"Not until a doctor contacted *you,* in fact."

"Yes, we heard from a doctor first. Tommy had told the nurse at school—"

"Even then, when you heard he'd gone to strangers with his story, you didn't believe him, did you? You thought he

321

was just letting you in for more embarrassment. Didn't you?"

Eliot had to add the little question at the end because it didn't look as if Mrs. Algren was going to answer. She hesitated even longer, the silence growing threatening.

"We weren't sure," she said.

"Because you knew he'd lied once before," Eliot insisted.

"Yes," Pamela Algren said in a small voice.

Eliot looked at her rather more compassionately than I had questioned her. But I suspect he was thinking about me, not about Pamela Algren.

"Pass the witness," Eliot said.

"But the first time Tommy accused someone," I said immediately, "he recanted the story almost as soon as he was confronted, is that right?"

"Yes," Mrs. Algren said. She was turning a little robotic, distancing herself from all of us.

"He didn't stick to the story even for a day."

"No."

"But *this* time, when he accused Austin Paley, he's persisted, even in the face of your and your husband's disbelief, hasn't he?"

"Yes," Mrs. Algren said. "He wouldn't let it go." I thought she still showed a tinge of embarrassment that Tommy *had* persisted; a faint, lingering wish that he'd let the whole thing drop. That was a good image with which to end: the cost to the family of *this* accusation.

"No more questions."

Eliot shook his head. "I have none either."

Pamela Algren kept her head down as she left the stand. I thought she might stumble into my table. She had one moment, though, just before she reached us, when she looked up, to the side, at Austin. She stopped where she was and stared at him. Her face turned bleak; not as if she was afraid of him, but as if she had just realized she had a terrible job to perform. Austin didn't see her expression. He wouldn't look at her.

Becky leaned close to me and said, "Are you sure?" At the same time, Judge Hernandez asked loudly if I had another witness. I stood and answered them both.

"We recall Tommy Algren," I said.

* * *

He was standing by. I'd had Tommy brought from school when I'd realized I was going to need him again, but I hadn't briefed him very much on why he was back. He took his place on the altar of truth ignorant of the use I planned to make of him. He looked nervous. His eyes traveled around the room, and questioningly over the faces of the jurors, as if they were keeping something from him.

"Tommy." My voice seemed to startle him. I pointed. "Is this the man who molested you? Austin Paley?"

Tommy glanced only once along the path my finger indicated, then back at me. "Yes."

"When did that happen?"

"In May, two years ago," he said quietly. He was leaning forward, his shoulders hunching.

"But about *one* year ago," I said, "you told your parents a different man had sexually assaulted you. Do you remember that?"

"Yes."

"Who was that?"

"Mr. Reese, our neighbor." Tommy was still speaking softly, but clearly, with a trace of defiance. He was prepared to be stubborn, as if someone had accused him.

I softened my tone. "Was that true, Tommy?"

"No," he said.

"Not at all?"

"He—" Tommy began quickly, then drooped. "No. Nothing about that was true."

"Why did you say it?"

There is always an explanation. For children, for adults; everyone has a good reason. The man who breaks into a home and strangles five strangers can tell you why they had it coming. Tommy was no different. As soon as he began explaining he became more animated.

"I shouldn't have said it, I know, but Mr. Reese was mean to me first. One time I was playing a game with Ronnie—his son—where we were trying to hit a volleyball back and forth over the fence, from my back yard into his and like that, and Mr. Reese came out and told us to knock it off, we were going to hurt the fence. Like we were going to knock down the fence with a ball! And Mr. Reese picked up the ball and took it inside his house. And it was my ball! And I told him, very nice, I said, 'Mr. Reese, that's my ball.' And he just kept walking, he didn't even turn around."

"Did he ever give the ball back?"

"No. I asked Ronnie for it the next day and he said his dad still had it."

"So that's why you made up a story about what Mr. Reese had done to you?"

"Not just that," Tommy said quickly. "Another time, I was coming home from school, running, and I cut across their yard, and I didn't see that Mr. Reese had some string laid out because he was going to build something there, and I tripped over the string, and Mr. Reese got mad and yelled and he *swatted* me."

"Swatted you?"

"He hit me on the—on the behind with his hand, and he told me to go home."

I was glad I had parents on the jury, but it was important to have people who could remember what it was like to be children, who could understand how large these offenses could remain in a child's mind; a child, who still expected the world to be just.

"So that's why you told your parents what you did about Mr. Reese?"

"Yes," Tommy said, a little sullenly, as if *he* felt justified, no matter what anyone else might think.

I sat silently for a long moment, until several pairs of eyes turned toward me. Then I did what I'd put Tommy on the stand to do.

"Pass the witness," I said.

There had been stirrings at the defense table ever since I'd announced Tommy's name, whispered consultation that had grown almost loud enough for me to protest. But one likes to hear consternation in the enemy ranks. Now I saw the end of the argument. Both defense lawyers were looking at Austin, who inclined his head toward Buster. Eliot sat back, composed as always, but his face was a tight mask of composure. Buster Harmony leaned forward eagerly, glanced down through his half-glasses at his notes, and glared sternly at my witness.

"Did you realize, Tommy," he asked, "how seriously grown-ups would take this accusation you made?"

Tommy looked as if he thought about it now for the first time. "I don't know," he said.

"You don't know? You didn't think about it at all before you told this lie about your neighbor? You didn't think about how much trouble you could get him in?"

"Well, I knew my parents would get mad, but I was mad, too."

"Why didn't you just tell your parents what had really happened? Why didn't you ask your father to get your ball back for you?"

Tommy screwed up his face in preparation for a lengthy explanation, then fell back on, "I don't know."

I think defendants have a hard time during moments like that. Austin knew how crucial this testimony could be. If his lawyer managed to destroy the victim's credibility, the case against Austin would be destroyed as well. But you don't want your defendant to sit there like a vulpine cheering section, his face exclaiming, "Yeah! Get the kid!" As a defense lawyer I've instructed people how to look during moments like that in front of a jury: stern but sympathetic, as if you're sorry for the victim but he or she brought it on himself. It requires a fine range of expression.

By leaning back I could look past Eliot's back and get a pretty good view of Austin. As I would have expected, he was in good control of his face. He stared at Tommy as if he were sitting in judgment of the boy. There was no one in the courtroom better able to sympathize with Tommy, but Austin wasn't putting himself in Tommy's place. He was thinking about where Tommy had put him.

"Tell us, Tommy," Buster said. "Didn't you think your father *would* get the ball back if you asked him to?"

"I don't know," Tommy insisted.

Buster was equally insistent. "You must have thought about it. Did you think your dad would side with Mr. Reese if you just told him about the ball?"

Becky looked at me, concern forming a crease between her eyebrows. I sat still.

"I thought—" Tommy hesitated, "maybe it wouldn't be important enough to him to make a fuss about."

"But it was important to you, wasn't it, Tommy?"

Tommy shrugged.

"Well, it must have been, for you to make up this story about your neighbor."

"And he hit me, too," Tommy whined. "It wasn't just because of the ball."

"Why didn't you tell your parents about that? Did you think that wouldn't be important to them, either?"

"No."

"No, what? It wouldn't have been important?"

"Not as much as it was to me," Tommy said.

"Didn't you think your dad would go over and say something to Mr. Reese about it, tell him not to touch you any more?"

Tommy made a face as if he'd said something ridiculous. Buster wouldn't let even that silent expression pass. "Why do you make that face, Tommy? What does that mean?"

Becky touched my wrist with her fingers. I ignored her, watching Tommy.

Buster had started out trying to tone his questions down to a child's level, but by now he was no longer treating Tommy like anything but a hostile witness. That, I was sure, was what the defense argument had been about. Eliot had been too soft on the boy the first day. Buster had convinced Austin that a firmer hand was needed. Buster had won the argument, and now he had to prove he'd been right.

"My dad doesn't like trouble," Tommy said.

His dad was in the audience. I didn't turn to look at him, but I could imagine his reactions. Tommy didn't search the crowd for him, either, but he knew he was there.

"He wouldn't want to make a scene," Tommy continued explaining, "over something like a ball or a little—" He moved his hand in demonstration of a tap on the bottom.

"So to get your dad to pay attention to what really bothered you, you had to make up something much worse than what had happened," Buster said, not bothering to lift his voice into a question at the end.

"Yes," Tommy said quietly.

If Buster had spoken softly to him at that point, he might have started crying. Buster maintained the same firm tone. "But it didn't work very long, did it, Tommy?"

"What?"

"Well, you told your parents the story, but all they did was talk to Mr. Reese and he said he didn't do it and they believed him instead of you. And that was it, right?"

"They wanted me to tell him I was sorry," Tommy added.

"And then things went back to just the way they'd been, right? Your father out of town half the time and both of them busy all the time and neither of them paid any attention to you."

Tommy shrugged. He looked understanding, but I could see through it to the miserable child within, and I was sure others could see it as well. "They have a lot of things they have to do," Tommy said.

I glanced again at Austin. He had taken on some of his attorney's hard look as he stared at Tommy.

"So time went by and things were just the same and you had to do something again to get your parents' attention, didn't you, Tommy?" Buster said relentlessly.

Tommy looked puzzled. "I tried," he said hesitantly. "I always made good grades and they always said they were proud of me. And I—I was good for them."

"But that wasn't enough, was it?" Buster's tone was growing harder. Becky was looking at me again.

Tommy shrugged. He was looking down, as if there were something in the witness stand with him.

"You never got enough of their attention, did you, Tommy?"

In a small voice, after a pause, Tommy said, "I wish . . ."

He trailed off. Buster didn't pursue it. He had his own program. "So after a while you had to make them pay attention again, didn't you?" Tommy looked up at him. "You heard about other children being sexually abused, and then you saw this man on television and you told your parents he'd molested you."

"Yes," Tommy said.

For a moment Buster thought he'd achieved his victory. But he quickly realized there wasn't yet a contradiction.

"Did you remember him from when he'd been looking over the vacant house in your neighborhood?"

"I remembered him from lots of times," Tommy said.

Buster veered quickly away from that. "So you lied again, to get your parents' attention?"

"No," Tommy said.

"Didn't you want your parents to pay attention to you? Isn't that why you told them?"

"No."

"You *didn't* want their attention?" Buster asked sharply. Now even Judge Hernandez was looking at me. I could weather his stare, too. "Isn't that what you just told us?"

"Yes, I did," Tommy said. "But I didn't lie."

"You *did* lie," Buster said, "the first time, about Mr. Reese."

"Yes," Tommy admitted. He glanced at me, but Buster's voice reclaimed him.

"And when that didn't work you lied again."

"No." Tommy kept shaking his head. He even looked at Austin, as if Austin would back him up, but Austin was giving him that judgmental stare, cold as an old painting's.

"And they *still* didn't pay any attention to you, did they? They didn't even believe you for a second."

"No," Tommy said. The pain of that rejection was perfectly visible on his face, as if it had just happened.

"So you had to do more this time. Is that why you went to your teacher, and the school nurse? You wanted them to help you get through to your parents?"

"I had to tell somebody else," Tommy said.

"Because if you didn't it would all just fall apart again, the way it did the first time? You needed other people to help you reach your parents."

"If they didn't believe me I had to tell somebody else," Tommy said.

Buster nodded. "So you got caught in the lie, because people who didn't know you as well as your parents believed it."

"It wasn't a lie!" Tommy's voice went shrill.

"When, Tommy? You've already told us you lied. You admitted it."

"I didn't lie about him." Tommy jerked his head at Austin. The movement seemed to draw tears into Tommy's eyes. He was suddenly blinking.

"You didn't realize how you'd be hurting him, did you,

Tommy? He was just somebody you'd seen in the neighborhood."

Tommy shook his head. That movement, too, made his eyes grow more moist.

Tommy's misery was blood in the water to Buster. He bored in relentlessly. Like him, his client was leaning forward, resting one arm on the defense table as if gaining leverage to leap over the table and get at the boy. Eliot was still in his initial position, having nothing to do with them. Buster's voice remained hard. "You didn't know all this would happen, did you, Tommy? The first time you lied it all went away without much trouble, didn't it? You didn't expect this second accusation to come to trial, did you?"

"I did," he said softly. "I thought that's what would happen."

"You were prepared from the beginning to tell this story in front of these people?"

"If I had to."

"To lie again?" Buster insisted.

"I'm not lying." He began crying, softly.

"—and again, and again, as long as it took to get your parents to notice you?"

"No." Tommy shook his head over and over, past making his point. He might have been on the verge of hysteria. "I wouldn't lie about this."

"Tommy," Buster said, moderating his tone as if Tommy had convinced him. Tommy stopped shaking his head and looked at him. "It's okay. It wasn't so terrible to lie about what happened before. It wasn't very bad. But lying here, after you've sworn to tell the truth, when this man could go to prison if you keep it up—lying here is very, very bad."

"I know that," the boy said solemnly.

Buster sensed a breakthrough. "Then don't. Tell us the truth now."

Tommy didn't hesitate. "I have," he said.

"Tommy." Buster was about to lose his patience with him. "You expect us to believe you lied once about the same thing, but you're telling the truth now?"

"I am," he said. Something in his face quivered. His nose, his lips.

"No. It was a lie. You lied about going inside the house with this man—"

"No."

"You lied about riding in his car, you lied about the other house. You made it all up, didn't you, Tommy?"

"No."

"Look at him and say that, please."

Buster and Austin were both staring at Tommy as if they could reach inside him and pull out what they wanted; as if they wanted the chance to try, anyway.

Tommy looked up. The quivering grew worse. It was apparent he was crying. Becky had hold of my arm again.

I didn't think Tommy was going to be able to break the silence. He was staring at Austin Paley, without a trace of hatred. His expression held sorrow and loneliness and longing. Austin looked back at him as if Tommy were someone he didn't want to be seen with.

"He did," Tommy said, softly at first. "He took me to that house, and he took my clothes off, and he hugged me, and he touched me, and he made me touch him." He kept looking at Austin. His eyes were liquid. "He told me he loved me."

"No!" Buster slapped his hand on the table. "Tell the truth."

"I am," Tommy said. His voice had grown firmer.

Buster should have known he had lost the moment, but he wouldn't let go. "Did it get you what you wanted?" he asked. "Did it make your parents pay attention? Was *this* lie good enough?"

I shook off Becky's hand and stood up at last. "I object, Your Honor. I believe defense counsel has hammered at the witness as long as he should be allowed to. He's growing repetitious."

At the defense table, Austin seemed to come to himself. He shot a glance at the jurors and saw that some of them were staring at him, rather than at Tommy. Austin touched Buster Harmony's arm.

"Sustained," Judge Hernandez said. Even he seemed relieved that I'd finally punctuated the interrogation with an objection.

When I sat down Buster was shaking his head, at something his client had told him. But he did as he was told.

"Pass the witness."

"Tommy," I said gently. He remembered his long-ago instructions to watch me, and he fastened his eyes on me. He swiped one forearm across his eyes. "You said you used to call this defendant Waldo. How did you find out his real name?"

Tommy himself seemed surprised by this turn of questioning. He sat up straighter. "When I was riding in his car," he began. I interrupted him.

"What kind of car was it?"

"Big and white," Tommy said. "A—what do you call it?"

"I don't know."

"Continental," he remembered.

"What color was it inside? The seats and the rest of the interior."

"Red," Tommy said. "Dark red."

"And how did you find his name?"

"There was a box between the front seats. Built in, like an extra glove compartment. I opened it and I found some papers with his name on them. Letters he'd gotten."

"What did they say?"

"Austin Paley."

"Did they say anything else, that you remember?"

"They said—" At first Tommy kept staring at me, just trying to see what I wanted. Then his eyes lifted, into the past. He was seeing an envelope in his hands. "They said 'attorney,' " he said.

"Thank you, Tommy. No more questions."

Buster's eyes were half-lidded. He stared at Tommy as if he could see the lever with which to open him up. But Austin's hand was on his arm. "I'm done too," Buster said.

Once again I escorted Tommy down from the witness stand. I put my arm around his shoulder, but before we reached the counsel tables I moved around him, so that I was between him and the defense table when we passed it. Karen Rivera met me to take the boy from me. I didn't even look at her. Halfway down the aisle Tommy broke away from her and darted into a row of spectator seats, where his father was sitting. Tommy lunged against him, clamped himself to his father's side, and James Algren hugged him with both arms, covered him up, hid him away from all the rest of us.

Everyone in the courtroom watched this reunion, except Austin and his lawyers, who sat in their different attitudes staring forward, waiting for the trial to resume.

While I'd stood watching Tommy and his dad, Judge Hernandez had said something, undoubtedly asking me to call my next witness. I leaned down to Becky, we exchanged a sentence apiece, and I straightened and said, "The State closes, Your Honor."

Eliot huddled with his client. Buster half-leaned toward them too, his job done. Eliot rose stiffly and said, "The defense closes too."

"Both sides rest and close," the judge said with satisfaction. He looked at the clock, then at the jury. "It is late and the attorneys and I still have work to do," he began. I stopped listening. I looked at Eliot. His chin was high. He was watching the jurors.

There'd been a potential trap for the defense in cross-examining Tommy. He was a child, you couldn't hammer him too hard, you'd lose the jury's sympathy for your own client. Eliot had avoided the pitfall the first time around. He'd been stern but not harsh with Tommy, almost grandfatherly.

But the case had still been close. I'd offered the temptation again. I'd given Tommy to the defense, first providing them with the fuel about his home life, his too-busy parents, that seemed to create a motive for him to lie, then I'd brought Tommy on again and offered him up.

Eliot hadn't gone for it, but Austin had. Buster had. He'd seen how he could open the boy up, and Austin had given him his head. But in trying relentlessly to break Tommy down, Buster had finally looked vindictive. With Austin beside him giving Tommy that same icy stare, the jury had seen, right before their eyes, adult men abusing that boy. I was counting on their imaginations to picture the different form of abuse to which one of those adults had subjected Tommy.

I'd also counted on Tommy, on his bearing up under the cross-examination. Because I believed in him. I was certain he was telling the truth. So I'd given Buster a free hand, sitting silent sometimes when I should have objected to spare my witness, hoping like hell he could take it. And he had. I hadn't prepared him for what was coming, I'd let him look confused and vulnerable in front of the jury, because that was best for my case. Even so, Tommy had stuck by his story. Under the relentless defense cross-examination, Tommy's insistence had looked even more truthful. That had been my hope. After the case Eliot had put on, I'd had to do something, and all I'd had to offer the jury, again, was Tommy.

"We will see you at ten o'clock tomorrow morning," Judge Hernandez was concluding his remarks to the jury. "Remember my instructions."

It took a while for the courtroom to clear. I wanted to see Tommy but found that he was gone. His father had whisked him away before anyone could get to him. In doing so Mr. Algren had violated my instructions to remain available at the end of the day. I was proud of him for that.

Becky and I waited around the court's office to pick up copies of the proposed jury instructions. It was a way of avoiding people. By the time we came back into the courtroom even the press had left. But there was one person I knew still waiting.

Becky stood undecided for a moment, then said, "I'll take these upstairs."

I accompanied her as far as the railing, where Janet was waiting. Waiting for me, apparently, but she didn't speak immediately.

"Did you watch? You shouldn't have, I might have needed to call you again and I couldn't have if you—"

"I wanted to see Tommy," Dr. McLaren said. She had that look that people get, weary but alert, when a crisis is well advanced. I wanted to ask her how her day had been, but she continued.

"Was it really necessary to bring him back, to ask him the same questions again, to let that despicable lawyer abuse him all over again?"

It was worse than she thought. I could have spared Tommy some of the abuse by objecting to the repetitive questions. But I'd needed him to look helpless; needed the jury to see him suffer.

"I thought so."

Her gaze went around the stark, empty courtroom and she hugged herself, hands holding her upper arms. I wanted to hold her myself, but my exquisite sense of timing told me the moment wasn't right. When she looked at me again I saw there was anger behind her sadness.

"You don't make my job any easier. This public carving up. He'll remember this after he's put aside the trauma of the rape. If he ever does."

"You told me I couldn't help Tommy. I could only try to prevent its happening to other kids. This was the best way I knew how. My best shot at conviction."

"I know what I said. I just—don't like seeing my advice acted out."

I heard the unspoken rest of the sentence, the part where she added that she didn't want anything to do with the kind of man who could put the theory into practice in the brutal realm of a criminal trial, where the victim often suffers more than the accused.

"Janet, could we—"

She made a negative sound and held up her hand to block me. She must have thought of more to say, but kept it to herself. She just walked away. In the echoing confines of the empty courtroom the rhythm of her heels came back to me with the staccato insistence of a message in telegraph code. She went out the door without ever looking back.

I perfectly agreed with her.

17

I should talk about the lie right off," Becky said. "Take it out of the case if I can, so the jury can have their minds made up about it before they even get to argue it."

"No. I need to talk about that. If I don't, it'll look as if it scares me. It's their strongest weapon, I've got to address it last."

I was speaking by rote, abstracted, already lost in the arguments I was going to make to the jury this morning, the arguments that had filled my head all night, making sleep only a thin, thin layer of cotton laid over my racing thoughts.

Becky snapped me out of it momentarily. "Damn it, Mark!" I was surprised to see that she was completely exasperated with me. "You want it all," she said.

She was right. I did want it all. I was scared to death. I had never wanted so badly to convince a jury.

What was this look of concern on Becky's face, underlying the anger? She looked as if she had worries, too.

After a moment I said, "I see. You want part of this."

"Yes!" She laughed, but the laughter didn't eradicate the anger, or the worry. Her worry, I saw, was not just for the case.

So I made myself do what a good manager is supposed to do—delegate. We divided the arguments more equitably, but it didn't calm either of us. We were sunk in silence when we walked out of my office.

* * *

I had the hardest role. I had to sit and watch the other arguments, waiting for my turn, feeling my burden grow heavier and heavier as I tried to remember everything I had to say, every response I had to make. Becky was luckier. She came quickly to her feet as soon as Judge Hernandez finished reading his instructions to the jury.

"These are the elements of this offense," she told the jury. She'd written them on a large tablet standing on an easel in front of the witness stand. "If you find that these things happened, then you will find the defendant guilty of aggravated sexual assault." She read off the elements she'd numbered. "This defendant penetrated the mouth of a child with the defendant's sexual organ, *or* caused the child's sexual organ to contact the defendant's mouth, and the child was younger than fourteen years old. That's all. That's all you have to decide. They're listed in the charge the judge will give you. You can look at them now, you can read them over and over again in the jury room, and one thing you will not find is anything about consent. In an adult rape case consent is an issue. In rape of a child—this kind of case—it is not. The legislature has decided that children *can't* consent to have sex with an adult. Children aren't mature enough to make a decision like that. The adult has to bear the responsibility, no matter what. So you don't have to decide in this case whether Tommy was physically forced to do what he did, or whether he was psychologically coerced, or whether he was seduced rather than raped. When a child is the victim, there's no such thing as seduction. There is only rape."

She walked along the railing in front of the jury box, making eye contact with each juror. She ended at the corner of the box closest to the witness stand. Becky turned and pointed at its chair.

"You will never see," she said, "a witness sit in that chair and tell you he's lying. They come here to tell you their story, whether it's the truth or a lie, and they're going to stick to it.

"But something almost as unusual happened in this case," Becky continued. "Our victim told you that he *had* lied. He sat here in front of you and admitted that he lied about someone else a year ago. He didn't have to admit that to you. He could have persisted in his lie, he could have tried to make you believe it.

"But as Tommy's mother told you, Tommy *never* persisted in that lie. As soon as he was confronted about it, he admitted he wasn't telling the truth. And that was the end of it. The lie never left the neighborhood. It barely left the house. When he wasn't telling the truth, Tommy couldn't keep it up. He didn't even try."

Becky paused. The jurors gave her nothing but their attention; no hint of their leanings.

"How different was what happened in this case," she continued. "This time, when Tommy saw the man who really had raped him, he wouldn't let it go. He couldn't. When he told his parents what had happened, and they doubted, like they had before, did Tommy break down and say he was lying? No. He went to someone else. This time he *had* to tell his story until it was believed. Because it was the truth. He went to his teacher, he went to the school nurse, he went to a doctor, he went to the police, he came to *us*. He never faltered. He never backed down."

Again Becky studied the jurors. "Do you think what you saw on this witness stand was a boy who was lying?" She shook her head. "You know better. You saw a boy who wouldn't break down, who insisted on his story in the face of devastating cross-examination. A boy who knew all the details of the story, who never contradicted himself. You know that." She had slowly backed up, until she was in front of the defense table. She pointed. Austin should have been expecting that, but nonetheless he looked startled for a moment. "This man knows it," Becky said.

She held her arm for long moments. When she dropped it she stayed in the vicinity of the defense table. She didn't want the jury forgetting Austin Paley. She wanted the crime very real to them. She wanted them to picture it, and she wanted Austin in the picture.

"There's one other way you can be sure Tommy Algren was telling you the truth," Becky said. "The proof is in the pudding, as they say. This truth is in the details of the story itself. Did it sound to you like something made up? No. Tommy knows every detail of what it's like to have sexual intercourse with a grown man. He described it to you. He described it to his mother a year ago. Because it had already happened by then. Tommy didn't say, 'He touched me in a bad place.' He didn't just drop a few phrases he'd heard somewhere. No. He described the sex act in such detail that his mother was horrified. She was convinced it had happened to him."

Becky gave the jury one last long stare. "It did," she concluded simply.

There was a long silence while she stood a moment longer, a silence that continued while she took her seat beside me. I laid a hand on her arm. I knew what she was thinking, what every lawyer thinks when she sits down again: There was something else I should have said.

I heard Eliot's voice before I knew he had come to his feet. "Yes," he said, "you know what it's like to see Tommy lie. You watched it happen."

And *he* had the jury's attention. "The prosecutor would have you believe the boy overcame great odds to bring you his story. But that's not true, is it? It was easy for Tommy. It was *too* easy.

"To whom did he tell this story? Whom did he manage to convince? His teacher, first of all. But remember when this happened. A few months ago, in August. August! School had just started. The teacher didn't know Tommy. She'd had him in class how long? A week, two? Barely time to learn the names of all her students. So when Tommy told her his story, she believed him. She had no reason not to, and with the hysteria that prevails now about child sexual abuse, she knew she'd better pay attention to his story, or her job would be in jeopardy."

"Objection," I said, without much force. "That's outside the record."

"Sustained," Judge Hernandez said. "Please ignore that argument."

Eliot wasn't thrown off stride. I had never seen him argue on behalf of a defendant before. He used that novelty to his advantage. He seemed to be appearing out of a concern for impartial justice. He spoke quietly but forcefully; reason was on his side. "Then Tommy told his story to the school nurse, who perhaps gave him aspirin two years ago. Again, a stranger. Next to a doctor, then to police officers who had never seen the boy before, whose job it is to take statements from people who claim to be victims, and pass them on. They didn't investigate Tommy's background, they didn't find out if there were reason to believe him or not. They just passed on what he'd told them. To these people." Now it was Eliot's turn to point at us, at Becky and me. "These people have a job to do: to present claims of crime to you. Not to question the supposed victim's story. They *represent* the victim. That's what they're supposed to do. That's how I trained one of them. And he did a fine job here. But again, Tommy was a stranger to the district attorney. He had no reason not to believe him."

I didn't feel a stranger to Tommy, not by this time, but that offered no basis for objection. I sat stolidly, waiting.

"So put no stock in the unquestioning acceptance of all these strangers. You heard the only real evidence about whether Tommy deserves to be believed. Out of all the people in this world, who knows Tommy best? His parents. And they were the only ones, out of this world of strangers, who did *not* believe him. They knew he had lied before, they knew he had told them the exact same story about someone else, and that it was a lie. They knew their son couldn't be believed. That's a sad fact for them, but it's even sadder for Austin Paley, who is here in front of you today because people who didn't know any better believed a lying boy, when his own parents could have told them Tommy couldn't be trusted to tell the truth."

Austin looked suitably saddened at his own predicament. I couldn't read at all what he was really thinking. His gleam of irony was completely suppressed. He was pure facade.

Eliot's head was lowered. When he spoke again his voice sounded troubled. "But the second time he persisted," he said, as if asking why. "Shouldn't we believe Tommy because this time he took the story much further?" He lifted his head. "Or did the story take *him?*"

He moved closer to the jury. "We have seen what Tommy's life with his parents is like. It's a common story: too little time to go around. His parents give him things, but not what Tommy craves most, their attention. After a while he took extraordinary steps to gain their notice." He was choosing his words carefully. "He lied. He told them the worst thing he could think of that had happened to him.

"And the first time, the lie worked wonderfully well. Tommy got exactly what he wanted, his parents' undivided attention. That first night, the whole household revolved around him exclusively. So when Tommy's parents suggested the scary idea of his actually facing the man he'd accused, Tommy could afford to back down. He could let go of the lie. It had already accomplished what he wanted.

"But then time passed, and things went back to the way they had been. Tommy lost the parental attention he craved so desperately. So he tried again. Tommy saw a story on television about children being molested, he imagined the attention those children were receiving, and he told the same story."

Eliot moved along the front of the jury box. He was being very careful not to sound as if he were attacking Tommy. He sounded sympathetic toward him, but removed. It was a sad story, but not of Eliot's making.

"This time, though, it didn't work. His parents didn't believe him. Tommy had to do more this time. He had to go to strangers to help him win his parents' attention. You saw Tommy. He is a smart little boy. He knew if he enlisted other adults on his side, his parents would have to take notice, too.

"And it worked beautifully. He got attention. You can imagine, Tommy's had more of his parents' time in the last three months than he had in three years before now."

I was watching the side of Eliot's face, cheek seamed with years of experience but still with a jaw muscle that tightened at the end of sentences as if he couldn't bear to let anything go. When he turned toward my end of the jury box I saw his eyes, which could be piercing but now were deeply concerned, wells of potential tragedy in which jurors could see a drowning innocent.

"And do you know what made it so much easier this time?" Eliot asked the jurors. He waved a hand at his client. "This time no one suggested Tommy might have to face the man he'd accused. Oh, no. He was perfectly sheltered. The man he accused this time wasn't a flesh-and-blood next-door neighbor, it was a man Tommy had picked at random off a

TV screen, because he remembered him vaguely from having seen him a few times at a vacant house in the neighborhood. The man was anonymous to Tommy, and he stayed anonymous. Tommy never had to see him, never had to think about the pain he might be causing with his lie. By the time he did have to face the man, here in court, it was too late to turn back. The lie had become the whole basis for Tommy's newfound closeness to his parents. This time he could not give it up. Even if it means sending a stranger to prison."

Eliot walked a few steps, thinking. I knew the pressure on him. He was responding to Becky's argument, but he also had to answer my final one, without having heard it yet. The prosecution would get two chances, but Eliot only had this one. He had to remember everything.

"The proof is in the details, the prosecutor has told you. And she would have you believe there is only one possible source for those details. But you know better. Some of you are parents. You know how children have changed. Today's children are nothing like what we were like growing up. They have some amazing details at their fingertips. They know things that astound us. That disgust us sometimes. And what is the first thing a child, particularly a close-to-teenager like Tommy, does when he learns something new and sordid and terrible?"

A lady on the front row of the jury knew the answer. Eliot spotted her knowing look and focused on her. "He runs to share it with other children," Eliot answered his own question, and the lady on the front row looked satisfied, as if she'd given the answer herself. "Especially if it's something grown-up and nasty, that you know you shouldn't be allowed to know, it *has* to be shared. If one child in the fifth grade learns some secret facet of adult behavior, soon they all know."

Eliot shrugged. "Perhaps this is how Tommy learned the details he passed on to his parents. Perhaps he once saw something himself. We can't know. We can only guess. But your verdict cannot be based on a guess. You must be certain *beyond a reasonable doubt*. That is not possible.

"Now," he said, "having talked about what is wrong with the State's case, I will remind you of the defense. The State's case is inherently flawed, but once you also consider the defense's testimony, your verdict is certain.

"Consider Austin Paley himself. He is not an ordinary defendant. He's not a multitime loser who comes to you already tainted by past convictions and brushes with the law. He is a grown man, and his record is unblemished. If it were otherwise, *they* could have told you about it."

Since I was the "they" referred to, I stood up for myself. "Objection, Your Honor. 'Brushes with the law' wouldn't be admissible except under certain circumstances that didn't arise in this case."

"Overruled," said the judge, and I wondered if any lay persons knew what we were talking about.

"Do you think a man reaches this defendant's age being the kind of lustful creature the prosecution has described, and never before been brought to trial for any sort of crime?" Eliot continued instantly. "No. You know better. Austin Paley is an innocent man caught in the most terrible accusation of which a man can be accused. He sat here before you and told you, without mistakes, without contradictions, that he had nothing to do with this boy. And the State has brought you no witness, except the admittedly lying boy, to contradict him.

"But the *defense* had another witness. Austin was very lucky in this case, after the terrible bad luck of being caught up in a boy's lie. He was lucky because he had a friend. How many of us can prove where we were on any given day? Our days blend so easily into one another, and we spend so much time alone, going from one place to another. But Austin was lucky because he has a friend who remembered that particular day, because it was unusual. You heard her testimony. Normally now I would speak in glowing terms of the character of this witness, but modesty prevents me. I've been married to her for more than forty years, and that should be testimonial enough to how I feel about her." The jury smiled along with him. "So I won't praise her character, but I will point out what you have not heard from the other side: a reason why Mamie Quinn would lie. The prosecution did not even suggest that she did. Austin Paley is an old friend of Mamie's, but he isn't her son. He isn't close enough that she would commit perjury on his behalf. Mrs. Quinn was as close to an impartial witness as you will ever see in a trial."

Eliot waved away what he was about to say next. "Yes, the prosecutor managed to confuse her momentarily about the date when Austin was at our house all afternoon, by throwing at her a string of different dates. Those are just numbers. But Mamie remembers the *day*. She had no uncertainty about that."

Thin ice. Eliot looked down so that his eyes were hooded. I was touched to hear him speak of Mamie. I couldn't stand the thought of attacking her. Eliot remained quiet. He had brought his hands up in front of his chest and folded them. His voice when it came was terribly sad.

"There may be no more horrible a crime than the one with which Austin Paley is charged. We recoil from it. We can't even look rationally at a man who would do that to a child. It is perhaps the oldest human instinct. When we hear that a lion is loose among the flock, we rush to the defense of the lambs with clubs and stones." He nodded as if he would lead the mob himself.

"But," he said, suddenly changing course, "this is also one of the easiest accusations to make. The State doesn't have to support it at all. They don't have to show you a corpse, they don't have to bring you other witnesses, they don't have to present medical evidence or *any* other physical evidence at all! They haven't, in this case. Only the word of a troubled, confused, lying boy.

"I know you feel sorry for that boy, as we all do. But you must look critically at the State's evidence. Because while this is a terrible crime, it is also terrible to be accused of it falsely. *This* man's life will be ruined if you make the wrong decision. How could he ever live down the stigma of it? You owe him a critical examination of the State's case."

He sounded short of breath. He was wrapping up. "And when you do look at it critically you will see on one side two adults, one of them completely impartial, sure of their facts, with completely unsullied backgrounds. On the other side you will find a confused child who is an admitted liar, whose own parents did not believe him. When you weigh those two sides, you cannot fail to have a reasonable doubt."

With all the trial's evidence boiled down to that uneven

balancing, he was right. If I hadn't known what I knew about the case, I think Eliot would have convinced me. And the jurors didn't know what I knew.

He was returning to his seat very slowly, looking enormously troubled. One would have thought he was the accused himself. I crossed quickly between Eliot's retreating back and the jurors' faces.

"*He* doesn't want you to do the job you're here to do," I said quickly. "He doesn't want to give you the chance to weigh the evidence."

Eliot hadn't even sat down. "Objection, Your Honor!" he cried. "That is a complete mischaracterization of my argument. It is striking at the defendant through an attack on his counsel."

"Sustained," said Judge Hernandez. "Ladies and gentlemen of the jury, disregard that argument of the prosecutor's."

I had been watching the jury throughout this exchange. I took up the thread of my argument as if it hadn't been interrupted. "He wants you to do it by the numbers. Two witnesses on one side against one on the other means you have to find his client not guilty. But that's not the way life works, is it? We have all seen in our lifetimes big lies that have lots of adherents, and sometimes only one small voice opposing them. And we know that sometimes the one small voice is right."

I was moving. I felt shot through with energy. I seemed to have grown a foot taller, so that twitches became gestures. I knew I had to restrain myself.

"Mr. Quinn wants you to believe that Tommy got caught in a lie, that the lie took on a life of its own so that he couldn't escape it, he was forced to repeat it to you in this courtroom. That's not his history, that's not how we know he behaves when he's confronted with a lie, but the defense would have you believe that it happened this one time, when he accused *their* client.

"But that's not what you saw happen here. Yes, Tommy told his story to strangers. He had to, to find someone to believe him, because his parents were understandably skeptical. But he didn't tell a bunch of credulous, naïve innocents. He told professionals, people trained to spot lies.

"And finally"—I put a hand on my chest—"the story came to me. Defense counsel has implied that I presented the story to you just because it's my job to do so. But do you think I want to put a reluctant witness on the witness stand? Do you think I want to risk losing a case like this by having it depend on someone I think is lying? Tommy could have called a halt to this at any time—*any* time—simply by telling me it was a lie, that this man never harmed him. A lie doesn't have that kind of momentum. It was the truth that carried Tommy through the ordeal of testifying."

I took a turn in front of the box, pacing as if thinking. My steps brought me close to the defense table. "And now for the defense evidence. I want you to do what defense counsel asked you to do. I want you to think about the defendant." I knelt beside Austin with my hand on the back of his chair, my arm almost around him. Austin looked sidelong at me, appalled at this family portrait opportunity. "Think about the predicament he found himself in. Put yourself in his place. Accused of raping a child. Caught. Imagine it. A successful attorney with a good life, good friends, nice car, money to buy houses for investments. All that suddenly at risk. What would you do? What would you do in his place?"

I stood up, putting space between Austin and myself again. "Anything," I said. "You would do whatever it took to save yourself. You would hire the best lawyer you could think of, you would investigate the hell out of the case, you would find anything you could to discredit the boy, you would lie with all the sincerity you could muster, you would do what*ever* you could think to do.

"Including looking for an alibi witness. In this case, because the boy's story is true, that meant *inventing* an alibi witness. And that's how Mamie Quinn was brought to you. I don't for a second accuse Mrs. Quinn of lying to this jury. She remembers that day. It *was* an unusual day, when Austin Paley spent the whole afternoon and early evening with her—exactly, conveniently, the time for which he needed an alibi.

"But Mrs. Quinn doesn't know the date. You heard her say the wrong one, and then guess at which one she meant. Because one day is much like another for Mamie Quinn.

She doesn't keep business appointments, she doesn't have deadlines to meet. So when her old friend Austin Paley came to her and said"—I put my own hands together in prayer—" 'Please, God, Mamie, I'm in trouble, terrible trouble, you're the only one who can help me,' and he told her that the day she remembered happened on the date on which he was sexually assaulting Tommy Algren, Mrs. Quinn took him at his word. Mamie Quinn wants to help her friend, and that's admirable, but the only date she knows is the date Austin Paley told her."

I pointed at the defense table. "They could have pinned down the date. They could have brought you Mrs. Quinn's diary, but it's been discarded. They could have brought you Mamie Quinn's husband if they'd really wanted to be certain about the date. Because *Eliot* Quinn *does* have appointments to keep. He would have calendars to consult to pin down that date. But the defense didn't offer *his* testimony."

I didn't look at Eliot. I was fixed on the jury.

But I still felt the force of his argument. He had gotten to the jurors first. Their minds might already be made up. I had to break them down.

"And that's the last time I'm going to ask you to put yourself in the defendant's place," I said. "Because ultimately, you can't. You and I cannot understand him. The forces that drive him. The desire that won't let him lead a normal life, that compels him to trap a boy like Tommy. The defense has told you Austin Paley shouldn't even be here, but it's *Tommy* who should never have been here. Tommy's life should never have taken this turn. He should still be an innocent ten-year-old boy. But a house went vacant in his neighborhood and a man appeared, trolling for children, for a lonely, neglected boy just like Tommy Algren."

I had lost my manic energy. My shoulders slumped. I returned, as I've been trained to do, to the weakest part of my case.

"Yes, Tommy lied once. Martin Reese made him mad, and Reese didn't know what he was messing with in Tommy, did he? Because by that time, a year ago, Tommy was no ordinary little boy. Yes, Tommy lied, but look at the ammunition he had for that lie. He knew precisely what it was like to be sexually abused. He could describe it to his parents step by step, every detail, what everything looked like, all the textures, all the feelings. It wasn't something abstract, something he heard. He knew exactly what it was like to be raped. And he knew the man who'd done it to him. He knew the house where he met him, he knew what the inside of the man's car looked like, he knew his face. He knew his name."

I was backing up, but I wasn't creeping up on anyone. Everyone knew where I was headed. When I came abreast of Austin he was looking at me stubbornly, his shoulders slightly hunched. I looked at him, too, looking for the trace of what I knew must be there.

Everyone boasts a guilty heart. We can't live five years without acquiring one. Even Tommy, the only complete innocent in the case, felt guilty about betraying Austin. Even Eliot, who'd done nothing worse than a favor for a friend, felt guilty toward Austin as a result.

I felt guilty over the way I'd raised David, by hit and miss and crucial absences. David probably felt guilty that he hadn't lived up to the ideas he'd imagined I'd had of a son.

Everyone appeared to feel guilty but Austin. He seemed to feel it was his due to live as he wanted, at anyone's expense; that the world could never pay off its debt to him for his anguished childhood.

But I could not believe that. If there was anguish in Austin's past it lived in him still, no matter with how nonchalant a face he hid it. It is the mark of humankind that we feel guilt toward those we have hurt, and guilt for having been victimized, as well.

"Think of that boy," I said. "No one can help him. He thinks no one *will*. He can't even trust his own parents. His father isn't there for him. Think about that boy alone in the dark at night. No one to comfort him.

"Is it any wonder he didn't tell anyone? Is it any wonder he lied? Imagine how the world appears to him. He thought he'd found one true friend, a new father, big enough to protect him, to explain the world to him. And then that man violated him. Raped him. Imagine the effect. Not just the physical horror and pain, but the confusion. Nothing in the world can be trusted any more."

There was one person in the room who understood perfectly what I was saying, for whom it took no leap of imagination to empathize with the victim. I was directing my argument at him. Austin looked back at me blank-faced. *You will not touch me,* he seemed to say. But he didn't take his eyes off me as I continued to address him.

"Then some time later, after he's begun to sort things out, after he thinks he understands a little how the world is, Tommy is deeply offended by something a neighbor does to him and he strikes back, with the rage that's been in him for a long time. He *uses* what happened to him, the pain he can describe with such horrible exactness. Do you blame him?"

Are you proud of the boy you made, Austin? It was akin to the transformation he had experienced himself. From victim to user. He understood the venting of pain. I hoped he understood, too, how he had made a legacy of his injury, hurt someone else exactly as he'd been hurt. I knew I could make him see, if not the jury. Austin was still watching me. His expression hadn't softened, but it was as if he had retreated behind the mask of his face. His eyes, I thought, were moist. A boy's eyes, still bright, eager, often confused.

I turned back to the jury. "Yes, Tommy used his pain to try to punish someone who'd offended him. But the pain was already there for him to tap. He lied about who had molested him, but he didn't lie about what had happened. He described it so vividly that his parents knew it was the truth. You know it too, don't you? An eight-year-old boy doesn't know those details unless he's experienced them. Unless he's been raped.

"And when he came in here and told you who had really done it, you recognized the truth, didn't you? You heard the sound of true, anguished memory. And you know that Tommy, try as he might, can never forget the man who raped him."

My voice sounded loud. The silence that followed it was equally loud. There were no rustlings from the jury, or murmurs in the crowd. Or maybe I had just grown deaf to them, as I'd grown blind, for just a moment, to every face in that crowded courtroom but one.

* * *

"I'd like Tommy to be here for the verdict," James Algren said. His face was stiff as he talked, as if he were a ventriloquist's dummy being inexpertly operated. "Well, to tell you the truth, he insisted on being here."

Algren probably disliked me as much as he did anyone else involved in his son's tragedy. I'd put on the evidence that told the world what a lousy father he was. But I was his only contact in the sordid world of criminal law, and he had questions.

"Will they handcuff him and take him to jail after the verdict?" There was an undisguised vindictiveness in the question.

I shook my head. "I'm sure the judge will continue him on bond until the entire trial's over. After all, he might get only probation. Anyway, I wouldn't count too heavily on the verdict. It might be one you don't want to hear."

"You think they might not convict him?"

"I think it's likely he'll be found not guilty."

"How?" James Algren asked.

Weren't you watching? I wanted to ask him. Didn't you hear the testimony that *you* didn't even believe Tommy? Instead I said, "It's very hard for a jury to take the word of a child against an adult's. In a case like this, with an emphatic denial and an alibi, it's almost impossible not to have a doubt."

"And that would be it?" Mr. Algren spat out. "Could you try him again?"

Sometimes I'm amazed by intelligent laypersons' ignorance of the law. "Not for this," I said. "You could file a civil suit against him, try to win damages. That would be easier, you'd be on an equal footing, you wouldn't have the burden of proving it beyond a reasonable—"

Mr. Algren sneered. "I wouldn't put Tommy through this again for money." He paused. His eyes slid away from me. "That's not what I was thinking of doing."

I took his arm. "Keep to yourself what you're thinking. I'm still the district attorney."

For another two months or so, I thought as I ushered him out. He stopped at the door. "Tommy and I'll be down in the courtroom."

"It might be a long wait."

"We'll be there."

He left me alone in my office. I stood beside my desk for a long moment, looking at the wall behind it, where my plaques and diplomas and pictures hung. The office already looked unfamiliar, as if I were returning to it only in memory, long after departing. I turned toward the corner where my view lay, the five-story drop to the city streets and a large slice of the old red stone courthouse across the street where I'd grown up. Soon I'd be dislodged from this perch. The television news had been on the night before while I'd paced my condo, rehearsing my argument. It had been interrupted by a commercial for Leo Mendoza, a newly made one in which he sat on the edge of a desk much like the one in my office, with crossed flags behind it. Leo had spoken confidently, already with the air of authority to which my job would entitle him.

There would be no more polls before the election. The most recent one showed Leo with the allegiance of almost half the people who claimed they'd be voting, me with the loyalty of only about a third of the prospective voters. A gap like that could be closed, but not in only a week, not by a well-publicized trial loss. The news this week seemed to focus on the trial I'd been conducting rather than on the election. I had no idea what citizens thought about that trial, but I was pretty sure what they would think if Austin was acquitted and began trumpeting his victory over my unjust prosecution of him.

Curiously, though, I couldn't keep my attention on the consequences of the trial. I kept returning to Austin himself. After it was over he would be free. His friends would embrace him, his practice would continue, his influence might even be extended. He would be more cautious than ever, perhaps for a long while, but not forever. Some day he would appear again in a new neighborhood, in the vicinity of a school where he'd never been seen, in an apartment complex teeming with children whose parents were too busy for them. By the time that happened I would be a private citizen, as powerless as James Algren. But I still felt the responsibility. I knew that weight would only grow heavier once I was out of office. Perhaps I would linger close to

Austin's life, to let him know he wasn't forgotten. Perhaps I might even have to take some action.

The jury had been out for almost an hour. In a case like this, a quick verdict would have been bad, it would have signaled a rapid agreement among jurors that they couldn't possibly decide who was telling the truth, so they must make a finding of not guilty. The time for a verdict like that was passing. If the jury continued deliberating too long, though, they would arrive back at the same point. Too much talk meant dissension, and dissension was good for the defense. They only needed one juror holding out for acquittal. I needed all of them voting guilty.

Without warning the office door opened and Becky walked in. She carried a paper sack, its top gathered and wrinkled as if it had been opened and closed again several times.

Gone was the deference Becky had shown me early in our partnership. We stared at each other like battlefield veterans meeting in a tent we would soon have to pack up or abandon. Becky dropped the paper sack on my coffee table. "Someone was nice enough to bring me a sandwich," she said. "I thought I'd share it with you."

I leaned over the sack, loosened its top with a finger. Inside was a barbecued beef sandwich that had been only loosely rewrapped in its waxy paper. The sandwich had been cut in half, and its filling was spilling out between the halves, as if the sandwich had vomited it out. White veins of fat gleamed amid the dark lumps of meat. No steam rose from it.

"You're too kind," I said.

Becky dropped onto the couch. For a moment she slumped there, her knees on a level with her waist, looking like a TV-stunned child late on a Saturday morning. The next moment she underwent a remarkable transformation. She pulled herself up straight, put her hands on her thighs, and looked up at me as if she were well rested and just beginning her preparations for trial. I don't think I ever had that resilience.

"Think we need to put Tommy on again at punishment?" she asked seriously.

I laughed, a burst of surprise.

"No, really," Becky said, frowning with concentration. "To testify about how this has affected his life. That's relevant to punishment. This time we can really let out all the stops. Bring in the other times it happened, have the psychological testimony about how he'll never recover from it even with—"

"Becky." When she stopped I just drew a hand across the air, a cavalry officer canceling a charge.

"We have to be ready," she said stubbornly.

"I know." But I didn't mean by it what she had, and she knew it. I sat in the chair next to her and leaned forward so our heads were close. "Listen," I said, looking at the floor. "I don't know how much Leo will clean house here. I think you could hang in if you try, but I don't know what your prospects for advancement would be. Maybe if you stayed on for a few months, so it wouldn't look like you were being kicked out, you could catch on with a civil firm. But if you want to get out right away, or have to, I know a few people who'd hire you, I'm sure. It wouldn't be one of the big firms, but—"

"What would *you* do?" Becky asked. Still optimistic, she spoke of possibilities, while I'd been discussing what *was* going to happen.

I shrugged. Go back to defense work, I started to say, but I heard the phrase in my mind and didn't like the sound of it. I left my answer at a shrug.

Becky was giving my face one long moment of close study. Then I saw a lessening of intensity in her look, a shade going down far back in her eyes. She gave me the knowing but benevolent look that passes between friends.

"Let's talk about the case," she said.

I smiled. We fell silent, but the subject of the silence had changed. We sat waiting for a verdict.

They took their damned time about it. Juries. What was there to discuss? Either they believed our boy or they believed the defense, or they threw up their hands and decided they couldn't decide. How could they keep hashing over those simple choices for hours?

At midafternoon, when the jury had been out for more than four hours, James Algren reappeared in my office.

"Listen, uh, I had no idea it was going to take this long," he said apologetically. "I need to run by the office just for a minute. It's not far, I'll be right back. Client's been waiting for me since one."

"Okay," I said. "If it's been this long, there's no telling."

"Tommy wants to stay," Algren continued. "Could I leave him with you? I promise it won't be—"

"Sure," I said simply. Tommy should have been sitting with Becky and me all along. The three of us were the trial team.

Mr. Algren looked relieved. He brought Tommy into the office, spoke to him quietly for a minute, then left, trailing more apologies. Even before his father was out the door, Tommy gave me a look. Here was the pattern of his life reasserting itself already. But Tommy's expression was indulgent. He was a little adult again, so much so that he showed an adult understanding of the demands on his father.

"Tom," I said, "I don't think things are going our way."

He nodded, lips pursed. I wondered which would be harder on him, a verdict of guilty or not guilty: seeing Austin off to prison, or learning that he was going to remain at large.

Tommy tried to reassure *me*. "I'll be all right," he said.

Becky and I glanced at each other. Tommy joined our circle of silence.

The jury seemed just to have been waiting for James Algren to leave the building. He hadn't been gone half an hour when my phone buzzed. Becky and I knew what that meant, because I'd told Patty I didn't want to receive any calls except the one from the court. Becky looked, for just a moment, panicked, as if we'd been caught together in a compromising position. I felt the same way. They'd tracked me down. I'd been in hiding from this verdict.

This was one I would have liked to receive privately, in a small office, where I could stand near the door. Instead it would be one of the most public verdicts of my career.

"I think it would be better if you wait here, Tommy," I heard myself saying. "I'll come back and tell you what happened as soon as we find out."

He was shaking his head. "I want to hear it."

I couldn't deny him. In the outer office I asked Patty if Karen Rivera was around. Patty pressed four buttons on her phone and, a few seconds later, shook her head. "Get Jack, then," I said, "or one of the other investigators. Have him bring Tommy down to the court. Tell him to get him out of the courtroom as soon as the verdict's announced, whatever it is. We don't want him being interviewed. I've got to head down."

I knelt to speak face to face to Tommy. "Whatever happens," I said, gripping his arms, "you don't have to be afraid. He'll never come near you again."

Tommy nodded, an ambiguous reply, but his mouth was a firm line.

I left him waiting for my investigator while Becky and I hurried down the stairs. Only one television reporter tried to elicit a statement from me outside the courtroom doors. The other reporters were already inside, jammed among a throng of spectators. It looked like the headquarters of a successful candidate on election night. I took Becky's hand to be sure she made it through the crowd with me.

Inside the railing, relative calm prevailed. The bench and the jury box were vacant. A bailiff lounged behind his desk opposite the jury box. "We have a verdict?" I asked him, and he nodded calmly.

Eliot was already seated, his client beside him. He looked up at me with very little expression: no hostility, no smile, no obvious nervousness. Just an acknowledgment, I thought, that we knew each other, that we'd been in this position hundreds of times. In a few minutes one of us would be elated, the other stricken. For a moment it seemed to me that Eliot wished me well, in that shared anxiety.

Beside him, Austin didn't look up. He was staring straight ahead, rigid in his effort to appear calm. If nothing else, I had the satisfaction of finally seeing him utterly robbed of his omnipresent devil-may-care sparkle. That didn't feel like a victory, though. I felt as if I'd seen an old friend transformed into congealed dust.

I scanned the crowd, looking for Tommy. He didn't seem to be there. Then a flutter of motion caught my eye. Tommy was waving from a seat in the far back corner of the courtroom. I waved back, and caught the eye of my investigator

Jim Lewis, kneeling beside Tommy in the narrow aisle. I gave him a significant look, glancing at Tommy again, and Jim nodded.

When I turned back the judge was just taking his seat.

"I am told we have a verdict," he said with great detachment, and nodded at the bailiff, who sauntered across the room and out the door behind the judge's bench.

I hate that moment. Even when I am confident of the verdict, I don't like to sit and wait to hear it from a stranger's lips, because any half-smart trial lawyer has learned that you can *never* be confident. Juries always find a way to surprise us. They hear things in testimony none of the rest of us hears, they find significance in details the lawyers didn't deliberately elicit, that just slipped out in a witness's offhand maundering. Sometimes juries seem to have based their verdict on the essential evidence, but just as often they offer us after trial an explanation for their verdict so bizarre it cannot be the truth, they must be covering up something flawed and ugly in their decision-making. I'd hate to have my life in the hands of a jury.

The bailiff reappeared, and behind him the jurors. They blinked as they walked single file into the courtroom, as if they'd spent the last few hours trapped in a dark hole. They didn't look at all familiar to me. The bailiff could have brought back the wrong jury for all I could tell. Then I recognized a middle-aged Mexican-American man with dark-rimmed glasses, whom I'd wanted on the jury because he had children and he'd looked so serious during jury selection. Behind him came an overweight Anglo woman who'd worn the same yellow dress every day of trial. She had trouble negotiating the step up into the jury box and the man I'd recognized turned to help her. They spoke briefly to each other and even exchanged quick smiles.

Now I recognized other members of the jury. Something had happened to them, though. They were no longer the stiff faces I'd watched covertly during testimony and intently during final argument. They had become a group of living people, moving, looking over their shoulders at one another, speaking hurriedly in asides, even in the glare of the attention they knew was focused on them. They seemed affected by the hostages' syndrome that binds people held at gunpoint for a daylong bank robbery.

They were moving too slowly for Judge Hernandez. "Have you reached a verdict?" he asked with an edge.

Another man stood, a very thin one wearing a short-sleeved white shirt on this dank, cool November day. "Yes, Your Honor," he said stiffly.

Judge Hernandez said, "Read your verdict." He moved his head fractionally and Austin and Eliot stood to receive the verdict.

The foreman unfolded the paper, as if his memory of their decision wouldn't do. He never looked up again as he read laboriously:

"We find the defendant, Austin Paley, guilty of aggravated sexual assault, as charged in the indictment."

For a second I didn't look up. If I did I'd see Austin smiling and shaking Eliot's hand and realize I'd heard an illusion. But Becky grabbed my wrist and I could feel in her grip that I'd heard right. We had a guilty verdict.

Never let the jury see you exult. To any normal citizen the sight of a happy lawyer is offensive. If I gave vent to my feelings, screamed "Yessss!" or even just smiled broadly, I might make the jurors feel I'd put one over on them. Instead I only looked at them. My lips tightened and I nodded slightly, as if they'd done their simple duty, as I'd expected them to do. Inside, I was jumping up and down.

The judge was beckoning me forward. There was noise from the spectators, but he didn't subdue it. The jury foreman was still standing as I walked forward. "Thank you," Judge Hernandez said to him, and I said the same thing.

"It would be nice to be done with this," the judge said quietly when Eliot and I stood before him. "You have many punishment witnesses?"

Though I'd thought it hypothetical, Becky and I had discussed it. "Two, Your Honor. Maybe three," I said.

The judge didn't even turn to Eliot. "And of course the defense will," the judge said. "All right. Let's do it Monday." He motioned us away. "It is late on Friday and this jury has worked hard enough today," he announced to the room. "We will begin the punishment phase Monday morning at nine o'clock. Sharp."

When I turned away from the bench I had my first good look at Austin Paley since the verdict. He had collapsed into his chair, collapsed inside his suit as if all his air were gone. For the first time he looked like that portrait he must have kept in his attic. He looked old, older than Eliot Quinn, older than a man on his deathbed. His chest was fluttering. He was breathing in quick, shallow gasps. At first I thought he was having an attack. Then I dismissed what I was seeing as a carefully rehearsed performance, designed to tell the jury they'd made a terrible mistake, so they'd go easy on him at punishment.

By the time I reached my chair there was pandemonium in the courtroom. People were pouring in through the gate in the railing. Some of them were reporters, thrusting microphones and questions at me. I lifted Becky to her feet beside me. I would have tried to shield her from defeat, but she deserved to share in the victory.

I heard myself, with heartfelt sincerity, mouthing stupid, shopworn phrases like, ". . . remarkably intelligent jury. And they worked very hard."

"And after the evidence we present at punishment," Becky added, "the jury will have no doubts about what should be done with this defendant." I turned to her, surprised at the hardness of her tone. *Yes, Monday,* I thought. Monday would seal Austin's fate. Monday the city would hear about his abused childhood, and I would try to convince the jury to send him to prison in spite of that sad background.

Monday would be the day before the election, too.

There is a back way out of the courtroom, which leads into a hall open only to lawyers and court personnel. We used that exit, to give ourselves a moment of respite. Becky and I looked at each other, grinned matching goofy grins, and threw our arms around each other, which after a few seconds was a little awkward, so we pulled apart, still smiling, and shook hands. I put my arm around her shoulders in another congratulatory squeeze as we started down the hall. "Punishment Monday," she said.

I laughed. "You're a killer. Give yourself a few minutes to be happy."

The hall was narrow and white and had an experimental look, as if at its end I'd be confronted with a choice of three unmarked doors. Instead I turned a corner and found myself face to face with Eliot. He was just coming out of the court's office.

He looked even neater than when the trial had ended, in his gray suit with a yellow vest, but he looked as if his heart wasn't in it, as if he was just wearing the clothes he'd found laid out this morning. There were deep lines in his cheeks. When he saw me he waited. Becky and I sobered immediately. Eliot took my hand.

"Congratulations, Mark."

Becky was excusing herself, but Eliot stopped her before she could turn away. "Young lady," he said, "I first used that trick of mixing other dates into a cross-examination before you were born. And it was taught to me by a man who used it before *I* was born. It's so old I didn't even think to warn my wife against it."

He spoke admiringly, as if to an apt student. Becky smiled slightly. "Really," she said. "I thought I'd invented it."

She left us, and Eliot turned his attention to me. "Powerful closing, Mark. You—were convincing."

"Thank you."

"I can't offer wholehearted congratulations on the verdict," he added.

"I know, Eliot."

"But I can't— I wanted you to know I bear you no ill will, either. You made a decision I . . ."

He couldn't say that, either. "I still owe him," he concluded softly.

"You didn't do anything wrong, Eliot. All you did was believe a friend. There's nothing wrong with that."

Of course, to make up for the guilt of that mistake, he *had* done something wrong years later. He'd killed cases against Austin Paley. He'd let him think he was immune to the law. He'd as good as put innocent children in Austin's path. I don't know how I could have lived with such knowledge.

"You put on a hell of a case," I said. It was a most oblique question, but Eliot heard it.

"Mamie went to Austin and Buster before I ever agreed

to be part of the case," he said quietly. "I wouldn't have let them call her if I hadn't believed her. I don't think for a moment—"

"No."

"On the other hand," Eliot went on quickly, looking down, "your child was quite convincing himself. Quite." I wished I could see his eyes. Eliot clapped me on the arm, but he wasn't looking at me. "But it's not our job to decide who's telling the truth, is it, Mark?"

After a quiet moment I said, "Austin may get lucky on punishment, after you—"

Put on your evidence, I'd started to say, then realized Eliot himself was the witness to Austin's childhood abuse, maybe the only witness other than Austin himself. And Eliot still felt he owed him everything he could do for him. Come Monday, I might be cross-examining my old boss.

"A lot of people in this town are fretting about what Austin will do now," Eliot said. "They're wondering if now that he has nothing to lose Austin will decide to take everyone else down with him. He holds a lot of dirty secrets, Mark, and he has nothing more to fear if he spills them.

"Don't think anybody will forget your part, either," Eliot went on. "If you'd done what they asked you to do there'd be no occasion for Austin to smear them. It's going to come down on you like the wrath of God, if they can manage it. The squirming, the pleas for probation, the lust for revenge." Eliot had recovered himself. He sounded almost jovial, talking about the wrecked lives just ahead. "Going to be a hell of a weekend," he said.

My office windows had gone gray by the time I returned from the courtroom and realized how weary I was. Becky was gone, Patty was standing beside her desk with her purse in her hand. I would have liked to call Janet, but in our last meeting in the empty courtroom I thought I'd heard that door firmly close. I wondered if there was anyone in the world who would have a drink with me, the winner.

I had on my coat, and was turning off my office light, when the phone rang. I shook my head at Patty, but she had already picked it up, in an automatic response. I trudged past her.

"Mark?"

Patty was holding the phone toward me. "It's Mr. Algren," she said. "He's down in the courtroom."

Instantly I felt guilty for having forgotten Tommy. I should have talked to him as soon as he heard the guilty verdict, but I'd been trapped in my own affairs. I knew I should run down and speak to him before his father took him away.

"Tell him I'll be right down."

"Mark." Patty stopped me with only that. She was still extending the phone toward me, stiffly. I suppressed a shudder, but it spread across my shoulders and down my back like melting ice.

James Algren was no longer unhappy with me. "Congratulations!" he shouted happily. "I heard the news on the radio. Listen, I'm down in the hall outside the court and it's locked, everybody's gone. I was wondering where you've got Tommy."

"He's with one of my investigators," I said with unfelt assurance. Patty was already on the phone at another desk. But she wasn't speaking. She shook her head at me. "Why don't you come on up?" I added to Algren, and hung up.

"Where's Jim?" I asked sharply.

Patty had gotten hold of somebody. While she listened she spoke to me. "They haven't seen him since he went down to the courtroom."

"Idiot," I said. Patty knew I wasn't speaking to her. She was already making another call. I started calling too. I couldn't find the man I was looking for. I even called Eliot. He hadn't seen his client since two minutes after the verdict.

We were expecting James Algren when the hall door swung open. Instead Jim Lewis was standing there. His face announced permission to panic.

"Is he here?" he asked loudly.

We found a few people still at their desks. We called others at home. When Algren came in we tried to keep the news from him, but he quickly realized what was up. The investigator had brought Tommy back to the offices right after the verdict. Jim had left Tommy with a secretary while Jim went to the bathroom. When we tracked the secretary down she said Tommy had gone down to the basement to get a Coke. Nobody'd told her she had to stay with him. When Tommy didn't come back she figured he'd found his father, or Jim.

We scoured the building, which was almost empty by that time on a Friday afternoon. While others looked for Tommy I was continuing my own search, which proved equally fruitless.

By six we were standing staring at each other, forced to admit that Tommy was no longer in the building.

No one knew where Austin Paley was, either.

18

For the first time in too long I remembered Chris Davis, Austin's youthful lover, who had vanished off the face of this earth after he became a threat to Austin. He'd drifted to the back of my mind because he'd fallen out of the case, but now his disappearance seemed a foreshadowing, an announcement of what Austin could do when desperate.

We had no evidence that Austin Paley had kidnapped Tommy, but as the quarter-hours crawled by with no sign of either of them, it began to seem certain. Police were poring over the neighborhood around the courthouse complex, anywhere Tommy might have wandered, but they found no one. Mrs. Algren, at home, hadn't heard from him. I sent an investigator—it was Jim Lewis, anxious to atone—to Austin's office and his home. Jim called me from Austin's house—I didn't ask how he'd gotten inside—to report there'd been no one at either place. Jim started trying to trace Austin's friends. Other investigators, and cops, were doing the same.

The DA's offices began to grow as congested as on a working day, though it was by now early evening. I wasn't surprised to see anyone. Becky was there, and Janet McLaren. The Algrens must have called her, in their panic. Janet stopped me as I paced past.

"Mark—" She lowered her voice, glancing at James Algren sitting stunned in my outer office. "It may not be as bad as it seems. Tommy may have gone with him willingly.

Tommy feels guilty, you know. And he still loves Austin. He may want to help him."

"I've already thought of that. But Tommy's willingness doesn't have anything to do with Austin's intentions. Austin doesn't love Tommy."

"Maybe he's trying to talk Tommy into recanting."

"Could be," I said, to let Janet retain that hope. I didn't. I'd seen Austin in court after the guilty verdict. I realized now his breakdown hadn't been an act. And his collapse hadn't been only physical. If he thought he could save himself by holding Tommy hostage, he'd lost his mind. Nor could the Austin Paley I'd known, the cool, efficient attorney for important clients, hold any rational hope that any of us would believe a new story he might force Tommy to tell. Austin couldn't hope to accomplish anything sane by snatching Tommy. That left me trying to fathom a madman's motives.

Seven o'clock took three or four hours to become seven-thirty. I had a sip of the coffee someone had made, felt it drop unimpeded into my stomach and begin burrowing into the lining, and tried to remember when I'd last eaten.

I have a private line in my office. Only four or five people know its number. When, sitting in the outer office in order to be closer to the lack of action, I heard the phone on my desk begin ringing, I knew something was about to happen. I sprinted past a blur of statues, paused with my hand on the phone to draw a breath, and answered.

"I've been calling you at home, like a fool," the man said. "Your answering machine will have a lot of hang-ups on it when you check it."

I was so expecting to hear Austin Paley's voice that I thought I was. It took that second sentence for me to identify the caller.

"Eliot?"

"I can tell you where he is, Mark. But he wants you to go alone, and *now*. Right away, so you don't have time to plan anything."

I thought of all those people in my outer office, some of whom were now crowding through my doorway to listen to my end of the call. "I don't know if I can manage the alone part," I said.

Eliot didn't respond. "Here's the address." He gave it to me. "It's south of downtown, you exit 37 at—"

"I know where it is."

"Yes, he said you would. Good luck, Mark."

"Eliot. Does he have Tommy? Is Tommy all right?"

Silence, as if our connection were bad. I hated his hesitation. Maybe it was because I'd asked two questions at once, which they teach you in law school not to do. "Eliot!"

"Yes," Eliot Quinn said quickly, and the line went dead.

I didn't even *drive* alone to the battered old house in the little cul-de-sac neighborhood. Two cops went with me, one a negotiator trying to give me the ten-minute course in talking a crazy out of his hostage. I wasn't paying much attention. His voice was just background noise to my thoughts.

When I'd first realized Austin had taken Tommy I'd been livid. If I'd seen Austin in that moment I could have strangled him. But rage is hard to sustain for hours. I'd had time to sit and think. I knew I was partly mad at myself, because I'd abandoned Tommy as soon as I no longer needed him. I'd allowed Austin to take him. I remembered the way Tommy had stared at me from the witness stand, looking to me at every moment of uncertainty. I'd told him to put himself in my hands and he had. My feigned friendship of the last few months had been effective. I'd beaten Austin for Tommy's trust. Then betrayed that trust at every step.

We'd given Tommy a hell of a preparation for manhood; his father, Austin, me. I remembered how quickly, it seemed to me, Tommy had responded to the role model I'd offered him. I'd straightened out his life as easily as I'd straightened out his batting swing. But Tommy must have realized by now why I'd grown close to him. I'd dropped him like a hot coal as soon as I no longer needed him. As Austin had. If Tommy was still alive, he had learned there was no one he could count on; no one motivated by uncalculated affection for Tommy.

My rage had given way to cold resolve. I would take Tommy from Austin again. Or if that was no longer possible, I'd have the revenge to which a father is entitled.

Sawhorses blocked the entrance to the short street. They didn't say POLICE, they said CITY PUBLIC SERVICE. Very subtle. Around the corner, barely out of sight of the house, was a squadron of cars: police cruisers, ambulances, a fire truck, and, pulling up just as I did, the *Eyewitness News* van. Not quite a circus, more like an open-air carnival whose power has just failed. There were no spotlights or flashing lights. We were all in the dark.

I met Lieutenant Paul Romano, whom I'd known slightly since he was a patrolman and I an assistant DA using him as a witness on a DWI. He took me to the corner, from which we could just see the house where I'd met Austin two months ago. Its porch light was burning, making it look like Grandma's house when company is expected.

"We got men in back," Lieutenant Romano said without preliminaries, "we got this end blocked off, we got a spotter in the culvert at the dead end of the street. He's not going anywhere. But we don't move 'til we know what's up. We don't even know who's in there. There's two cars in the driveway, and a garage in back, so he could have twenty men in there. We don't know if the boy's there or not. We're going to try to send in a negotiator—"

"He won't let anybody in. Except maybe me." It had been obvious that Eliot had spoken to me with permission. Austin wanted me to know where he was.

Lieutenant Romano was looking down. He rubbed a thumb on an eyebrow. He'd been waiting for me to say it, unwilling to make the suggestion himself. He wouldn't even endorse it. "I wouldn't recommend it," he said. "Trading one hostage for another never works. He'll end up with both of you."

"But I'll be inside."

Romano nodded. He'd exhausted his opposition. "We'll put a wire on you," he said. "If you can just get up to the door and talk to him, maybe he'll let slip who else's in the house with him. While you've got him distracted, we might ease up closer. And we'll have shooters across the street. If he even opens the front door with a gun in his hand—"

I felt strangely like a traitor while listening to these plans, even as I nodded and approved them. While ready to kill Austin myself, it seemed cowardly to serve as the bait to lure him to a spot where he'd be vulnerable.

"Let's get you ready," the lieutenant said. "Then—" He handed me a cordless telephone.

Ten minutes later I was dressed again. My tailors assured me the wire under my shirt was invisible, but I could feel it. The adhesives holding it in place itched. They warned me not to scratch, which made scratching the most desirable sensation on earth.

I stepped away from the others to dial the phone number they'd told me. It rang three, four times. I was beginning to think they'd given me the wrong number, or that Austin didn't want to talk. I was disappointed, but it would also be a relief to step back and let the SWAT team take over.

Then a voice answered, a slow, calm voice with its irony restored. "Hello, Mark."

"Hello, Austin. I'm here, right outside."

"With all your friends," his voice drawled.

"They don't matter. It's me you want to talk to, isn't it?"

There was only slight hesitation. "Yes. Come on in, Mark. Um—" He paused, as if he were going to ask me to pick up a bag of ice for the party, but didn't like to impose. "Naked, please," he said.

"What?"

He was smiling. I could hear it. "I'm not going to let you come in here armed, or broadcasting. So just take off your clothes, please."

"Like hell. Austin, if you brought me here to humiliate me *and* kill me, I'm not going to give you both satisfactions. If that's what you want, you can go fuck yourself."

I was surprised to hear myself arguing about this. The wire was already gone as an idea. Austin would frisk me and disconnect it as soon as I got inside. But I was the district attorney and he was a criminal. I was damned if I was going to let him make me look ridiculous. I knew that if I gave up the upper hand to Austin I would never recover it.

We compromised. After I'd disconnected the call, I walked back to Lieutenant Romano.

"Give me a chance to work it out peacefully," I told him. "See if I can get the boy out of there. But if anybody fires a shot it will be him, Austin. It'll be too late to help me then. If you hear a shot, one shot, come in blasting. Shoot every man in the room. There won't be time to make distinctions. Everybody over five feet tall, kill them."

A lieutenant is a high-ranking police officer. He reports to a captain, to assistant chiefs, to the chief of police. I was nowhere in that chain of command. But I was an elected public official, to whom he could legitimately pass the buck for whatever might happen. He looked at me as if he hadn't calculated all that, as if making a personal promise.

"All right," he said.

A few minutes later I stood in the street in front of Austin's rental house, wearing my pants and holding my shirt in my outstretched hand. My chest was bare in the cool night. The marks where the technicians had stripped off the wire were already fading. Down the street, a spotlight sprang into life. I knew I was being videotaped. But the spotlight served to assure Austin of my harmlessness, too. No one made the cameraman shut it off. There was no longer a pretense that I was alone.

I turned to display my bare back to the house as well. Then I walked up to it, up the three steps onto the creaking wooden porch. I didn't knock. A voice called, assuming the role of hearty host, "It's open."

I went in. After standing on the well-lighted porch, I was blind momentarily in that dim living room. My skin felt icy. I was certain I was about to be shot, or stabbed, or struck.

So when a hand did touch me, I jumped. "Relax," Austin said. "I just need to check. If you'd taken off your pants, like I asked, this wouldn't be necessary."

He frisked me briefly but thoroughly. By the time he finished my eyes had adjusted. I found myself looking not at Austin but at Eliot Quinn. He sat in the old damask-covered armchair directly in front of me, under a fringed floor lamp. Thank God he nodded when I looked at him. For a moment I'd thought he was dead.

Eliot was fully dressed in a suit and tie, but he was missing his traditional hat. His bare head, with a faint gleam of skull through the white hair, made him look vulnerable. He was sitting in front of the large front window of the living room. I didn't think his position accidental. Gunfire from outside would find Eliot as its first target.

But Eliot didn't look like a hostage. He looked like an adviser, even a cohort. He watched me sadly.

I turned to Austin. He had stepped back away from me, well out of reach, but he still held the silver-plated automatic pistol pointed at me. Austin, too, was formally dressed, in the suit he'd been wearing in court. He wore his old smile, too, the self-deprecating one that contemplated the possibility he'd made a social blunder. But the smile didn't touch his eyes, which were perfectly self-satisfied and looked me over coldly. I drew on my white shirt. Austin's hand twitched, as if that small self-protective gesture of mine were justification enough for him to kill me.

"Where's Tommy?" I said. Austin continued to regard me amusedly. I took a step toward him, anger my only protection. Austin made a small gesture toward the back of the house. That was with the hand holding the gun. With the other he made a calming gesture toward me. But I was not to be calmed. Rage had owned me since I'd stepped into the house, certain I was going to die.

"That boy loves you, Austin," I said. "After everything you've done to him, you're still the most important person in the world to him. If you've hurt him I'll kill you. I'll find some way, believe me."

"This isn't about Tommy," Austin said.

"He's all right," Eliot Quinn said, the first words he'd spoken since I'd arrived. But the nervous glance he gave Austin as he said it scared me.

I heard a faint sound from the back of the house that made me think someone was back there. That calmed me slightly. Calmness was not my friend. It meant I had to think my way out of this, instead of doing something crazy.

"This isn't about Tommy," Austin repeated. "Who was Tommy to you? Nobody, you'd never heard of him. But you and I were friends, Mark. We'd been friends a long time. But when I needed your help, you preferred some strange boy to me."

"You never came to me for help, Austin. You just tried to trick and intimidate me. I want to help you. What can I do?"

He told me, very explicitly. "I want you to dismiss the case. I want you to join in a motion for a new trial and then dismiss the case, all the cases. I want you to announce, very publicly, that you've uncovered new evidence that conclusively proves my innocence."

He wanted, in other words, to go on being the person he'd always been, not some vile convicted felon. His demands were insane. How long did he think he could hold a gun on me? I studied him as if I were thinking it over. I asked a question, remembering the police negotiator's suggestion that talk might be all a man holding a hostage wanted to do.

"Why didn't you just quit, Austin? You seem to have been inactive for a few years. Why didn't you just stop while you were safe?"

"Why don't you?" Austin replied. "You're a single man now, you don't have a readily available sexual partner. You have to go looking. Why don't you just throw it over, declare celibacy, stay home with a good book? Wouldn't it make life simpler?" He looked at me as if he knew everything about me. He could see the answer. *Yes, but.* Austin smiled. "It's no different with me, my friend. The urge doesn't die. The urge is the same, even if the object is different. Maybe my urge is stronger, even, because it's forbidden. Why should I stop?"

"Because it's illegal."

Austin shook his head. "Not for me."

"Because it's wrong, then," I said, watching him closely. "Because it scares the children. Who can know better than you how it hurts them?"

He stopped bantering. Austin's expression grew more intense. His gaze held me. He could make me see. "The children never resisted, Mark. I've never raped anyone. They knew it wasn't wrong. They knew it was natural as swimming. Just another skill to learn. Have you ever really thought about it? You're not one of these robots, you don't think with your gag reflex. Think about it. That soft skin, their clear eyes. Completely unsullied by experience. Utterly open. You don't have to worry about why they're doing this, do they want something from you, are they out to get you? Children are full of love, and curiosity, and they are hungry for any gesture of affection. No one gets enough affection, Mark, no one's capacity is ever filled. Especially children, especially today. Have you ever walked into a daycare center and seen all their eyes light up, seen them all come running to the stranger, begging for attention, pleading for love? They'll come up and stroke your legs, just to say, Look at me, touch me. Love me.

"Where are their parents?" Austin held out a helpless hand to me, forgetting it was the hand that held the gun. "Where are the aunts and uncles and grandparents who should be lavishing love on them? All working, all too busy. Too busy for the children they've spawned and set loose in the world. I try to take up some of the slack. I love them, Mark. I do. And they love me."

I felt chilled, not because he was raving, but because he was telling the truth. I *had* been to daycare centers recently, enough to see that Austin was right. And I believed he loved them. I didn't try to argue with him, partly because I didn't want to antagonize him; partly because I had no response.

Eliot cleared his throat. We looked at him. He was looking down at the floor, his face red.

"Why don't you go, Eliot?" I said, then to Austin, "He doesn't have to stay, does he?"

Austin looked at Eliot with no sympathy. "Not on my account," he said. Eliot just shook his head, still not looking at us. It was obvious he hadn't been brought here, he had come on his own, still feeling responsible. "We have a history in my family of involving old friends in our crises," Austin said, just to watch Eliot grow more miserable.

There was another sound from the back of the house. I couldn't make it out, but I believed it was Tommy. Austin would have him close. What was keeping Tommy back there?

"I'm going to get Tommy," I said. Austin stood up straighter in my path. "There's no reason he has to be here." Austin shook his head. "Austin, think of him. He's scared, he's a boy. He needs our help." Silently I was thinking, expecting him to hear the thought as well, *I can save him, Austin. I can't save you.*

Maybe he did hear me, but he wasn't willing to give Tommy up. For all I knew, Tommy wasn't alone in the back of the house. Perhaps Chris Davis was with him, or someone like Chris Davis. The idea restored my fear, and fear renewed my anger. And I didn't believe in Austin's threat with the gun. With all I'd uncovered about him, I'd never heard he was violent. I didn't believe he could bring himself to shoot me.

"I'm going back there," I said quietly, "and get Tommy. If he's all right I'll take him out of here. If he's not, you'd better start running now."

Austin moved, toward Eliot, so that he was no longer blocking the far doorway with its beaded curtain, but he kept the gun leveled at me. He was sweating, I saw for the first time, and it terrified me. "I can't let you do that," Austin said.

His answer scared me even more. *Why* couldn't he let me see Tommy? I turned away from Austin, starting to run. Flight made me feel safer. But before I got halfway to the doorway the gun went off. I thought I'd been hit. Instinct threw me aside, almost knocked me off my feet. Instinct was stupid. It killed my momentum, left me standing. I looked back and saw Eliot Quinn on his feet, struggling with Austin. The gun was pointed toward the ceiling. Eliot's hand was on Austin's wrist, but Austin was a much younger, stronger man. He was already turning the gun.

My first instinct was to leave Eliot to his fate while I ran to find Tommy, but I didn't want to leave this maniac with a gun at my back. I ran back to them. The gun was swinging wildly, pointing at me, then to the side, then back at me. I had no time to make distinctions. I just gave both struggling men a shove, the momentum of my run behind it. I hoped to throw them both to the ground and grab the gun as they scrambled up.

But I was stronger than I knew, crazed by adrenaline, and my push was desperate. We all careened toward the window. Eliot and Austin crashed through the flimsy curtain and the old glass and fell out onto the porch. I pulled up just in time. The porch light was still burning, spotlighting the two of them in the black night. Eliot lay where he'd fallen. Blood was starting from half a dozen cuts on his face.

Austin was dazed but still conscious. And the gun had gone out the window with him. He looked down at Eliot, who was no longer struggling, then back at me. There was a wild but perfectly aware look in his eye. He looked down, saw the gun, and picked it up, and started to his feet.

I dived to the side, away from the open window, down to the floor. In the next second, in the time it would have taken Austin to rise, the gunfire came. Rifle shots, both remote and piercing. They came in a burst, too many to count, and died as abruptly as they'd begun.

I stood, with some trouble. I was shaking. I didn't go near that shattered window, but I got a sidelong glimpse of two bodies on the ground. I ran the other way, through the beaded curtain, skidding on a scarred kitchen floor.

"Tommy!" I screamed.

A voice answered. Behind the kitchen was a short hallway with a dark hardwood floor and peeling print wallpaper on the walls. I burst through a closed paneled door with an old glass doorknob.

Tommy was on the antique brass bed. He was still wearing the dress slacks and shirt I'd last seen him wearing in court. He was sitting up on the bed. Nothing bound him to it. I grabbed him, ran my hands over his arms and legs. "Are you okay?" I was asking, more than once, too loudly for him to interrupt with an answer. I remembered to look around the room, and saw no one else.

"I'm fine," Tommy said, and he seemed to be, except that I was scaring him. I made myself calm down.

"He didn't hurt you?" I asked.

Tommy shook his head. "I just wanted to talk to him," Tommy said. "I just wanted to tell him I was sorry."

I looked at him sharply. Tommy didn't look or act like a kidnapping victim. He might have arranged this meeting himself.

"Is Waldo all right?" Tommy asked.

I pulled him to me and held him. I couldn't lie to him, but it didn't seem like the moment to tell him the truth, either.

I felt a gathering tension, as if the whole house were leaning in above me. There was no sound from the front room. The police might still be afraid to rush the house, not having seen me or Tommy.

I picked Tommy up, along with a blanket and pillow off the bed. Tommy was light, too light to be the almost-grown boy he was. I carried him back through the kitchen. Sure enough, the living room was still empty. By the front door, I set Tommy on his feet for a moment, but kept him facing me, the broken window behind him. I opened the front door of the house and held the white pillow out through it. When gunfire didn't tear it out of my hand I stepped into the open doorway and waved. No one shot at me, either. I heard running footsteps.

I stepped back in and picked Tommy up again. He was looking curiously at the window. From that angle I didn't think he could see anything outside. After he was in my arms I draped the blanket over his head. "Cold out here," I said.

I stepped out onto the porch carrying him. Tommy's face was covered, but *I* could see the two men lying on the porch. Eliot's eyes were still closed. As I watched, an EMS technician ran up and knelt beside him. He didn't even bother with Austin, who was lying a few feet away. Blood had turned his white shirtfront black in the glare of night. Austin's eyes were open, but there was no question that he was alive. The bullets had left his face unmarked. It was smoothed in death, his unnatural youthfulness regained. I didn't stare at him. I hurried down off the porch with Tommy. I was aware that there was plenty of light now. The headlights and flashing lights of the various official vehicles and the lights of the television cameras lit the scene like day. A man ran toward me and tried to take Tommy away from me. I resisted until I saw that it was James Algren. He lifted Tommy out of my arms. "Don't let him see," I said. Algren shot me a look so compounded of emotions it looked like hatred, the way all colors blended together make black. He looked as if he were grateful to me but didn't like it. I didn't blame him.

Without the warmth of Tommy's body against me I felt suddenly cold. My shirt was thin. Someone handed me a jacket. It wasn't my suit coat, it was a police windbreaker. I was glad to have it, especially as I thought it had started raining. My face was wet. When I reached to wipe it off I discovered another EMS technician beside me. "Don't touch it," he said authoritatively. He turned a bright flashlight on my face and probed at a spot on my temple with a cold bit of metal. "Ow," I said.

"I don't think the glass is still in there," he said, "but we'll need to look again. Just hold this on it for right now." He pressed a clean piece of cloth to my temple, put my hand on it like a child's, and ran off to attend to someone else. From the bustle and the number of people spreading through the night one would have thought a dozen hostages had been held.

Lieutenant Romano took my arm. "I'll have someone drive you to a hospital," he said.

I resisted automatically. "I'm not leaving 'til it's over."

He shrugged. "What's left to do?"

He had a point. "You did our work for us," Romano added. I looked back the way I'd come. Tommy was gone. His father must have hustled him away, avoiding the postcrisis interview. On the porch of the house, someone had draped a jacket over Austin Paley's face. A medical examiner's investigator was kneeling over him, pulling back the jacket. The porch was otherwise empty. A uniformed police officer stood inside the broken window, talking on a portable phone.

A television cameraman was filming the carnage. At his side, the reporter turned and saw me, and started down off the porch. The cameraman needed a dead body for maximum impact, but the reporter needed a live one.

"Where's Eliot?" I asked Romano. He nodded toward the ambulance, which stood thirty yards away, its light off and its loading doors standing open.

"Why isn't it taking off?" I asked. I knew the answer. There was no rush.

But Romano shrugged and said, "It's not that serious. Few cuts from flying glass, I think that's it."

I grabbed his arm. "He's alive?"

The lieutenant looked offended. "Nobody shot him. He stayed on the ground. Nobody'd've shot the crazy one, if he'd stayed down. What kind of men you think I give rifles to out here?"

I started toward the ambulance. But that was where the majority of the reporters were congregated. A technician stepped out of the ambulance and waved them away. One or two, discouraged, turned and saw me. Romano pulled me back again. "You want to give a press conference here?"

He was right. I could talk to Eliot later. I could avoid reporters' pointed questions until there was an official version of what had happened here tonight.

Voices called my name as I turned away. "In the morning," I muttered.

As it became clear I wasn't going to stop, questions replaced my name. As I ignored them, too, the questions grew uglier. "What happened inside?" "Are you glad he's dead?" "Do you think this will improve your reelection chances?" I didn't turn.

Until Jenny Lord's voice pierced the buzzing of the others. "Why was your old boss here?" she asked.

I stopped. The clamor died. "Was he trying to continue the cover-up?" Jenny Lord asked softly.

I turned. There were four of them, with eager or patient or knowing expressions. A camera flash glared in my face as I looked at them.

"Eliot Quinn was here to try to defuse the situation and help out two old friends," I said. "That was all."

Jenny shook her head. "We know, Mark. About the old cases. Austin Paley went back a long way."

"What happened to the old cases?" asked the hairdo from Channel 4. I just looked at him for a moment.

"That was before my time."

"But you know how the system works," Jenny said, and the other newspaper reporter added, with the smugness of someone who only writes about the slime and doesn't have to step in it, "Were you part of the corruption or were you trying to stop it?"

It was Eliot's reputation they were talking about shredding. He had already connected himself to Austin by defending him. That had made someone start digging. I wasn't going to give them anything they didn't have, except maybe the right perspective.

"This isn't about corruption," I said. "What happens isn't always because of money, or sleaze. Sometimes, even when something bad comes of it, it started just from trying to help. To do the best you could. Our judicial system is no more corrupt than, say"—I groped for analogy, gazed around at all the official vehicles around us—"the auto parts business. The trouble is, we're entrusted with something precious—

justice—but we run the system the same way the auto parts business is run: You treat some customers preferentially because they're your friends, or because they can do you some favor in return. You make do with the stock you have when you don't have the right part. You try to make a living."

I felt myself growing taller, rising above the scene, into the starry sky. I'd forgotten to keep the cloth pressed against my head, and blood was trickling down my cheek again.

"But our stock is human lives. People count on us. When we make do, someone's life could be ruined. A prosecutor gives away a case because it's too much trouble to pursue it, or would step on someone's toes; so a criminal is loose in the world. And a little respect for the law dies. The hope of ever achieving justice withers. People say there's no point in trying to do the right thing. And everybody suffers."

Jenny Lord was looking at me thoughtfully, not writing. But the TV hairdo just wanted to keep me babbling. "So you're saying covering up somebody's crimes is just part of the game?"

I hated his self-righteousness. He was maybe twenty-five years old. If he'd ever been confronted by an ethical dilemma, he probably hadn't noticed. "Have you ever killed a story as a favor to someone?" I asked him hotly. "Maybe you did it because you thought you could get a better story later in return. So does that make it just business, or corruption—or just a favor for a friend?"

He looked alarmed. "I've never done that."

"Oh no?" I asked quietly, staring at him. He shut up.

But there's always someone with another question. "So does that still go on?" the *Eyewitness News* reporter asked. "Do *you* do favors for friends?"

I raised my chin, indicating the old house behind them. "What do you think?" I said. "Austin Paley was my friend."

19

The news coverage of the evening's adventure was interesting, not for the divergence of angles, but for the similar spin all the news outlets put on what had happened. I'm sure the reporters hadn't colluded. But practicalities dictated the outcome. My light-headed speech didn't make it intact into print or on the air. It was too wordy for TV, and didn't fit the print stories.

They all made me the hero, because that's the image that fit the footage they had: the district attorney going in half-naked to face an armed madman and emerging with the child victim in his arms. The images were striking. Without too closely examining the background, they made a good story.

Jenny Lord's piece had a quiet tone that didn't match the vivid photos, one of which was a shot of Austin's body on the porch, with the caption, THE DA'S FRIEND. There was no mention of a possible cover-up in the dead man's past. I wondered, but never asked, if Jenny had omitted that as a favor to me or because *she* had understood my implied threat to the bubblehead TV reporter. We had all known each other long enough to harbor secrets. I *knew* stories they'd all killed, or favors done. And so it continued. The web of favors can take a hit from a cannonball, and by morning the spiders will have repaired it completely.

Leo Mendoza was in the news too, commenting on the end of the strange case in which he had declared the defendant innocent—the defendant a jury had found guilty of child rape just before his crazed death. Asked for his reaction, Leo sounded huffy: "I'm certain voters are tired of Mark Blackwell's brand of cowboy justice, that ends in a shootout rather than in a courtroom."

He spoke like an upholder of legal order, and I'm sure Leo was confident he was still riding high in the polls, but a lot of voters prefer cowboy justice to any other kind. Before the weekend was over I'd received four invitations to speak to citizens' groups. People I'd never met greeted me on the street and shook my hand. I decided I was the darling of the lunatic fringe.

Monday night, election day eve, I had my long-deferred dinner with David and Vicky. We ate in a Chinese restaurant where we'd all been before, but never together, never while I was still married to Lois. We ordered sesame beef and kung pao chicken and a pupu platter and ate family style. Vicky was gorgeous, in a tossed-back way that as a young man I'd thought indicated effortlessness. Her blond hair was freer than usual, swept back from her face. Her eyes and cheekbones and lips were prominent, but when I greeted her she was cool as ever, as if she'd come under duress.

David wasn't wearing a tie, but he looked as if he'd just rushed into the house, torn it off, and rushed out again. "Tough day?" I asked, and he only nodded.

So we all had a drink, then wine with dinner. "Good luck tomorrow," David said dutifully. I shrugged.

"You do want to win, don't you?"

"Sure," I said. "But it wouldn't be so terrible if I didn't. It would be nice to have a life again, not see everything I do on videotape the next day."

"But you have to win," Vicky said. "What if one of us gets in trouble again?"

I just looked at the girl. Either she was a complete dullard or she had a quirkier sense of humor than I'd ever realized.

We didn't talk about me after that, we talked about David's business venture and Vicky's job and their latest charity involvement. I noticed that they left things out of the conversation, they glanced at each other and mutually, silently agreed to skip ahead; once she even nudged David's arm and they snickered in unison. "What?" I asked, but they wouldn't say.

Vicky and I reached for the last piece of sesame beef simultaneously, I with a fork, she with chopsticks. "Go ahead," I said, "I don't need it," patting my stomach.

"Hey, I saw you on TV and you didn't look bad," she answered. "And they say TV adds ten pounds."

"Only if you have clothes on," I said.

She said to David, "See, I told you it was only his clothes that make him look like that."

"Like what?" I asked, glancing down at what I was wearing. "You think I need help?"

"Doesn't David look better since I started going with him to buy clothes?" Vicky replied.

I looked at David. He *did* look better. Even rumpled as he was at the end of the day, his shirt was not only nice-looking but did something to his face that diminished his habitual paleness. And his jacket didn't hang awkwardly on him as if he'd taken it from someone else's closet. I tried to remember when he'd stopped dressing like a teenager. It wasn't just his clothes, either. David seemed at ease. He leaned back in his chair, stepping into the conversation only when he had something to say. He didn't feel responsible for it. This ease was a recent addition to David's personality. He had an adult assuredness. Maybe David was growing old enough to put aside his adolescent resentments, or at least to view them more critically. You don't have to be adult very long to realize *you* can make mistakes too.

The food was gone, but we had another round of wine. I was in no hurry to get back to my barren condo. David and Vicky didn't seem to mind staying with me.

After the check was already on the table, David leaned forward and said, with his old hesitancy returning, "You haven't asked about Mom."

"I have my sources, David. I have a whole staff of investigators, you don't have to be one of them."

He grew easier in his manner again after I relieved him of the duty of reporting. "She's good," he said, "she seems happy."

"I'm glad."

David was watching me to see how I took the news, then he and Vicky exchanged another of those looks. I couldn't see what she was telling him, but after the exchange David added, "But I'm not sure if she's happy because things are going well or because they're not."

"What?" I directed the question as much at Vicky as at David. It was David who answered.

"With the new boyfriend. Sometimes when she seems to be spending a lot of time with him you can see her draw back, like she doesn't want to get too involved too fast."

"Well, I guess that's—"

"I think she enjoys keeping him off balance," Vicky said confidentially.

I looked at her, then decided, what the hell, to say what I was thinking. "Oh, you know something about the pleasure of that, Vicky?"

It could have been a bad blunder, ending a pleasant evening. But Vicky's smile broadened. She laughed. I laughed with her. "I have my memories," she said, putting a hand on David's shoulder. He rolled his eyes. "Me, too."

Damn, I thought. *I could get to like this woman.* David seemed to have discovered that he liked her too. Amazing thing, how their lives seemed to be blossoming, with no help from me.

On election day I went to work, but I didn't spend much time in my office. I roamed around the old courthouse and the new Justice Center in a valedictory way, reminiscing with acquaintances of long standing or sitting in empty courtrooms alone. Here was where I'd tried my first case. Here was my old office. Here were the stairs down which I'd thrown my briefcase after an especially bitter loss. I'd left my marks on the buildings, and they on me, even if I'd never have an official position in them again. That was what hurt most about the prospect of losing the election, the thought of being exiled from this world I knew best, by strangers who didn't know it at all.

I stayed until after six, then walked a few blocks across downtown to the old Menger Hotel, where Tim Scheuless had rented a suite for me and, optimistically, a ballroom for my supporters. Avoiding the latter, I went straight upstairs, where I found a small group of campaign organizers whose quiet cheer at my appearance was rather dispiriting. I joined them in a drink.

At seven o'clock the polls closed and, a few minutes later, the first results were announced. It was a presidential election year, my race came well down the ballot. The screen showed the numbers while the commentator read them. I was leading 53 percent to 47.

No one said anything, so I said it. "Not enough," I said. These first figures showed only the absentee voting, which had already been counted. The conservative north side of San Antonio, which should have been my most solid base of support, votes disproportionately heavily in the absentee voting period. I should have had a very big lead in that first announcement, which would be whittled down gradually throughout the evening as the rest of the city's votes were counted. Six percentage points were not enough of a lead to endure that whittling.

An hour later I had retired to the inner bedroom, and no one disturbed me there. Oddly enough, I couldn't keep my thoughts on the election. I was standing at the window, staring down at the narrow street that ran between the hotel and the grounds of the Alamo next door, thinking of Austin Paley. I don't like to view the body at a funeral. I'm always afraid that last glimpse of the departed will overlay all my memories of him, so that I will never remember him any other way. That had been happening to my memories of Austin: It wasn't that last view of him on the porch that had been superseding everything else, it had been the last weeks, when he'd been a defendant and I a prosecutor. But Austin and I had had twenty years before that. We hadn't been close friends—I wondered now if anyone had really shared Austin's life—but he'd had a gift for making me feel close to him in a few snatched moments. It wasn't only me on whom he'd exercised this gift. I remembered an occasion ten or twelve years ago, long enough ago that Austin had been representing a DWI defendant and I'd been a defense lawyer, when I'd overheard Austin talking to the prosecutor of the case. Austin never made what he did sound like plea bargaining, but that's what it was, and the prosecutor was being a hard-ass, insisting on some jail time. Austin started talking about the number of drinks the defendant had had—too many, but not enough to justify nights in jail. Then he'd leaned closer to the prosecutor. "Confidentially," he'd said, "I was at the same party. I'm lucky it wasn't me arrested afterwards."

The prosecutor had smiled with him. In a few words Austin had turned the courtroom into a confessional and the discussion of the crime into a reminiscence of a social occasion. The threat of jail time had gone away. And when he'd seen me watching Austin had winked, out of the prosecutor's sight, taking me alone into his confidence. Austin's life was layers of confidences, none of them real. Or maybe all of them real. He was a complex man. I didn't like the simple creature he'd been made in his obituaries.

The door opened behind me. It seemed quite natural that the man behind me was here, as if my thoughts had conjured him. "Hello, Eliot," I said before I turned.

"If I'd known you were psychic," he said, "I'd have never tried to put anything over on you."

I indicated the window. "I saw you in the glass."

He glanced past me and shrugged as if he were turning stupid. He still looked rather battered. He had a Band-Aid on his forehead and another on his cheek; other cuts were healed enough to remain uncovered, but they still marked him.

"I just came to say good luck."

"Thanks." Eliot knew where the luck lay in this campaign, and he must have seen the first returns and known what they meant, so I appreciated his appearance. He showed no inclination to leave. A minute later I was saying, "I watched him, Eliot. He was never unconscious. He knew exactly what he was doing. He knew who was out there watching his every move. And he knew what picking up the gun would do."

Eliot sat silent for a moment, as if even now he felt bound by some confidence of Austin's. But then he said, "I knew he had no designs on the boy. That was just a way to get you there. And he knew you wouldn't come alone."

"You're saying—"

"He wasn't going to prison, Mark. There was no way he could let that happen."

In the silence that followed, Austin Paley seemed to be in the room with us, smiling silently, as we tried to fathom his mind. "But he still might have gotten probation," I finally said. "He was an ideal candidate."

"The conviction was all that mattered to Austin," Eliot said. "Having his life spread before the whole city like that. He could never have been what he was again. In the end he just couldn't face it."

"Like his friend Chris Davis," I said.

Eliot's lips tightened again; he had the secret-holding habit, even after the cause was gone.

"Chris volunteered to fade the heat for Austin," I said, and I waited long enough that Eliot answered.

"Yes. Because he loved Austin. And he thought it didn't matter where he spent his last days anyway." Eliot looked at me. "You realized Chris was dying?"

"It crossed my mind. He looked worse every time I saw him."

After a moment Eliot said, "But he couldn't go through with the plea. And I don't know if Austin would have let him in the end. He loved Chris, you know. He loved—"

He stopped. Putting Austin into words was too painful for Eliot.

"Mark?" It was one of the campaign workers at the door, a Young Republican type whose name, I was proud of myself for remembering, was Jesse. "Could you come out here for a minute?"

I followed him out to the living room, which seemed brighter than it had been. Tim Scheuless waved me over to where they had the traditional three televisions set up. "Quick, quick," he said, and as I joined him, "They're about to show it on Channel 4. They just showed it on 5."

I didn't have to ask what he meant. The new numbers. I wondered if this was the round that would drop me below 50 percent. It must be nerve-racking for Leo Mendoza to watch this, sure he was going to win but starting from behind.

"And in the race for Bexar County District Attorney," the newsreader intoned, then waited for the numbers on the screen to flip, "latest returns indicate the incumbent, Mark Blackwell, leading with fifty-five percent of the votes."

"Fifty-*five?*" I said.

"It's true," Tim assured me. "That's what the other channel just reported too."

My lead was growing, not shrinking. "Cowboy justice," I muttered, but no one heard me. The half-dozen people in the room were clapping.

I looked back at Eliot, in the doorway of the bedroom, who wore a little smile. I wondered if he was thinking what I was thinking. In an ugly case like Austin's, the public couldn't really be satisfied unless the defendant ended up dead, and immediately. Screw all the official support I didn't have, the political kingmakers who were furious with me. I'd not only prosecuted a monster, I'd killed him. Good job, the voters were replying.

The numbers continued to climb through the short evening. With the new electronic ballot counting no one has to stay up all night any more to know who's won a local race. It was only nine-thirty when my percentage of the vote hit 57 percent and the rumors began that Leo had already conceded. It was clear that I had won when other elected officials began showing up in the hotel suite and the ballroom below was reported to be filling. Tim told me, laughing, that the bumper stickers and yard signs we couldn't give away a week ago were suddenly in demand. Tomorrow morning everyone would look like one of my lifelong supporters. I laughed with him. Let everybody climb aboard.

They let me go into the bedroom alone to straighten up and prepare a few remarks—ones I hadn't expected to deliver. Jesse tried to shoo out the old man in the chair who was the last person in the bedroom. "Please, sir, the district attorney needs a few moments alone."

"It's okay, Jesse," I said. He looked at me puzzledly—he had no idea who the old man was—but left, shutting the door.

It seemed fitting that I be alone for a minute with Eliot. Paradoxically, he was still one of the few people I trusted.

He came up to me and clapped me on the arms, exactly like a father congratulating a son. "I will leave you alone," he said. "I just wanted to remind you of one thing. Everybody's on your team now, because you're a winner. But don't you ever forget who your real friends were, when you needed them."

I stumbled over the words. "I know, Eliot. I—"

"Nobody," Eliot said firmly. "Nobody turned a finger to help you. Everybody was against you. And that's still who you're going to have on your side in a crunch. Nobody. The ones who come up and shake your hand, they're the ones you can trust the least. Unless—" He studied me. "What are you going to do with what Austin told you? The recreation center, the dead man in the basement?"

"Dig," I said. "Find where the body's buried, to start. Get enough on somebody to make him turn on the others. See how far I can take it. Prosecute the ones who should be."

I was sure of my answer, but I couldn't tell from Eliot's face that it was the right one. "Austin's dead," he reminded me needlessly. *"You* could be the man with the secrets now. Something like this, you keep it in your pocket, it'll be better than money in the bank for years to come."

It was a strange speech from Eliot, so much so that I thought I was being tested. I just shook my head. Eliot looked at me sadly. "Then I've got nothing to tell you," he said. "I wish I could offer you some advice, but there's none that would do you any good. I'm not even sure which of the people in power will be after your hide. But they will be. You're what they hate most: a loner with popular support. You watch your back."

And he was gone, in his black suit, knowing he would be a troubling specter at the feast. I thought about what he'd said to me for two minutes, until the mob came in and started carrying me down to my beloved friends in the ballroom. As I laughed and shook hands and recognized faces I was startled to see there, smiling at me, I was rehearsing in my mind my victory speech: *Well, I won for the wrong reasons, but I still won. I got very, very lucky. And some people are going to be very sorry about it.*

When I found myself at the podium, in front of a serpent's tangle of microphones, I looked out on a crowd of hundreds of people, so many I couldn't see individual faces, all beaming at me. I opened my mouth and said:

"Well, children, we did it."

They went nuts. When the noise died down I put on a

more serious expression and said, "We got our message out to the people, and the people liked what they heard. They heard that this is an administration committed to one thing: the truth. They heard . . ."

It was a ridiculous speech. You don't want to hear any more of it. It went over very big.

If I could have asked for one person to come congratulate me on my victory the next morning, it would have been the one Patty ushered into my office without warning. I thought I'd seen her for the last time the night of Tommy's kidnapping.

Janet even came in person rather than phoning, which was delightful. She was pleasing to eyes that had had only three or four hours' sleep. She took my hands for a moment but let me go.

"I should have come last night," she said.

"No, you shouldn't have. It would've made you sick." Not like a criminal trial, but a political campaign victory party is in its way just as disgusting.

"I did see you on the news, with Tommy." She was scrutinizing me closely—trying to see, I imagined, if I'd acted out of concern for Tommy or in order to look like a hero in the last days of my reelection campaign. I didn't say anything. I was sure I couldn't convince her of anything she didn't already believe.

"No one else could have saved him," Janet said. Then I realized it was my forehead she was studying. She reached up to almost touch it. "It looked like you were hurt."

"I'm all right."

She looked at her own hands. "Mark, let's make an agreement. Let's not ever see each other again," she said, looking troubled, "professionally."

Thank God for the last word. "Absolutely," I said seriously. "Because let me tell you, you were a great flaming pain in the ass to work with." I liked the way her eyes went wide and her mouth came open and color rushed into her face. "Sashaying around here the way you did while we were supposed to be having a professional consultation," I went on. "Flirting with me like a schoolgirl, doing those things

386

with your eyes and the way your voice would drop when you looked at me, like I was the most wonderful—"

She rolled her eyes. "You have a rich fantasy life."

"Oh, you mean you did it all unconsciously? You know what Freud would say about that."

"No, and neither do you," she said. "And he was probably wrong."

"It may take some study, but I'll find it. You have a professional library, don't you? Maybe if I browsed through it ..."

We were standing close. Janet turned serious again. "But one thing," she said. "Have you been to see Tommy yet?"

I felt reproached by the question. "I've tried to call him a couple of times, but—"

"Good. Don't go see him. Not yet, maybe not ever. Don't keep being part of his life. They're trying to put their lives together. They don't need you there to remind them what they've been through. Or to compete for Tommy's attention just when James Algren is finally trying to be a real father."

"Is he? That's great. I wish—"

I didn't finish. I'd almost said I wished David and I had had a tragedy like that earlier in our lives, something to make me stop and question what was important in my life.

Janet didn't ask me to finish the thought. She finally gave me a smile. Business was done.

"And if this advice leaves you with a lot of free time you don't know what to do with," she smiled, "I have another suggestion."

I stood lost in contemplation of her, as if her voice were speaking my thoughts aloud. When she stepped forward and held me I relaxed for the first time in days. No, weeks.

She left too soon. She was a busy person, after all, a doctor. She had sanities to save.

Her departure left me free to renew my study of the single sheet of paper on my desk. It was handwritten, on the stationery of my own office. Two crisp sentences, following a formal salutation.

"Patty?" I asked the intercom. "Is Becky Schirhart by any chance waiting to see me?"

"She's not out here."

"Find her and ask her to come in, would you?"

It seemed so strange to be sitting behind my own desk, in the office of the district attorney, with no boxes in sight, no packing to do. Everything felt brand new. I couldn't wait to get started.

When Becky arrived she walked briskly into the office, as if I'd taken her away from something important. There was an assurance about her movements I hadn't seen before. She didn't feel called on to speak first. She came up to the desk and looked at me, questioningly, then a little more intently, with a touch of concern.

"I had a hard night," I said.

"You had a great night."

"I didn't see you there."

"I wasn't there," she said, not dropping her eyes or explaining further.

"I'm glad to hear it," I said. "It confirms my opinion of you."

She looked questioning again at that, but I changed the subject, pushing her letter of resignation toward her across the desk. "I wish you'd take this back," I said, "and tear it up, or maybe keep it until you need it."

"I think I need it now," she said slowly.

"Found a good job?"

"I haven't started looking yet." She frowned, disliking to say more. She'd wanted it to be cleaner. "But after what happened between us"—she laughed slightly, not smiling—"or *didn't* happen, it would be too uncomfortable for me to go on working here. For both of us."

"Not—"

She continued doggedly, "I don't think you could get over the lingering suspicion that I did it to gain an advantage, when I had the chance."

I shook my head. "You obviously didn't do it to advance yourself at work." I touched her letter of resignation again. "This proves that."

Becky's mouth moved. She didn't want to argue. "Maybe I'm just being sly."

"If you're that cunning, I want you on my side. Becky, winning another term was the first shot in a war. Things could get ugly around here. I have to be very careful now to have around me only people I completely trust."

Her eyebrows went up. "And that's me?"

"That's you."

She finally picked up the letter, read it, and tore it in half. She glanced at me and away. She was happy and didn't like to let me see it, or maybe didn't like to let herself feel it.

"Sentimental old fool," she said.

Jay Brandon

Author of **RULES OF EVIDENCE** and
LOOSE AMONG THE LAMBS

LOCAL RULES

Available in Hardcover
mid-April 1995 from

POCKET
BOOKS